# TELESMA

# TELESMA
# A NOVEL

# Dalton Keene

# G𝓑
## GLADIUS
## BOOKS

TELESMA Copyright © 2010 by Dalton Keene

Published by Gladius Books

ISBN-13: 978-0-9829100-9-2

Printed in the United States of America.

Library of Congress Control Number: 2010933597

www.gladiusbooks.com

Second Paperback Edition, March 2018

*In Dedication to Shirley Ann Mulvaney,*
*The First to Believe*

# TELESMA

# PART ONE

1

The Wazir Valley, Afghanistan
Winter, 2001

THE BLANKET OF stars over the Wazir Valley bathed the frozen mountain peaks in numbing shades of blue. Captain Tanner stared up at the magnificent field of stars, amazed by their sheer number. Even the bright Arizona constellations he was accustomed to seeing were lost in the great multitude.

Tanner pulled his gaze from the heavens and wiped away the frost from his GPS unit, then recorded his team's position. He nodded to the entrance, and the five-man squad slipped into the cave, each a misshapen form of white against the icy-gray mountainside. Behind them, the wind, clean and bitterly raw, swept past the entrance at a crazy angle.

Lowering his night-vision goggles, Tanner positioned them snuggly over his eyes, then turned and appraised the tunnel ahead. In a flare of green, he could see the ragged earth jutting out from the ceiling and walls like monstrous canines. He checked his footing. The rocky ground sloped downward at a bothersome angle, but if his team moved cautiously and with precision, it would be a manageable descent.

"Footing," Tanner whispered into his comm device. He stabbed his hand at the cavern floor, signaling the others, then crept forward, loose rock crunching under his feet. Al Qaeda may as well be damned, he thought as he cautioned ahead, pondering the seclusion of the cave and its bleak interior. Living their lives in a shit-hole like this couldn't be much better than living in hell.

Slowly, the team edged around a slight bend.

Tanner stopped and studied the cave's layout, simple in its design. It sloped and it curved, but little else. Most other caves he'd been sent to clean were maze-like in their complexity, with countless passages breaking from the main, a warren of smaller recesses and cubbies. Clearing the enemy from this one, Tanner thought, would be easy, like clearing snot from his nose. One blow. Two blows. Out it goes; out *they* go. And no doubt when he was finished here, his team's success would be another feather in his cap.

Among expeditionary squads, explorations weren't supposed to be a competition—at least according to Command they weren't, the logic being over-eagerness equaled sloppiness, and sloppiness equaled dead soldiers. But in reality, the competition among squads was fierce. In three short weeks, Tanner's strike team had already neutralized over four dozen al Qaeda operatives and secured a sizeable quantity of munitions. Few squads had achieved as much. And soon, Tanner knew, there'd be medals awarded. And he wanted his share.

The sudden skid of rock against rock broke the silence behind him. Tanner pivoted, extending his arm in anticipation of a falling body. Childress had lost his footing, then quickly regained it. Rivulets of sand trickled from under his feet, disappearing into the darkness.

"Great going, Childress," Baker whispered into his comm. "Why not just announce our arrival with a frickin bullhorn? It would be more effective."

"Give me a break. You ain't ever slip before?"

"Sure as shit not under these circumstances."

"Quiet," Tanner said, "the both of you." He paused, discerning the tunnel ahead.

"See anything?" Baker said.

"No, we're good to go. Let's move."

The team stalked forward.

Tanner's eyes resolved the greenish haze ahead, where the tunnel floor leveled out, running straight into the murky darkness. As he moved, the cavern walls seemed to close in around him. His mind pushed back the fear that somewhere beyond the next curve he'd run his men into a trap, into a place where the walls and ground had been rigged with high explosives, or some other hidden device—equally as deadly. To ease his concern, Tanner kept his eyes on the tunnel, but his mind upon something else, something more pleasant. He thought about home, about the wild parties he'd throw as soon as his tour ended. He had it all figured out, how to impress his buddies. He'd display his medals strategically around the house: in the living room, in the den, places they'd be sure to notice and make jealous comments.

Baker said, "I know why Childress slipped back there. He's been on edge ever since he caught his wife banging that car salesman."

"Not cars," Childress said, "RV's. And she wasn't banging him. They were chatting, online."

"Yeah, right, chatting." Baker snickered. "About what? The date of their next rendezvous? Or maybe whose turn it was to bring the KY?"

"Screw you, Baker. We get back to camp I'll knock your teeth out."

"Mouths shut, the both of you," Tanner said. "Stay alert." He stopped and held up a fist. The men froze behind him. With his teeth, Tanner tugged off a glove and ran his fingers over the coarse surface of the tunnel wall. The cold air suddenly became filled with a sweet, herbal smell, something burning, like incense. No question, somewhere ahead the cave was occupied. Adjusting his grip on his M16, Tanner moved again, at first slowly, but then with longer, bolder strides. Soon, the narrowing passageway began to level out.

On the ground thirty feet ahead, two burning bowls, registering as flashes of brilliant jade, revealed an opening to a small cavern. Before Tanner could fully assess the tactical environment, one of his squad members knocked away a cluster of stones embedded in the wall, sending them skittering to the ground, spoiling any chance the team had of surprise. Tanner signaled an immediate advance. In pairs the soldiers raced through the cavern opening. Baker and Stenton dropped back, lending rear support. Tanner quick-scanned the area, the barrel of his weapon trailing his vision. The space was a dead-end cave approximately fifteen meters in diameter, lit by a flickering campfire. Wooden crates and straw-woven baskets lined the far wall, adjacent to generous stacks of chopped wood. An empty bedroll of some sort—wool, maybe fur—lay bunched inside an alcove. In the campfire, a glowing wedge of firewood broke apart and excited a small flame, throwing up green and white embers. Sweet smoke rose from a metal bowl hanging over the flame.

"We've got a safe-house here," Tanner said into his comm. "Watch for an ambush, concealed aggressors."

At that instant, the bedroll stirred, and in a great sweeping motion, a blanket fanned out from the alcove, obscuring Tanner's line of sight. A scream echoed inside the cave, followed by the sound of a man's hurried footsteps.

"We've got al Qaeda!" Childress called out, "He's going for a weapon!"

But none of what Tanner saw made him believe it. Al Qaeda operated in larger numbers. This looked like a one-man show, a non-combatant, maybe. "Hold your fire," Tanner shouted, but his words were suddenly buried in a haze of rapid bursts. Bullets flew, and quarter-size chunks of rock sprayed from the far cavern wall. The man, a dark form against the wavering flame, twisted and spun uncontrollably as his body took the force of the rounds. A bullet struck the smoking dish, sending it flying end over end.

Abruptly, the gunfire ended, followed by a riot of brief echoes. Tanner's heart drummed wildly, and he could feel a burning pulse in his fingertips. As the cloud of cave-dust settled, he threw off his goggles and took in the scene. The man they'd shot lay prone, his dark form stretched out like an acrobat, reaching toward the licking flames of the campfire.

"Dammit," Tanner said, rushing to the body. "This ain't al Qaeda." He knelt beside the man and rolled him belly up. His face, temple to beard, was streaked with dirty sweat. The grisly hair below his lips had become matted with bloody drool. "For chrissake it's just an old hermit."

There came a faint gurgle, followed by a wet sucking sound, and the old man forced open his eyes, staring past Tanner, unseeing.

Childress rushed up, dropped his backpack, then began fumbling through a side compartment. "I'll get the medkit."

"The medkit's useless." Tanner reached out and grabbed Childress's arm. "Poor bastard's beyond help."

The old man struggled to raise his head.

Among the sickening gurgles, Tanner thought he heard a string of words. "Quiet, he's trying to speak." He braced a hand under the old man's neck and leaned closer, listening to the wet sounds.

"What's he saying?" Childress asked. Tanner silenced him with a gesture, and for a quiet moment, he listened.

Then the old man's body convulsed and his head lolled to the side. There was a final spasm, and from his mouth bubbled a raw stream of blood.

Tanner eased the dead man's head to the ground, angry, confused. How could this have happened? How could they have killed an old man? He wasn't a terrorist. This never should have happened.

A tense minute passed as the team looked on. Then Childress stirred, dragging the back of his hand across his forehead to wipe away the dampness. "What did the old man say?"

Tanner pointed to the scattered blankets. "Cover the poor guy up, lay him in the alcove."

"What did he say?" Childress asked again.

"He was dying. He didn't know what he was saying." Tanner scooped up his M16 and goggles, then stood to his feet.

Childress scratched his head, a look of worry in his hound-like eyes. "He didn't curse us or anything, did he?"

"Curse us?" Tanner said.

"Yeah, you know… may Allah bend you over, anything like that?"

"You're a piece of work, Childress. We just killed this guy, and you're worried about a goddam curse."

"I just want to know what he said, that's all. It could bear some significance on our mission."

Tanner stared at his team, slowly, from one man to the next, the orange glow of the fire playing against their faces and casting their sweat-streaked features in strange relief. "I told you the old man was dying. He didn't know what he was saying. At least it made no sense anyway, something about time. He said we can't let it end."

"He was worried about the time? Maybe he was meeting somebody? Maybe he's al Qaeda after all. Maybe we didn't fuck up."

"Look around you," Tanner said. "There're no weapons. This isn't a terrorist operation." He hurried across the cavern and began slapping off basket lids. "Look." He kicked them over, one after another, spilling bundles of dried plants. "What was the old man going to do, burn incense and sedate us to death?"

Childress paced the room, kicking at loose stones. "Okay, okay, so we blew it. What are our options?"

Before Tanner could answer, Stenton interrupted, "What the hell is that?" Everyone turned and followed his gaze toward the ceiling. High over the winking embers and scattered ashes of the fire pit, obscured within a soft glow, a black, spherical object hung suspended from the ceiling by a leather cord. Thinning smoke roiled around it, like a nebula around a lifeless star.

The team stared at the object silently, discerningly.

A chill rose in the cavern.

"Fire's dead, better get a halogen going," Tanner said at last, his eyes never straying from the curious piece. "Let's comb this place for drill."

"What is it?" Baker asked.

"Some kind of a crazy necklace, I think," Stenton said.

"No." Tanner shook his head. "More like a talisman."

Childress, who'd begun digging through a woodpile, turned back and stared at the strange object.

Tanner said, "Definitely a talisman, and an odd looking one." He considered its spherical form. Carved from obsidian, the stone was slightly elongated, twice the size of a hand grenade. A band of relief encircled its center, depicting scenes of an ancient warrior and his prowess on the battlefield. "It looks old, real old."

"Now how could you possibly know that?" Stenton said.

"I don't. I'm just saying that's the impression I get."

"Give it to Childress," Baker said. "Maybe he could use it as a gift to woo back his wife."

"Go to hell," Childress said.

Baker laughed, then finished rigging a halogen lamp at the center of the cave. He flipped it on and the area exploded in bright light.

Tanner turned from the talisman and surveyed the rest of the team. Each man had set about routinely checking the cavern: its floor, its walls. Stenton and Owens had assembled metal-detectors and were sweeping in long, careful arcs over the old man's bedding and the spilled bundles of incense.

Tanner turned back to the artifact and followed its length of cord up into the shadows of the ceiling. "Bring me the halogen."

Baker picked up the lamp and brought it over.

With it, Tanner looked up into the ceiling and strained to see the end of the leather cord. "Look there," he said, "a hook of some sort. I'll bet I can climb up and slip it off." He hurried to the woodpile and carried back a load stacked like a pyramid, then made a few more trips and began constructing a square brace.

"Why not just cut the cord?" Baker asked. "Save yourself the time and trouble."

"Because," Tanner said, stacking the brace, "as far as I know, that cord is as old as the talisman. I don't want to damage it."

"Maybe you're right," Baker said. "It might be worth something."

Tanner finished the brace, then picked up and slung the halogen lamp over his shoulder. "Lend me a hand, would you?"

Baker stepped forward and Tanner gripped his shoulder, pushing himself onto the top of the brace, thinking about what Baker had said, how the stone might be worth something. Christ, did everything have to be about money? Some things, like this talisman, had intrinsic value. Tanner wouldn't sell it, not in a million years. He'd hang it in his locker at Pendleton, next to his Girls Gone Wild calendar. Or better yet, take it home and display it on the mantel, next to a few of his medals. He removed the halogen from around his shoulder and lifted it high toward the ceiling. The intense light revealed the detail of the craggy rock, and Tanner could now make out every peak, every valley of its miniaturized ranges. "There's the hook," he said, "and there's the loop." He reached up high, stretching himself at the legs and arms. But he couldn't quite reach it. "Slip another block under me, would you?"

Childress brought over more wood and added another lattice to the tower.

Tanner stepped up higher and reached again for the loop. His fingertips played against the knot, and he managed to nudge it over the end of the hook. "Got it," he called out triumphantly.

Stenton and Owens cheered and clapped sarcastically.

Holding out the talisman in a Roman-like salute, Tanner gave an awkward curtsy, then he stuffed the stone into the leg pocket of his fatigues.

The wooden tower suddenly shifted. Tanner's delight turned to panic as he overcompensated for his abrupt change in balance. There was a quick jerk, and in an instant, the fragile array tumbled from beneath his feet. His legs kicked out, upending him, sending him crashing backside to the ground.

A glassy shatter echoed through the cavern as Tanner's body and piles of wood crushed against the halogen lamp.

Darkness smothered the cave.

For a moment only the faint and distant whistle of the valley wind could be heard. Then, stretched over a bed of firewood, Tanner began to shift, gingerly.

"You okay?" he heard Baker call out in the darkness.

"No bones broken," Tanner said. He pulled out a piece of the lamp from under his back. "The halogen's seen better days, though." He struggled to sit up. "Someone burn another one."

"I can't see a thing," Childress said. "Where the hell did I put my night vision?"

Tanner could hear fumbling and cursing as his men searched for their goggles. And then he felt a strange, violent tug against his pant leg. "Jesus, what the hell was that?"

"What was what?" Childress said.

Everyone stood still, listening.

The cavern became quiet.

Tanner scrambled to his feet, brushing aside pieces of wood.

Suddenly, the air around him shuddered, and at once the cavern was drowned in a terrible, high-pitched shriek.

Someone screamed in agony.

Tanner said, "For chrissake, someone burn a halogen!"

Then, as if on queue, another member of the team wailed, his cry pain-filled and horrific.

Moved by fear and confusion, Tanner dashed from his position, unsure where he was going, but unwilling to stand idle while his squad was assaulted. He'd just hit his third stride when there came another sickening cry. Childress, maybe? What was happening? A flood of panic overwhelmed him. Where in the hell were his goggles, his M16?

Racing across the cavern floor, he felt his boot drop upon a piece of wood. His foot rolled and his body pitched. His ankle twisted and snapped. Searing pain coursed up his leg as he drove headfirst through bundles of dried incense, sliding wildly into the cavern wall, crushing his head and shoulder against the rock.

Tanner felt his heartbeat pulsing through his eardrums, and as he listened, he became vaguely aware of the surrounding silence. A numbing wave slapped across his face. And for a brief moment, he imagined himself standing at attention, his superiors stripping him of well-deserved medals. He shut his eyes and slipped into unconsciousness.

# 2

Phoenix, Arizona
June 2002

THE GENTLE SOUND of surf lapping the shore woke Rick Lowell, chief engineer at station KSND in Phoenix. His mind in a fog, he swung his arm over the nightstand and tapped the alarm button. The ocean waves abruptly ended. Gently, he reached out to feel for Beth, to touch her hair and to caress her warm shoulders, but when his hand fell upon the cool surface of the sheets, the empty space scattered the remnant haze of a dream. He realized, as was often the case when he awoke in the morning, that he and Beth had ended their relationship months ago. For a time Rick lay on his side, hands folded between his head and pillow, staring at the white walls. Damn things looked so bare. Maybe paint them green, he decided, or better yet, the color of the open sky.

He swung his feet to the floor and sat up, his hands forming shallow depressions in the mattress. Again he thought of Beth. She was gone. And damn if it still didn't hurt. He lifted a glass of water from the nightstand, sipped it to break the dryness in his mouth, then stared again at the bland walls. To hell with them, he thought bitterly. They could stay white for all he cared.

In the kitchen, Rick pulled a pre-mixed milk and egg concoction from the refrigerator, tossed in a banana and a handful of walnuts for good measure. He noted the time on the kitchen clock. He had a good hour before work. He considered taking a run along Williams Field Road, maybe get in a little exercise before the day heated up. He tightened the pitcher lid, flipped on the blender, and shook the mixture to get things churning.

The telephone rang, followed quickly by the greeting of his answering machine. The voice on the other end was hurried and strained. It was Elliot O'Connor from the station. "Rick, we've got a problem." Elliot paused as though considering what to say next. "That sound tech Mason hired called in sick again, says it's viral this time. Anyway, I can't get anyone to cover, and Mason's screaming like a goddamn orangutan. Can you get in here ASAP and run the board? He's on the air in less than an hour. We've—"

Rick grabbed the receiver. "I'll be there in twenty minutes."

He took a few quick gulps of the shake, feeling cold lumps of banana sliding down his throat. Already a problem at work. This was going to be another one of those shoulda-stayed-in-bed kind of days. He snatched his keys from the hutch and left for the station.

By the time Rick arrived at KSND, the sun had broken the horizon, throwing long shadows over the parking lot. He pulled into his marked space and cut the Explorer's engine, then sat back and shifted uneasily in his seat. The thought of a morning with Mason, the shock jock from hell, etched his nerves. Every other word the man breathed seemed laced with venom of one sort or another, which, surprisingly, seemed to be an asset in the radio talk-show business. It was also the reason Mason had become so successful. Rick considered the dynamics of it all. Though Mason was an asshole, he was also profitable. That there was no denying. The way the station saw it, a disc jockey that brought in high ratings could do no wrong.

Rick sighed.

He shook Mason from his thoughts and threw open the car door. Outside, he breathed deeply, taking in long, steady streams of air. The morning was dry, and a breeze stirred from the north, carrying the faint scent of pine from the desert's creosote shrub. With the temperature already topping eighty, Rick hurried to the entrance. He slid his clearance card through the door's electronic lock and stepped into the lobby.

Security nodded as Rick walked toward the elevators. A smile crossed Rick's face as he thought about the guard and his ironic name. Security Hayworth was a tall, middle-aged black man with a forehead mole that would make Aaron Neville blush. He'd suffered his childhood years in Watts, the oldest of eight children. His mother had named him the night a burglary induced her into labor. A couple thieves jimmied a rear window and slipped inside the house. The experience scared the hell out of his mother, or as she liked to put it, scared Security out of her. She later told him the cramps had been so intense, so unbearable, her wails drove away the thugs. Coming up with a name for her boy had been a piece of cake.

Rick noticed Security poring over a page of the Value Line Survey. "Any recommendations?"

Security closed the booklet and rolled his chair to the kiosk's edge. An eager look formed on his face. "Three words, Rick: Abercrombie and Fitch."

Rick scratched his head. "Clothes?"

"Company's got a strong balance sheet, and earnings over the last five years have grown annually at least twenty percent." Security patted the VL notebook fondly. "Not to mention, I see a winning trend in their marketing strategy."

"And that would be?"

"Using what amounts to kiddy porn to sell overpriced pieces of shit to spoiled rich kids."

"Hey, sex sells," Rick said. "Listen to Mason's broadcast sometime and you'll know what I mean." He gave Security a nod, then walked to the open elevator, where he stepped inside and punched the third-floor button.

When the doors opened, he saw Elliot pacing up and down the hall, running his fingers through his thin, silver hair.

"Good morning, Elliot," Rick said.

The skinny, second generation Irishman dashed over, waving a clipboard in the air. "A lifesaver, that's what you are, a goddamn lifesaver."

"You can take it easy. I'll see about hiring a new sound technician after the show." Rick placed a calming hand on Elliot's shoulder. "I warned you against letting Mason hire people without my approval."

"Look, Rick, the last thing I need right now is an I-told-you-so."

The two men walked shoulder to shoulder toward the studio, Elliot exaggerating his stride to keep up.

Passing the guests' lounge, Rick could hear Andrea Yacker, the station producer, talking with a guest, reviewing the on-air do's and don'ts.

"Who does the little pain in the ass have lined up this morning?" Rick asked.

Elliot turned his head, flopping his silver trim from one temple to the other. "I know Mason can be abrasive, but that *little pain in the ass* is the key to this station's success. His ratings charts over the past six quarters are through the roof. A person doesn't pull in a seven-figure salary and grow to become nationally syndicated without having some kind of talent. Wouldn't you say?" Elliot glanced around to see who was listening, then spoke under his breath, "Look, God only knows why people listen to his brand of insult, but the fact is they do. They love it; they eat it up. And since it's my job to keep this station running profitably, as long as Mason's ratings continue to skyrocket, he's our man."

Rick and Elliot stopped at the studio door—an oversized, soundproofed slab of steel. Rick looked down at Elliot and said, "I understand the station's priorities. And I know the kind of bullshit Mason dishes out. I accepted it when I signed the contract. Just don't expect me to swallow it gracefully. On air or off." He gave the knob a twist and pushed open the studio door.

Inside, he immediately felt Mason's miserable presence. The room, small and windowless, sat under a pall of dim lighting. Cinnamon incense burned near the door, and as Rick made his way inside, curls of brown smoke wafted a trail alongside him.

A waist-high retaining wall divided the studio into two areas. Where Rick would be working, it was clean and organized, the soundboards and patch panel forming a convenient U-shape. Mason, in sharp contrast, sat among filth, as content as a rat atop a garbage heap. He was busy working alongside a litter of Pepsi cans and Ding Dong wrappers, tapping his dough-like fingers rapidly across a keyboard. An idea of some kind seemed to materialize in his head, for he shook his balding red pate approvingly and began mumbling kudos to himself.

Across from Mason, a young female intern was busy clearing away crumbled papers and empty coffee cups from the guest couch. She worked quickly to adjust the three microphones hanging conspicuously overhead.

Rick waved to her, then cleared his throat to signal his arrival to Mason.

The deejay lifted his chin, peering at him with closely set eyes. "It's about time you showed up." He glanced down again with a look of contempt.

Rick shrugged off the usual welcome, then sat down at the board to run a quick sound check. "Any problems with the audio feed?"

Mason ignored him.

Likely a no. Had there been a problem, Mason would be kicking and screaming. Rick spun around and began running a cue mode test, adjusting a field of slides. Then he worked a few knobs, checking the meters. When he finished he reclined back and swiveled his chair one-eighty, observing Mason.

As the little deejay worked, sweat broke from his freckled face, glistening under the faint light. He picked up a pair of massive headphones, squeezed them around his head, then ran a mike check. A moment later he said, "The opening mix is cued. We go live in ninety seconds."

Rick sat up and readied himself. Four hours and he'd be done, able to get to work searching for a more reliable sound technician.

Mason glanced at him sidelong and twisted his thick lips in a crafty grin. The intro music finished running and the on-air light flashed green. Mason began to speak, settling into his low-pitched radio voice. "G-o-o-o-d morning, Phoenix! As promised, I have a great line-up for you today. My first guest is one of those Internet babes with a website to plug, so let's see if we can't take advantage and coax her into putting on a little show for us. See what she won't do to get her web address carried over the airwaves." Mason pushed a button, calling up a pre-recorded S&M mix. The sound of groaning women and wet, slapping flesh echoed through the studio.

Rick shook his head.

"Then later on, during my daily conspiracy hour, we'll have an opportunity to speak with an interesting young man, a soldier. And boy does he have a story to tell. We'll find out if our government's been keeping secrets from us." Mason grinned and eyed Rick. "But first I want to welcome back KSND's chief station engineer, Rick Lowell, filling in for Mel the Mouse, our very own chromosome-shy sound tech. Why don't you give Phoenix your very best how-do-you-do, Rick?"

Words had barely formed on Rick's lips when Mason cut him off. "Uh, uh, this is radio. Have to be fast on the mike." He punched up the sound of a snoring man. "We'll see if we can't wake up my engineer and get him speaking like an adult later on in the show."

Rick's body stiffened. He dug his fingertips into the cushion of his chair, debating whether or not to hit the cough switch. That'd really piss Mason off. The little guy obsessed over controlling everything that went on the air. Which as far as Rick could tell was anything flattering to himself, and anything humiliating to others. Weeks before, when Rick had been asked to cover for Mel, he'd discovered this the hard way. An hour into the show Mason had fixed him between his crosshairs, taking shots at everything from Rick's love life to his education and time in the military.

But since then, Rick had prepared. He'd installed a kill switch to temporarily disable Mason's edit circuitry. He'd also tapped into the shock jock's office line and recorded dozens of personal telephone calls. A few of which turned out to be real gems. Let the little weasel get out of line today. The airwaves would be fair game.

A few minutes before eight, the studio door opened and a petite blonde in a tight miniskirt walked into the studio. Her hair was short and gel-combed straight back, giving the impression she'd just emerged from a dive into a swimming pool. With excited eyes, she hurried across the room. Rick followed her gaze, eager to witness her reaction to the sight of Mason.

As the blonde drew closer to the couch, there was a sudden change in her expression. Straight lips replaced the smile and her rear end lost its swing. Rick reclined in his chair, savoring the moment. She'd seen the mighty shock jock, and like all his other fans who met him in person, she was immediately disappointed.

Mason ogled the woman, then said into his mike, "I'd like everyone to close their eyes and imagine this gal, except of course my listeners at the wheel. Strike that, especially my listeners at the wheel." He tapped a button, and the sound of crashing metal shattered the studio calm. "When I say she's hot, folks, I mean she's smoking hot, a tasty little morsel...."

Rick shook his head in dismay, then went to work adjusting levels on the soundboard, while Mason proceeded with an anatomical inventory of the woman.

After a thirty minute barrage of obscene questions and answers and a series of broadcasted ass-slaps, Mason mercifully pulled back the third degree and allowed the woman to plug her voyeur-cam website.

Nearing the last hour of the show, Andrea walked in followed by a lean man in his late twenties, wearing faded blue jeans and a yellow tank top. As the man took a few steps inside, Rick noticed he moved with a pronounced limp. Still, when offered the okay, he walked to the couch confidently, gave the cushions a quick appraisal, then took a seat. Gently, he rested an old Vans shoebox at his side. He crossed a leg, ankle to knee, then began looking around the studio.

Rick punched up the morning schedule on the computer: Captain Jake Tanner, United States Marine Corps. The notes indicated the segment was to be an interview, an account of the man's military experience in Afghanistan. It said Mason had read about an incident involving Tanner and his strike team. And after learning the man was a local, Mason contacted him and convinced him to come on the show to share his experience.

This was the flip side of Mason's radio persona. As much as he was obsessed with sex, he was equally paranoid over government conspiracies. Since the start of the Afghan conflict, he'd been bringing in guests with political and military affiliations, trying his best to un-cover X-File type plots and cover-ups.

The commercial track ended, and the on-air light flashed green. Mason cleared his throat, then punched his cough switch to edit it from the broadcast. "Two words—government cover-up. That's the topic of our next segment. I've been telling you all for months how these trigger-happy dictators in the Middle East are itching to blow a little kiss our way. Today, I have a man in the studio who knows first hand the horror and devastation these bastards are willing to inflict up-on Americans. With me is Jake Tanner, a captain in the United States Marine Corps." Mason looked over at the seated man and gave him a thumbs-up.

Tanner acknowledged the gesture with a nod.

"What I would like to know first," Mason asked him, "is a little background. Tell my listeners about yourself."

The intern adjusted Tanner's microphone, dropping it nose level and a few inches from his face.

"I'm a soldier, a U.S. Marine."

"You married?"

"No sir, I'm not."

"Have a girlfriend?"

"No sir."

Mason grinned from behind his mike. "Prefer blondes or bru-nettes?"

Adjusting his position on the couch, Tanner said, "I guess blondes, but I don't see—"

"Of course you do. If you couldn't see, they never would've made you a Marine." Mason grinned devilishly. "What's your girl-friend's name?"

"Sir, I told you, I don't have a girlfriend. We broke up in April."

"Oh, you broke up?" Mason pointed across the partition. "Then you and my engineer have quite a bit in common. You're both military men and you were both dumped. You see, Rick here was a hotshot in the Army, just like yourself."

"I'm a Marine."

*"I apologize if you're not satisfied, however—"*

Rick stopped the tape.

Instantly, an army of switchboard lights blinked alive, callers eager to comment.

Mason's nostrils flared, and behind the mike he squared his shoulders like a football player set at the line of scrimmage. "I seem to have struck a nerve bringing up Beth, eh, Rick? I notice you didn't answer the question. Why'd she dump you? Not enough fuel in your rocket?" Mason grinned, happy to be back on the offensive.

Rick shrugged, coughed Mason's reply from the broadcast, then calmly queued another tape. "Let's see what else we have for your listeners." He pressed a button, running a second telephone conversation:

*"You can't just make claims, then not deliver,"* came Mason's voice again, loud and grainy. *"I'll have my lawyers stuffing your ass so full of lawsuits you'll feel like a Thanksgiving Day turkey. Do you understand me?"*

*"Sir, we market our supplement honestly. The ad doesn't guarantee three inches, it guarantees* up to *three inches. The relevant phrase being 'up to'."*

*"But it says I'll get results or my money back."*

*"Within six months, Mr. Manning. Our records show your bottle was purchased nine months ago."*

*"Christ almighty! I was giving it time to work."*

*"I'm sorry, sir, but—"*

*"It's not about the money, don't you understand? It's about the promise."* Mason's voice was laced with desperation. *"Come on, I didn't expect a full three inches, but damn it, I got nothing. Hell, it may have even shrunk!"*

Rick stopped the tape and looked over at the switchboard. The call lights blinked furiously.

Mason sat stunned, red-faced and motionless.

A long moment passed.

Then the shock jock's eyes refocused and he began to speak, "Dead air. We can't have dead air. Go to commercial."

"Commercial?" Tanner said from the couch. "Then when are we gonna get around to talking about this?"

Rick turned his attention to the Marine, who seemed little interested in their on-air confrontation. Through the dimness of the studio lights, Rick could see dangling from Tanner's outstretched hand a peculiar black stone.

# 3

RICK RAN HIS fingers across the soundboard, punching buttons, and adjusting slides. "The commercial track is running," he announced, standing to his feet and preparing for a confrontation with Mason.

But oddly, Mason wasn't firing back. He'd already shaken off the humiliation and was walking to the couch with a Ding Dong in his hand. He dropped down next to Tanner and examined the object. "It's awesome, like a black jewel," he said. "I'll bet it's old."

Tanner raised it eye level and nodded. "Yep." He swung it back and forth as if it were some sort of tool of hypnosis. Then he shrugged. "Well, at least I think it's old. I haven't been able to figure that out yet."

Rick approached the couch slowly, trying to read Mason's face. He was clearly absorbed with the strange looking stone, not the least bit of anger in his eyes. Either he'd a short memory for insults or remarkably thick hide, much thicker than Rick had given him credit for.

"It's a talisman, found it in Afghanistan," Tanner said. "In a cave."

"In a cave?" Mason said.

The Marine nodded. "Same place where," he paused, a sick expression forming on his face, "where me and my men…" his voice trailed off.

"Why don't you tell me what happened?"

Tanner lowered the stone back into the shoebox, covered it up. "Last December—"

"On the air, my boy, on the air." Mason stood and headed to his mike, but then stopped a few steps short and turned as-a-matter-of-factly, his index finger curled like a question mark to his lips. He eyed Rick. "I'll admit, engineer, you took me by surprise. I didn't think you had it in you." He spun back around and marched to his chair, stomping over Ding Dong wrappers and bellowing like a politician, "I shall not forget, though. I shall not forget."

As the commercial track ended, Mason carefully adjusted his headset. The on-air light flashed green, and he shifted again into radio mode, speaking confidently under the mike. Rick was baffled. It was as if the man controlled his emotions with a switch.

"Thanks for staying with us," Mason said. "We're back with Captain Tanner, who's ready to intrigue us with his story. A true story." Mason pulled a notepad from the console and flipped it opened to a tagged page. "Most of you know I support our government's position on terrorism. I believe military action is an important component in dealing with these douche bag terrorists. My guest this morning is one of those faceless men who work hard to keep our nation secure. The kind of man most of us never get a chance to thank." Mason twisted his chubby body toward Tanner and saluted.

The Marine tipped his head, acknowledging the kind words.

"Earlier this month, I read a news article about a man who'd gone through hell last winter during a military operation in the Afghan mountains. That man was Captain Tanner. When I learned he was a local hero, I booked him immediately. At my request, he agreed to come on the air and describe the horror our soldiers are facing in these ass-backward countries." Mason turned and spoke directly to Tanner. "That *is* what we're facing isn't it, Captain? Horror?"

"No question about it," Tanner said into his mike.

"You told us that last winter you were involved in a military operation."

"That's right."

"Anything unusual about it?"

Under the studio's dim light, Rick could see Tanner's face beginning to harden. The Marine rested a hand on the shoebox. "Yeah, it was unusual alright."

"How so?"

"My men were killed."

Mason didn't reply, letting the dead air heighten the impact of Tanner's revelation. After a few seconds he lightly cleared his throat and said, "Would you mind telling my listeners about this mission, Captain?"

"It was simple, really. I led an MEU—"

"You'll forgive us for not knowing the military jargon."

"MEU, a Marine Expeditionary Unit," Tanner said. "It was our job to clear caves, neutralize al Qaeda. That's what we were doing when we ran into the hermit."

"Hermit?"

"Yeah, the cave, it had a hermit living inside it." Tanner dropped his head and spoke under his breath. "There weren't any munitions or any terrorists, just an old man who'd made the place his home."

"So there was a hermit in the cave, so what?"

"So we shot the poor bastard, that's what."

"Jesus Christ, why did you do that?"

"He spooked my men," Tanner said. "It was an accident."

Rick was trying to put a read on the Marine. There was regret in his voice, of that he was sure. But there seemed to be something more inside him, something Rick couldn't get a handle on.

"Why on earth would someone be living alone in a mountain cave?" Mason asked.

Tanner shrugged. "No idea. But if I was to guess, I'd say he was just a crazy old man."

"He say anything to you?"

"No."

"Nothing at all?"

"Nothing that made much sense," Tanner said. "Seconds before he died he became agitated, worried about the time."

"The time?" Mason said.

"Yeah, nutty, ain't it? I mean, here's this guy lying in his own guts, bleeding out from a hundred holes, and what does he fuss over? The time."

"Maybe he was expecting someone?"

"In the midst of a storm? In a remote Afghan cave? I doubt it. The fact is the old man was dying, and he knew it. His time was growing short, and he didn't want it to end. Had to be what he meant."

Rick could see Mason scratching his head, trying to make sense of it.

"Okay, not to downplay your encounter with this hermit," Mason said impatiently, paddling his hand in circles, "but could you get to the part where your men were killed?"

Tanner looked across the room, sweeping his sight from Mason to Rick, then back again to Mason. The Marine looked pale, like he was ready to puke. "It was after I'd broken the halogen lamp. Everything went black. None of us could see." He paused, absently stroking the shoebox. "That's when it happened."

"That's when what happened?" Mason said, his eyes growing wide.

Tanner thought a moment. "I don't know for sure. I remember a strange sound, kind of a high-pitched wail, like something you might hear in a nightmare, something echoing in the halls of an asylum. Then came an awful vibration, intense. Felt like I'd been grabbed by the head and shaken like a rag doll. Thought my eardrums were gonna explode."

Mason riffled through pages in his notebook. "It's my understanding you had an accident and were knocked cold."

Rick noticed an immediate change in Tanner's demeanor, a hint of shame. The Marine glanced down at his lap, tugged at the couch's purple nap. "That's right. I busted my ankle, fell and slid headfirst into the cave wall. I don't remember anything after that."

"When did you learn your team had been killed?"

"When I woke up in the medevac chopper, hours later."

"You see their bodies?"

Tanner swallowed, staring blankly into the mike. "No."

"Then how do you know they were killed?"

"Because when I came to in the chopper, none of my men were with me. I knew something horrible had happened to them. I could see it in the eyes of the crew."

Mason nodded impatiently. "Yes, yes, but when did you get the details? I mean, how exactly were they killed? Who briefed you?"

"Technically," Tanner said, staring wondrously at Mason, "nobody. All I was told was that my men hadn't survived the operation."

"You're telling me you haven't a clue? Doesn't that drive you crazy, not knowing? It seems to me any number of things could have happened to them. No one really knows, except maybe the brass in the military, and they don't want you, or the American people, to find out about it."

"In Germany, while recovering from my injuries, a couple investigators from Medical Research Command came by and grilled me about the events. I told them everything I could remember. When I asked how Childress, Baker, and the others died, they told me the details were classified, not to ask any more questions."

"You see," Mason said. "It's a conspiracy. The government's up to their eyeballs in 'em, which is why we have the daily conspiracy hour here on the Mason Manning show." He punched a button, running theme music from the Twilight Zone. "American soldiers were killed, and our own military refuses to tell us the truth about it." He leaned into his mike. "They've even gone so far as to send a goon squad to silence our good Captain here."

Rick could see Mason's words were having an impact on Tanner, who was staring absently, nodding.

Mason said, "These men who came to see you in Germany, were they from the Marine Corps?"

"No, the Army," Tanner said. "They'd flown in from Fort Detrick, Maryland."

Mason rubbed his chin. "I smell a rat," he said. "Soldiers don't just drop dead, especially not highly trained U.S. Marines. Something unspeakable killed your men, something the military is hiding."

"What do you think it was," Tanner asked. "And why didn't it kill me, too?"

"I don't know, at least not yet I don't. But you can bet I'm going to find out."

For a second, Rick was taken aback. Mason Manning, a serious investigative reporter? He'd pay to see that show. Rick looked across the room at Tanner, who was staring at the shoebox. His mind seemed to be on sabbatical. Rick decided to give the guy a break, change the subject. "Tell us a little about that talisman of yours."

Tanner blinked. "Oh, yeah, the talisman," he said. A smile returned to his face.

                    *          *          *

After the show, Rick found himself traveling instinctively up the warm, hollow stairwell of the station building, loping contently over the concrete steps. He thought back to the show. Confronting Mason may not have been a wise career move, but it sure made him feel good.

At the top landing, Rick pushed open the roof access door and stepped out under the powder-blue sky. He stretched back his arms, feeling unfettered, eagerly taking in the dry Phoenix air. A shadow streaked overhead, and he looked up to see a flock of finches riding the wind currents eastward across the sky. From somewhere in the bunch, he heard a faint twittering. The sound was soft and pleasant. Then quickly the song began to multiply, even as a few playful strays darted from the ranks, spiraling in crazy directions, later resuming a position in the wedge-like formation. The birds needed each other, Rick realized, as his gaze traced the flock across the sky. Each was an individual, but in the scheme of survival, they were bound to one another for comfort and protection. The finches soon disappeared against the eastern horizon, over the muted greens of the Sonoran Desert.

Rick turned his sight toward the southeast, where a hundred miles distant lay the city of Tucson, Beth's new home. Whether Rick could accept it or not, she had made her choice and had left him. And he was responsible. He'd been a fool to expect Beth to give up her career for a family, to turn down an associate professorship at the university. It was a step in the right direction for her. She was brilliant and hard working, everything a woman needed to be these days to make a mark in the world. Marriage and kids just weren't in the cards. He should have accepted that instead of pushing her, instead of insisting she be something she wasn't.

"Thank you, sir." Rick heard Tanner's voice resonating up from the parking lot outside the lobby.

Rick stretched himself over the roof's parapet and looked down. Five stories below, Tanner was crossing the parking lot, half waving, half saluting Security, who was lounging at the station entrance, sucking the tar from a brown cigarette.

"Hold on a minute!" Rick shouted down.

Tanner glanced up, raising a hand to shield his eyes from the harsh sun. "That you up there, Rick?" he said, shifting the shoebox under his arm.

Rick eyed the box thoughtfully. Beth would love to have a look at that talisman. What archaeologist wouldn't? "Wait there, I'm coming down."

A few minutes later, he met up with Tanner next to his car. "You know, I was thinking, considering you found that talisman in Afghanistan," he pointed to the shoebox, "I know a person I think might be able to identify it for you, maybe give it a date."

"I'm already sure it's old."

"Yeah, but how old? That part of the world has a long history. Muslims have lived there for hundreds of years. And before them, Romans, Greeks, and Persians. Wouldn't you like to narrow things down a bit?"

Tanner stared at the box.

"I'll bet you'd like to know what the talisman meant to the old man, too."

Tanner's face stiffened, and he grew a shade redder than could be accounted for by the sun. "What makes you think I care?"

"In the studio, I could hear it in your voice. Killing that old man rattled you." Rick leaned against the car. "The talisman is gonna stir that memory for as long as you keep it. Learning something about it might help you make sense of things. Trust me, as an ex-military man, I've been there."

"Mason mentioned you were in the Army. Where'd you see action?"

"Panama."

"That was a bitch of a conflict."

Rick shrugged. "Panama in '89, Afghanistan in '01, it's all the same to me."

Tanner limped closer to the car, rested the shoebox on top of its hood, and fished in his pockets for the keys. He turned and leaned against the car next to Rick. They stood quietly, taking in the empty sky.

After a minute Tanner said, "My men and I, we should've been more careful." He shifted his weight, easing the burden on his injured ankle. "I can't help but think something I could have done might have changed what happened that night."

Rick didn't respond, figuring it best to let the Marine speak his mind.

"Oddly enough though, I don't feel guilty about what happened. I never have. I suppose to a lot of people that makes me an asshole." He glanced at Rick. "What do you think?"

"It doesn't matter what I think."

"I'm asking."

Rick dragged a palm across his forehead, wiping away the sweat. "You and your men had a job to do and you did it. That's what I think. It worked the same way for me in Panama. And it's worked the same way for every soldier in every war in every century since man discovered how to piss on one another. It's the nature of the beast."

"Guess that's one way to look at it." Tanner pushed away from the car, the corner of his lips stretched long in an acquiescent grin. "But with me, the issue was perfection. I run through that night over and over again in my mind because it was a failure. I blew what should have been a perfect record." He grabbed the shoebox from the hood and unlocked the car door.

Rick stepped aside.

"But still," Tanner said, patting the box, "I'd like to learn more about this stone anyway."

That's what Rick wanted to hear. He pulled a pen and business card from his shirt pocket, flipped it backside and scribbled a note: Dr. Beth Harper, University of Arizona, Tucson. "Call the school and get in touch with this woman. I guarantee you, if there's anyone who can tell you about that talisman, it's Beth Harper."

# 4

PETER ECKERMAN concentrated on taking slow, deep breaths, his chest still heaving beneath the ill-fitted cardigan. The climb up the steep Chanoines steps had taxed his lungs dearly, and so it was with great satisfaction that he planted himself comfortably on a wooden chair at a storefront table along the rue de la Reine Berengere. From a leather satchel, he removed a bottle of Evian and a porcelain cup. His meaty hands shook as he filled it.

The flight to Le Mans had been a tiring one, but one he'd made for good reason. Investigating every lead, no matter how small, was crucial if ever he wished to find what he was looking for. And the call he'd received from the Frenchman sounded promising. Hope stirred, but Eckerman promptly suppressed it. No sense getting too excited until he had a chance to examine the book.

He watched through the café window as a young waitress with thick, golden hair finished a sale and hurried from behind the counter. Adjusting her apron, she quickly emerged from the café and greeted him with an honest smile.

"Good afternoon," she said in melodious French. "May I offer you a pastry?"

"Café au Lait will be fine, my dear," Eckerman said. He admired the young girl's vitality, her dash from behind the counter, her immediate response to a customer. Such initiative was rare among today's youth.

She acknowledged his order with a polite nod, then shuffled off, leaving behind her a magnificent view of the Cathedral St-Julien. Eckerman stared in awe at the stony leviathan, its flying buttresses pressing like claws into the ashen walls. The cathedral dwarfed the adjacent place St-Michel, rising tall against a background of silvery cirrus clouds.

Eckerman finished his water and returned the cup to his satchel. He watched through the storefront window as the young waitress frothed his milk, shifting impatiently on her feet. The café clock chimed 9:30 a.m. Soon morning Mass would end and the square would fill with parishioners. He pulled a fistful of coins from his pocket, sifting through it for a couple of euros. The waitress emerged from the café with his drink.

It was 9:45 a.m. when the cathedral doors finally opened and small groups of the faithful streamed into the place St-Michel. At first only a few scattered groups spilled out into the plaza, buzzing over the morning service, but as the seconds turned to minutes, the entire area filled, thronging with men and women engaged in cheerful conversation. Children played tag, darting artfully over the cobblestones and slipping between the crowds, excited into action by the conclusion of Mass.

Eckerman sipped his coffee, recalling similar scenes many decades ago in Munich when he himself was a child. On Sundays, he would accompany his mother and father to the Frauenkirche, and after services caper about Market Square in much the same way as did the children here. He sighed wistfully. It had been a blissful time in his life, a time of innocence and naivety. Ah, to be young again, he mused.

The waitress emerged from the café. "Would you care for another drink?"

"No no, thank you," Eckerman said. "If you don't mind, I'd rather you direct me to this address?" He produced a scrap of paper and showed it to the young lady.

"Yes, the rue St. Flaceau. It is just beyond Place St. Pierre in the Old Town, le Vieux Mans. Not far." Her thin finger pointed across the crowded plaza, to where a series of cobbled lanes disappeared between the buildings.

"Thank you kindly," Eckerman said. He added another euro to the table and lifted himself from the chair. The day was young and a cool breeze stirred. But still he perspired. After pulling a handkerchief from his pocket and dabbing his forehead, he strolled across the plaza to where the waitress had indicated.

It was a short walk along a series of paths to the rue St. Flaceau. There, Eckerman's eyes studied the cobbled lane. Old timber-framed houses rose sheer on either side of him, smothering the storefronts in deep shadow. The upper windows of the buildings were fronted by wrought-iron balconettes, upon which hung potted flowers of yellow and red, a smidgen of color against an otherwise gray façade.

The lane was deserted.

For several minutes Eckerman strolled, pausing occasionally to double-check the address. *Ah, there was the shop, just ahead.* He walked to a recessed doorway, over which hung a weathered sign with faded script: *LIVRES RARES ET MANUSCRITS*.

Eckerman felt a growing anticipation. It was a feeling he'd come to know very well over the past few decades. But all of the leads, all of the searching he'd accomplished, it always seemed to end in disappointment. He reminded himself of this fact, so as not to get overly excited, then reached for the handle of the door.

In keeping with the atmosphere of the Old Town, the room inside was dark and cramped. To Eckerman's right, a narrow staircase ascended into blackness. Shades covered the windows, even as an old-fashioned oil lamp burned dimly on a table heaped high with manuscript rolls. Shelves filled with dusty volumes divided the shop into sections, and the smell of old leather hung in the air. It was a scent Eckerman knew quite well.

He searched for the dealer, but aside from the many books and manuscripts, the shop was empty. He looked again at his paper and read the name: Monsieur Laval, the gentleman he'd come to see. Eckerman was about to call out for assistance when at the top of the staircase a door opened. There was a flash of bright light and the door shut again. In the shadows, a figure descended.

Eckerman gripped his satchel and said, "My name is Ecker-man, Peter Eckerman. I have come from Munich. Please, where may I find Monsieur Laval?"

"I am Monsieur Laval." The voice was soft and effeminate, which quickly put Eckerman at ease. The descending figure resolved into a young man, perhaps thirty, with short curly hair and a long sloping nose. He wore jeans and sneakers and a T-shirt with a slogan that proclaimed: M'm! M'm! GOOD!

"Pleased to make your acquaintance." Eckerman offered his hand.

Laval shook it, then stepped back, hands rested on his hips. He studied Eckerman with large oval eyes. "Forgive me if I seem taken aback, it's just that, well, I'm a little surprised to see you."

"But we spoke, you answered my inquiry, do you not remember?"

"Yes, yes, of course. What I mean is that I'm surprised you actually came, and all the way from Munich."

"What I seek is very important."

"Yes, it must be."

"I brought the volume you requested."

Laval's eyes grew wide. "After we spoke, I asked myself why a man would go to so much trouble—and expense—all for information that seems quite innocuous. You brought the book you say?"

"Of course." Eckerman patted his satchel. "The History of the Indian Tribes of North America, the second of a three-volume set."

The Frenchman beamed.

"This is a very valuable book," Eckerman added.

"I'm aware," Laval said. "And most difficult to acquire. I own volumes one and three. This will complete the set. Your shop must contain an impressive collection."

Eckerman smiled. "Let us just say your shelves are humble in comparison."

Laval ignored the slight, gaping at the satchel. "The book, may I see it?"

"Yes, of course." Eckerman opened the satchel and withdrew a volume bound in red leather. "Leaf thirteen has a one-inch tear, leafs one hundred six through one hundred nineteen have nibbles, and a few of the pages are lightly foxed. But over all, the tome is in excellent condition."

Laval reached for it.

Eckerman pulled it back. "You'll forgive me if I first insist on seeing your book."

"My book?" Laval wrinkled his long nose. "I'm afraid there's been a misunderstanding."

"A misunderstanding? When I called, you said you'd come across something which fit the bill. I must say, if this has been some sort of a scheme, I shall be very—"

"No, no, of course not. The object you described, I have information you should be very much interested in."

This was all confusing to Eckerman. "If you've come across a relevant passage, then—"

"A passage? No, no, perhaps it's best I simply show you," Laval said. "Come with me." He turned and retreated back to the staircase.

Eckerman followed him, laboring up the creaking steps. When Laval opened the door, bright light again poured from the room beyond. Eckerman shielded his eyes and entered. The young Frenchman shut the door behind them.

Eckerman's first sensation was that of a chill. But it was refreshing. He breathed in the crisp air and exhaled pleasantly. As his eyes adjusted to the harshness of the light, he quickly realized he was in a place altogether different from the antiquated bookstore below. Cleanliness was the order of the day here.

The white, sterile walls were decorated with all sorts of American memorabilia. Pinned up on display were items of clothing: a pair of faded Levis, a T-shirt with the picture of a guitar-wielding rock star, and a white, jewel-encrusted jumpsuit. "Long live the king," Laval said, noticing Eckerman's stare.

Large prints hung over the wall to his right. One showed the '69 moon landing, while another, a cowboy smoking Marlboro cigarettes. A replica of Warhol's famous soup can painting was here as well. And there was plenty of other memorabilia, all an assault on Eckerman's eyes.

The only books displayed were on a shelf to Eckerman's left. At their center were two red leather volumes and a space between them for a third. A few feet from the shelf, protruding far from the wall, Laval had mounted a horse saddle, complete with stirrups and saddlebags.

At the room's center was an island of tables upon which were arranged a ring of computers and monitors. A large air conditioning unit rumbled above them.

"As you can see," Laval said, "I'm a bit of a nut for American popular culture."

That, Eckerman thought, was an understatement, but it did explain the Frenchman's interest in the book he'd brought. "What exactly does all of this have to do with the object I seek?"

Laval gestured to the computers.

Eckerman stared at them. His shoulders slumped. Coming here, he was now certain, had been a waste of time. "I may be an old man, but I have heard of the Internet. I've already conducted a thorough investigation. What I'm looking for cannot be Googled, my dear boy." Exasperated, he turned to leave.

"Then this object, it no longer interests you?"

Eckerman stopped at the door. "As I've said, I've already tried the Internet, have hired professionals in fact, people who can dig in places you and I cannot."

"Indulge me," Laval said. "If after five minutes you're still no longer interested, then you may leave and take that wonderful book with you."

"I can leave and take it with me now."

"Five minutes, it's all I ask."

Eckerman sighed. He'd come a long way. There would be no harm in hearing the boy out.

Laval led him around the island of computers. On most of the monitor screens were video games, paused in mid-play. On one screen, Eckerman saw what appeared to be a virtual juke-box, an old-fashioned model, like the ones found in American diners of the 50's.

Laval planted himself on a swivel chair in front of the computer and began to type. The jukebox blinked alive with color. "One of my passions, you understand, is American talk radio. I particularly enjoy listening to what they call shock jockeys. These are fascinating radio personalities who seem little restrained by modern social norms. For them, no topic is taboo. You may have heard the names Howard Stern, Don Imus, or Mason Manning. They dominate their field. I listen to their webcasts regularly." As he spoke, a virtual record fell onto a turntable and the speakers crackled to life.

Eckerman heard the voices of men.

Laval spoke over the recording. "The one calling himself Tanner is a U.S. military officer who led a team of soldiers into an Afghanistan cave, apparently searching for al Qaeda operatives. They encountered not terrorists, but rather an innocent old man."

Eckerman found himself intrigued. "May I sit?"

Laval pulled up a chair.

Eckerman eased himself down.

"This old man was in possession of a stone, one that matches remarkably well the details of the one you seek. Here, listen, this is where Tanner describes it." Laval clicked up the volume.

Eckerman paid close attention to the Marine's story and his description of the talisman. With trembling hands he removed his cup and water bottle from the satchel. He listened intently, growing excited with every passing detail. There was no doubt. There could be no coincidence. This had to be the artifact he'd spent decades searching for.

"So," Laval said, scratching his long nose. "Am I right? This talisman, is it the stone you seek?"

Eckerman poured more water and took a deep gulp, quickly calming his nerves. When he finished he set the cup on the table. "Yes, my dear boy. And I should say you have more than earned this." He withdrew the rare volume from his satchel and handed it to the Frenchman, whose eyes glowed with delight.

Laval leapt from his seat and hurried to the bookshelf, where he carefully inserted the tome between the two others. He stepped back and beheld them, as if admiring a Monet. With a nod of satisfaction he turned to Eckerman. "What you have given me is quite valuable. So I can only imagine this stone, it is important for you to find?"

Eckerman stood from the chair, gathered his satchel, and smoothed down his rumpled cardigan. He walked to Laval and rested a hand upon his thin shoulder. "Let's just say, my dear boy, I must not fail to retrieve it. A great many lives hang in the balance."

# 5

CARSON BENNETT LOOKED down again at his summer session schedule, made sure the room number matched up, then entered the lecture hall, still pissed that university counselors didn't know their keisters from a hole in the ground. Three of his buddies had already flown out this afternoon to London, beginning a six-week backpacking trip across Great Britain to celebrate their graduation. Carson by all rights should have been with them. Follow the four-year schedule I've outlined for you, his advisor told him. Trust me, you'll be just fine. What a joke. Transcript evaluations came back last week and it turns out he was missing a science requirement. Wouldn't graduate until he met it. Now, while his friends were halfway across the Atlantic, hours away from tossing back pints and putting the moves on European girls, he was here at the university taking some good-for-nothing field archaeology course.

Shoulders slumped, Carson surveyed the lecture hall, running his sight along ascending rows of ancient chairs, each equipped with an itsy bitsy foldout slate that the university had sense of humor enough to call a desktop. The room was only a quarter full with students sitting in clusters, grouped by what Carson figured were probably common personality traits: a few loud-mouthed and destined to flunk jocks hidden in the top seats, a scattering of semi-serious undergrads near the center, and a few nerdy ass-suckers in the front. The ass-suckers, they'd be the worst, the ones delaying the break, asking the professor a million questions that each of them already knew the answers to. Carson scanned the schedule for the professor's name, wondering which stuffy old windbag would soon be blowing hot air up his kazoo. Dr. Harper, Beth. Great, the old windbag was a woman. He could imagine her now, hours in the excavation pit, miles from a shower and a toothbrush. Christ, she'd have skin tougher than leather, and her breath probably smelled like crap. He ascended five or six rows, just in case he was right about the breath, and found a seat cattycorner up from a couple of cute blondes. He shrugged off his backpack, removed a pencil and note-book, then began flipping through the text for interesting photos.

The hall quieted and Carson instinctively looked up from the book. A lean woman in a white T-shirt and faded Levis entered the hall, striding across the floor carrying a worn leather briefcase. Her hair was as black as midnight, glowing with a healthy sheen and falling in feath-ered waves across her forehead. Her olive skin was smooth and un-blemished, the perfect compliment to deliciously rounded cheekbones. And as she reached the lectern, her piercing green eyes swept over the hall. She laid down the briefcase, smiled, and in a voice as sweet as honey said, "Welcome everyone to the Archaeology of the Persian Em-pire."

Tears welled up in Carson's eyes and he had to resist the urge to clap. *There was a God after all.* He was graduating as a psych major. Why on earth hadn't he considered going into archaeology? Harper would have been the advisor to kill for.

Instantly, the blondes below him changed their perky tone, and Carson could now hear them whispering snide remarks: "She oughta dress like a professor," one of the bimbos said, "not like a twenty-something wannabe."

"Uh, huh, obviously she's just trying to get a rise out of the guys," another answered back.

"See the way she strutted in here like she's God's gift?"

Whatever Harper's reasons for going casual, Carson thought, one thing was clear—she was hotter than a summer sidewalk.

Dr. Harper pulled a notepad from her briefcase and flipped through its foxed yellow sheets. At the dry-erase board she began num-bering lecture points. Conversations mingled behind her as she rapidly scribbled. Then, a sharp, ear-splitting whistle rang out from somewhere behind Carson, hushing student conversations. Before he could turn and hone in on the moron, a male voice, thick with conceit, carried down from a higher row. "I hear archaeologists love doing it in the dirt. Is that a fact, Teach?"

Dr. Harper continued writing, ignoring the idiot. She capped the marker and turned to face the class. "Morning everyone, I expect we're all anxious to begin the course and learn a little about the science of archaeology." Her stunning green eyes searched the upper rows accusingly. "A bit about myself. I hold a Ph.D. in Near Eastern Archaeology, with a specialty in Ancient Persia. I've spent the last few years—"

From high in the hall, a rumble of voices interrupted the professor's introduction. Carson twisted around to zero in on the offenders. He could see a small group of jocks huddled in a tight knot spanning a portion of two rows. They ignored Dr. Harper, talking and carrying on as casually as if they'd been kicking it in the student center. None of them had supplies, no notebooks, no textbooks, no nothing, just the clothes on their backs and the marbles in their heads. A bunch of mouthy apes, all of them probably on football scholarships, expecting to skate through their classes.

Dr. Harper continued. "This summer I hope to accomplish two things: First, I would like everyone to walk away with an understanding of how an archaeologist collects and interprets evidence of the past."

The jocks continued their conversation.

"Excuse me," Dr. Harper called out to them. "You really should pay attention. You might miss something important."

The jocks turned and glared, annoyed that Harper had the nerve to interrupt them.

As Carson looked on, the boy in the center of the group waved a hand. He was big and ugly and loaded with vein-laced muscles. "A couple of questions, Teach."

"Dr. Teach, if you don't mind," Harper said.

A few polite chuckles.

"Right, whatever." The jock propped his elbows onto the desktop and began flexing his biceps in an alternating rhythm. "I got a question that can't wait."

Great, here comes the wisecrack, Carson thought.

"You university people must think students can shit cash or something," the jock said. "This is nothing but a summer class. Why should we fork out two hundred bucks for a bunch of crappy text-books?"

If Dr. Harper was bothered by the asinine question, she didn't show it. She rested the marker on the lectern, held her hands prayer-style over her lips, and appeared as though she were giving the question serious consideration. "Why should you buy a textbook?" she said. "That's a very good question. The answer, I suppose, is so you might learn a little something. Do you mind if we move on?"

The jock rolled his eyes and let out an exasperated breath.

"The second thing I'd like everyone to come away with," Harper continued, "is a greater understanding of the Persian Empire, its culture and its political organization. Through the use of archaeology, scientists are coming to learn more and more about an incredible civilization that to date has been sorely overlooked by historians."

"Overlooked?" said a kid with acne scars sitting in the front row.

"Yes," Harper said. "Strangely enough, the Achaemenids did not sufficiently record the history of their own empire. Apart from a few inscriptions, most notably the Behistun columns, there exists no Persian narrative. Because of this, historians tend to jump from Babylonia and Assyria right to the empire of Alexander, as if there were nothing in between. Fortunately, archaeology is changing that."

The jock interrupted, "Hey Teach, do you work out?"

Dr. Harper's green eyes observed the boy with indifference.

"Because if you do," he added, "you and me, we could go work out together, if you know what I mean."

"Maybe if you pay attention, you'll find this to be an interesting course."

"Yawn, yawn, yawn," the jock called out. "Bor-ring."

"Boring?" Dr. Harper said. "You would call boring an empire that exploded into prominence, conquering in two generations the whole of the Near Eastern world?"

"No shit?" The jock straightened in his chair.

"No shit."

More chuckles.

"They must've had a bad-ass army."

"Theories for their success range from the more credible military brilliance of the Achaemenid kings to the far less credible explanations of the supernatural."

*Supernatural?* Carson's interest was piqued. "What sort of explanations?"

Harper said, "Most of what we know of ancient Persia comes to us not from the Persians themselves, but rather from the written records of the nations they conquered. In these records we find references to the Achaemenid kings and their practice of the occult. It's been said they possessed a divine artifact capable of manipulating nature, of conjuring fierce storms and deadly plagues."

"What sort of an artifact?" Carson asked.

"A mystical stone," Harper said. "Because its depiction was first discovered in the treasury of the Persian capital, it's been called the Talisman of Persepolis."

"Are any of the legends true?" Carson asked.

Harper smiled at him. His stomach fluttered.

"The ancients' belief in the supernatural was the order of the day," she said. "In much the way we use science to understand and control our environment, they used magic and ritual. Today, sophisticated medicines cure illness, back then, it was potions and incantations. And so if you ask me am I shocked that ancient chroniclers explained the Persians' success in terms of the supernatural, I would tell you absolutely not. On the contrary, it's to be expected."

"Makes sense," Carson said.

"What we have here is the ancient equivalent of modern-day spin control. Nations were beaten badly by the Persians. And so it couldn't possibly be they were simply outmatched and outmaneuvered. Much better to claim King Cyrus was in league with evil spirits, that to gain victory he'd resorted to spreading plagues."

Carson noticed the nerds in the front row scribbling furiously into their notebooks.

"But of course today, giving any of these antiquated claims serious consideration would be silly," Harper said. "People who do, I'm afraid, suffer from overactive imaginations. Credible historians will tell you the Persian conquests were the result of a growing cultural unity within the Near East, as well as the superior military prowess of the Persian kings."

"That's right, Teach." The jock in the upper row flexed his thick biceps, raising each one in turn and giving them a smack with his lips. "The Persians used good old-fashioned muscle power."

"Exactly my point," Dr. Harper said. "The armies of the Achaemenid kings had brawn, as well as brains. Their ranks swelled with strong men. Becoming a soldier was no simple task, you understand. There were challenges to meet."

"Challenges?" the jock said. "What kind of challenges?"

"Arduous challenges, ones far too daunting for a modern man such as yourself to attempt."

The jock looked around the hall, unsure whether or not he'd just been taken to task. "I could do anything some old Persian stooge could do. I'm sure of it."

"Don't be ridiculous. Soldiers back then were in peak physical condition. In fact, they were capable of bearing the weight of two grown men. It was required of them, should the need have arisen to carry injured soldiers from the battlefield."

"I could carry two dudes, no problem." He glanced around at a few of the girls, looking to see who was impressed. His gaze fell upon an attractive redhead. He winked.

"No, no, it's best we just move on," Dr. Harper said. "I'm not sure of the liability, if you were to... hurt yourself."

"Hurt myself? Lady—"

"Not to mention we have no volunteers for you to carry."

In a heartbeat, the jock's three buddies jumped to their feet. "We'll do it," one of them called out.

Harper looked unsure. "But if you hurt yourselves...."

"Not a chance. If some ancient Persian dude could do it, then sure as shit I could, too."

"Alright," Dr. Harper said, still appearing skeptical. She took a step back and stared at one end of the lecture hall, then at the other end, where the open door stood propped. "The breadth of this room is about thirty yards. The ancient challenge required the men to bear the weight a full one hundred. From this wall—" she glanced through the door "—to that cottonwood tree there." She pointed outside. "That's about one hundred yards. You would have to make it the entire distance you understand, without allowing either of your friends to drop, not even for a second."

"I could do that."

"Maybe, but I'd need a judge to be sure."

The jock's third buddy called out, "I could follow them, make sure nobody drops. I won't cheat."

"Alright," Dr. Harper said. "Really, though, I honestly doubt you gentlemen can do it."

Faces eager, the jocks had already descended the stairs and grouped up at the far end of the hall. The loudmouth who'd begun the spectacle was now preparing himself, rolling his shoulders and exhaling in violent bursts. "Alright, already," he said. "Let's do this. Houp! Houp! Houp!" he cried out, in an effort to produce an adrenaline rush.

"Alright, then," Dr. Harper said, "since you insist."

The jock crouched low, allowing the bigger of his two buddies to jump up piggyback style. His face flexed in an awkward grimace as he took the weight. Next, he scooped up the other kid in his arms, holding him as would a man crossing the threshold with his new bride. He grunted under the tremendous burden, and his face turned red as a ham. He began staggering forward, one foot kicking past the next in obvious discomfort. Halfway across the hall, he picked up momentum, his breathing coming in quick, labored gasps. Suddenly, he screamed in a manner reminiscent of a powerlifter hefting up a great load, and a moment later, buried under the flesh of his friends, he rushed through the door and into the glaring heat of the day, the fourth boy side-stepping along, observing the ground at their feet with great precision.

Dr. Harper strolled to the door, gave the four idiots one final glance, then lifted the stop and watched as the door shut with a self-locking click. She turned and brushed off her hands as if she'd just emptied the garbage, then walked back to the lectern, her head shaking in disbelief.

There was a moment of silence as the class processed what had just happened. Then there came a rise of scattered laughs. Even the nerds in the front row managed a snicker.

Harper smiled and swept a tangle of loose hair behind her ear. "Now that I've cleared away the dead wood," she said, "what do you say we get started."

The hall erupted in laughter.

Wow, Carson thought. Not only was this lady a looker, but she was as sharp as a tack, too. He was beginning to accept the fact he wasn't gonna make it to Europe this summer. But what the hell. Spending the next few weeks here with Dr. Harper wouldn't be so bad after all.

# 6

IT WAS NEARING five o'clock when Beth arrived at her office, having just spent the better part of an afternoon in the museum archives searching through catalogues and copying imprints of ancient cuneiform tablets.

On the fourth floor of the Emil W. Haury building, tucked away in a neglected corner of the Anthropology Department, her office was little more than a hovel. Beth had overheard some of the professors with similar workplaces complaining over the cramped conditions and Spartan furnishings. They saw it as an insult, a sort of blatant disregard for their years of academic preparation and fieldwork training. But to Beth, a small office didn't seem like much of a problem. She considered it a temporary nuisance, like having to deal with those immature boys in class this afternoon, one of many she'd have to accept on her climb up the ladder of academia.

After coaxing her key into the lock, she worked open the door and stepped inside. She unloaded a stack of journals onto her desk, then switched on the fluorescent lamp and watched as it flickered and died. With an open hand she banged its metal casing. Electric light sputtered to life.

She pulled a bottle of water from the mini-fridge, then began scanning her office area, counting off items on her mental to-do list. The space she'd originally envisioned had not yet come to fruition. Against the wall opposite the desk, she planned to erect a bookcase,

where she would shelve and catalogue a small library of texts and journals. And in a cabinet alongside it, she intended to store the product of
her tedious research: numerous volumes of Old Persian cuneiform
transliterations. These changes alone would cut her workspace in half.
Then there was always the wall over her desk. She could—

The office door creaked open and Beth turned, startled. Doris
Heckel, the department secretary, stood at the threshold, her great mass
centered in the doorframe like a bear looming at a cave entrance. Light
reflected from the sweat on her face. She took a step into the office and
hefted up a chunky arm, offering Beth a manila envelope. "Take it,
doll. It hurts just lifting the thing."

"An envelope?" Beth asked, figuring it couldn't weigh more
than a few ounces.

"No, my arm."

Beth laughed and snatched it away. She glanced at the return
address. Jake Tanner, Surprise, Arizona. Didn't know the guy. She
turned back to Doris. "Sorry you had to make the trek all the way to
this end of the floor."

"Don't you worry," Doris said. "In time they'll move you
closer to the action. I mean, look at Dr. Bailor. Four years ago I needed
a backpack and a canteen to reach his office. Then he published that
book about them Indians who lived in the cliffs."

"The Anasazi," Beth said.

"Yeah, that's what he called them. Anyway, Dr. Chendekar
ended up rewarding him with prime office space."

"Publication has its perks."

Doris tapped her nose. "See, you understand the politics, don't
you, doll? If you don't mind me saying, if I were you, I'd find something people want to read about. Then write it." Her eyes widened.
"Hey, why not them Indians?"

"I think I'll stick to ancient Persia and leave the Anasazi to Dr.
Bailor."

Doris shrugged. "Whatever you say, doll." She scanned the
office, as if trying to gain insight into Beth's studies. "Anything in the
works?"

"I'm speaking at a conference in two weeks, but what I'm presenting isn't anything to write home about, I'm afraid."

"You don't sound too enthused," Doris said. "What's the trouble?"

"No trouble, really," Beth said. "I've prepared a paper on some cuneiform transliterations that deal with various royal decrees and economic transactions."

"Yuck," Doris said. "Sounds stuffy."

"That's the problem," Beth said. "It *is* stuffy, nothing groundbreaking. Like most everything else at this symposium, my presentation will be vanilla, it won't stand out. It'll end up lost in the mundane."

"Hey, mundane ain't so bad," Doris said. "It pays the bills, don't it, doll?"

Beth frowned. In academia, the mundane was like a disease, and it could be the death of a scholar in her field. How could she ever explain to a person like Doris how it felt to be driven to achieve something great. Doris was somewhere in her third decade here in the department, and she'd never aspired to anything more than being a secretary. How could she ever understand the passion—

Beth stopped, angry with herself for having become so condescending in her thoughts. What was she thinking? Doris was just trying to be helpful. She was a sweet lady and Beth had no right judging her. "You know, Doris, you're absolutely right. These transliterations are going to pay the bills."

Doris smiled and took a step back, peering down the hall. She sighed. "Alright, doll. Knock 'em dead at that conference. And if you'll take a little advice, don't be afraid to use what the good Lord gave you. That petite figure of yours, and those green eyes, they can be an asset. Flirt a bit with the head honchos and maybe this time next year, I won't have to drop a crumb trail to find my way back from your office." She winked and turned away, then lumbered off down the hall.

For now, Beth decided, she'd forget about the conference, focus on other things, like getting her office in order. She turned her attention back to the envelope. Jake Tanner from Surprise, Arizona.

She sat in her chair and grabbed a letter opener. With a flick of a wrist, she split the envelope, reached inside and pulled out a letter.

A photo slipped out from between the paper and glided zigzag to the floor. As she bent forward to snatch it up, her sight fell upon a name in the letter: Rick Lowell. *Rick,* Beth thought. Quickly, she sat up and began to read:

*Dear Dr. Harper,*

*My name is Jake Tanner, Captain in the United States Marine Corps. The object in this photograph was recovered in the Wazir Valley, Afghanistan, back in December of last year. I recently met Rick Lowell at station KSND in Phoenix, who told me you might be able to identify the stone, given your area of expertise. I've taken quite an interest in it and thought maybe you could tell me about its history. If so, please call me at the number above. Any help would be greatly appreciated.*

*Sincerely,*
*Jake Tanner*

Beth's eyes traced back up the letter to the name Rick Lowell, her ex-boyfriend. A man she still cared for deeply. And for a moment, she couldn't help but slip into the past and recall some of their fonder times together. Memories of their camping trips always seemed to stand out. Often during weekends, they'd hike into the high Arizona desert, where the air was crisp and the skies were clear. In the twilight hours they'd assemble Rick's telescope and sit side-by-side, sharing their thoughts and dreams and waiting for the heavens to darken, for that moment when stars blinked to life and flickered by the thousands.

With some difficulty, Beth pulled herself back to the present. Their breakup had been over priorities. Rick wanted marriage and a family, a commitment impossible for her to make if ever she wanted to achieve lasting success in her field. By taking the faculty position at the university, she'd chosen another path, another life altogether. Still, Beth couldn't help but feel a certain warmth whenever she thought of Rick. And whatever their differences, he was still a wonderful man.

She took a sip of water and reclined in the chair, her brain feeling like overcooked spaghetti. She kneaded her temples, and after a time recalled the photograph that had slipped under the desk. She rolled back in her chair and fished it out with her foot, then took a quick look. The image in the photo was lost in the shadows of the office. She laid it on her desk and angled up the lamp, immersing it under a wash of pale blue light. A shiny black object of indeterminable size came into view, but there was nothing in the photo to give the thing scale. Still, something in its shape and design seemed familiar to her. She leaned closer and stared hard at the image. Instantly, she became aware of the office clock, its miserable ticking. She yanked its plug, then focused back on the photograph. Looking closer, she thought she could make out detail around the object's center, some sort of relief. Beth wheeled her chair to a basket on the floor and dug through it for a magnifying glass. Under its lens, the image in the photograph exploded in size.

And what Beth saw nearly knocked her out of her chair.

The object was clearly an artifact made from obsidian, and the band around its center depicted scenes cut expertly in relief. Her eyes slowly followed the pictorial story. The first scene depicted a man in a chariot surrounded by an army of warriors, battling under a blazing sun. The next showed the charioteer thrusting an object high into the sky. Tanner had not photographed other angles of the stone, so the remaining scenes were impossible to discern, but nonetheless, Beth had seen enough.

Her hands began to tremble.

She set down the magnifying glass and took a long drink of water, then rolled the cold bottle against her neck. Looking down again at the picture, she considered the object's size and shape. She jumped from her chair and removed a leather-bound book from a stack on the floor. Quickly, she leafed through the pages until she reached a series of photographs detailing various stone relief and cylinder seal impressions found in excavations at Persepolis. Beth flattened the book on the desk and traced her fingertips down the page, reading each of the photograph's descriptions:

*Cylinder Seal Impression on a Clay Tablet, Seated God and a Priest Standing on Opposite Table Sides, Assyrian, Found in the Treasury*

*Cylinder Seal Impression on a Clay Tablet, Hero in Combat with a Winged Monster, Assyrian, ninth to eighth century B.C., Found in the Treasury*

*Cylinder Seal Impression on a Clay Tablet, Hero Holding Two Winged Monsters, Achaemenian, Found in the Treasury*

*Cylinder Seal Impression on a Clay Tablet, Winged Monster Chasing an Ibex, Achaemenian, Found in Eastern Fortification*

*Cylinder Seal Impression on a Clay Tablet, Hero Triumphant, Darius Inscription, Achaemenian, Found in the Treasury*

Beth's eyes stopped on the next photograph. She glanced at its description:

*Cylinder Seal Impression on a Clay Tablet, Darius Holding the Talisman of Persepolis, Achaemenid, Found in the Treasury*

She studied the talisman in Darius's hand. Though small, she could tell it was the same shape as the artifact in Tanner's photo. She continued scanning the page, looking for one photograph in particular. On the next page she found it:

*Cylinder Seal Impression on a Clay Tablet, the Talisman of Persepolis, Achaemenid, Found in the Treasury*

The picture was clear, and because of the large size of the impression, so was the talisman's detail. Again, Beth held Tanner's photograph under the magnifying glass, and she compared the relief in his photo to the relief found at Persepolis.

There was no doubt.

The details were the same.

For a moment, she couldn't think. Her mind was a tangle of emotions. Excitement and disbelief welled up from somewhere deep inside her, and again she became aware of her trembling hands. The object in the photograph bore a striking resemblance to the Talisman of Persepolis. No, not a striking resemblance, she thought—it was an exact copy. Could it possibly be? A find like this would be amazing. No, not just amazing, it would be extraordinary, a crowning achievement for any archaeologist.

Beth considered the artifact again, the Talisman of Persepolis. She had mentioned it to her students this very morning. In the eyes of the ancients, the talisman was the conduit between a king and his god, believed to be the physical manifestation of his right to rule an empire. And as such, it was the subject of much intrigue. Many a Persian prince had given his life in pursuit to capture it. It was the greatest of all Near Eastern relics, and if by some miracle Beth could acquire it, there would be no telling the excitement it would generate. She glanced around her tiny office, at its stained walls and chipping paint, and she laughed. Dr. Bailor, she thought. Eat your heart out.

Beth rolled her chair across the floor and locked the door. Then she stood up and stretched, dipped her chin down and rolled her head from side to side, thinking, considering all the angles.

That's when the doubt set in.

A rotten feeling grew in the pit of her stomach. The object in Tanner's photo couldn't possibly be the Talisman of Persepolis. The stone was only a legend, like the Ark of the Covenant or King Solomon's Tablet, or any other number of elusive relics. And even if it was real, artifacts like this didn't just turn up in people's hands, especially the hands of a Marine living in Surprise, Arizona.

Beth drew in a deep breath, angry at herself for having indulged in such a silly fantasy. She was weary and growing more tired with each passing second. Far more likely, she thought, someone—a history enthusiast—had crafted a fine looking copy of the stone. She closed the book and tossed it back onto the pile, then slumped into the chair, closed her eyes, and thought of the upcoming symposium and her boring cuneiform transliterations. A few minutes later she was asleep.

\*          \*          \*

When Dr. Beth Harper awoke she felt disoriented. The electric light on her desk was flickering, casting the office in a pale, strobo-scopic gloom. She banged the light's casing to get it working again, turned and looked at the clock. The second hand wasn't moving. Of course not, she'd unplugged the darn thing. Her head throbbed, and all she could think about was a cool shower and a comfortable bed. As she stood, memories of the talisman returned, and she recalled Tanner's photograph. She imagined the upcoming symposium, rows and rows of critical colleagues, all sitting under dim light, watching near death's door as she ran through slide after slide of cuneiform transliterations, doing her best to infuse excitement into a lecture on livestock trade and emerging money economies. She'd make about as much splash as a pebble in the Pacific.

She lifted Tanner's photo and looked again at the image of the talisman, wondering if it could possibly be.

Just maybe.

What the heck. It wouldn't hurt to take a firsthand look. She snatched up the note, found Mr. Tanner's number, and picked up the phone and dialed.

## 7

MASON MANNING WALKED the six steps to the ornately carved antique bar and took a quick inventory of his snacks: One twelve pack of Pepsi—check. Two boxes of Ding Dongs—check. Three bags of Doritos—check. If he didn't overindulge, it was just enough to get him through the day. Popping open a soda can, he returned to the upholstered armchair and took a seat. He stared around the room wondering what the parlor had cost to furnish. The paneled walls, like the fancy furniture, appeared to be solid cherry. The rugs covering the floor, if he didn't know better, were comparable in quality to a few he'd laid out in the living room at home. And God knows they weren't cheap.

Through the glass-paned doors leading onto the caboose's open-air platform. Mason could see the station's crowd beginning to thin. He glanced at a brass clock and noted the time: nine forty-five. The conductor had seemed confident the train would leave as scheduled, which gave his buddy Jarred about fifteen minutes to get his ass aboard. Mason slurped his soda, then jerked back the can, nearly spilling onto his khakis. It was warm—still. Christ, he'd put the damned things on ice nearly thirty minutes ago.

There was a knock on the door. Mason turned. "Be my guest."

The door opened and a man in a black suit leaned inside. He wore a conductor's cap and was palming a gold pocket watch with a chain that disappeared inside his vest. "We depart the station in five minutes." He smiled and ducked back out.

Mason snickered. Did people still actually carry those old timepieces, he wondered, or was the guy just playing a role. Admittedly, it did add a certain Old West atmosphere to the trip. It wasn't often Mason rode to the Canyon in this, a turn-of-the-century locomotive. But on the occasions he did, he usually had a radio segment in the works. There was something about the rhythm of the train that helped him to clear his mind and figure the angles.

A horn sounded, followed by a blast of steam, and the train lurched forward, beginning its crawl from the station. Mason peered through the caboose window. Only a few interested observers still remained on the departure platform, staring wistfully at the historic locomotive. Jarred wasn't among them. Maybe there was a problem at the military base. Or maybe he didn't have the security access he'd bragged about having. Could be he was saving himself from a good chewing. Mason reached into his carry-on and pulled out a box. He opened it, removed a cigar, then stepped out onto the platform. As he patted his pockets for matches, the parlor door opened. He turned, ready to rip the porter a new asshole for not knocking. Instead, Jarred walked in, tall and hulking, squeezed tightly into a faded-blue Polo shirt. He carried an attaché that brushed coarsely against his jeans as he walked.

Mason pocketed the cigar and hurried back into the parlor, rubbing his hands excitedly. "To be honest," he said, "I had doubts you'd show, buddy. Thought maybe you were blowing smoke about your security clearance."

"Come on, when have I ever lied to you?" Jarred sat down and rested the attaché on his lap.

As the big man worked open the case, Mason studied him. He was dark-skinned and leathery, with a thick neck and a square jaw. But it was his hair that amused Mason the most. Military cuts were, without question, the most pathetic haircuts on the face of the planet. And Jarred's cut took the blue ribbon. Shaved flat on top and tight on both sides, his head reminded Mason of a caramel apple pulled fresh from the wax paper.

"We gonna be alone?" Jarred asked, nodding at the two empty chairs.

"I reserved the entire caboose," Mason said. "There'll be no one else around. Let's talk where we can get some air."

Outside, Mason stood on the platform, watching the dry countryside retreat at an impressive forty miles per hour. He scratched alive a match and lit the cigar, fighting against the seesawing motion of the train. "So what do you have for me," he called back to Jarred.

"Something you're gonna like." The big man appeared at Mason's side, double-fisting a red folder. "The Marine you wanted information on, Jake Tanner, I got his bio."

"Good," Mason said, blowing away a cloud of smoke. "How about the others on Tanner's team? The dead men. They're the meat of the story. I need cause of death."

"I was able to access standard information: bios, ranks, assignments, military honors and disciplinary actions, the usual. But once I dug a little deeper and tried to get dirt on Operation Cold Strike, I hit a brick wall. Something big must've happened that night, something the Corps found important enough to involve specialists at MRMC and DARPA. The file's been turned over to Command at Fort Detrick. Its contents have been sealed."

"What do you mean sealed?"

"Sealed. Inaccessible. The mission's classified. Access has been upgraded to Top-Secret."

"Is that unusual?"

Jarred shrugged. "All operations are military classified, that's not unusual," he said. "But the fact something so routine was handed over to the Army's Medical Research Command, well, let's just say that doesn't happen every day. Then there's the issue of DARPA."

"What's DARPA?"

"The Defense Advanced Research Projects Agency," Jarred said. "The boys there are the brainiacs of the U.S. Defense Department, the scientists responsible for creating all sorts of sophisticated war technologies. From what I understand, they've dabbled in everything from hybrid biosystems to genetically modified soldiers."

Mason turned toward the rapidly retreating landscape, lost in thought. He'd suspected something ugly was going on, and now he was sure of it. His instincts told him to dig deep, that a whale of a story would turn up, something big enough to skyrocket his already impressive program ratings.

He took a long, thoughtful drag from his cigar, absently scanning the thickets of brush growing under the ponderosas. A passing tree shuddered with activity, catching Mason's attention. Ground squirrels darted across needled branches, shaking loose pine cones. Why the scare? He wondered. Squinting against the sun, Mason searched the ground for a predator. Then he heard a shriek from high above the treetops and glanced skyward. A red-tailed hawk fell slowly in descending circles over the trees, scouting for a meal. The thought of nature's brutal food chain quickened Mason's pulse, and for a moment he considered his own place in the hierarchy. He couldn't help but smile, thinking of the hawk-eat-squirrel kind of world he lived in. Among the squirrels of the broadcasting biosphere, he liked to think himself a hawk.

"What's got you grinning?" Jarred asked.

"Never mind," Mason said. He flicked away ashes and considered his next move. "Okay, this is the plan." He turned to Jarred, pointing his cigar at the big man's chest. "I want you to dig deep, access those MRMC and DARPA files, find out how those men died. I want specifics. If it's horrible news, it's great news. My guess is—"

"Hold on," Jarred interrupted. "You don't seem to understand."

"I understand just fine," Mason said. "Last year in the Wazir Valley, something killed a group of American soldiers, something awful, something our military doesn't want people to know about. I say that's bullshit. People in this country have a right to know the threats they face. We can't allow our government to keep secrets." Mason narrowed his eyes and inched the cigar closer to Jarred. "For chrissake, we're supposed to be a free nation."

Jarred stepped back from the glowing butt, shaking his head. "These documents are inaccessible."

"Inaccessible? Baloney. Access is a privilege of the wealthy." Mason dug a hand into his pocket and pulled free a money clip loaded with cash. "Where there's a bill there's a way." He eyed Jarred discerningly. The big man clutched the folder protectively against his chest.

Mason turned toward the tracks and flicked away a lump of ashes, watching it scatter into a glittering cloud. "How's your mother?"

"She's fine," Jarred said, his voice barely audible over the roar of the moving train.

"I'm sorry, I didn't catch that," Mason said, turning back. "Did I hear you say she was fine?"

Jarred relaxed his grip on the folder and stood with his head cocked slightly downward. "Yeah, she's doing great."

"I take it my radio plug helped her business, what's it called again?"

"Mona's Psychic Readings."

"That's right, Mona's Psychic Readings. Your mom's little 900 scam."

Jarred stepped forward. "Hey, watch what you say about my mother. Her business ain't a scam."

Mason shrank back, mindful of Jarred's hulking size. The big guy was his friend, but he was also stupid and impulsive. Mason didn't want to feel the back of his meaty paw. "No, right, that's not what I meant."

"Then what *did* you mean?"

Mason snubbed out his cigar on the railing and tossed it onto the retreating tracks, watching it bounce crazily from tie to tie. "Only that a thirty-second radio spot doesn't come cheap, especially in my market."

"I understand that," Jarred said. "Look, there's no question me and Mom are both grateful. Business has really picked up for her."

"That warms my heart," Mason said with a hint of sarcasm.

"But I'm still not authorized to access those files."

"Christ, Jarred, didn't you hear me? I want answers. Do what it takes." Mason leaned against the railing, staring fiercely at the big man. Then he softened his expression for effect. "Look, buddy, imagine what a weekly plug would do for your mom. I could arrange it. In a few short weeks, she'd find herself ass deep in palm sweat, the money rolling in. Hell, in a year or two she'd probably be able to retire."

Jarred stood quietly, thinking.

"You love your mother, don't you?" Mason said. "If I remember right, she's coming along in years. Sometimes a son has to do what it takes to provide for his parents."

A long moment passed.

Finally Jarred spoke up, "I know someone that might be able to help me access the database at Detrick, maybe dig up a little more on Cold Strike." He stared hard at Mason. "That's it though, just one last time. I'm taking a huge risk."

"Of course, just one last time," Mason said, his lips stretched in a wide grin.

## 8

EARLY THE NEXT MORNING, Mason sat quietly under the dim glow of the studio lights, poring over lists of books and periodicals he intended to have his intern dig up for him at the library. He yawned, letting the cool air of the studio stream into his lungs. The oxygen gave his brain a temporary jolt. He blinked down at the papers, then paused to consider again the incredible news Jarred had given him: Tanner's mission in Afghanistan had been coded top-secret, and details of the op were now being overseen by DARPA, the central research and development unit of the Defense Department, the same cunning men and women responsible for creating all sorts of cutting-edge war-fighting technologies.

Mason had been trying all morning to settle on the most effective angle to air the developing segment. He rested an arm on the soundboard, carefully avoiding the sliders, figuring how best to word the commercial lead: U.S. launches new anti-terrorist technology in Afghanistan. Attempt fails. Four U.S. soldiers dead. Mason scratched his head. Nah, polls still showed Americans overwhelmingly in favor of the war. Best not to imply U.S. incompetence. Probably better to go the other direction, blame the bad guys: Terrorists in Afghanistan test new weapon prototype. Devastating technology kills four American heroes.

Much better.

He decided to go with it, be vague about the details of the technology, at least until Jarred fed him more information. Mason wasn't sure exactly what had killed Tanner's men, nor was he sure which side was responsible. But what he *was* sure about was that he had tapped into something big, and as soon as he figured it all out it was gonna make a helluva story—whoever was to blame.

The studio door creaked open and that young intern Mason had been dreaming about walked in carrying a box of Ding Dongs and a twelve pack of Pepsi. Instantly, he forgot about the lead. "Set 'em right there, darling."

She turned her big brown eyes to the table, tossed back curls of long, sandy hair, and sauntered over.

Mason eyed her rear end as she bent low to put everything down. *Oh, yeah. The way she strolled into the studio, the way she swung her hips. What a tease. She wanted him, real bad. He could tell.* "Come over here, baby."

She frowned, then crept toward him, uncertain.

"No, seriously, darling, hurry up. I have real work for you today."

She picked up her pace.

"Take this list and get your pretty little tush to the library. I want you to bring me back every periodical and every textbook I have highlighted there. Can't find them at the first library, skip your cute little self to another, as many as it takes to get everything on the list." Mason grinned at her, wishing she'd come closer so he could smell her hair. "You understand what I just told you?"

She nodded.

The intercom crackled. "You there, Mason?" It was Elliot.

"Of course I'm here, numbnuts. Where the hell else would I be?"

"I got this German fellow in my office wants to see you. I told him you don't see people, but he insists, says it's important."

"Dammit, it's five in the morning." Mason tore open the Ding Dong box. "Besides, you know my rule, Elliot: tits or ass, preferably both. Anything else you send away."

Papers in hand, the intern pivoted to leave, but Mason held up a finger to stop her.

Static over the intercom. "Gotcha," Elliot said. "I'll tell him you're unavailable."

Mason waved the girl closer. "Let me ask you a serious question, darling." He reached out and took her hand, caressed it. "How far, exactly, do you intend to go in this business? You know, radio's a highly competitive field. If you please the right people, the right... person, you could go far, real far."

The intercom crackled again. "This guy says—"

"Jesus frickin Christ, Elliot." Mason dropped the girl's hand. "Just call Security and eighty-six the loser."

Static. "Mr. Manning, I'm sorry for bothering you." The voice was laced in a thick German accent.

Mason could hear Elliot objecting in the background.

"My name is Peter Eckerman, and I—"

"I don't care if you're Peter Pumpkin-Eater," Mason said. "I'm busy, and I don't talk to screwballs. Take a hike, before I have security bounce you back to Berlin."

"If you'd be so kind as to answer a few questions."

Mason waved the girl away and turned back to the intercom. "Be so kind? Do you know who I am? Do you have any idea what my time is worth, you sorry son-of-a-bitch? Elliot, get rid of him."

"Right away."

The intercom sputtered, and Mason could hear what sounded like a small struggle. "Please, Mr. Manning. If you'd simply point me in the direction of one of your recent guests."

My God, Mason thought. How hard could it be to get rid of an old Kraut?

Static.

There was a tangle of voices, "...his name was Captain Tanner."

Static.

The intercom went dead. At the sound of Tanner's name, Mason dropped his half-eaten Ding Dong, lurched forward, and slapped the intercom. "Elliot, send that guy in here, right away. What was his name? Peter Pumpkin-Eater?"

*        *        *

A minute later, Mason found himself standing face to face with the old man. "I'm sorry about the little misunderstanding. So, you're a friend of Tanner's?"

"A soon to be acquaintance, I hope."

Mason was surprised how well Eckerman spoke English. And he was especially pleased to find that the guy didn't reek. He'd heard most Euro-trash despised taking showers and stunk to the high heavens. But this guy had no smell at all, not unless it was hiding under his layered clothing. He seemed to have forgotten it was summertime in Arizona, wearing a navy blue cardigan over a white collared shirt. He had a pear-shaped frame Mason figured would tip a scale at two-twenty. Despite his size and age, the old man seemed to have fared well with the hair. Whitened by time, it was as thick as a coyote pelt.

Mason pulled a Pepsi from the pack, thought about offering Eckerman one, then decided against it. If he gave one up he'd only have ten left, barely enough to get him through the day. "Why you here?" Mason asked. He popped open the soda can.

"I'd be most grateful for a transcript of the radio broadcast you aired three days ago with Mr. Tanner. And, if you don't mind, a telephone number where I can reach him."

Mason took a long gulp, sat in his chair and leaned back. "What's your business?"

"It's concerning his military experience in Afghanistan."

Mason blinked. Military experience? "You understand I can't just give out home addresses and telephone numbers. My guests count on me to be discreet."

"Perhaps in this case you could make an exception."

"What is it about his military experience you want to know?"

Eckerman paused, thinking. "The purpose of his mission, events that transpired, details for a news article I'm piecing together."

"You came all the way from Germany to ask questions for a news article? I don't buy it. All that could have been done by phone. What do you really want?"

"If you would simply provide me with his telephone number."

"I won't give you squat until you start talking straight with me." Mason slurped from the can, his eyes trained on Eckerman.

Perspiration broke from the old man's wrinkled forehead. His breathing became labored. "Mr. Manning, I am not at liberty to discuss the details."

"Then I'm not at liberty to give you his telephone number. The transcripts you can buy from the station. They're public domain." Mason hoped he wasn't pushing too hard. In reality, he didn't want Eckerman leaving before he could pry out some useful information. The guy seemed too old to be German military intelligence. Maybe he had some kind of affiliation with a defense contract company or something. One thing was for sure, he had an interest in Operation Cold Strike.

"Alright, Mr. Manning, I must apologize." Eckerman pulled a handkerchief from his pocket and dabbed the back of his neck. "You seem to have me—how do you say?—at a disadvantage. Your instincts are correct. I haven't been completely forthright."

Satisfied he was beginning to get somewhere with the old man, Mason folded his arms and listened.

"As I told you, my name is Peter Eckerman. That much is true. However, I am not a news reporter. I am a rare books dealer, a specialist in ancient and medieval manuscripts."

"Okay," Mason said. "That's a start. But tell me, why does a rare books dealer come all the way from Europe to powwow with a U.S. Marine?"

"During your broadcast, Mr. Tanner had in his possession a black stone. A talisman. Do you remember it?"

Mason straightened up. *Remember it? How could he forget it? The damn thing was mesmerizing.* "Yeah, I remember it."

The old man's blue eyes sparkled.

"You came all this way for the talisman?"

"Indeed, I did," Eckerman said.

Well that sucked, Mason thought. He was hoping the old man would be a connection to the mystery.

"You seem disappointed."

"You're not what I was expecting."

"What were you expecting?"

"I'm not sure exactly," Mason said. "Another piece of the puzzle, I guess. During a reconnaissance-op in Afghanistan, Tanner and his team were caught up in some sort of intrigue. I'm trying to figure out what happened. I thought you might be a link."

"I'm sorry I can't help you, Mr. Manning. I've come simply to offer my assistance in safeguarding the talisman."

*Safeguard the talisman?* Mason's disappointment turned to curiosity. "What are you talking about?"

"If you please, I must contact Mr. Tanner."

"Not a problem. I have his number and address. And I'll share—right after you explain what's so important about the talisman."

"Forgive me, but I haven't the time to explain."

Mason pointed to the door. "There's the way out."

Eckerman's blue eyes gazed at the door. He appeared to be in the midst of a dilemma. A moment passed and the old man sighed, unfolded his handkerchief, then began dabbing his brow.

"Come on, make up your mind," Mason said. "I'm a busy man."

"Yes, of course." Breathing heavily now, Eckerman looked about the studio, his eyes searching. "May I have a seat?"

Mason rolled up a chair. "Be my guest."

Eckerman eased himself down. "As I told you, I deal in manuscripts—rare and priceless. Nearly two decades ago, an associate and dear friend of mine was murdered, and a very important tome was stolen from me. I've been searching tirelessly for it ever since."

Mason narrowed his eyes. "I don't see the connection. What's this book have to do with the talisman?"

"They are intimately connected," Eckerman said. "They share a very long history."

"Exactly how long?" Mason asked.

"Well, the talisman's precise age is unknown, but certainly it's been in existence since the time of the Achaemenid kings, over twenty-three hundred years."

Mason whistled. Twenty-three hundred years. That was a hell of a long time. "This book you mentioned, tell me about it."

"It was compiled sometime in the first century before Christ and is known as the *Telesma*. The word itself is from the Classical Greek meaning the talisman."

"What is it, like a history book?"

"A history book, yes," Eckerman said, "but much, much more. It's a sacred liturgical text that details the ceremonies and rituals of the Mithraic religion. It is, in short, the Mithraic bible. One of a kind."

"The Mithraic religion? Never heard of it."

Eckerman chuckled. His belly shook under the cardigan. "No, of course you haven't. Mithraism, like so many other religions, has been lost in the shadows of Christianity. But I can assure you, my friend, you have certainly felt its influence."

Mason popped open another Pepsi and took a sip, listening carefully.

"Mithraism was widely practiced in the Near East centuries before the rise of Christianity." Eckerman considered for a moment. "Please, if you would, describe for me a modern Christian church."

"What for?"

"Indulge me."

Mason shrugged. "I don't know. The churches I've seen usually have a long nave with aisles on both sides, an altar at the end."

"Yes, of course," Eckerman said. "And hundreds of years before Christian services, Mithraic gatherings were held in much the same sort of place. Its followers, too, sat on benches running either side of a narrow nave, with an altar at the end. You see, Mr. Manning, the Mithraeum was the forerunner of the traditional Christian church."

Mason considered a moment. "Okay, even if that's true, I can't say I'm much influenced by it." He grinned sheepishly. "Haven't been to church since I was a little boy."

"Do you celebrate Christmas?"

"Most people in this country do, in one way or another."

"December 25th then, an important date, yes? Perhaps you could tell me why."

*Was this guy an idiot? Who didn't know the significance of December 25th?* "It's Christ's birthday."

"It is, is it?" Eckerman chuckled. "Read your Bible, Mr. Manning, then explain to me the discrepancy in seasons. Jesus was born in the springtime."

"Well, December's when everyone celebrates it."

"Right you are, but do you know why?"

Mason scratched his head. "No."

"In the early centuries after the birth of Jesus, Christian leaders were concerned over the growing influence of an equally popular and longer standing religion—Mithraism. The Church saw it as a serious threat, and so it entered into competition with it."

"How so?"

"By choosing the most prominent day of the Mithraic calendar, and then eclipsing it, establishing in its place a new day of Christian celebration."

"Let me guess. December 25th."

"Precisely," Eckerman said, "December 25th, an immensely significant day: The Birth of the Sun. The Birth of Mithra."

"You're actually telling me the Church stole the day…just like that?"

"Indeed, making it Christ's own."

Mason was quiet again, thinking. None of what the old man said surprised him. Whether it was man exploiting man or religion exploiting religion, it was all the same, the way of the world. "I know how the Establishment works. People, belief systems, they're suppressed all the time. The powerful reign supreme. You don't need to convince me. But what does any of this have to do with the talisman? Why do you want it so bad?"

"That's a bit complicated, Mr. Manning. To understand my motivation, you would first need to understand the history of the stone." Eckerman paused and folded his hands. "It is not known precisely when the talisman came into being, but legend holds that it was first wielded by Cyrus, a leader of the Persian peasantry. He used the stone to depose the Median overlord, Astyages, and with it, Cyrus and his successors legitimized their rule, hastening the Persian's rise to power. But in time, rulers of the empire began indulging in excess. As a result, they lost Mithra's favor, and shortly thereafter, the talisman fell into the hands of Alexander the Great."

Mason straightened in his chair. "*The* Alexander the Great?"

"That's right."

"How?"

"Precisely how, I'm afraid, is unclear. What is known, however, is that his possession of it was brief, as one of his officers, a Greek scholar by the name of Tacticus, stole the relic and secreted it away into the mountains, convinced that its misuse would somehow bring about the destruction of civilization."

Mason leaned forward, muscles tense. "The destruction of civilization?"

"Yes, you see the talisman is a divine artifact, Mr. Manning. And as such, it is capable of harnessing immense power."

"You mean like fire and brimstone?"

"Yes, something like that—withering crops, violent storms, devastating plagues." Eckerman leaned close and spoke in a wondrous tone. "And on a fantastic scale, my dear boy."

Taking great care, Mason unwrapped a Ding Dong. "How do you know all this?"

"It is prophesized in the *Telesma*."

Mason took a bite, swallowed. "What else does this book say?"

"That Mithra's Chosen, the Brotherhood, will one day reclaim the talisman and rise to prominence as leaders of a New World Order."

"A New World Order? The Brotherhood?"

"Yes, the *Telesma* describes them as a fraternity of priests, the Keepers of True Knowledge. Their order was prominent during the height of the Persian Empire. They were the spiritual advisors of the kings, and as such they greatly influenced the course of world history. They are known by the mark of their order, the black sun."

"A black sun?" Mason said. "Sounds sinister."

"You must understand, these people are fundamentalists, practicing Mithraism in all its primitive aspects: bizarre ritual, human sacrifice, and the male domination of society."

Mason grinned. "Hey, one out of three ain't bad."

"Please, Mr. Manning. If the Brotherhood finds the talisman, I can assure you it will be no laughing matter. Human suffering will be substantial."

"Hold on," Mason said. "Are you telling me you think this Brotherhood organization is still around?"

"Of course."

"You mean you've come all this way because you're afraid of some crazy, two thousand-year-old prophecy?"

"It's not so crazy," Eckerman said.

"That's ridiculous. The Brotherhood may have been around twenty-three centuries ago, but I think it's safe to say time's put an end to their plans. Trust me, nothing lasts forever. These people are a memory."

Eckerman's eyes darkened. "It was not a memory that murdered my friend, Mr. Manning. And it was not a memory that stole the *Telesma*. You see, the night my partner was murdered, I was there. We were together in the shop working late, appraising a collection of newly acquired manuscripts." Eckerman seemed to fall into an uncomfortable reverie, staring blindly past Mason. "A stranger entered, young and so very tall. I explained we were closed, that he would have to return another day. But the man stood firm, unwilling to leave. He was quiet and without emotion, in a frightening sort of way. I repeated we were closed, but my words fell upon deaf ears. The man approached, menacingly. My friend and I became panicked and demanded once more that he quit the premises."

Body rigid, Mason stared into the old man's eyes, sharing the fear of his memory.

"It was then I saw the garrote." Eckerman began to sweat. He wiped his forehead. "Still, my friend summoned the courage to stand fast."

"What happened?"

"The stranger attacked, brutally. I was powerless to help. I fled, seeking assistance. But when I returned with the police, the assassin was gone, and my colleague, my dear friend—dead."

There was a long, uncomfortable silence. Mason could hear the ticking of the studio clock. "And the book?" he said at last. "What happened to the *Telesma*?"

Eckerman flinched, his eyes refocusing. "It was gone."

"You think this killer was part of the Brotherhood?"

Eckerman nodded gravely. "I'll never forget the fear I felt as the stranger loomed toward us. The scene is etched into my memory. And I'll never forget what I saw. There on the assassin's hand, inked into the flesh between his thumb and forefinger was the mark described in the ancient tome, the mark of the Brotherhood—the blazing black sun."

For a moment, Mason was at a loss for words. The old man's story was incredible, and it would make a great tie-in to the Tanner segment. Not only did Mason have a cover-up involving a failed U.S. military operation, but now an ancient religious artifact had been thrown into the mix, as well. The question was how to proceed? How could he best connect the two stories and present them to his listeners for maximum impact?

"So, Mr. Manning, if you please."

"Huh?" Mason shook away his thoughts and looked at the old man.

"The telephone number and the address of Mr. Tanner. I have been honest and forthright, so may I have what you promised in return?"

"Oh, that, sure," Mason said. "But first..." Casually, he strolled to the table and plucked up another Ding Dong. "You know, Mr. Eckerman, Peter. I can call you Peter, right? Your story has given me a fantastic idea."

The old man arched his bushy white eyebrows.

Mason returned to his chair, leaned close to Eckerman and grinned. "I have a proposition for you."

# 9

CLARK STEWART SAT in the climate-controlled sanctuary of Walter Enterprise's company jet. With a loathing eye he stared through the small, tinted window at the waves of heat radiating from the Tarmac. Stewart scowled. Phoenix was a desert, for chrissake. What would possess men to build a city in the middle of a god-forsaken desert? The attendant's voice interrupted his thoughts.

"Shall I call for your car, Mr. Stewart?" She asked.

"What's the temperature out there?"

"The pilot tells me one hundred four degrees."

Stewart considered the woman's stiff, expressionless face. Not a frown, not a twitch, not a single damned wrinkle of emotion. How could she be so oblivious to his crisis? He'd soon have to step out of the plane, and for the love of God, it was a hundred and four degrees outside. Didn't that faze her? He gave her a rude stare. "Yes. Call for my car. And make certain the air conditioner is running high."

Like an automaton she nodded, straightened her posture, and with measured steps, made her way down the aisle.

Stewart stood from his seat and despite the temperature outside, slipped his suit coat from its hanger. In the heat or in the cold, a custom-tailored Dormeuil was meant to be worn and exhibited, not toted. Besides, the car would be cooled, and only if this Tanner fellow was suicidal would he live in Phoenix without air conditioning. Stewart picked away a tiny piece of lint from the corduroy coat, pulled it over his thin frame, and prepared to deplane.

*         *         *

The white Mercedes sped along Sun Valley Parkway in the Phoenix suburb of Surprise. With mild interest Stewart noted the squat buildings as they streaked by, shades of brown against a powder blue sky.

So this was Surprise, Arizona. He snickered at the ridiculous name, but after giving it some thought, he concluded that indeed it was quite fitting. It was a surprise anyone would choose to live in such a dreadful place.

Minutes later, the Mercedes pulled curbside in front of Tanner's house. Stewart glanced around the neighborhood, observing the dreadful homes surrounded by pitiful yards. Rock gardens dotted with succulents and cacti seemed to be the design a la mode. And everywhere he looked, nothing stirred. Not a gardener pruning a bush. Not a retiree walking a dog. Not even a child riding a bicycle. He turned to Tanner's house, a brown-washed little nothing, like all the rest of the little nothings, with peeling paint and shuttered windows, surrounded by a swath of dead grass. But no matter, Stewart thought. If the artifact Tanner possessed was real, he'd soon have little trouble affording a new place, assuming, of course, the man had sense enough to sell it.

From car to porch, Stewart bled heavy streams of sweat. He readjusted a slippery grip on the handle of his briefcase and poked twice at the doorbell.

When the door opened, Stewart smiled at the fit young man standing before him. "Mr. Tanner, I presume?" he said, pushing his way into the air-conditioned house. At the edge of the foyer, Stewart turned and extended a hand. "Very pleased to make your acquaintance."

Tanner shook his hand. "You must be Walter's man."

"Indeed," Stewart said, "at least the part of me that hasn't yet melted."

The young man grinned. "You shouldn't be wearing a suit coat. But anyway, to each his own, why don't we talk in here?" He led Stewart into the living room. Situated next to an open kitchen, it was a small space, made smaller by a sectional sofa and a big screen television set.

Tanner picked up a remote and muted the television's volume.

"I'm sorry," Stewart said. "Did you say you had refreshments?"

"Sure thing." Tanner started for the kitchen, his walk betraying a mild limp. He opened the refrigerator and peered inside. "I got Coors in the bottle or Coke in the can."

"The pilsner will be fine."

"Sorry, buddy. All I got is beer or soda."

Stewart sighed. "The beer, thank you."

Tanner grabbed two bottles and kicked the refrigerator shut. "I appreciate you coming out here."

"Yes, well, I certainly hope it was worth the flight."

Tanner walked back into the living room, a surprised look on his face. "Did I hear you right? You flew out?"

"Indeed, from San Francisco."

"I got the impression you were local?"

"Yes, well, when you own a private jet, everywhere is local."

"An expensive trip. On the phone Walter said the appraisal wouldn't cost me any money."

Stewart fell silent, considering for a moment his strategy. He'd been here less than ten minutes, and already he'd sized-up Mr. Tanner. The young Marine would be easily manipulated. And money would be his weakness. "Sir, when Mr. Walter called, I'm afraid he wasn't being completely up front with you."

"Oh, so here it comes," Tanner said, "the old bait and switch. First you say the appraisal's free, then you slap me with a bill."

"No, no, nothing like that. You see, what I mean is Walter has a special interest in this artifact, and he wishes to purchase it from you."

"Stop right there," Tanner said, pointing at Stewart with a bottle in his hand. "I never said anything about selling it."

"Mr. Walter considers it crude to negotiate by telephone. Too impersonal, you understand. He feels business is best conducted face to face. I happen to agree."

"Or maybe he didn't say anything because he was afraid I'd shop around before he had a chance to fly you out here and make an offer himself."

"I can assure you that is not the case," Stewart said. He straightened his posture. "Indeed, you will find the artifact has very little value outside of a select circle of antiquarians."

"I wouldn't be so sure about that," Tanner said. "In fact, an archaeologist at the university wants to examine it. She's coming by this afternoon."

Stewart maneuvered around the sofa, shaking his head. "My dear Mr. Tanner," he said. "University researchers struggle to fund even their most promising projects. Believe me when I tell you, this archaeologist has no intention of offering you any money. Likely she'll try to persuade you to donate the artifact to the university, probably by appealing to your sense of philanthropy."

Tanner listened thoughtfully.

"Mr. Walter, on the other hand, is in a much different position. He's a very wealthy man and is prepared to make a generous offer."

"I told you, I'm not selling it."

"You said no such thing," Stewart shot back, unintimidated. "You said you were not *planning* to sell it. Plans change. Indeed, a promising sign for Mr. Walter."

"You're twisting my words." Tanner held out the beer.

Stewart stared at it with a critical eye. Had this man nothing imported? He set the briefcase at his feet, accepted the beer, then settled onto the sofa.

"If the stone is worthless, then why's your boss willing to buy it?"

"The talisman is worthless to traditional collectors, but to a select few it holds a special value."

Tanner kicked off his shoes and dropped onto the couch. "I may not be a big shot like your boss, but the talisman means something special to me, too. A lot of my buddies were killed in the cave where it was recovered, and I'm starting to believe it may have been the reason I wasn't croaked along with them. Sort of a good luck charm, you see." He took a swig of beer. "I'm not selling it."

Stewart acknowledged Tanner's resistance with a polite nod.

"Mr. Walter said he would appraise the stone and tell me about its history. Does that offer still stand?"

Stewart set his beer on the coffee table and leaned forward, hands in a knitted embrace. "Let's talk reality," he said. "To people like you and I, the talisman is a stone and nothing more. But to someone like Mr. Walter, it is a lure, an original objet d' art. Something impressive to display in his collection. You own it, and Mr. Walter desires it."

"Man, you don't hear so good." Tanner leaned back on the couch and folded his arms. "I'm not selling."

"Put it this way," Stewart said. "Hypothetically, if you were forced to sell it—for whatever reason—how much would you demand?"

"You don't give up."

"Please, indulge me."

"Alright," Tanner said. He considered for a moment. "I know it's gotta be real old, so I'd have to say…" He stared at Stewart. "…five thousand dollars."

"If you agree to sell the stone, Mr. Walter shall double that figure."

Almost immediately, the young man's eyes betrayed a huge internal dilemma. And Stewart knew he had him.

"Ten grand, huh? I never would've figured that much."

After a long moment, he gave a sharp nod and said, "Okay, you have a deal."

Stewart smiled and lifted his beer eye level, watching the drops of condensation roll down the bottle's neck. The boy was making it too easy. Clearly, this Marine needed to develop negotiating skills. "No, no, no, you're doing this all wrong," Stewart said. "After I asked for your price, the proper response would have been, 'Tell me, sir, exactly how much is Mr. Walter willing to pay for such a precious piece?'"

"Excuse me?" Tanner said with a puzzled expression.

"And in response to your inquiry, I would have offered a number, perhaps twenty-five percent of Walter's ceiling figure. Then, assuming you rejected the offer, I would have analyzed your physical response and approximated my next value based upon how closely I believe I came to your selling range."

"Wait a minute. Don't you work for Walter?"

"Of course I do."

"Then what the hell are you telling me this for?"

"Because it is in your best interest," Stewart said, smiling. "And it's in my best interest, as well."

Tanner scratched his head. "I don't understand."

Stewart reclined against the couch and held up the Coors bottle, allowing stray bits of sunlight to play through the glass. Staring into the amber liquid, he said, "Perhaps you understand $80,000?"

Tanner slammed his bottle onto the table. "Stop fucking with me," he demanded. "I ask for five grand, you say Walter is willing to pay ten. I say okay, and you tell me I'm an idiot, that I should've asked for more?"

"Indeed," Stewart said evenly. "I should say a great deal more. $80,000 to be precise."

"What the hell kinda game are you playing?"

"Allow me to explain." Stewart paused to take another sip of beer. "My client is a very wealthy man. And when he sets his sight on a piece, he always invests generously to ensure its acquisition." Stewart waited a moment, allowing his point to penetrate the Marine's thick skull. "Don't you see? Walter wants the talisman and is prepared to pay a considerable sum to get it. He has given me $100,000 cash with which to negotiate. If I return having paid $10,000 for the artifact, I will be congratulated with a handshake and a 'well done'. If I return having paid $100,000—eighty thousand net to you, and twenty thousand net to me—I will be deprived the kudos and the handshake, but I will also be $20,000 wealthier."

Tanner's expression suddenly turned contemplative.

"And what is needed from you is simply an assurance, which I am now purchasing for $75,000 above your original asking price. For this to work, I must convince Mr. Walter that you were a formidable

negotiator, stubborn and stalwart. If in the unlikely event you are contacted, you must play the part well."

"I could do that." Tanner's eyes glistened.

"Excellent, then we both win," Stewart said. "You, my friend,
become eighty thousand dollars richer, simply for selling an object that
is worthless to all but the most eccentric of men. And I retain twenty
thousand dollars, a consulting fee, if you will." Stewart smiled thinly.
"And, of course, Mr. Walter, he gets his talisman."

*          *          *

When Tanner returned to the living room, he was clutching a
battered shoe box. Stewart was still seated, nursing a second beer. He
watched as Tanner eased his way to the coffee table, gently resting the
box on a stack of *Outdoor Living* magazines.

"Here it is," he announced.

Stewart nodded approvingly. "The agreement, then, is as fol-
lows: upon confirmation of the talisman's authenticity, we shall telephone Mr. Walter and confirm the $100,000 figure. A handshake and a
gentlemen's agreement will bind our transaction."

Tanner sat down and leaned forward, listening carefully.

"I will then give you $80,000 U.S. dollars, large denomina-
tions. I will keep $20,000 for myself. This latter figure represents my
fee."

"I'm game," Tanner said, rubbing his hands and smiling slyly.

"I trust you fully understand the discreet nature of this transaction," Stewart added, "and further that you understand the privacy of
my consulting fee. It is a payment to be recognized only by the two of
us. Discuss it with no one, especially Mr. Walter."

"What consulting fee?" Tanner said. He winked.

"May I see the artifact? I should now like to verify its authenticity."

"Sure. Let's wrap this up."

Indeed. Wrap it up, Stewart thought. The sooner he left this
hellish desert and returned to the mild climate of San Francisco, the
sooner his twenty thousand dollars would find a home in one of a dozen

safe deposit boxes he had hidden throughout the city. And over the years Stewart had accumulated a healthy sum to be sure. It seemed nearly every transaction he negotiated for his clients ended with success. He always returned with a good portion of the ceiling figure. This case was no different. What Tanner didn't know was that Walter had in fact entrusted him with $250,000 in negotiating funds. Returning with $150,000 would be seen by Mr. Walter as a great success.

Tanner opened the shoe box and removed the talisman, then handed it to Stewart.

The stone's spherical form was intriguing. It was as he had seen it in the sketches. Every curve, every detail was as Walter described. Turning it over in his hands, Stewart examined it from every angle. The sun shone through a break in the plantation shutters, pouring radiant energy over the talisman's glassy black surface. He held it to his nose and inhaled deeply. Oddly, Stewart thought it possessed a smell, sweet and vaguely exotic. He pinched the leather strap, and pulled its coarse surface across his fingertips.

"Is it authentic?" Tanner asked, eagerly.

"It seems to be. The lighting is poor. Open the shutters completely and I shall compare each relief with its corresponding sketch. If they all match up, precisely, I'm authorized to complete the transaction." Stewart removed a folder from his briefcase.

Tanner stood from the couch and limped to the shutters. Flipping a hook, he threw them wide open, letting in a flood of brilliant sunlight.

"Yes, yes, much better," Stewart said. He laid the sketches side by side on the coffee table and lifted the talisman, washing its obsidian surface in the light. As he rotated the stone, Stewart compared each relief, every minute detail, as demanded by Walter. One after another each scene matched, and without a single discrepancy.

Upon finishing the examination, Stewart felt satisfied. He rested the talisman on the coffee table, collected the sketches, then turned to Tanner. "Sir, I am confident that this object is indeed the artifact Mr. Walter wishes to purchase."

Tanner grinned.

"Furthermore, Mr. Walter reserves the right to conduct further scientific research, and if it's found to be a forgery—

"Wait a minute," Tanner said. "It's real, I found it myself, in a goddamn cave."

"Further analysis is just a formality," Stewart said. "In all likelihood, this artifact is real. Mr. Walter assures me that much of the relief on this stone is unknown to modern scholarship. Since my client is the only man who possesses illustrations in their entirety, an accurate forgery would be impossible." Stewart turned a hand toward the talisman. "And from what I can see here, each relief is precisely depicted."

Tanner smiled, clearly placated by the assurances. "Then I guess we could say it's my lucky charm after all."

The talisman lurched a few inches across the coffee table.

"Did you see that?" Tanner's smile disappeared.

"Yes, very strange."

They both leaned closer, staring.

Then again the talisman jerked, this time with greater force, moving itself nearly a foot across the glass.

"There it went again," Tanner said. "How'd it do that?"

"How should I know? I'm an attorney, not a physicist."

Suddenly, there came a horrible, high-pitched shriek.

Stewart slapped his hands to his ears and turned to Tanner, whose face had become stiff, drained of all life. The Marine looked as if he'd heard the voice of the angel of death.

The shriek came again, and Stewart hurried to scoop up the sketches. Disoriented from the mind-splitting noise, he called out to Tanner, "The thing must be possessed."

But as he turned, he saw that Tanner had already risen to his feet and was half running, half limping to the front door. "Don't just sit there, Stewart! Can't you see? The nightmare's returned. It's happening again!" In his rush to flee, and with only one good leg, Tanner tripped and went tumbling to the floor.

Quickly, Stewart stuffed the sketches and the cash back into his briefcase, but as he reached for the talisman, what he saw materialize from it shocked him.

His chest seized up and his throat began to swell. The loss of air to his lungs and the crushing pressure against his heart threw him into a panic.

*Cripes! What was the thing?*

He didn't dare touch the stone. Instead, he turned and sprinted for the entry, his briefcase banging wildly against his hip.

Halfway to the door Stewart passed the fallen Marine, who was stretching out a hand. "Help me, please, my leg, for the love of God!"

But Stewart wasn't about to delay, not for the love of God, not for some pathetic Marine, not for anybody. He bolted past the doomed man, reaching for the door handle.

*             *             *

Anthony Jones sat in the air-conditioned Mercedes that idled curbside in front of an old ranch-style on Desert Canyon Drive. Stewart had told him he'd be only twenty minutes. That was nearly an hour ago. What could be keeping the man? Jones glanced at the house thoughtfully. Just look at the bright side, he told himself, without a passenger in the car, he could listen to whatever kind of music he liked. He zipped open a vinyl case and flipped through stacks of scarred CD's, until he came to his favorite, Pink Floyd. He slid in the disc and punched a few buttons, then reclined back, melding into the soft leather upholstery.

This job was sweet, no dipweed supervisor breathing down his neck. Plus, at times like this, it had a special little perk. Privacy. He took a quick look around to be sure no one was watching him, then pulled a dented flask from inside a coat pocket. A few harmless sips of Jack to the mind-bending insights of Floyd's "Comfortably Numb," then he'd check in on Stewart, make sure everything was okay.

A rogue cloud passed between the sun and the Mercedes. In its deepening shadow, within the confines of the chilled cabin, Jones rocked his shoulders and absorbed the song's profound melody. Beautiful man, just beautiful. He sang along, "I, I, I've become, comfortably numb." He took a slug from the flask, allowing the satisfying heat to settle into the pit of his belly, then he leaned into a vent to enjoy a blast of cold air.

A sudden, high-pitched howl, like an injured coyote, pierced the music's melody. What the hell was that? Jones popped to attention and capped the flask. He punched off the stereo and jerked around, looking in every direction, trying to see if anyone else had heard the noise. But there *was* no one else. The street was deserted. The neighborhood was a frickin ghost town.

Jones looked back at the house. Maybe he was just hearing things. He had the radio up pretty loud, after all. He settled back into his seat, uncapped the flask, and took another slug, keeping his eyes peeled on the front door. Everything seemed okay. He turned up the music.

A few seconds later, the song ended and another began. Jones tapped the steering wheel and hummed the new tune. He glanced at the house, eyed the windows, then looked at his watch. Been an hour since they first arrived, he thought. He'd better knock on the door and see if Stewart was doing alright. Wouldn't hurt. In fact, showing a little concern might actually earn him a good rating on the customer satisfaction survey. He tucked the flask back into his jacket, popped a breath mint into his mouth, and opened the car door.

A rush of scorched air enveloped his body, and for a moment he felt like a kernel being popped in a microwave. One of these days, he thought, he'd crawl out of this desert, maybe drive for a company in Alaska.

Standing at the door of the Mercedes, Jones studied the house, eyeballing the shuttered windows. Waves of heat pulsed against his back. He felt a twinge of irritation. Babysitting clients wasn't part of the job. He considered getting back in the car, where it was cool. He wiped the sweat from his neck. Then sang softly, "Hello, is there anybody in there? Just nod if you can hear me. Is there anyone home?"

A sudden high-pitched cry pierced the neighborhood silence. It came from inside the house. Jones started for the porch, but then hesitated. Man, could this have been something illegal, like a drug deal gone bad? He began backing away, cautiously. Hold on. Get a grip on reality, man. Stewart didn't mention what he did for a living, but he sure as hell didn't look like a drug dealer. Quit being a goddamn wimp. Go up there and knock on the door, see what's going on.

As he rounded the front of the car, another terrible wail shattered the silence. Instinctively, Jones jumped. It had been a crazy noise. His mind began searching for a rational explanation. Then, at that moment, there came a flurry of scrapes, like rocks being dragged against glass. Looking up, he saw the windows of the house, every one of them, cracking from the center outward to the edges.

To hell with this shit, Jones thought. He wasn't going to put his ass on the line for some career as a glorified taxi driver. Time to go.

As he turned back to the car, the house door flung open and Stewart came tearing outside, eyes wild with panic, screaming incoherently. Behind him inside the house, Jones could see a strange dark mass, rising and unfolding, slowly, grotesquely, like an obscene apparition. And below the horror, a man on the ground scraped and crawled his way forward. Then the door banged off the wall and slammed shut behind Stewart, and Jones could see no more.

But he'd seen enough. He dashed back to the car and threw himself into the cabin, hesitating long enough for Stewart to jump inside, screaming and barking orders.

Jones gave the house a final glance, jammed the gearshift into drive, then punched the accelerator.

## 10

BETH STUFFED AN extra bottle of water into her backpack and opted for the stairs to the faculty parking lot. Since seeing the photograph of the talisman, she'd become intrigued and decided that a trip to examine the stone was well worth a shot. A firsthand look might actually put to rest the question of its authenticity. An obvious fake would be easy to spot.

It was just about noon when Beth broke from the doors of the Anthropology building and hurried into the parking lot, the sun beating down from high overhead. She slipped on her shades, shouldered her small pack, and trudged toward her 4-Runner, noting with mild interest the crystalline patterns that seemed to boil from the car's sun-baked exterior. Her mind returned to the talisman. The mere possibility that such an extraordinary artifact could surface here in Arizona, and without so much as a shovelful of dirt being tossed, seemed impossible to her, yet she couldn't explain away the photograph, not completely. The image was too precise, too real. She opened the car door and tossed her pack onto the passenger seat.

*       *       *

Two hours later she exited Highway 60 in the city of Surprise. As she drove along Sunrise Boulevard, she divided her attention between the road and the backpack, one hand on the wheel, the other digging for Tanner's photograph. She stopped at a red light and flattened the picture against the wheel. She stared at it discerningly, looking for any detail she might have missed, anything that would betray the artifact as a fraud. She tried a fresh angle, rotated the picture forty-five degrees, considered it again. But there was nothing. Everything matched up precisely with the prints published by the Oriental Institute. If the object Tanner had was a fake, it would only be revealed by a closer physical examination.

A long, angry horn startled her. She looked up to find a green light, then waved an apologetic hand to the driver behind her. Tossing the photo on the passenger seat, she punched the accelerator and continued toward Tanner's house, feeling a growing excitement over the possibility that the stone might actually be the Talisman of Persepolis. It was a delicious thought. And if by some miracle it turned out to be true, the upcoming Symposium on Persian Archaeology in Chicago would be the ideal venue to unveil it. Assuming, of course, she could convince Tanner to relinquish it to the university. That could prove difficult if he didn't appreciate ancient cultures or recognize the importance of preserving their relics.

When Beth finally pulled in front of Tanner's house, she kept the car idling, and gave his place the once over. This guy was no Bob Villa. The dead lawn was understandable—it was summertime, after all, but what was with the shattered windows? It was a peculiar sight. Every one of them, split like a cobweb. She cut the 4-Runner's engine, grabbed her purse, and hurried to the porch.

She rang the doorbell.

A long moment passed with no answer.

She glanced at her watch to make sure she wasn't too early. They'd agreed on three o'clock, and it was five minutes till. She ignored the doorbell and knocked.

As she waited, she became increasingly uncomfortable. The heat was smothering. She pressed a finger against her skin and watched as the flesh turned milky white, then slowly darkened to its original color. She looked back at her car and wondered whether or not she had any sun-block in the glove compartment. She turned back and banged on the door again. "Hello? Mr. Tanner? Answer the door please!" She set down her bag, shifted on her feet, and wiped away the sweat leaking like a faucet from her forehead.

This was ridiculous. She was going to bake to death out here. She tried the doorknob. It turned. Great, it was unlocked. She twisted the knob and cracked opened the door. "Hello? Mr. Tanner?" She opened it a little more. It swung a few inches, then stopped, blocked by something soft, something heavy. She leaned forward and yelled inside, "Mr. Tanner! I'm Dr. Harper from the university!"

Still, no answer.

"I talked to you on the phone about examining the talisman! Hello?" She peered through the narrow opening and heard the steady hum of the AC. Her face could feel the cool air rushing down from the vents. She took in a refreshing breath.

Low, in front of her, something fell with a thud. She glanced down. A man's hand! Startled, she stepped back. The hand was red and blistered. The thumb twitched.

*My God.*

The obstruction was a body! She lowered her shoulder and heaved her weight against the door. It gave, opening about a foot. She squeezed inside.

Lying on the floor facedown was a young man. She quickly knelt beside him and took an assessing look.

What she saw made her gasp. She drew her hand to her mouth.

Though the body lay chest down, the neck had become hyper-twisted, offering a full view of the man's face. Eyes swollen closed and lips frozen in a hideous snarl, his visage sent a chill down her spine.

Red sores covered the poor man's skin, which had become inflamed and pillowy. Beth's fingers moved to his neck, searching for the carotid. They explored desperately for a pulse, but found nothing. A sticky substance oozed onto her fingers. Quickly, she jerked them away, rubbing her hand violently against her jeans.

*He was dead.*

She scrambled from the entryway, fighting the urge to run. Calm down, she told herself, calm down and think. Call 911 and get emergency people here right away. She fumbled in her bag and pulled out her cell phone.

When the operator answered, Beth did her best to speak clearly and calmly. "I have an emergency. There's a man here, and I fear
he's dead. Send help, quickly. Please."

"Are you in immediate danger?"

"No, at least I don't think so." Beth looked deeper into the
house.

Everything was still and gray.

She listened to the operator's questions and could hear the
hollow echo of rapid keystrokes at the other end.

"You're calling from a cellular telephone, I can't fix the location," the operator said. "What is your address?"

"It's… oh God, what is the address here? I'm at Desert Canyon Drive in Surprise." She squeezed back through the door, ran out to
the curb and read the street number, then hurried back inside, listening
carefully to the operator's dispassionate voice.

"I'm not sure how he died," Beth said. "It looks like he had a
reaction to something. His neck and face are badly swollen, and he's
covered with sores. I don't know what happened, just hurry." She
dropped her phone back into her bag, then stared at her hands, remembering the ooze. What if it was something communicable? She needed
soap. She glanced around and spotted the kitchen, hurried to the sink.

Searching inside the cabinet, she knocked around a clutter of
plastic bottles until she found some liquid detergent, then she wet her
hands and began scrubbing them hard, clean. She wiped them on a dish
towel and started back for the door.

At the threshold to the living room, Beth stopped, noticing a
glass-topped coffee table. Like the windows of the house, it, too, had
been shattered, and in a similar pattern.

A siren cried in the distance, and she felt a sudden swell of
relief. Turning to run outside, she caught a glimpse of something black
and reflective, like glass. Obsidian.

Thoughts of the talisman came rushing back.

Hesitant at first, Beth slowly maneuvered her way around the
coffee table and knelt down for a better look.

On the floor behind the table leg is where she saw it. Shadowed by the furniture, yet enveloped in an aura of aged beauty, the

ancient relic lay peaceful, almost majestic. She reached out and grabbed hold of its leather cord, then stood and raised the talisman high, at arm's length, playing it against the golden branches of sunlight streaming through the open shutters.

She studied the stone as it dangled and spun by the cord, examining it from a variety of angles, admiring the smooth etchings that encircled its center.

She felt a sudden thrill.

The rending wail of emergency vehicles broke her trance, reminding her of the gruesome body she had discovered. She searched around for something protective she could use to wrap the talisman. On the sofa, lining a shoebox, Beth saw a terrycloth towel. She pulled it from the box, quickly swaddled the stone, and slipped it into her purse. She'd just taken her first step toward the entryway when an army of firefighters burst through the door.

# 11

EARLY THE NEXT morning, the 4-Runner rolled into the staff parking lot at the university. Beth quickly parked and hopped out, eager to get to the lab. She'd hardly slept the night before, her mind filled with images of that poor man, Mr. Tanner. He was so young, and she couldn't begin to imagine what he must have suffered from. What could have caused such a gruesome reaction? The EMT's weren't sure either, however they had seemed confident respiratory failure was the resulting cause of death.

But today was a new day. The sky was cloudless, and a gentle breeze carried the sweet scent of creosote. Beth decided to put the nightmare behind her and focus on moving forward with the talisman. The Symposium was in less than two weeks, and she knew if she was to have any chance presenting the artifact, she'd have to authenticate it, immediately.

Beth took the service elevator to the basement floor, the location of the laboratory, and stepped out into a prison-like hall, a long tunnel constructed of whitewashed cinderblocks. Activity was brisk. Men and women in suits and lab coats hurried up and down the hall, moving between research rooms. Some were university employees, but most were unaffiliated research scientists, specialists from across the country. With every step deeper into the tunnel, Beth became filled with a sort of awkward anticipation. She would have to convince the lab manager, Eddie Sorini, to give her priority use of some of the lab's most sensitive equipment. And Beth was well aware of Sorini's reputation. He was a procedures man, and took pride following the rules. Gaining immediate access to the QuanX, she knew, might not be easy. And she dared not use the talisman as a bargaining chip either, as Eddie would certainly be familiar with it. If word spread that she'd gotten hold of an artifact of its caliber, the university might very well step in and take credit for its discovery. As far as Beth was concerned, the world would know soon enough about the Talisman of Persepolis, but it would be *she* who unveiled it, not some hot-shot university spokesman with an expensive suit and a flashy smile.

When Beth reached Eddie's office, the door was open. She took it as an invitation and stepped inside. The office was clean and organized, just like every other room in the lab. It was the product of an obsessive-compulsive manager, who Beth suddenly realized was nowhere to be found. She glanced around the office, wondering what filled the rows of storage boxes stacked neatly against the walls. The desk and tables were fashioned in the style of Mission Revival, indicating Eddie's preference for straight angles and perfect symmetry. He was a real square guy. Beth took a seat and waited.

Nearly ten minutes passed and she could feel herself becoming restless. The sooner she was given the okay to power up the spectrometer, the sooner she could settle the issue of the talisman's authenticity. The wall clock showed 8:30. Beth had begun tapping the chair's armrest when a ledger book on Eddie's desk caught her attention. She scooted closer and slid the ledger in front of her. She glanced at the door. Still no Eddie. She looked back at the ledger. Upside down she could read the label affixed to the front: *Lab Reservations and Equipment Inventory*. Hurriedly, she turned the book and opened the cover. The first half of the ledger appeared to be an itemization of the lab's non-consumables, everything from beakers and test tubes to printers and computers. Beth flipped past a tab in the center of the book, where she found a record of analysis equipment, along with dates and times for their use. After leafing past six or seven pages, she stopped and read the header: *QuanX Energy-Dispersive X-Ray Fluorescence Spectrometer (EDXRF)*. It was the spectrometer she needed to complete her analysis, but it appeared to be booked solid for the next five weeks. There was entry after entry of scientists and organizations. Beth scanned down the list: the United States Forest Service, the Bureau of Land Management, the Institute of Archaeology and Ethnography, Instituto Nacional de Antropologia, the Russian Academy of Science (Siberian Branch), and a long list of American universities and museums.

Beth sunk into her chair and moaned. This wasn't good. A reservation list this impacted would make it difficult to convince Eddie to allow—

A throat cleared behind her.

Beth spun around to see Eddie standing under the door jamb, his arms folded across his tiny chest. He wore a white, freshly starched lab coat with a picture I.D. clipped level over his right breast pocket. His creased black slacks hung loosely to the floor, stopped short by a pair of machine-polished wingtips.

"Well, well," Eddie began, the pitch of his voice shrill. "It takes some nerve, Dr. Harper, inviting yourself into my office and snooping through my personal effects."

Beth slapped closed the ledger and jumped out of the chair. "Eddie, I was just—"

"Dr. Harper, we don't know each other well enough for such informal address. You'll refer to me as Mr. Sorini, if you please."

Beth fumbled with the chair, trying her best to straighten it to its original position, but the grinding screech of the metal legs against the laminate floor only intensified Eddie's pinched look of irritation. "I'm sorry," Beth said, reaching out a hand, not so much an offer to shake as it was a plea for kindness. "Could we start over, Eddie? I mean, Mr. Sorini?"

"You disappoint me, Dr. Harper. I should think as a member of the faculty, you would know enough to exercise discretion. My office is not a public library, nor is it a rest stop for weary researchers."

Having walked into the lion's den, Beth had to think quickly. "And you're absolutely right, Mr. Sorini. I apologize for coming in uninvited, but the door was open and I couldn't help but notice how well-organized and proper you kept your office. I was very impressed and wanted to see more."

Sorini's face was like stone, his upper lip arched in a permanent snarl. Flattery seemed to have had little effect.

"Perhaps, then, I should get to the point of my visit," Beth said. "I would like to book time with the QuanX Spectrometer. When could you fit me in?"

"You've already browsed the reservations ledger, so perhaps I should be asking you that question, Dr. Harper." Sorini marched past her and took a seat behind his desk. He smoothed a wrinkle from his lab coat, squared the ledger in front of him, then pulled open a drawer and removed a crisp sheet of paper. "Purpose of visit?"

"I just told you," Beth said. "I'd like to reserve time with the QuanX."

Sorini plucked a pen from his breast pocket and glided it carefully across the paper, crossing T's and dotting marks of punctuation with the gentlest of taps. "Description of your research?"

It was clear to Beth what Eddie was doing. This was his way of punishing her. He planned to prolong her suffering with ridiculous formalities. She sighed, then took a seat. "I'll be sourcing obsidian."

"Who will be operating the machine, you, a trained undergraduate, a graduate student, or a qualified lab employee?"

"I'll juice the baby up myself," Beth said, smiling, trying her best to put Eddie at ease.

He lifted his eyes from the paper long enough to scowl. "Could you please take this a bit more seriously, Dr. Harper?"

Beth ditched her smile and sat up straight. A sickening feeling began to grow inside of her. The reservation list clearly showed the QuanX booked far beyond her two-week window, and all attempts to appease Eddie seemed to be backfiring.

He asked several more irrelevant questions about payments and grants, then opened the ledger book and scanned down the list. "Let's see here, Dr. Harper. I could schedule you as early as...July 28th, or anytime thereafter."

"July 28th? That's over a month from now. Couldn't you squeeze me in sooner?"

Eddie stared back at the book, glided his hand down the page, then looked up at Beth. "No."

For a second, she thought she saw the hint of a smile cross his face. The little twerp. He was enjoying this.

"Shall I book you for July 28th, or is our business here concluded, Dr. Harper?"

Beth thought for a moment, searching for other options. But there were none. There was no other way to verify the authenticity of the talisman. At least no other way that would be faster than this lab. She could send a sample off to Berkeley, but their turn around was about the same as Eddie's. She had to convince him to give her lab time now. There would be no other way. Beth folded her hands respectfully on the desk, leaned forward slightly, taking care to mind Eddie's space. "Mr. Sorini, the research I'm conducting has the potential to be groundbreaking. And since I'm in the employ of the university wouldn't it be possible to reschedule another of your reservations? I'm sure the Bureau of Land Management could wait a few more weeks."

At this, Eddie grew visibly angry. His snarled lip rose to a sharp curl and his face darkened. "You may not be aware, Dr. Harper, but my laboratory has been taking steps to attract non-research based clientele, all in an effort to increase revenue for the university. And as you have seen in the ledger, I've been quite successful thus far. Canceling our client's lab time would set a miserable precedent. Bad for business. I refuse to do it, all on account of your...*groundbreaking research.*"

The sarcasm in Eddie's voice was so thick Beth could almost touch it, and she abruptly felt an unsettling urge. She wanted to reach across the desk and slap the smile off Eddie's smug little face. It was then the words of her department secretary, Doris Heckel, came rushing back to her: *Don't be afraid to use what God gave you, doll. Your figure could be an asset.*

*Doris, you're a genius.*

"So then," Eddie continued, "can I help you with anything else?"

Beth perked up in her chair, smiled, then drew a finger softly down the side of her neck. "July 28th, let's see... what day of the week is that, Eddie?" She stood from the chair and strolled around to his side of the desk, staring curiously at the calendar in front of him. She leaned in, pretending to get a better look, not concerned so much with the calendar as she was with getting closer to Eddie. She wished she had dabbed on a bit of Tresor.

"Miss Harper, Dr. Harper." Eddie corrected himself. "My space, if you don't mind, please."

Beth was summoning the courage to brush her arm against his shoulder when the phone suddenly rang, startling her.

Immediately, Eddie grabbed for the receiver. "Sorini here." He listened intently. "Uh huh, sure, yes, not a problem." He removed another sheet of paper and began scribbling furiously, ignoring Beth.

Defeated, she returned to her chair, listening to him grovel on the phone. Flirting had never been her thing.

"Yes that date will be fine," Eddie said. "And Mr. LeBroche, may I once again thank your firm for using our facilities. I'm sure you'll be pleased with the turn around time, and of course you'll find that our experience in all spatial and temporal contexts is top notch."

When Eddie finally hung up the phone, he made a quick entry into the ledger, replaced the pen, then tented his hands on the desk. "Where were we, Dr. Harper?"

Beth sighed. "Well, Eddie, we were just—"

"Dr. Harper, I think I've made it abundantly clear that such personal address is inappropriate. You will address me as Mr. Sorini, if you don't mind."

That was it. This man was impossible. Beth's hope for presenting the talisman at the upcoming symposium began to fade. She took a deep breath. It seemed a cruel twist of fate that she'd been given the talisman just weeks before the largest gathering of Near Eastern scholars in the world, and yet she had no way to authenticate the artifact and prepare it for presentation.

"Dr. Harper?" Eddie said. "Is our business here concluded?"

"I guess so." She stood to leave. "Go ahead and put me down for July 28th."

Eddie opened the book and scanned down the page, acting as if he hadn't seen it in days. "I'm sorry," he said, "it seems Mr. LeBroche has taken the last slot for July. Will August 1st do?"

# 12

WHAT WERE THE odds? Andrew thought as he stood outside the customs gate at San Francisco International Airport. What were the odds of buying two hundred lottery scratchers, and not a single one of them paying out? He wasn't sure exactly, but whatever the odds were, last night he'd defied them. He'd come up dry. And it didn't quite seem fair. In Andrew's estimation, even the world's unluckiest bastard should have scratched at least one winner. Like the guy he'd seen on the news last night, the one back east who'd had his nuts burned by a bolt of lightning, even he would have scratched a winner. It was all an odds thing, odds and karma.

Yeah, karma.

Just minutes ago, driving into the airport, he'd given the right-of-way to a group of old ladies crossing the terminal parking lot. He could have just as easily hit the gas and blown past their puckered asses. What he'd done was a good thing. Positive karma. So if he bought two hundred more tickets tonight, he couldn't possibly scratch another two hundred losers. Could he? No way. He had odds on his side—odds and karma. He straightened his black driver's cap, held up the nameplate, and reminded himself to stop by the 7-11 and pick up some more scratchers before heading home tonight.

The crowd pouring from customs had begun to thin. Andrew lowered the sign, read the name again. Sarth. What the hell kinda name was that? Sounded biblical. Abraham begot Isaac, Isaac begot Jacob,

Jacob begot Sarth. He peered back up. The gate was empty. Maybe the guy missed his flight. Maybe his name was Aramaic for "Shit out of luck." Andrew's eyes strayed down over his bulging gut, and he checked to make sure his shoes were tied. Earlier in the day, he'd stepped on a lace and taken a digger in the parking lot at Wendy's. As if a tear in his pants and a bloodied elbow wasn't bad enough, some pothead kid in the drive-through had seen the whole damn thing, laughed all the way to the window.

Andrew's laces were tied, double-knotted, in fact. He looked up again and stumbled back a step. A man stood inches in front of him.

"Holy mother of… I didn't even notice you walk up, mister," Andrew said, trying to explain away his surprise. "Can I help you with something?"

But the stranger didn't answer. He just nodded to the name-plate. He was an odd looking fellow, tall, real tall, a skyscraper of a man. His skin was smooth and tan, naturally dark, a Middle Easterner, Andrew figured. Short wiry hair lay plastered to his skull, and his eyes looked like cold, muddy raindrops.

Please, Lord, Andrew thought. Don't let this be the client. He smiled theatrically, trying to hide the fact that the guy gave him the creeps. "You ain't Sarth, are you?"

"I am."

The answer disappointed Andrew. He gave the guy a second look, glancing down at his long arms which hung relaxed at his side. On his left hand, inked in the fold of flesh between his forefinger and thumb was the image of a black sun. A swath of grotesque scarring covered his knuckles. Andrew looked away, figuring it best not to stare.

"You're to drive me to the Russ building in the city's Financial District. Are you familiar with this location?"

Andrew nodded.

"Very well, then." The tall man grasped him by the shoulder and turned him toward the exit. "Come, let us waste no time."

                    *          *          *

A short while later, the black Town Car pulled up curbside at 235 Montgomery Street. Sarth opened the car door and stepped out into the deep shadow of the Russ building.

An impressive neo-Gothic construction, the high rise sprawled an entire city block. Men and women in business suits swarmed the streets, entering and exiting nearby buildings with clockwork regularity.

Sarth took in a lungful of cool June air and stared appraisingly at the building that loomed before him. It was an impressive structure, with curtain walls and columns of arched windows that rose nearly four hundred feet, dark against the late afternoon sky. Brick and terra cotta stonework lent the façade hundreds of years of unearned maturity.

The building was nearly as impressive inside as it was out. Pendant lighting blanketed the lobby in a gentle glow, highlighting the reds and coppers of the ornate area rugs outspread over the marble floors. Sarth moved through the lobby, past huddles of men and women, some loitering quietly, others engaged in quiet conversation. At the security station he identified himself as Jonathan Walter's five o'clock.

The security guard seated at the kiosk looked down on his desktop and consulted an appointment book, then quickly stood and said, "Right this way, sir." He led Sarth to an elevator lobby, passing four open carriages and stopping at a private car. He swiped a security card over a small black plate and looked up at the annunciator lights, staring blankly as the elevator descended floors. When at last the steel doors parted, the guard gestured Sarth to enter, stepped inside after him, and quickly swiped the card again. He backed out and the doors whooshed closed.

The elevator began its climb. With each passing floor, Sarth felt a growing sense of anticipation, an intense desire to know the purpose for which he was summoned. He'd been told nothing of the assignment, only that he was to meet with Father, an act that alone raised the importance of his presence. Sarth's expertise was seldom used in the States, but on the occasion it was, the stakes were always considerable.

A moment later, the elevator opened onto an empty foyer. At the far end was a maple door embossed with gold letters that read

WALTER ENTERPRISES. Sarth opened the door and entered quietly, surveying the room, a small reception area with mahogany-paneled walls and a sweeping, marble-topped desk. To his right, an arrangement of leather armchairs and side tables abutted a display wall crowded with framed photographs, each showing Father consorting with heads of state and other Fortune 500 company CEO's.

Behind the desk sat a sleekly dressed woman with blonde hair pulled tightly into a bun. Her attention was focused on paperwork.

Sarth glided to the desk and waited.

After a time, the woman glanced up from her work. "I beg your pardon," she said. "I didn't realize anyone had entered. As she studied Sarth, her gaze fell upon his scarred knuckles. She blinked wide, then quickly turned her eyes. "You must be—"

"Indeed, I am."

She nodded and touched a button on the intercom. "Mr. Walter, your man has arrived." There was an immediate buzz and the door behind her clicked open.

"Straight down the hall, last door on the right." Her eyes fell again upon his hands, and with a pained expression, she turned away, busying herself once more with her work.

Sarth tipped his head to the woman, then moved around the desk and through the door. Beyond the reception area, the corridor ran long and was brightly lit. Sarth walked its length, passing entrances to nearly a dozen offices and conference rooms. To his left he noticed a glass-walled suite with chairs surrounding a long table. A frail and nervous-looking man in a finely tailored suit paced from one end of the room to the other, glancing repeatedly at his watch. Sarth continued down the hall. The door at the end was slightly ajar. Quietly, he pushed it open and stepped inside.

Jonathan Walter stood with his back turned, pouring brandy into a small snifter. He lifted the drink to his nostrils, inhaling deeply, staring through a large window that offered an impressive view of the San Francisco skyline.

Sarth moved deeper into the room, noting its dimensions, points of entry, and the position of its furniture. It was a conditioned response to an unfamiliar environment. Crucial in his line of work. He remained standing, head slightly bowed, waiting for Father to acknowledge him.

Walter drew the glass to his lips, held it there as if lost in thought, then tipped it back and drained away the amber liquid. He turned to Sarth and lowered his head slightly in a gesture of respect. "It is good to see you, my son. It's been many years."

"Far too many, Father."

"May I offer you a drink?"

Sarth held up a hand, declining.

Walter poured himself another, then walked across the office, settling himself into a chair behind a large mahogany desk. He shuffled some papers into a drawer, then pointed across the room to an arrangement of Victorian armchairs with intricately scrolled arms.

Sarth crossed the room and took a seat.

Walter stood from the desk and moved to join him, seating himself pleasingly. Sarth observed Father. Though a man of sixty, his auburn hair remained thick and defiant to age. His build was strong, and his skin's vibrant tone did much to hide away the years.

"I acquired a new piece," Walter said. He pointed to a far wall, brandy glass still in hand. "Opinion?"

Sarth maintained eye contact with Father. "You refer to the rosewood cabinet?" He had noted it when he entered.

"Yes."

"I find it stimulating," Sarth said, "particularly the battle scenes depicted on the marble inlays. I've always found artifacts of Assyrian warfare to be refreshingly candid, appealing in their uncensored brutality."

Walter smiled thinly. "Indeed."

As much as Sarth desired to learn the reason for his summoning, he understood the required pleasantries among members of the Organization. And as Pater Patrum, the Father of all Fathers, Walter ranked senior. It was he who possessed the ancient tome—the *Telesma*, and it was he alone who interpreted the will of Mithra. The fact that Sarth now sat before him indicated his reason for being here was of critical importance.

Slowly, Walter rolled the brandy.

Sarth gazed through the western window. Beyond lay a magnificent view of the city. The sun was low, topping a jumble of skyscrapers, reflecting pearls of light from their dark, featureless windows.

Walter seemed to have sensed Sarth's growing anticipation, for he stood and walked to his desk. Behind it, a wooden mascaron was affixed to the wall. The face in relief was twisted and distorted, of medieval origin, Sarth judged. Walter slid aside the panel, exposing a titanium safe. With a nimble play of fingers, he punched a code into a digital keypad. "I have a gift for you, my son, tools of your trade so to speak." He pulled out a cherrywood container, closed the safe, then slid the mascaron back into position.

Sarth moved to the desk and squared the case. Carefully, he opened it and peered inside. Nestled in a rubber mold was his firearm of choice, the Heckler & Koch .45, equipped with a wet suppressor and Laser-Aiming Module. He lifted the pistol and examined the LAM mounted at the trigger guard.

A smile turned up the edge of his lips.

A dagger lay next to the impression. With great satisfaction, Sarth lifted it and pulled away the sheath, admiring its long, glistening blade, which had already been sharpened to razor perfection. He imagined, with mild interest, the blade sinking into a man's flesh, spilling the warm essence of his soul.

"If I'm not mistaken," Walter said, "the object there is of particular interest to you." He pointed into the case.

Sarth eyed a small drawstring purse. "Yes, of course." He drew open the purse and pulled out a long, silver wire with knotted leather ends—a garrote, his preferred tool in the field. He wrapped the leather ends around his knuckles, first his right hand, then his left, pulling taut the cord, feeling its intense vibration course through his hands.

It was a divine sensation.

"I trust everything is to your liking?"

"You have done well, Father," Sarth said. "I am grateful for the opportunity to serve."

After finishing their inventory, the two men returned to the armchairs.

Walter reached for the intercom button. "Ring the conference room and tell Mr. Stewart I am ready to see him."

"Yes, Mr. Walter," the receptionist said.

Stewart? Sarth searched his memory. The name was not familiar. Perhaps someone outside the Organization.

Moments later, there was a rap on the open door, and Sarth turned to observe the man he'd seen pacing the floor of the conference room.

"Ah, thank you for your patience, Mr. Stewart," Walter said. "Do come in."

The man drifted inside. "I have an appointment later this evening. If you don't mind I really must be—"

"Nonsense," Walter said. "No one compensates you as well as I. Stay. I insist."

"Yes, of course. I didn't mean to imply—"

"Sarth, may I introduce you to Mr. Stewart—one of my attorneys specializing in acquisitions." He motioned for the man to take a seat.

Stewart's eyes darted back and forth between the two men. He hesitated, but after a moment settled into a chair. "In regard to the events at Mr. Tanner's, if you prefer I could draft a written account. Everything I told you is—"

"True?" Walter said. "Of course it is, Mr. Stewart. Of course it is."

Sarth noticed perspiration beading below the man's hairline.

"The talisman's relief matched perfectly with your sources," Stewart said. "It's authentic, I'm sure of it. It's just that…" his voice trailed off.

"Since you were unsuccessful, I called in my associate to handle the acquisition personally." Walter gestured to Sarth.

Stewart shifted uneasily. "I see, but what about—?"

Walter raised a hand, silencing Stewart, then he turned and peered at Sarth. "The news is extraordinary, my son. The Talisman of Persepolis has resurfaced." Walter's eyes grew wide with excitement. "After two thousand years, Mithra calls us into action."

There was a charged silence in the room.

Sarth considered the full weight of what Father had just revealed. The Talisman of Persepolis, Mithra's gift to man, had been lost since the days of Alexander. If in fact it had resurfaced, it would mean the coming of a New Age, a rebirth of the Brotherhood's ancient glory. Indeed, its recovery was the cardinal objective of the Organization. Sarth clenched his fists. He could feel the pressure of his blood as it coursed through his veins. Never could he have imagined that in his lifetime the prophecy would come to fruition.

Stewart said, "But, but the stone, what I saw, the evil."

"My dear Mr. Stewart. What you witnessed at Tanner's house was a cleansing of sorts. The artifact can be handled only by a person of consequence, a devotee of Mithra. It was a mistake for me to have sent you. I realize that now. You see, Mr. Tanner's hands were morally impure." Walter paused. "As are yours, Mr. Stewart."

"I beg your pardon?"

"Your soul, Mr. Stewart, it is unclean."

The attorney stood to his feet, his neck and face beginning to flush. "How dare you."

"I'm curious," Walter asked. "How long did you think I would stand for your treachery?"

"Treachery? Really, I have no idea what you're talking about. As a representative of Walter Enterprises, I've always taken great pride in comporting myself ethically."

"For years I've sent you around the world, at great expense, and in comfort, conducting my affairs and acquiring antiquities. I've compensated you well. And in return, how have you repaid me?"

There was silence.

"Perhaps you can explain these bank accounts." Walter removed an envelope from his breast pocket. "I have here a list of safe-deposit boxes."

Stewart gawked at the envelope, his face becoming rigid.

"Each account contains a sizeable deposit, and each deposit coincides with dates that I've sent you to conduct my personal business."

Stewart suddenly paled. "I can explain."

"I need no explanation," Walter said. "For your failure to secure the talisman, an object so very precious to me, I will tolerate your betrayal no longer." He turned and nodded to Sarth. "My son, if you please."

Teetering on his feet, Stewart looked at Sarth, then collapsed into a chair, his body trembling.

A most unexpected turn of events, Sarth mused. But not wholly disagreeable. He stood to his feet and stared into Mr. Stewart's eyes, two glassy orbs, sick and corrupt. Sarth stepped forward. He was rather going to enjoy this.

## 13

BETH TRUDGED INTO her office and ignored the light switch, settling for the faint electric glow spilling in from the hallway. She nestled into her chair, folded her arms on top of the desk, and lowered her head. It was early still, but she felt mentally exhausted. She had in her possession what could very well be the Talisman of Persepolis, and all that was needed for confirmation was a few hours of simple lab work. Lab work she couldn't perform, at least not before the big symposium.

She sat up and sighed.

How ironic it was that she worked at a university whose campus housed one of the most sophisticated materials dating laboratories in the country, and for the time being she was powerless to use it. Beth took a deep breath, exhaled slowly, and thought about Eddie Sorini. The little man was a jerk, and there was nothing she could do about it, nothing except put it all behind her.

She straightened up, hands on her hips, and slowly arched her body, stretching the knotted muscles in her back. At the edge of the desk, she noticed a pinpoint of light reflecting from a telescope eyepiece. Picking it up, she couldn't help but smile. Beth kept the small ocular as a reminder of Rick and the moonless nights they used to spend together under the desert sky, stargazing and sharing each other's dreams. And although now those nights were over, Beth knew there would be no letting go of the memories. She turned the eyepiece over in her hand, staring at it absently.

Then a thought occurred to her. Maybe she ought to call Rick and give him the news of Tanner's death, in case he hadn't already heard. It had been months since they last talked, and the prospect of hearing his voice brought an unexpected feeling of joy. She lifted the receiver and dialed.

When Rick answered the phone, Beth hesitated, surprised at just how much she missed his reassuring tone. Lightly, she cleared her throat. "Hi, Rick."

There was a pause. "Beth, it's nice to hear from you, it's been a long time."

"I've been meaning to call you," she said. "But with summer classes and this upcoming symposium—"

"I understand," he said. "You're a busy woman, you have important work."

His response surprised her. Where her job was concerned, six months ago, he never would have said anything so understanding. He'd always discouraged her from working, said she'd never be able to raise their children if she spent all her time in the field or at the university. Maybe now he was coming around, beginning to recognize the importance of her career.

"Beth," Rick said smoothly, interrupting her thoughts, "what's wrong?"

*       *       *

It was nearing midnight when Rick arrived at Beth's apartment and knocked on the door. Word of Tanner's death had come as a complete shock to him, and he couldn't help but feel a little guilty for having involved Beth. The horror of stumbling upon a corpse could weigh heavily upon a person. In Panama, he'd witnessed his own share of grisly scenes—soldiers dead in the streets, brain matter scattered from their skulls; bodies of opposition rebels lying twisted and contorted in roadside ditches. It was a horrible experience, but Rick had been able to put it behind him, been able to cope with the images. Unfortunately, not everyone fared so well, and that's what worried him. How was Beth taking this?

The apartment door opened and Rick nearly gasped. Standing before him was the woman he loved, stunningly beautiful with black feathery hair and rich olive skin. She leaned pleasantly against the doorjamb, her sharp cheekbones glistening under the honey-glow of the porch lamp. With some effort, Rick stopped his eyes from tracing the curves that ran down her lean figure.

"Mr. Rick Lowell," Beth said, "the most handsome radio engineer this side of the Rio Grande." She smiled slyly, then stepped forward and greeted him with a tight hug.

He hugged her back, relieved to have found her in such good spirits.

*         *         *

Inside Beth's apartment, Rick settled onto the couch. Beth had made coffee and was fixing him a cup in the kitchen. He stared around the living room, glancing at some of the familiar furnishings they'd once shared together. Beth had been selective when she moved out, taking only a few small pieces of furniture. He fixed his sight upon the old wicker armchair, where he remembered her spending countless evening hours reading books and deciphering journals. Adjoining the chair was a glass-topped end table with a stack of battered paperbacks. When they were together, Beth read more often than she slept. Apparently, old habits died hard. Rick closed his eyes and ran his fingers along the wooden armrest. The hour was late, and he was tired. Still, he was happy to be here, happy to be close to the woman he never stopped loving.

Beth walked into the room. He opened his eyes and watched her cross to the couch, balancing two coffee mugs in one hand, and a plate of biscotti in the other. "Here's a little pick-me-up." She handed him a mug, set the biscotti on the coffee table, then nestled onto the couch next to him.

Smiling like buffoons, they stared appraisingly at each other, the moment feeling immensely long and a bit awkward.

"I'm happy you're here," Beth finally said, breaking the uncomfortable silence. "The last few days have been tough. I didn't know who to call."

"You knew who to call," Rick said. "You just had mixed feelings about doing it."

She gazed affectionately at him, then after a long moment, abruptly asked, "How well did you know Tanner?"

"Not well, met him at the radio station. He was one of Mason's guests." Rick dabbed the surface of his coffee, testing the temperature. "Still, he was a Marine and a decent person. He didn't deserve to die, especially as young as he was."

"And in such an awful way," Beth added.

"Any idea how it happened?"

"Asphyxiation," she said, "possibly from a severe allergic reaction. At least that's what the EMT's were saying. I've never seen anything like it. That poor man, his neck and face were covered with oozing pustules."

A nasty image formed in Rick's mind. He forced it away, trying to imagine something more positive. "Sorry you had to go through this. I should never have given him your number."

"No, no, I wouldn't say that." She leaned closer, her stare becoming hard and penetrating.

Rick knew that look all too well. It was the look he'd seen two summers ago at Lake Powell, when he'd first taught Beth to water ski; when, despite taking dozens of nasty tumbles, she'd refused to give up until learning to stand. And it was the same look Rick had seen the day he accompanied Beth to the university to watch her defend her Doctoral dissertation. In a stuffy room full of grumpy old men, she had answered every question and defeated every objection. In a word, the look on Beth's face was determination. "What's on your mind?" Rick asked.

Beth nudged even closer. "It was an awful thing what happened to Mr. Tanner," she said. "But I'm glad you had him call me. It was a brilliant move."

"I don't understand."

"That artifact I was to examine, the talisman, it's the break I've been waiting for. It's sure to make a huge stir at the university."

She stood and hurried to the table, opened her backpack, and pulled out an object swaddled in cloth.

Rick studied its dimensions, quickly making the connection. "Is that what I think it is?"

Beth hurried back and pulled away the cloth, exposing the same wondrous stone Rick had seen at the station. Even under the room's dim lighting, it was still an incredible sight, glassy black with expertly engraved etchings depicting ancient battle scenes.

"How did you end up with it?"

"At Tanner's, I found it lying on the floor."

"Should you have taken it?" Rick asked. "I mean, maybe it should be given to his next of kin."

Beth's eyes quickly narrowed. "In all likelihood this is the Talisman of Persepolis. Tanner may have been the one to find it, but an object like this certainly doesn't belong to a single man. It belongs to everyone, to the world, in a museum where thousands will have an opportunity to admire it."

Rick shrugged. Looking at it that way, it made sense.

She lowered the stone into his cupped hands. "You're holding what is in my opinion the greatest of all ancient relics."

Rick glanced at it again. It was impressive, but still, it was just a rock. "This is going to make you a big shot at the university?"

Beth paced the floor, rubbing her hands. "I wouldn't say a big shot, but it'll certainly... oh, who am I kidding? Yes, it'll make me a big shot."

Rick smiled, watching her fuss about the room.

"Next year during deliberations, I'll be a shoo-in with the tenure committee."

"That's great news, but I don't see how one artifact could generate that much attention."

"I'll explain." She scrambled to the coffee table and plucked up a biscotti. "The Talisman of Persepolis is not just a piece of obsidian, you see. It's an artifact that defines a civilization—the Persian Empire. You have to understand that the Persians rose from obscurity in a remarkably short period of time to dominate the entire Near Eastern world. Their achievement was phenomenal, historic. Do you know the two things they credited for their success?"

Rick shrugged, turning up the palm of his hands.

"The first, of course, was their god, Ahura Mazda. Take a stab at the second."

Rick smiled. "Eating their Wheaties?"

"Come on, I'm serious," Beth said. "Imagine it, nearly every nation conquered by the Persians recorded stories about the talisman. You find mention of it in Median and Babylonian sources, Egyptian and Greek sources, as well. And these stories all share a common theme. They tell of an incredible power harnessed by the stone, a power so intense, a power so absolute entire armies would succumb before it."

"Ancient superstition," Rick said.

"Of course, but you're missing the point. It's not the legend that intrigues modern scholars. It's the historical context surrounding it. The influence of myth is an integral concept in the study of ancient cultures. For that reason alone the talisman would be a remarkable find."

Rick considered what Beth was saying. Though it made sense, he still thought she was putting too much faith into one artifact. An artifact she wasn't even sure was authentic. But then again, what did he know? She'd managed her career pretty well up to this point. Who was he to question her tactics? "Okay, you've convinced me," he said. "It's an important find."

At Rick's words, Beth hurried back to the couch and knelt beside him. She took his hand and cupped it, as if protecting a captured butterfly. Her expression was warm and sincere. "I need your help at the lab."

Rick blinked, a little surprised. He knew nothing about archaeology. What kind of help could he possibly be? He chuckled. "What, you need me to wash your test tubes?"

"Be serious," Beth said. "What I'm asking, I'm asking because I know you. We've shared part of our lives, and I know I can trust you."

Her talk was beginning to concern him. Pleas that began 'I know I can trust you' were never good. Rick stood from the couch, pulling away his hand. "What kind of scheme are you hatching, Beth?"

She sprang to her feet. "Please, I need your help."

"Doing what?"

She stepped closer.

"Doing what?" he repeated.

"Getting into the lab at the university."

Rick was confused. "You're a professor there. Don't you already have access?"

"Not the kind I need."

"What kind would that be?"

She hesitated.

"Beth?"

"The kind that requires circumventing an alarm system and getting past a locked door."

Rick moaned. Now it was all becoming clear. Beth needed his help with something clandestine. That's why she'd called him. He'd come here concerned for her well-being, maybe even to test the waters and see if their relationship still had life. But in reality, she didn't need his shoulder to cry on. She needed it to bust down a goddamn door.

"Forget it, Beth."

"Rick, please."

He reached into his pocket for his keys. "I never should have come."

"No, don't leave." She nudged him back onto the couch, then dropped down next to him. "You have to hear me out."

"Okay, I'm gonna hear you out," he said. "Then I'm gonna say no, then I'm gonna leave."

Beth smiled, apparently missing the part where he said he'd say *no*. "It's not like I don't have authorization. I do, it's just that the lab's booked solid until August. And Eddie's being a real jerk about it. There's a very important symposium coming up, and I have to meet the deadline for submitting my presentation."

"What do you need the lab for? You already seem sure it's the real McCoy."

"True, the paleographic evidence is conclusive. And the scenes that encircle the stone match up precisely with known relief designs."

"There you go, done deal." Rick started to get up.

Beth shoved him back down. "But that's not enough. The paleography alone won't stand up to peer review. There'll be those who claim it's a forgery. To remove any doubt, I'll need to run Obsidian Hydration tests to determine its age, and X-ray Fluorescence Spectrometry tests to determine the source of the stone."

"Why not make life simple for yourself? Go to the university and tell them what you have. If it's as important as you say, I'm sure they'll authorize the use of whatever you need."

"No, you don't understand. If I go to the department and show them what I have, they'll claim the talisman as university property, assemble a team to analyze it, and assign the lead to a tenured researcher."

"And you think a better alternative is to break into the lab and test it in secret?"

"One alarm, and one little door, that's all I'm asking, Rick."

"Easier said than done."

Beth's jade eyes narrowed. "Don't you dare tell me you can't do it. I spent five years of my life with you. I know what you did in the Army, in Panama. The only thing that could stop you from getting us into that lab would be your own unwillingness to help me."

Rick didn't say a word. He knew Beth was right. Breaking into a basement lab would probably require little more than disabling circuitry and punching a lock. He'd done a lot of it in the Army, as a Ranger in the Special Forces. Still, this wasn't the compound of some corrupt government official, this was an American university, and Beth's idea was insane. He shook his head. "I'm not going to do it. I won't risk us going to jail over a harebrained idea. It's for your own good."

Beth stood up, pushing off the cushions with a heavy sigh.

Rick knew it was for effect.

"You kept your promise," she said, shoulders slumped. "You heard me out. Thank you, Rick."

He snatched his keys from the table and stood to his feet, purposefully avoiding her gaze. There was a look she could reveal, her head cocked slightly to one side, lips closed in an innocent pout. It was a look that was hard for him to resist. He kept his eyes on the carpet and walked to the door.

As he reached for the knob, Beth spoke again. "I've been doing a lot of soul searching these past few months," she said. Her tone was soft and caring. "I think you and I splitting up may have been a selfish act... on my part."

Rick grabbed the door handle.

"And I'm not just saying that to get your help. It's true. I still have feelings."

Rick turned and looked at Beth. In the shadowy glow of the living room, she stood motionless, like a helpless fawn, her dark liquid eyes beautiful and sincere.

"I realize now I made a mistake," she said. "I still love you, Rick." She walked to the door and stood tiptoed, giving him a gentle kiss on the lips. "I respect your decision, and I know you're trying to look out for the both of us. I just feel that if I could achieve something big, if I could do something to make a mark in my field, I'd be able to relax enough to begin considering other areas in my life that are lacking."

"Other areas?" Rick said.

Beth reached out and stroked his cheek. "Our relationship, a family, children."

The keys slipped from Rick's hand and struck the carpet with a dull clank.

"I'm glad you came over tonight, I really am."

Rick was suddenly overcome with feelings of anticipation. This was what he'd always dreamed to hear her say. He imagined the two of them together, with children. A family. His stomach burned with an intense longing. "You're sure with the talisman authenticated you'll make that mark?"

"If this artifact is what I think it is, there's no question."

Rick let out a deep breath and turned away from the door. He crossed the room and scooped up the talisman. It was definitely an impressive looking thing, no question about it. And if it was the key to getting Beth noticed at the university, the key to getting the two of them back together again, well then, he'd have to go along with the plan. He swaddled the stone in the cloth. "Okay, I'll do it. Just this one time, that's it."

Beth grinned, then threw her arms around him in a big hug.

"I'm serious, just one time," Rick repeated. "Because when people start bending the rules, things have a crazy way of spiraling out of control."

# 14

FRANCISCO PULLED MARIA along by the hand, scampering through alternating bands of light and shadow cast down by the streetlamps lining Desert Canyon Drive. He needed to hurry, to get her there fast. He could wait no longer.

It was nearing 2:30 a.m., and still Francisco could feel the intense heat of the day. It surrounded and smothered him like a woolen poncho. Maria was moving much too slowly. He could sense her reluctance and was becoming angry with her Latina stubbornness, the same stubbornness that seemed to poison every other girl he'd tried to make a move on. After tonight, he'd find himself a *gringa*. His friend Eduardo had hooked up with one and said they didn't tease boys like the Mexican girls did.

"*Mas rápido*, Maria," Francisco said, pulling her harder by the hand. "It's up here, only a few houses more."

Passing under the glow of a streetlamp, he could see her face, her eyes bulging and chin quivering. She seemed frightened, maybe a virgin after all. Word around school was that she'd been with three other boys, two in one night, but Francisco couldn't be sure it was true. At Willow Canyon High, rumors spread like wildfire.

No matter, scared or not, he would taste her tonight, every inch of her delicious body. And he knew the perfect spot, a place they would be alone. "Ay, Maria, hurry. You move like a turtle." Within the shadows, he whisked her along.

When at last they reached a dark house with broken windows, he stopped and pulled Maria close, whispering into her ear. "Here it is, we'll be safe like I promised."

She stared at the house, gray in the darkness, her eyes narrowed with concern. "Are you sure it's empty?"

"No doubt about it," Francisco said. "The owner didn't pay his bills. A deadbeat like my Uncle Jorge. The bank made him leave."

As Maria passed through a wedge of moonlight, Francisco caught a fleeting glimpse of her body, hard and thin and fitted tightly into a floral pattern summer dress. He could see her panty lines, how they curved up and disappeared between her legs, into places Francisco could only imagine. He took her by the arm and pulled her to the side, under the deep shadow of a magnolia tree.

"It doesn't look safe," Maria said, her face hidden in darkness.

"I promise you it is," Francisco answered quickly. "Eduardo came here with his girlfriend last night."

"Eduardo's a liar," Maria said. "Everything he tells you is bullshit."

"We will be alone inside." Francisco draped his arm around her shoulders and nibbled at her neck. The scent of her perfume was sweet, and he felt a stir in his pants. "There will be no one to bother us."

Maria remained quiet, uncertain.

Francisco licked her neck, tasting her salty skin. They had run for nearly a mile and already Maria was damp with perspiration, which only intensified the smell of her perfume. He had to get her inside. There would be a bed or a couch, something they could use. They would hook up—ay, it would be *fantástico!*

Because of the darkness, Francisco was sure Maria couldn't see his pants. He allowed himself to harden. God, he had to get her inside the house. "I will jump the fence, open it for you."

"I don't like this," Maria said. Her eyes fixed upon the shattered windows, and the grayness beyond. "This place, it has bad energy."

"I want to be your boyfriend," Francisco said. "We'll just kiss." But he was sure if he could get her inside, onto a couch, he could do so much more. Without waiting for an answer, he dashed to the fence and scaled over, all in one burst. Seconds later, the gate creaked open and he whispered for Maria.

After a slight hesitation, she crept up to meet him. They skirted the house to the rear, Francisco pulling her along at a fevered pace. He tried the back door but it was dead-bolted. They scampered to the other side, where they found a large, splintered window, hidden deep in the shadows under a canvas awning. Closed shutters made it impossible to see inside.

"Look there," Maria said, pointing to the far end of the window.

Francisco looked carefully to where she was pointing. He could see a two-foot wide section of glass that was missing. Behind it, the shutter was open.

"Eduardo really was here," Maria whispered, her voice filled with surprise. "That must be where he entered, with his girl."

Francisco, too, was surprised. To comfort Maria, he had made up the story of Eduardo sneaking inside. But no matter, he was happy for an easy way in, and soon he'd have her all to himself, no one to bother them.

He crept to the end of the window and stopped. "Be careful," he said, pointing near his feet. A pile of broken glass lay neatly stacked against the stuccoed wall. "Someone, I mean Eduardo must have pulled away the glass."

Maria nodded.

He turned his attention back to the window and pushed on the shutter. It creaked open. Inside, the house was dark, hopelessly dark, with only a few stray shafts of moonlight lancing through splits in the awning. Francisco had hoped for more light. He wanted more than to just touch Maria's breasts, he wanted to see them—their rounded form, their brown nipples.

He turned back to her. "I'll climb inside and help you through, okay?" He didn't wait for an answer. It no longer mattered what she wanted. She'd come this far and that was as good as a promise. With a single leap he was on the sill, taking care to avoid the glass edges that jutted out inches from his shoulder. And with another leap he was standing inside on the plush carpet.

"Help me," came Maria's nervous voice from outside.

Francisco turned and reached his arms through the window, grabbing her by the forearms. In one thrust he pulled her through and into the house, catching her dress against the jagged window edge. A large piece flicked free and shattered on the patio.

Maria landed on her feet, then quickly bent down and slapped a hand to her thigh. "Ay, it stings." She held her palm up against a moonbeam. An inky shine covered her hand and she let out a weak groan. "You've cut me," she said.

Francisco stared at her hand, then knelt and lifted her dress. "It's a small cut, not deep. He pulled off his T-shirt and pressed it against her thigh. After a minute, he removed his shirt and examined her leg. "The bleeding stopped, it's nothing." He lifted her dress higher, pretending to search for more wounds. Maria slapped down the fabric, but not before Francisco caught sight of her white panties. He clenched his teeth and jumped to his feet, swinging Maria into an embrace. "Let's sit there." He pointed to a sectional sofa in the living room.

But Maria did not answer. She'd become interested in the house and its furnishings, staring at the dark, lifeless shapes blending quietly throughout the rooms.

A hum broke the silence. Maria drew a quick breath.

"Take it easy." Francisco put his hand against her chest to feel her heartbeat. It thumped rapidly. "It's just the refrigerator, through there, in the kitchen." Maria had become too frightened to notice his hand inching toward her breast. He held it there a moment, until she realized what he had done and slapped it away.

He took her by the waist and led her into the living room.

"Just kissing," Maria said. "You promised that was all we would do."

Francisco pulled her onto the couch. He was moments away from having her. He was sure of it. It felt like a hammer in his pants, and he could no longer wait.

Sitting, Maria crossed her legs and leaned close to Francisco, her face turned to kiss him.

*Click, click, click.* A strange noise sounded from behind them. They turned to look, peering toward a darkened hallway.

"What was that?" Maria asked.

Francisco wasn't sure, but he knew it wasn't the refrigerator. "It must be a clock," he said after a moment of thought. "You know— tick, tick, tick."

"You sure?"

"Of course, see there." He pointed to a towering shape, dark against a lighter wall. "The noise came from that, a grandmother's clock."

"Ay, stupid," Maria said, slapping Francisco's hand away from her thigh. "They're called grandfather clocks."

"Grandmothers, grandfathers, let's not talk of old people now," Francisco said, his thoughts returning quickly to Maria's body. He would need to arouse her if ever he hoped to remove her dress. He had a thought. He could move her hand to his pants and let her feel his desire.

Their kissing became fierce. He felt like an animal, licking and sucking her neck. Gently, he took her hand and maneuvered it to his knee, then ever so slowly he inched it up, higher, to his thigh, further still, to his—

"Ay, disgusting!" Maria yelled. She pushed him away and rubbed her hand against her dress, wiping as if she'd touched a dead slug.

"What's wrong with you," Francisco said. "You act like it was out of my pants or something." There was no way she'd been with three other guys, he decided.

*Click, click, click.* The sound echoed through the house.

Maria sprang to her feet. "Did you hear that?"

"A grandmother's clock, I already told you."

"Two clocks?" Maria said doubtfully. "The noise came from there." She pointed toward a closet door, opposite the entrance to the hallway.

*Click, click, click.*

She turned her head and froze. Taking a step back, her face split a shaft of moonlight.

All thoughts of sex disappeared when Francisco saw her eyes. They were opened wide and frozen with fear, fixed upon the wall where the clock had stood. He turned, expecting to find el Diablo himself, but instead he saw nothing. Nothing at all. Why was Maria panicked?

He reached for her hands, to pull her back to the sofa, but she had balled them up and drawn them tightly against her chest. "Why you so afraid?" he said. "There's nothing there."

"Yes," Maria answered. "There's nothing there. So where did the clock go?"

Francisco looked again and realized something was wrong, terribly wrong. Where seconds ago there stood a tall clock, there was now nothing. Nothing at all. It was gone.

*Click, click, click.*

Francisco jumped to his feet, suddenly realizing they were not alone.

A crouching form moved in the darkness behind Maria. Then as if by witchery, it grew larger, much larger, only inches away from her.

Francisco tensed.

Led by a wicked flash of steel, the dark form broke through the moonlight.

Francisco tried to scream but was overcome by terror. In one swift motion the figure swept in front of Maria, and when it passed, Francisco could see a change in her expression—shock replacing fear.

There came a grotesque gurgle, and Maria's hand reached for her neck. The flowery print on her dress slowly began to darken, and a grotesque blackness spread across her chest. Lifeless, she slumped to the carpet.

Francisco wanted to run, but his feet were like cement. And when he finally moved it was too late.

He could see it now, a tall form outlined in the darkness, quiet yet menacing. At its side hung a cord with two bulbous ends that swung and clattered in the moonlight. *Click, click, click.* Then instantly the cord was taut, stretched out by two claw-like hands.

*El Diablo!* But before Francisco could beg for his soul, he felt a pinching squeeze around his throat. He struggled desperately to free himself, clutching at his neck, gasping for air.

But none came.

Was this punishment for his lies?

Francisco reached out into the darkness, everything around him becoming a blur.

Suffering for his sins?

As his muscles weakened, Francisco could feel only a pressing chill. He had deceived Maria, and now this was his punishment: Death at the hands of el Diablo himself.

# 15

IN THE GRAY stillness of the house on Desert Canyon Drive, where only a few bolts of stray moonlight penetrated, Sarth knelt motionless over his sacrifice. How fortunate he was to have two gentle lambs present themselves so conveniently and yet so unexpectedly. Using a dry portion of the girl's dress, he finished wiping clean his blade, then stood and walked back to the hallway, carefully avoiding the blood that had spilled from her neck onto the carpet.

Before the interruption, he'd searched the kitchen and common rooms thoroughly for Father's talisman. He'd found nothing. Now, all that remained was the bedroom. He crept down the hall and with a gloved hand removed a small Maglite from his pocket. He switched it on and opened the bedroom door.

Inside, the flashlight revealed what Sarth assumed to be typical American bachelor furniture—a portable television, two fold-up chairs, a secondhand dresser, and an unkept bed. He moved to the bed and lifted the mattress, searching for any sign of the relic. He found nothing. Next to the bed a small lamp surmounted a stack of boxes, the arrangement doubling as a crude nightstand. With the penlight between his teeth, Sarth knocked aside the lamp and opened the boxes, digging through clothes, toiletries, and an assortment of pornographic magazines.

Still, there was no sign of the talisman.

After completing his search of the bedroom, Sarth stepped across the hall to a large nook. Set into one end of the space was a desk with a computer, a monitor, a printer, and stacks of CD's and software manuals. Sarth pulled open the desk drawers and searched inside, riffling through papers. He reached behind the computer and flipped on the power switch, waiting patiently as the system beeped and whirred to life.

Once the operating system booted, he slid the chair away from the desk and knelt at the keyboard. Rapidly, he stroked the keys and watched as file after file scrolled over the glowing screen. After minutes of reading, a file caught his attention, a document addressed to a Dr. Beth Harper at the University of Arizona, Tucson. He snatched the mouse, raced the pointer across the screen, and stopped on the icon. With a click, he opened the file and began to read:

*Dear Dr. Harper,*

*My name is Jake Tanner, Captain in the United States Marine Corps. The object in this photograph was recovered in the Wazir Valley, Afghanistan, back in December of last year. I recently met Rick Lowell at station KSND in Phoenix, who told me you might be able to identify the stone, given your area of expertise. I've taken quite an interest in it and thought maybe you could tell me about its history. If so, please call me at the number above. Any help would be greatly appreciated.*

*Sincerely,*
*Jake Tanner*

How very wonderful, Sarth thought. A route of inquiry had presented itself. Perhaps this Dr. Harper was the archaeologist of whom the pathetic Mr. Stewart had spoken. Now that Tanner was dead, it seemed entirely possible this woman had taken possession of the relic. Sarth re-read the letter, carefully, making a mental note of its contents. When he finished he closed the file, deleted it, then shut down the computer.

He stood and observed the time. The hour was late and soon the sun would creep over the horizon and brighten the desert cityscape. Sarth had much to do before his departure from the house. Mithra had seen fit to bless him with a gift, and Sarth would first have to show his gratitude. He returned to the living room, where the bodies of the children lay in silent waiting. He knelt near the boy, touched his smooth black hair. *As Mithra honored the bull with the spilling of its blood, so too, gentle child, shall you be honored.* Sarth stroked the boy's lifeless head one last time, then removed his blade.

*        *        *

Gabe Carter braked to a sudden stop in front of his rental property on Desert Canyon Drive. His brother Theo lurched forward, nearly spilling his iced tea. Gabe was still a little peeved that Theo wouldn't stop clamoring on about selling the place. It was a stupid idea, and he'd have to put his foot down. Theo didn't know crap about investment. This house and their other two rentals were all the two of them had. And all three properties had been Gabe's brainwork, not his idiot brother's. He'd involved Theo cuz of his wallet, not cuz of his figuring skills.

Gabe kept the car idling and the air conditioner running at full. It was only a little after eleven, but already a scorcher. Shrill laughter turned Gabe's head. In a fenced-off yard across the street, he could see a bunch of kids throwing themselves around on a bright yellow Slip'N Slide. There were half a dozen of 'em, and they were all white smiles and as brown as berries. The garden hose ran at high, spilling waves of water onto the sidewalk. A mother stood on the porch, holding a tube of tanning lotion in one hand, while shielding her eyes with the other. She watched the kids with interest. Gabe figured the woman was thirty, maybe thirty-five, lean and sexy in a white one-piece swimsuit with one of them sarongs draped around her waist. She opened the lotion, squirted a bit into her hand. The way she rubbed circles over the exposed part of her chest, he was starting to get a boner.

Gabe began to feel a little guilty, with Margaret at home—bless her heart—no idea he was thinking dirty about a woman he'd never even met before.

"I'm telling you we ought to sell the place," Theo said. "It'll be too hard to rent it out again. I'm pretty sure the law says you gotta come clean with tenants when someone goes and croaks inside."

Gabe, still angry with Theo, turned away from the woman and glared at his brother. "Yeah, well, then we'd probably have to disclose it to people buying the place, too. Think of that, genius?"

Theo stared back, a blank look on his face.

"Yeah, you didn't, did you? I say we clean the place up, do our best to rent it out again, keep the cash flow coming. If we sell, we're down to only two rentals. I don't know about you, but I'd like to retire someday without having to eat Friskies for dinner. Can't do that without cash flow."

Gabe only planned to be inside for a few minutes, have a quick look-see, find out how bad the Tanner boy had beaten up the place. During the weekends, him and his Marine buddies probably did a real number on it, hell, just look at the outside windows, every one of them busted. Gabe clenched his fists and cursed the kid, but then reminded himself it wasn't a good idea to wish ill of the dead. That poor boy never hit thirty and already he was a goner.

*Sorry son.*

As far as Gabe knew, Tanner had no immediate family, so until someone came knocking to collect his things, he and Theo would have to move everything in the garage. Then they'd patch up and spot-paint a few walls, have the carpet cleaned, maybe Pine-Sol the bathrooms. Place would be ready to go within a couple days.

"Still, I say we sell it," Theo said. "What do you figure we have in equity? Thirty, forty thousand? I've been hoping to float a new pontoon on Havasu next spring. If we sold the place, I'd—"

"Listen, we ain't selling it, we ain't talking of selling it, we ain't even thinking of selling it. So get the idea out of your thick skull, you got it?"

Theo shrugged, took a drink from his bottle of iced tea.

"Now let's get in there, do what's gotta be done, so I can get back to the shop before the place goes to hell."

Gabe kept the car running and the air conditioner humming on high. They hurried to the door, Gabe glancing back to get another look at the greased up woman, who was now sitting on the porch turning the pages of a magazine.

Inside the house, the air was muggy. Gabe sucked it in through his nostrils, noticing what he thought was an odd kind of odor—kinda like spoiled meat. Damn, the kid must've been letting the dishes stack up. He looked at Theo, who was standing with his shoulder slumped, wrinkling his nose in disgust.

"What do you figure Tanner's been doing in here?"

"Don't know," Gabe said. "He's probably got rotten food in the kitchen. The coroner took care of the kid's body, but they ain't maids you know."

Gabe and Theo took a step into the entryway and stopped, staring at the carpet in the living room. A huge black stain five, maybe six feet in diameter lay smack in the middle.

"Shit, the kid must've really done a number on the place," Gabe said. Then he noticed an area at the center of the stain, where the carpet was still clean. It looked as if whatever had spilled had spilled around something lying in the middle, leaving a clean spot.

"Think one of them motorized carpet cleaners will take that up?" Theo asked.

"That stain ain't coming up, no way, no how."

"Dad-blasted, then we'll have to replace the carpet."

"Look there." Gabe pointed to some smaller stains leading away from the large one toward the bathroom. They were lighter, not black in color, more of a deep red.

"Christ, ain't that blood?"

"Sure as shit is."

They both walked a little further into the entryway. Gabe could see that the trail leading away had been made with bare feet, and he figured from their size, whoever it was that made them had to be incredibly tall.

He looked back to the larger stain. There was something odd about its clean center. There wasn't nothing in the room that was small enough to make it, the sofa, the coffee table, the television set, all of them square and pretty big pieces of furniture. Then Gabe noticed two sets of handprints in the stain, just outside the clean center. His mind formed a quick image. Using hands for balance, someone had knelt down low, getting a good bath in—*holy shit*. "Theo, this ain't good, I got an awful feeling."

"What kind of kinky parties you think that boy was throwing, screwing up the carpet like that?"

Gabe didn't answer him. He just inched forward, trying to get a clear view of the vaulted ceiling in the living room. Stepping from under the low ceiling of the entryway, he peered up high.

And then he saw it.

A feeling of nausea stirred in his gut. Gabe slapped a hand over his mouth to hold in the barf. Hoisted high against the vaulted ceiling was a scene unlike any other he'd ever witnessed before, grotesque and horrific.

"Damn if your face ain't gone sour," Theo said. "What is it you see?"

Despite Gabe's best effort to prevent it, a burning stream of vomit erupted from his mouth, spraying out between his fingers onto the floor. He wiped a hand across his sour lips, unable to tear his sight away from the hideous spectacle. Hoisted high against the ceiling hung two human bodies, all carved up and butchered like animals. They swayed gently from a mess of nylon cords, their intestines dangling out of their bellies like fresh links of sausages.

Gabe's feet shuffled back, and before he realized it, he'd run into Theo. He spun around and grabbed his brother, hands covered in hot chunks. "Let's get the hell out of here," he sputtered. "We're gonna sell this house, just like you say, Theo. Best idea you ever had!"

## 16

"HE'LL MAKE a good technician," Elliot was saying, staring down at the resume on his desk. "He's got the education and experience. But I still think you'd better run him by the czar. If we move on this without Mason's say-so, he'll bitch and moan for a month, regardless of how good the guy turns out to be."

Rick nodded, vaguely aware that Elliot was still talking to him. All morning he'd been trying to wrap his mind around Beth's scheme to break into the university laboratory. It was important to him that he justify taking such a drastic action on better grounds than simply wanting to make her happy. He considered the talisman. Clearly it was a significant artifact. Beth said its discovery would make news around the world. Maybe getting inside the lab so she could make the deadline on this upcoming symposium would—

Hell, he wasn't being honest with himself. Breaking and entering was still breaking and entering, any way he tried to spin it. He could kick himself for going along with it. But damn if Beth hadn't been persuasive, working her magic. How he'd felt last night, hearing her voice, touching her cheeks. It had been months since he'd felt so happy. Not to mention, whenever it came to Beth, he'd always had a hard time saying no. The thought of the two of them getting back together and starting a family filled a void somewhere deep inside him. It was too much to resist.

"Sound like a plan?" Elliot asked.

Rick shook himself out of his reverie. "Oh, sure, I'll run his resume by Mason first thing Monday morning."

"Why not now? He's in his office."

Rick frowned. "Mason's here? Now?" That was odd. He never worked on Saturday, said his weekends were far too important to spend in the company of morons—meaning everyone at the station who didn't wear a bra.

"I'll take care of it," Rick assured Elliot.

*       *       *

Rick gave a quick rap on Mason's office door and opened it. Inside, the diminutive shock jock sat hunched behind his desk, books and papers heaped up high. An old man with a plump physique and a mane of thick white hair stood next to him, pointing between pages. Rick didn't recognize him. They both peered up, blinking.

"Christ, Rick, why bother knocking if you're not gonna wait for an answer? You know the meaning of the word *privacy*? What if I'd been taking a shit or something?"

"At your desk, in your office? Are you insane?"

Mason scratched his head. "You know what I mean. It's a matter of etiquette."

"Listen, speaking of etiquette," Rick said. "The other day, on the air, I took things a little too far. I shouldn't have—"

"Forget about it," Mason said. "Anyway, it worked out fine. Got hundreds of listener emails, everyone thinking it was a gag, part of the show."

"Well anyway, I'm sorry."

Mason waved a dismissive hand, then nodded to the old man. "Someone I want you to meet, Rick. This is Peter Eckerman, a rare books dealer. He comes to us all the way from Munich. That talisman of Tanner's, Peter's somewhat of an expert on it."

The mention of Tanner's name made Rick cringe. It was an unwelcome reminder of what Beth had gone through yesterday—not to mention what the two of them were planning to do tonight. He took a calming breath. "Here's the resume of the new sound tech we're hiring."

"Put it wherever." Mason said. "I don't have time to worry about it."

Rick slipped the paper into the in-tray, turned to leave.

"Hold up," Mason said. "Since you're here, you don't remember Tanner mentioning anything about leaving town, do you?"

"No."

"Peter and I have been calling him every hour since yesterday afternoon. We can't seem to get ahold of him. We're driving out to his house in a few minutes."

Rick hadn't planned to tell Mason about Tanner, but there was no sense having them waste their time. "I hate to break this to you, Mason, but Tanner's dead."

Rick's words hung in the air.

Both men's eyes grew wide with shock.

After a moment, Eckerman lowered his head as though in prayer, mumbled something under his breath.

"What do you mean, dead," Mason said. "Like six feet under dead?"

"Is there any other kind?"

Mason stood up, his eyes tiny slits. "How do know this?"

"I saw Beth last night. She'd called me, rattled. It turns out Tanner had contacted her about the talisman. When she went to examine it, she found him on the floor of his entryway, dead."

"How?"

"Not really sure. Beth says his body was covered in sores. He seems to have suffocated, a bad reaction of some kind."

Mason hustled around his desk and grabbed the handle of the open door. He peeked down the hall, then quietly shut it.

Rick said, "What's going on?"

"The stone…Tanner was cursed," Eckerman said.

"We could go with that," Mason added. "But I'd much prefer the military cover-up angle. More punch. Plus, we have just enough facts to make the story believable. What happened to Tanner was no coincidence. He was the only Marine left who'd been part of Operation Cold Strike, and he wasn't keeping his mouth shut either. Christ, he was blabbing about it right here on my radio show. Now he's dead, just like the rest of them."

"You honestly think the military's involved?" Rick said.

"Have to be a fool not to," Mason said. "They're playing loosely with new technology. I'm sure of it. And they didn't want word to get out. Tanner's memory was improving. They had to tie up loose ends."

Eckerman pulled out a handkerchief, wiped sweat from his forehead. He peered at Rick, his blue eyes large. "The talisman, do you know what's become of it? Please, it is very important."

"You're an expert on the artifact?"

"That's right." The old man was breathing hard.

"It's in good hands," Rick assured him. "Beth has it. She's an expert, as well. She works at the university."

"Please, I must be allowed to see her."

"I think it's best to let her handle it."

"You don't understand," Eckerman said, moving around the desk, closer to Rick. "There are forces at play here that operate beyond the scope of your understanding."

That was an odd kind of comment, Rick thought. He didn't really know what to say. The old man was sweating and his hands trembled. Clearly, the news had had a disturbing effect upon him. "What are you talking about?"

"Don't mind Peter," Mason said. "He's got some extreme ide-as. Anyway, I was thinking, with Tanner dead, I mean it's tragic and everything, but I can see all sorts of new angles opening up. I need to get this story shaped, find some experts willing to go on the air. If I get busy, I could have it ready for Monday morning's broadcast."

Eckerman clasped his hands together. "I must see the stone. It is critical. You could arrange a meeting with this woman, yes?"

"Beth," Rick said, "her name is Beth, and I don't think I ought to be arranging anything. I can assure you, the talisman's in good hands."

"I don't doubt this woman's—Beth's—expertise, my dear fellow. But as Mason said, Tanner's death was no coincidence. While the stone is in her possession, I believe she's in grave danger."

Rick looked at Mason, who threw up his hands and shrugged.

Eckerman inched closer. His blue eyes shined with a fierce intensity. He seemed crazed, in a controlled sort of way.

"So please tell me, how I can contact her, this Beth."

"What do you mean she's in grave danger?"

"The Brotherhood."

Mason stepped between them. "Look, Rick, do you mind if Peter gives her a call, has a quick chat?"

"Yes, I do. I don't think she would appreciate being interrupted. She's busy working to authenticate the stone." Rick nudged Mason aside, then peered at the old man. "What are you talking about, she's in danger?"

"The Brotherhood," Eckerman said, "an ancient society dedicated to the worship of Mithra, the God of Light. They consider the talisman their sacred relic."

Mason bulldogged himself back between them. "It's complicated, Rick, but what he's telling you is that there's a nasty group of people whose organization has existed for thousands of years. The talisman's like their treasured penis or something, and they're gonna do whatever it takes to get it back."

"Indeed," Eckerman said.

Rick glared at Mason, wondering why he was letting a kook like this run around the studio. Then Rick realized Mason had to be playing an angle. The little guy didn't sit on the toilet without careful calculation. Eckerman was here for a reason. Rick stared over their shoulders to the desk. "What are you two working on?"

"The Tanner segment," Mason said.

"Right, your conspiracy theory—the U.S. government, al Qaeda, whichever one's panning out to be the better story. But how does Mr. Eckerman here fit into it?"

"I'm trying to shape the beats—the war, this mysterious technology that killed the Marines, Tanner's relic. It'll add more dimensions to the cover-up. I'm sure it'll draw huge ratings. Peter's agreed to go on the air, as a sort of expert on the talisman."

"Yes, yes," Eckerman said, "but our agreement, Mr. Manning. Remember our agreement."

"Right, of course," Mason said. "Rick, we were expecting to link up with Tanner this afternoon, but since that's no longer a possibility, maybe you'll do us a favor. I've agreed to help Peter find the talisman, or at least get in touch with the person who has it. Right now, that seems to be Beth. I'd like for you to arrange a meeting."

Rick laughed. "Sorry, like I said, she's too busy. But good luck on the story anyway. I'll see you Monday morning."

Perspiring heavily, Eckerman bound forward, stopping himself inches from Rick. "No, you mustn't leave. The Brotherhood, they will come. And I can assure you, they will stop at nothing to retrieve the talisman."

"We'll take our chances." Rick stepped away from the old man, turned, and left the office.

*      *      *

A few hours later, Rick was standing in Beth's kitchen. He watched her from behind as she fussed over a bowl of chicken salad, violently stirring mayonnaise into a mixture of chunked meat, celery, and onions. It was midday and a brilliant light shone in through the dining room's bay windows, accentuating Beth's raven hair and highlighting her lean figure in hues of yellow and gold.

"Met an old man at the studio this morning," Rick said. "Comes all the way from Germany. He claims to be an expert on the talisman."

Beth stopped stirring.

"Says it's an ancient artifact."

"Well, duh," Beth said. "That's common knowledge. Anyone with a history book or Internet access could tell you that."

"He also says it's a religious relic, claims there're people looking for it. A secret society. He calls them the Brotherhood."

Beth laughed. "What university did he say he was from?"

"He's not," Rick said. "His name is Peter Eckerman. He's a rare books dealer."

"Oh, that explains it." Beth spread the salad onto the bread, cut them into diagonals, then squeezed the pieces into zip-lock bags.

"*Voila*, lunch. We'll eat at my office."

"What do you mean that explains it."

"I mean this Mr. Eckerman is not a professional scholar, and I doubt he's a sanctioned researcher. I'll bet he's an artifact hound or some sort of illicit antiquities dealer."

"You think he was feeding me a line to get his hands on the talisman?"

"No doubt about it."

"I don't know. Germany is a heck of a long way to come. Why go to all the trouble?"

Beth frowned. "Look at it this way," she said. "The black market in antiquities and fine arts is a five billion dollar a year industry."

"I wasn't aware."

"It's the fourth largest criminal enterprise in the world. Only illegal drugs, weapons, and money laundering surpass it. And a discovery like the talisman—a high profile piece—could easily fetch several million dollars."

Rick whistled. "Jesus, I had no idea. That would certainly explain Eckerman's motivation."

"Yes, it would." Beth took a deep breath and sighed, her jade eyes gazing absently through the window.

"What's wrong?" Rick said. "If it's the old man you're worried about, I could easily tell him to get lost."

"No, it's not him." She pulled up a chair, sank down. "I was up most of the night tossing and turning, thinking about our plan, about the lab."

"Hey, we can call it off," Rick said. "We're not guilty of breaking and entering—yet."

"I wouldn't call it breaking and entering. I have access to the building, just not the laboratory facilities."

"Right, it's locked up, and you don't have the key. That's breaking and entering."

"Come on, Rick. What would you have me do? This archaeology symposium is the biggest gathering of the year, a real who's who of Near Eastern scholars and researchers. If I miss presenting the talisman, I'll blow a huge opportunity."

"Why not just go to this symposium and announce it? Then when the lab becomes available…"

Beth shook her head. "If I announce the find without first authenticating it, you can bet your bottom dollar Chendekar will assemble a team for study, and as a non-tenured member of the faculty, I'll be relegated to some minor task. Who knows who'll end up getting credit for the talisman's discovery?"

"Tanner," Rick said. "That's who'll get the credit."

"Right, of course," Beth said. "I'm talking in terms of introducing the artifact to the academic world."

"Then that would be you." Rick smiled and took Beth's hand from across the table. "Alright, it's settled. We go tonight and take care of business. Be done with it. Since we already have access to the building, it's just a matter of getting into the lab. We'll be in. We'll be out. I mean, what's the worst that can happen?"

## 17

IT WAS 2:00 A.M. when Rick rolled the Explorer into the staff parking lot adjacent to the lab building. Never in his college career had he seen a parking lot so deserted. Back when he was going to school, finding an open space was like winning the lottery. Of course, he'd never taken a class at two in the morning, either.

He turned to Beth. "Everything you need to do the job is here, right? I mean, we're not going to have to hopscotch to different buildings, are we?"

"Everything's here. This laboratory houses some of the most advanced research equipment in the country. The university is ranked one of the leading research institutions in North America. In large part because of this lab."

"I'll take your word for it," Rick said. "You ready?"

Beth nodded.

They opened their doors and stepped from the car. Beth hung closely to Rick's side as they walked across the warm pavement to the building's entrance. With a quick swipe of her keycard, the door's lock disengaged. She opened it, and they slipped inside.

"Which way?"

Beth pointed down the dimly lit hall. "The freight elevator to the basement."

"Stairs?"

She turned and indicated a set of steel doors.

"Let's take them," Rick said.

Beyond the steel doors was a concrete stairwell. It was hot and smelled of must. A flickering bulb in a metal cage lit the stairs, which fell sharply to a landing, before switching back and disappearing into shadows.

Beth descended, with Rick following carefully behind. Her knapsack was fitted tightly across her back and blended seamlessly with her body. As she bound down the steps, Rick smiled. It had been quite some time since he'd seen her move so fast, and with such determination. She was on a mission, and it seemed nothing was going to stop her. "Slow down there, Flash," he whispered. "One misstep and you'll take a tumble. If you bust up that talisman, none of this'll be necessary."

Beth shot a look over her shoulder. "A gentleman would've offered to go first."

"A gentleman, maybe. I'm just the cretin who's concerned about our rear." He stabbed a thumb back over his shoulder. "If security saw us come in, they'll follow us from that direction."

Beth turned and continued downward, her strides now slow and measured.

The bottom of the stairwell ended at a landing with another steel door.

"Beyond is the main tunnel to the lab," Beth said. "Most of the perimeter rooms are used for materials and storage. There's also Eddie's office and a computer room for number crunching and data analysis, but we won't bother with them. Everything we need will be in the main laboratory." She pushed through the door and stepped into a long, cinder block hallway.

Rick followed her through. The elevator landing was straight ahead to his left. Heavy metal doors were spaced along the right wall, each fitted chest-high with large steel-meshed windows. Low-watt security lights hung from the high ceiling, casting a yellow glow into the rooms. Inside them, Rick could see banks of file cabinets and long, squat specimen drawers.

He and Beth hurried down the corridor, their footsteps falling softly, rapping like faint chatter.

The entrance to the lab was through a large set of double-doors. Rick peered through the small windows, searching. After a minute he stepped back. "There doesn't appear to be any active sensors. The alarm's gotta be a circuit design."

"That's good, right?"

"Well, circuit systems work on a simple principle, but they're popular because they're also very effective."

"So it's not good?"

"It'll require jumpering," Rick said. "I'll have to drill for the wires and connect a bridge across the circuit to bypass the switching mechanism."

Beth frowned. "Can you do it?"

"I think so." He knelt down and shrugged off his backpack. After unrolling a heavy cloth, he began laying out the needed tools— power drill, concrete bit, cutters, jumper wires, duct tape, and wax. He took a long deep breath and went to work.

For the next forty minutes Beth paced the hall behind him, setting his work tempo with the rhythm of her footsteps. Finally, after defeating the lock, Rick stood up and scratched his whiskers. "Hopefully, that'll do it," he said.

Beth stopped pacing and stared at him with big green eyes. "Hopefully?"

He gripped the handle, and with a quick jerk threw open the door, spilling in light from the corridor.

Beth covered her mouth in anticipation.

"Wait, hold on a second," Rick said, peering into the hall beyond. "Do you hear that?"

Beth tensed, listening. Her eyes darted back and forth as she struggled to discern the noise. "I don't hear anything, what is it?"

"Silence," Rick said, grinning. "The sound of success."

She frowned, then whacked him on the shoulder. "You nearly gave me a heart attack."

"Just wanted to add a little excitement."

"I don't need excitement, thank you very much." She peered through the door, and slowly, her lips turned up in a broad smile. "The lab, we're in." She threw out her arms and squeezed him with a big hug. "You did it."

*         *         *

Cal Dempsey sat on a chair in the security pillbox at the southern end of the campus, a portly man of fifty-five, with a balding crown and pepper black hair. He kicked his feet onto the counter, opened the sports page, and scanned down searching for the score to yesterday's Diamondback game. "Son-of-a-bitch," he blurted out, seeing the awful numbers. His team had lost their third in a row. How the hell did they expect to have a winning season, putting up scores like that? Christ, they were playing like sloppy little-leaguers. Cal glanced over the top of the paper, through the dark window. One of the lamp-lights in the parking lot sputtered. At this hour in the morning, the campus was like a ghost town. He half expected to see a tumbleweed blow by. Cal glanced at his watch. Almost time to make the rounds. Ah, heck, why bother? Nothing exciting ever happened around here. Plus, the tires on the electric cart were low again, making every speed bump a real ass-banger. He turned back to the scores.

*Click. Click. Click.*

Cal jerked up with a start. What in tarnation? He set aside the paper and looked out the window.

But there was nothing to be seen but a few trees and a whole lot of empty asphalt. He shrugged and leaned back in his chair, gazing into the night.

*Click. Click. Click.*

This time the sound came from behind him. He swiveled around, looking through the window. Couldn't have been his imagination, not a second time. He grunted to his feet, edged up close to the tinted glass, and peered out. But all he could see was a long, deep shadow created by the museum building. Nobody was around. Still, maybe he oughta have a look. Adjusting his utility belt, he slid open the door and stepped outside.

The pillbox was small, only about ten feet on each side. Cal lifted a flashlight from his belt, flicked it on, and walked along the perimeter. Up the first side there was nothing but a huge parking lot, and up the backside, just the museum building. Walking along the last side he saw more parking, the security cart, and his old Chevy pickup.

No one around. Go figure, he thought. Maybe he was hearing things, after all. He decided he could use a serious caffeine fix. There was a coffeemaker inside. He'd throw in some grounds and make a fresh pot.

The flashlight's yellow beam traced a path along the front of the pillbox, to the door where he'd come out. When he reached it, he holstered his flashlight, stepped back inside, and nearly shit.

In the chair with his back turned was a man, had to be real tall, too, his shoulders rising a good two feet over the backrest.

Cal quickly composed himself and reached for the mace clipped to his belt. "Who the hell are you and what do you want?" he demanded, fumbling for the canister.

"Who I am is of little import to you," the voice said with a chilling calmness. "As for what I seek, your access card to the laboratory building, if you please."

"I'll be damned if—"

"Indeed." The chair swiveled around, and Cal was astonished to see a man of such dark demeanor. He had cold black eyes and a drawn-out face that carried a look of controlled insanity. In his hand swung a garrote, its bulbous ends striking in a rhythmic clatter. *Click. Click. Click.*

Cal struggled to uncap the mace.

At once, a gun appeared in the stranger's other hand. A thin laser beam leapt from its sight.

Cal looked down to see a red bead flash upon his chest. "Oh, for the love of God."

\*          \*          \*

The alarm was disabled, but what was truly amazing, Rick thought, was that the task had been accomplished with hardly any damage to the cinder block wall—just a borehole the size of a quarter. A small patch of grout and no one would ever know the difference.

He peered beyond the door, searching for the unexpected. But everything looked secure. Access to the main lab was gained through a twenty-foot long causeway raised thirty feet above the floor and walled on both sides with thin sheets of Plexiglas. From this vantage point, he had a complete birds-eye view of the stations below. At the end of the causeway was a glass door, and beyond it, a metal staircase descending into the lab.

Rick stepped inside and fumbled his fingers over the wall, feeling for the banks of switches that powered the quadrant lighting. He looked at Beth. "Which one?"

"Light the fourth quadrant," she said. "Everything we'll need: reagents, thin-section saws, research microscopes, x-ray fluorescence spectrometer, it's all there."

Rick flipped the switches on the fourth bank, and immediately columns of high-watt lighting burst over the upper right section of the lab. Below him, the space was vast, probably every research scientist's dream. Though only a fraction of the lab was lit, the strong incandescent bulbs crisscrossing the ceiling performed double duty, offering plenty of light for Rick to see the entire complex. In a grid pattern between the ceiling and lights ran a massive network of gray ducts and sprinkler pipes. Metal and glass fume hoods were prominent in three of the stations. The fourth was a computer-intensive area webbed with cables and wire tubing. Aside from the workbenches, the sinks, the computers and oversized microscopes, the equipment was utterly foreign to him.

"Let's move," Beth said, interrupting his thoughts. She jogged to the end of the causeway and pushed open the door. Rick quickly followed. He glanced at his watch, a little after two-thirty. If Beth was accurate in her time estimate, they'd be finished and back to the car by 5:30. That was cutting it close. Though it was Sunday morning, people still conducted university business—and not all of them, Rick knew, would be late starters.

When he reached the bottom of the stairs, he saw that Beth had already removed the talisman from her pack. Its glassy black surface shined under the bright light. She rested it on a metal tray, then placed the tray gently on a wheeled cart. Rick had accomplished what he'd been asked to do, and now he felt at a loss to help. He glanced around the workstations, trying to guess the function of all the strange equipment. He paced across the floor to a large machine. Had it a paper feed and a print button, he would've figured it for a copy machine.

"It's a wavelength-dispersive x-ray fluorescence spectrometer," Beth said, sensing his curiosity. "It's state-of-the-art. Feed it a sample of obsidian and you'll have a complete chemical analysis in minutes."

Rick gave it a second look. Impressive, however the hell it worked. He turned back to Beth, who was busy lining up bottles of chemicals and hot plates. "You'll be using it for the talisman?" he asked, pointing to the big copy machine.

"No, that particular spectrometer performs destructive analysis. We'll use the QuanX." She finished arranging a series of slides on the workbench, then pointed across the room to a box-like contraption Rick might've mistaken for a large icebox. "That instrument's a bit more sophisticated and non-destructive. Secure the talisman on the sample plate, power-up the x-ray generator, run the results through the WinTrack software, and we'll have a complete chemical analysis of the obsidian—without any damage to the specimen."

"How does figuring the chemical composition authenticate the stone? Isn't obsidian just obsidian?"

"Actually, no. By conducting laser ablation ICP-MS tests, I can quantify trace levels of caesium, thorium, and scandium. Depending on where the glass was formed, it will exhibit its own characteristic levels of these elements. I'll be able to cross-reference my data results with known sources used by the ancient Persians. I've already worked up the figures for absorption rates based on six Near Eastern climate and soil regions, and likely the talisman will be linked to either the Cappadocian, or the Nemrut Dag, or the Bingol Supply Zones."

"Gotcha," Rick said. "So if the source of obsidian turns out to be from somewhere in... say... Hawaii, you'd know right away it wasn't Persian, and therefore couldn't possibly be authentic."

"Exactly."

"Then that's it?" Rick said. "We can clean up our mess and get out of here?"

"Not quite," Beth said. "Then comes the actual hydration analysis, which is done there." She nodded to a large microscope fitted to a long workbench. "After I've prepared the samples, I'll measure the thickness of the hydration layers with ten and forty power objectives."

"What's the point of that?"

"It's how archaeologists date obsidian," she said. "You see, whenever the glass is chipped, like to form a tool, for example, the freshly exposed surface begins to absorb water at a fixed rate. Calculating the period the artifact was crafted is accomplished simply by measuring the thickness of the hydration layers."

"Clever."

"Yes, but absorption rates are dependent upon environmental factors as well—temperature, humidity. To compensate for not knowing the talisman's precise recovery location, I've calculated a range of estimated matrixes. I won't get an exact date, but rather a range of dates."

"Will that be good enough?"

"With the obsidian sourced and dated, and given the undisputable iconic evidence, I'll be able to demonstrate beyond any doubt this little jewel here is indeed the Talisman of Persepolis."

"Great, and you'll be ready for the symposium?"

Beth reached over and squeezed Rick's hand. "Yes, and I'll have the ammunition I need to go to Chendekar. There'll be no risk of a forgery, and no looking foolish. With the analysis complete, he wouldn't dare reassign the project to a senior researcher."

"It's nearly three o'clock," Rick said. "I think we'd better hurry up."

Beth's eyes shifted focus, and she quickly turned back to the workbench, surveying the materials. "Everything is here. I'm ready to make the cuts."

"What would you like me to do?"

She thought for a moment. "Nothing really. I need to take the specimen to the gem saw." She reached for the talisman, but in her rush, she struck the edge of the metal tray, flipping it from the cart and sending the black stone airborne.

Instinctively, Rick's eyes followed it. The talisman soared like an arcing missile. He heard Beth gasp in horror. He dove, throwing out his hands to the point of intercept. The ground met his body quickly, and he landed with a hard slam, just as his fist closed tightly around the stone, inches away from the concrete floor.

Dazed, he could hear Beth kicking away from her stool, its metal legs scraping hard against the floor. He rolled over and looked up, trying to focus. She dropped beside him and threw her hands around his cheeks. "Are you okay, Rick?"

He nodded, her hands cupping his face. He could feel her trembling.

"My God, I'm sorry," she said. "How could I have been so clumsy?"

He held up the talisman, its leather cord dangling over his chest. "I'm not an expert," he said, gasping to get his wind back. "But my guess is this thing is more valuable in one piece than it is in a hundred."

Beth pulled him onto his haunches and embraced him. "I'd be helpless without you," she whispered into his ear. Her voice was weak and broken, the late hour clearly taking its toll. She helped him to his feet. "There *is* something I need for you to do," she said.

"Clean test tubes?" He couldn't hold back a smile.

"No," Beth said. "I need you to be here for me, like you used to be."

Her words had a sudden and deep effect upon him. He hooked his arm around her waist and drew her close. For a moment they stared lovingly at each other. Then she closed her arms around him and pressed her lips to his. And for the first time in a long time, Rick knew everything would be okay.

There was a beep from his watch. He gently separated their bodies and dangled the talisman between them. "It's three o'clock. What do you say we date this bad boy and get out of here?"

*        *        *

Over the next hour, Rick watched as Beth hustled about the lab, prepping slides and hot plates, onto which she carefully cemented obsidian samples. He'd become interested in a few of the machines she calibrated. He approached the gem saw, having paid close attention as she cut tiny, wedge-shaped samples from the artifact. He fiddled with one of the knobs, fascinated by its operation.

"I won't have time to fix anything you break, dear," she told him, her eyes never straying from the microscope's oculars.

Despite his curiosity with the saw, Rick knew she was right. There'd be no time for her to deal with any accidents. He found a cushioned stool, planted himself, and watched as she continued her analysis of the obsidian.

"Interesting," Beth said a few minutes later. She looked away from the microscope and rubbed her eyelids, then peered back into the ocular, occasionally changing the specimen slide. "The sample wedges I removed from the talisman seem to be filled with microscopic holes approximately forty microns in diameter. They're present on each of the samples."

"I never noticed them," Rick said.

"And you wouldn't. The eye can't detect particles smaller than fifty microns. The diameter of a human hair, for example, is only seventy-five."

"Are the holes a problem?"

"Not really a problem, but I can't think of any natural process that would account for them." She straightened up on the stool and stretched her back. "I'll have to make a note to speak to someone in the geology department." She photographed the samples, then hunched forward and continued her work.

Shortly after three-thirty Beth shut down the microscope and video-caliper system. "I've finished measuring the hydration bands of the slide samples. The computer will calculate the arithmetic mean and standard deviation. In just a moment, we'll have the date the talisman was crafted." She turned to the computer that was crunching the hydration numbers and began tapping the keyboard. A moment later, with her eyes still fixed to the monitor and a stream of rapidly scrolling data, Beth began to read aloud.

Rick could hear the rising excitement in her voice, her words coming in chunks. "… Near Eastern climate zone… effective hydration temperature… mean rind thickness… plus, minus one hundred… two thousand three hundred years." The stream of data suddenly stopped and Beth stood motionless.

Rick wasn't sure what to think. Was the news good or bad? Twenty-three hundred years was an awful long time. He would think that with—

Like a boxer at the bell, Beth turned and charged toward him, her arms stretched out in front of her. He could scarcely react before she was upon him, squeezing him tightly.

The news had to be good.

She pulled herself away and planted a kiss on his lips, then turned and dashed to the computer, eagerly re-reading the data. A moment later she printed the findings and carefully sealed the papers in an envelope. "Protect these, please," she said, handing Rick the results. Her voice was official, yet electrified. "I'll get started on the spectrometer."

He watched as she carried the talisman to a large, boxy machine, the one she'd called the QuanX. She lifted a compartment lid, nestled the artifact inside, and made a few adjustments.

Interested, Rick approached and peeked inside.

"Remember I told you I could associate the obsidian with its lava flow, and ascertain where it was formed?"

Rick nodded.

"This is the machine that'll do it, a spectrometer." She finished securing the talisman on a shelf that sat flush with two openings. She pointed to one opening. "From there the machine filters and beams radiation to the sample." With a slender finger, she traced a line to the talisman. "The sample is then irradiated with high-energy x-rays, which eject electrons, sending them here." She continued tracing a line to the other opening. "This plate detects the emission results, creating what's essentially a fingerprint of the specimen material. Concentrations of the sample's constituent elements are then sent to the computer, where a comparison will be made to the obsidian sources used by the ancient Persians."

Rick smiled, nodding as she spoke. He'd never really taken the time to understand the complexity of her work. It surprised him a bit, and, in fact, it impressed him. He began to realize archaeology wasn't just a matter of digging up bones and cataloguing potsherds. The science behind it was intense. He watched the passion in Beth's eyes as she spoke. Her face glowed with excitement, and he realized, maybe for the first time in their relationship, her work was equally as significant as his own, maybe more so. He felt like a hypocrite. He'd never offered to give up his career to stay home and raise a family, how could he have expected it from her?

Beth closed the compartment housing the talisman and double-checked the settings. Then, crossing her fingers, she started the machine.

The QuanX hummed to life. She stepped back and stood next to Rick.

Soon the testing would be over, and they'd be able to get out of here. It was too late to drive back to Phoenix. He'd see about staying at her place. In the morning they could go out for breakfast and discuss—

Rick noticed a red bead moving against Beth's shoulder. A laser. He looked at the spectrometer to locate its source, but it didn't appear to have one. He turned back and saw that the bead had moved up to her neck, and was still rising. Suddenly, his gut wrenched, and memories of '89 flashed in his mind. He could almost feel the hot, heavy air of Panama around him. He swung to his right and caught a visual of the beam. His eyes traced its path up to the entrance of the lab, where, on the landing, a man stood cloaked in black. He was tall and he was set in a stance to fire a weapon. And gripped in his outstretched hand was the source of the laser—an HK semi-automatic pistol.

# 18

FROM BENEATH THE drawn shades of Information Technology Specialist Jarred Dyer's office, a dim, cactus-green glow escaped into the desert night. Inside, Jarred squirmed in front of a network terminal, shifting from side to side, trying to mold his aching rump into the cushion of a brand new swivel chair. His fingers typed rapidly over the keyboard as he balanced an open notebook between his thighs. He tapped the return key twice and waited while the VPN at Fort Detrick loaded the MRMC's remote-access-user authentication page—remote access that Jarred knew he wasn't authorized to establish. He watched nervously as the system scrolled gibberish, running the encryption algorithm that protected Medical Research Command's vast, top-secret database.

Second thoughts began to manifest themselves as he worked, and he shuddered to think of the consequences if he were caught. Breaching MRMC's database to ensure Mom's business success no longer seemed like such a brilliant idea.

But she'd finally begun generating extra cash through her psychic-reader business, and whether Jarred wanted to admit it or not, much of that success was due to the free air-time on Mason's radio show. A few more months of rush-hour commercial spots and Mom would be sitting pretty. Jarred would finally be able to stop worrying about supporting her in her golden years.

The Medical Research Command's authentication page loaded onto the screen:

> **\*\*MRMC, Fort Detrick\*\***
> **\*\*Active Investigation (AI) DATABASE\*\***
> *//Access restricted to approved users*
> *//User Identification:*
> *//Password:*

Jarred stared numbly at the screen. It was almost 4:00 a.m., and he could feel the ache of the late hour creeping into his shoulders. He rubbed the nape of his neck, then peered down at the notebook, straining his eyes to discern the scribble: *FIRSTBLOOD. Christ, how could he have forgotten?* Looking back at the screen he typed:

> *//User Identification: TS000441*
> *//Password: 135firstblood753*

He punched return.

> *//Unauthorized User //Access Denied*

*Access denied?* Jarred swallowed hard. Had he been given the wrong user information? It seemed unlikely. He'd known Sergeant Major Ellis, his contact at Detrick, since '86, when they'd been assigned together to coordinate cross-training exercises between their bases. They'd become good friends and Ellis was as reliable as they came. Jarred double checked his notes. The ID number was correct, as was the password—

The password. It's case sensitive, you idiot. He laced together his fingers, cracked his knuckles, then slapped the sides of his face in a sort of flat-handed drum roll. Come on, wake up.

He blinked at the screen, then re-entered the password:

> *//Password: 135FIRSTBLOOD753*

Return.

Immediately, a blaze of green characters scrolled up the monitor. Jarred's eyes widened. I'm in, he thought, suddenly pleased, but still a bit petrified. Feeling naked, he glanced around the room, then looked at the door, half expecting heavily armed MP's to bust in and grapple him away from the computer.

He leaned back in his chair, scratched his head.

The code name of Tanner's Afghan operation was Cold Strike; that much Jarred knew. He scanned through pages of access instructions and military disclosures until he found the database search engine:

*//Abstract Report Field [Report#, Abstract Title, Operation CodeName]:*

Jarred typed rapidly.

*//Abstract Report Field [Report#, Abstract Title, Operation CodeName]: Cold Strike + Abstract Summary*

Return.

The screen cleared black, and for a moment, Jarred sat in the inky darkness of his office. The computer hummed and his heart knocked. Then the monitor blinked alive with a wash of data, causing him to lurch forward and read:

REPORTNUM: [MRMC]-86-113

*DATE: 22 JUNE 2003 [update]*

> *Operation:*      *Cold Strike*
> *Classification:*      *Top-Secret*
> *Investigation Status:*      *Open/Priority*
> *Findings Submitted by Dr (Lt Col) Osbourne*
> *Sub: Findings for MEU Failure: Operation Cold Strike*
> *Encl:*

*(1)        Overview*
*(2)        Operation*
*(3)        Casualty Report*
*(4)        Research Focus*
*(5)        Conclusions*

*(1)        OVERVIEW:*
*Enclosed report provides partial insight into breadth and scope of MEU Operation Cold Strike.*

*MRMC research facilities requested by USMC. All previous findings submitted.*

*Operation objective: Visual inspection of caves in Afghanistan's Wazir Valley, with goal of finding and eradicating al Qaeda cells and munitions.*

*MEU led by Captain Tanner successfully neutralized twenty-two al Qaeda-occupied caves.*

*In early morning hours on December 14, 2001, Operation Cold Strike suffered severe casualties [see findings in (2) and (3) below.] Captain Tanner's team entered cave designated WVC 212 and was subsequently overcome by unknown threat, resulting in 5 casualties [see (3) Casualty Report for findings.] Captain Tanner later transported by medevac helicopter to secure location. Remaining members of team pronounced deceased on site by medevac crew.*

Jarred scanned down the page, searching for the casualty report. Whatever killed Tanner's team would surely be found there. As he read deeper into the electronic text, he felt a growing sense of unease. He couldn't believe it. It was right smack in front of him, every one of the autopsies—the external/internal examinations, toxicology, biochemical tests, all of it! He knew he'd found something big, definitely big enough to please Mason. Jarred reached for the phone, fumbled it off the hook, and dialed.

Moments later he heard an angry grunt.

"Mason," Jarred said, "were you sleeping?"

There was a brief pause, then a raspy throat cleared. "Of course I was sleeping, you goddamn idiot! It's four in the morning. What did you think I was doing, mowing the frickin lawn?"

"Sorry," Jarred said. But he wasn't really. He knew Mason would forgive him soon enough, once he heard the news. "Listen to me, I just accessed the MRMC database and you're not going believe what I found. This goes deeper than either one of us ever would have guessed."

# 19

RICK WATCHED THE point of the gun's laser inch closer to Beth's head. Instinctively, he lunged forward, throwing himself between her and the beam. The report of the gun reverberated sharply, and Rick felt a bullet tear through the sleeve of his shirt and burn across his flesh. His hands clutched Beth's shoulders, and together they slammed to the floor, Beth screaming.

In the confusion there came a sudden, high-pitched wail, followed by a glassy shatter from somewhere inside the QuanX spectrometer. They needed cover! Rick drove himself like a plow against Beth, sliding her twisted body behind a row of storage islands, putting hard cover between them and the shooter. Quickly, he pulled open the tear in his shirt and assessed the wound. It stung and it bled, but it was only superficial.

He turned his attention to Beth, who looked dazed, blinking wildly, a trickle of blood running from her scalp down her cheek. In the fall, she'd taken a blow to the head. "Don't move," he said.

Stealing a look over the island, Rick tried to get a fix on the shooter. A second shot rang out and a bullet skipped off the steel countertop, inches from his head, shattering a stack of beakers behind him. Glass fell to the floor, spreading in an arc and glittering like diamonds. The shooter had moved half-way down the stairs and was advancing with caution.

Panicked, Rick searched around for anything he could fashion into a weapon.

Then again, from the QuanX, there came another high-pitched shriek, followed by more shattering. "My God," Beth said, slowly regaining her senses. She bolted up in a sitting position next to Rick, fear and confusion in her eyes. "What's happening?"

"We're being shot at." His eyes continued searching for something he could use for defense—anything at all. Across the aisle he spotted a cabinet with a sliding glass door. It was packed with clear bottles, each filled with liquids of assorted colors. "Any of those flammable?" he asked Beth.

"We're being shot at?" she said incredulously. "Maybe it's campus security, I could show them my I.D. badge."

"I saw the guy, and he sure as hell wasn't security. And besides, security would never fire at us without provocation."

Beth touched a finger to her scalp, probing the cut.

"You okay?"

"Yeah, I think so."

"Any of those compounds flammable?" Rick asked again. Then, in the hollow reflection of the glass cabinet, he saw the dark figure stepping from the last flier of the staircase onto the lab floor, forty, maybe fifty feet away. The tall assassin moved with grace and precision.

"There," Beth said, pointing obliquely to one of the shelves. "Acid."

Rick scrambled low to the cabinet door, tried sliding it open. It was locked. He turned away and thrust an elbow through the glass pane. Shards fell to the floor. He pulled out a clear, heavy bottle marked *sulfuric acid, 94% concentrate.*

It wouldn't be easy to score a hit with it, especially since he couldn't risk lifting his head over the tabletop again. The bullet had come inches from hitting him, and the shooter was now much closer.

Rick turned back to Beth and could see her jade eyes narrowed by fear, looking to him for reassurance. He remained hunched between the islands, and glanced back at the reflection in the pane.

The shooter was closer, maybe thirty feet.

There was no time to delay.

With one hand, Rick lifted and lowered the bottle, getting a feel for the weight. A direct hit would be ideal, but he'd settle for an acid splash, anything to make the son-of-a-bitch think twice. He hefted up the bottle, took a deep breath, and lobbed it over the island. He spun back to the reflection in the pane. In its hollowness he saw the ghostly figure dart back. The bottle shattered on the floor several feet in front of him, spraying in a semicircle at the intersection of the lab.

*Damn it!* Rick had missed. The bottle was too heavy, the shooter too quick. From a distance greater than ten or twenty feet, there'd be little hope of hitting the bastard.

The laser from the gun's sight played back and forth across the island, and Rick could see the man had stopped short of the acid spill, his free hand holding a black cloth over his mouth to stifle the fumes.

Even from a distance, the pungent odor of the acid was intense. Rick wrinkled his nose and looked at Beth, who'd risen to a knee and was scanning the long row of glass-faced cabinets behind them. She'd obviously recovered from the fall, and her mind was beginning to work.

Rick turned back and eyed the reflection. The man had not moved, apparently assessing the danger of the chemical. It had bought them a few seconds, but Rick knew there'd be little time before the assassin made another play. It seemed the only option was to have Beth sneak to the far end of the aisle, while the shooter approached. Rick figured if he could make enough noise to draw the guy's attention, she'd be able to circle around to the stairs and make a break for the outside. How he'd save himself he had no idea. Maybe let the guy get close, then bull rush him and hope for the best. With a little luck he wouldn't get shot, but either way Beth would get out alive.

It wasn't the best plan, but he didn't have much choice. He turned to explain to Beth, but she'd crawled to a cabinet ten feet down the aisle and was kneeling under a fume hood marked *Perchloric Acid Use Only*. She swiveled around on her haunches and kicked out the glass, then she reached inside and removed a bottle. The gun's laser whipped over the island above her, and she ducked lower, cradling the bottle.

Rick looked back at the reflection. The assassin resumed his approach, moving across the acid spill, slowly, quietly. There was little time. Beth would have to start circling. He heard a whisper and turned to see her next to him.

"Take this," she said anxiously, "and throw it."

"He's too hard to hit."

"Screw him," Beth said. "Aim for the spot you hit before."

Rick could see the wispy reflection of the shooter inching ever closer. He'd reached the intersection, in the middle of the spill. If Beth was to have any chance of getting out of here, she'd have to go now, no time to waste. "Listen to me," he said. "I have a plan to get you out."

"No, you listen to me." Her voice had taken on a surprising sternness. "Throw it, and make contact with the spill."

There was no time to argue. Rick turned back to the reflection. The assassin had almost crossed the acid, and was beginning to move with greater speed.

In a fluid hooking motion, Rick launched the bottle over the island, aiming for the intersection. The dark figure nimbly sidestepped the missile and leapt backward. The bottle crashed to the floor, over the sulfuric puddle, and exploded in a cacophony of energy that rocked the lab's stations and equipment. All around, glass-faced cabinets shattered. At the point of impact, a column of fire curled upward, and Rick could feel its blistering heat against his face. He leaned into Beth and threw his hands over his head as the rush of flames intensified.

Then, in an instant, the flash died, followed by a piercing siren that rang from somewhere above. A white light blinked madly and a gush of something cold, something wet rained from the ceiling. Rick looked up. A spray of water fell from the sprinkler system.

The laser had disappeared. Risking a look, Rick peered over the steel counter, ignoring the rush of water splattering on his head and his shoulders. In the opposite quadrant, lab tables burned, orange flames rolling up their legs and over their black tops.

No sign of the shooter.

Without hesitating, Rick turned to Beth and grabbed her wet hand. "Let's go."

She nodded.

They shot to their feet, remaining slightly hunched, and ran down the aisle. Rick glanced behind them as they moved, scanning the floor for signs of the shooter. But aside from shards of glass and shallow pools of water, the floor was clear.

"What was in the bottle you gave me?" he asked.

"Concentrated perchloric acid," she said. "Mix it with sulfuric and it becomes highly explosive."

"You think?" He adjusted his grip on Beth's slippery hand. She acknowledged it with a squeeze. They slowed to a more cautious pace.

Gauging the force of the explosion, Rick knew the assassin had to be hurt, but how badly, he couldn't be sure.

As they rounded the last station and turned back in the direction of the exit, he noticed a small flame rising from the top flier of the stairs. A few steps closer and he could see what was burning—a small, dark cloth, the cloth the assassin had been holding to his face. Clearly he'd fled the lab, hopefully with a good chemical burn.

"He's gone." Rick stopped and turned to Beth. Her eyes were dark in the shadows, as was her hair, which fell in wet tangles just above her shoulders. She drew long, labored breaths, not so much from running, Rick assumed, as from the stress of what had just happened.

And now he had to give her more bad news.

"We'll have to stay here," he said, "until the police and fire department arrive."

"Impossible," she said. "How would I ever explain this to the university? Besides, we're drenched and there's a fire in the second quadrant."

"It's nearly extinguished, and the water won't hurt us."

"But we'll be arrested."

"I doubt it," he said. "You're a professor here, you can explain to the police."

"But I can't explain to the university."

"Beth, you'll have to try," he said. "If we go up those stairs, we could be walking into an ambush. Whoever was shooting at us, there's no guarantee he's gone."

"The police are coming, he'll be gone."

"We can't risk it. Once the cops are here, we'll know for sure."

"Rick." Beth was on the verge of tears.

He pulled her close and squeezed her into his chest. "We're just going to have to explain," he said, ignoring the deluge of water spraying violently around them.

# 20

THE DOME OF blue and white stars that hung over the southwestern desert shone with a fierce brilliance that not even the red, rhythmic flash
of the fire engine lights could disturb. It was nearing 5:00 a.m., and to
the east, a faint glow rested above the dark folds of the Rincon Mountains, grading the horizon in bands of blue and indigo. Rick would have
found the sight beautiful, even awe-inspiring, had it not been spoiled by
the rush of firemen running back and forth between the trucks and the
lab. Two police officers stood uncomfortably close, notepads open and
faces twisted with irritation, having been forced to launch a pre-
breakfast investigation. A university security guard hovered nearby,
glancing here and there, unsure of his role in the questioning, but trying
nonetheless to look busy and official. One of the cops held a flashlight
snug under his arm, the beam angled up at his notepad. He finished
scribbling down Beth's information, then handed back her I.D. badge.
"So," he said, "you always make it a habit to work this late?" It was a
thinly veiled accusation.

Beth's jade eyes narrowed. A fireman had given her a blanket
and she pulled it tight around her shoulders. "It's not a habit, but necessary under the circumstances."

"And what circumstances would those be?"

"I'm working against a deadline," she said. "An important
symposium's coming up, and I have a ton of research to finish before I
present."

"Look, she's already given you her I.D.," Rick said. "And it's obvious she's working on a big project. Isn't the important thing finding the guy who shot at us?"

The officer peered up from his notepad. "If you don't mind, I'd like to establish a few things first, like why you and Dr. Harper are here this early on a Sunday morning. Some would say that's a bit unusual."

"She told you she was working," Rick said irritably. "And I was interested in her research, so I tagged along."

"I see," the officer said, sounding suspicious. "Before the two of you entered the building, did either of you notice anything unusual, a person loitering outside?"

Rick recalled when they had first arrived, the dark, empty campus, and the feeling of desolation. "No, there was no one."

"Any unusual vehicles?"

"No," Beth said. "The campus was deserted."

"Alright," the officer said. "How about a description of the perp: his age, weight, height, skin color, clothing.

"He was tall, real tall," Rick said, "well over six feet. Thin, too. He had short black hair and dark skin. Wore black clothes."

"Any other distinguishing features: tattoos, piercings, scars, anything at all?"

"Not that I noticed," Rick said. "It's hard to get a close look at a guy who's pointing a gun at you, which by the way was an HK .45, fitted with a laser sight."

The officer raised an eyebrow. "You didn't get a close look at the guy, but you know the make of his gun?"

"That's right."

"And you're sure it was an HK .45?"

"Positive."

"How can you be so sure?"

"I'm ex-military," Rick said. "I've seen, heard, and fired enough of them to know."

The officer scribbled more notes, then turned back to Beth. "Why do you think someone would follow you inside and try to kill you?"

Beth shrugged. "I don't know, maybe the plan was to rob us?"

The officer rubbed at a blanket of whiskers covering his jaw. He looked doubtful. "What bothers me is the laser sight," he said. "It's not the hardware of a gang-banger or your typical thief. There may be something more to this."

A short, squat officer with an overloaded utility belt rattled over, nodding to the other cops. "Dr. Harper checks out. She's current staff alright, an associate professor in the Anthropology Department." He hooked a thumb in his belt and adjusted the load. "I left messages with university people telling them what happened, also put in a call to the lab manager, a Mr. Eddie Sorini. The fire's completely extinguished, and the hazmat people say they have things under control. No question, though, a lot of damage was done."

Beth closed her eyes and moaned, color draining from her face.

"How about that missing security guard?" the officer asked. "What's his name?"

"Cal Dempsey," the squat officer read from a notepad. "No sign of him yet. His cart and truck are still here on campus, but another guard tells me Cal's been known to find a place and doze off. We've got people looking."

The officer investigating turned back to Rick and Beth. "We'll put out an APB on a tall, dark-skinned male, in black clothes, possible fire injury, armed with a handgun." He shook his head. "But if I'm being honest here, folks, with a sketchy description, no other witnesses, and no surveillance cameras picking up the guy, I doubt there'll be much in the way of an arrest. Not anytime soon anyway."

Rick nodded that he understood. The fact was the officer was right. The shooter would never be found, at least not by the police. This was no thug looking for a quick score. The guy was a professional and there was a reason he'd come after them in the lab, and Rick was confident he knew what that reason was. The words of Eckerman echoed in the back of his mind: *The Brotherhood, they will come. And I can assure you, they will stop at nothing to retrieve the talisman.* Rick swallowed hard, trying to purge away the thought. The important thing was that he and Beth were safe. They'd escaped from the lab with their lives.

Still, a sick feeling was growing in Rick's stomach, a feeling born of one fact, a fact he couldn't ignore: This relic Beth had become obsessed with appeared to be the obsession of others as well. Others who were willing to kill for it. Perhaps the old man wasn't as big a fool as Rick had originally assumed. He looked at Beth, her dried black hair hanging in tangles over her forehead, her tan cheeks and her pink lips trembled gently. Rick imagined similar concerns were crossing her mind, as well.

"I have no other questions," the officer said. "But if you don't mind, I'd like you to keep yourselves available should I later need to contact you. And in the meantime, call me if you think of anything else, anything you may have forgot to mention." He nodded to Rick, then to Beth, then he turned away to confer with his partner.

Rick rested a hand on Beth's shoulder. After a moment, he took her hand and walked her to the car. By the time they drove out of the university parking lot, the stars had disappeared, replaced by a powder blue sky and ten degrees of Fahrenheit.

They sat in silence as Rick guided the Explorer over empty surface streets. Beth stared unseeing out the passenger window, now and then bringing up a finger to spread away a tear forming in the corner of her eye.

"The university will have questions," she said.

"I understand."

"My credentials may have worked with the police, but they'll do nothing to satisfy Chendekar. The lab was locked and alarmed. He'll want to know how I got inside."

Rick sat quietly. Listening was all he could do. There was nothing he could think of to say, nothing that would change how Beth was feeling.

"I can't begin to imagine the extent of water damage to the lab: electrical and data wiring, computer hardware, all kinds of expensive analysis equipment. Then there's the fire. I think we may have completely gutted station two."

Beth wasn't being fair to herself. Sure, the damage was real, but it was the gunman who'd caused it, not them.

"Then there's the QuanX. My God, did you hear that burst?"

Rick nodded.

"Before the police arrived, when I retrieved the talisman, I took a quick look inside. The glass plates covering the x-ray tube and detector had been shattered, and the primary radiation filter was in pieces. What on Earth could have caused it?"

Rick rolled to a stop at a red light and turned to Beth. "You can't beat yourself up over something you didn't do."

She stared at him, anguished. "I'm finished at the university."

"Beth, don't get ahead of yourself."

"Ahead of myself?" A nervous smile crossed her face. "Heck, it's all behind me, breaking into the lab, destroying the place. It's over and done with. I might as well clear out my office."

"We have more urgent things to consider," Rick said. "I'm afraid Eckerman was right, others are after this talisman, and clearly, they're willing to kill for it."

"I should have seen this coming," Beth said. "Tanner's discovery was broadcast all over the nation. Of course people would come for it, like that old man you met. I just never thought anyone would actually try and kill us. Jerk treasure hunters."

"And as long as we have the treasure," Rick said. "We'll be the hunted."

Beth stared at him, her jade eyes full of concern.

The light turned green and Rick accelerated toward the freeway. "We need to get rid of the talisman, give it to a museum or the police—somebody."

"No way." Beth was shaking her head. "The talisman's the granddaddy of all Near Eastern artifacts. I'm not turning it over to the police or anyone else."

"Beth, people are trying to kill us. We can't just keep it."

"Keeping it's my only option. After what happened in the lab tonight, it'll take a miracle to salvage my career. The talisman's the only bargaining chip I have. I give it away now, I'm finished." She turned back, folded her arms across her chest.

Rick considered Beth's point. Holding on to the stone was a dangerous proposition—no question—but she was right, to keep her job, she'd need something to bargain with. And the talisman seemed to be the only something she had. "Okay," Rick said, "we keep it, but only as long as it takes for this lab incident to resolve itself."

"What do we do until then?"

"I'm not sure, but we can't go back to your apartment, and we can't go back to mine. The shooter knew where to find us tonight. Likely he also knows where we live. We'll have to get a hotel room."

Beth nodded. "Sounds like a reasonable precaution."

"In the meantime, we need to talk to Eckerman, learn more about this Brotherhood."

"Is that really necessary?"

"Absolutely, we have to get a handle on these people. I mean, we can't just ignore what happened and pretend it'll go away. They've come at us once, they'll come at us again."

"Alright," Beth said, "but under no circumstance do we give this man the talisman. It stays with me."

"I understand," Rick said. "I'll call the station and talk to Mason, see if he knows where to find Eckerman."

"If we're going stay at a hotel, I need to pack a bag." Beth jabbed a thumb behind her. "You passed my exit two streets back."

"We can't risk it."

"Not even for a few minutes, just to pack a bag?"

Rick glared at her. "You worry about the relic. I'll worry about our safety."

"But I need dry clothes, and my hair, it's a mess."

Rick didn't answer. He exited the freeway and turned onto the main road. The day was just beginning and a string of green traffic lights ran along the empty boulevard. The air appeared crisp and clean and a pair of finches darted across the sky. Rick imagined how wonderful it would be if he and Beth were together right now, without the talisman, without the events of the past few hours lingering in their minds. He couldn't help but feel they were getting caught up in something bigger than themselves, something dangerous. He looked at Beth and decided not to mention the extent of his concern. "We'll check into a hotel, clean up, and get some rest. Later, I'll run out and buy you some clothes. Then, we find Eckerman and learn what we can about this Brotherhood."

Beth was nodding weakly.

"Agreed?"

"Agreed."

She peered through the windshield, staring into the distant sky. After a long moment she turned to Rick and said, "I can't believe I actually destroyed Eddie's laboratory. He's going to have a conniption fit when he sees it." She began to laugh. "I'm screwed."

## 21

IT WAS EARLY morning and Mason stood in the office of Elliot O'Connor, manager and program director at KSND. Gripping a thick folder, Mason was eager to pitch his brilliant idea. He watched as his boss stacked and paper-clipped a pile of account ledgers, then busied himself with a mess of advertising invoices and payment receipts. Mason edged up close to Elliot's desk, stood tiptoed over him in an attempt to appear intimidating. He'd seen this move in the old westerns. A classic maneuver, it never failed to work for John Wayne. Mason leaned over the desk as far as he could, toes feeling like they were gonna snap, but at five feet two inches, he just didn't seem to make the same impression as the Duke.

"Jesus Christ, Mason. What are you doing?" Elliot said.

"Trying to pitch a segment."

"You're going to pull a hamstring stretching over my desk like that. Have a seat, let's hear your idea."

Mason took a seat, peering up at his boss from across the desk. "Got something big, real big, something I might be able to fluff into a dozen segments."

"Let's hear it."

"Okay," Mason said, "imagine this—"

"Wait a second." Elliot lifted the phone and dialed his secretary. "Hold all phone calls. Except, of course, for the rep from that new equipment manufacturer. That's right, the one based out of Israel. Oh, and Dr. Hasham, it's okay to put him through, as well." Elliot turned back to Mason. "You have my undivided attention."

"Right." Though Mason was responsible for much of the station's success, and though he had the authority to approve his own bits, when it came to controversial editorial pieces, Elliot insisted on hearing the pitch firsthand. High ratings or not, Mason had to consider the station's reputation. "This is what I have—"

"Keep that thought." Elliot searched through the top drawer of his desk until he found a box of tic tacs. He rattled them around a bit, then tapped a couple out. He popped them into his mouth and breathed in deeply. "You were saying?"

"I was saying—"

"Have you been spraying on that Hair-In-A-Can shit again?" Elliot was staring at Mason's head.

"Christ, Elliot, enough with the diversions. I have a big story, and I want to run it by you. It's fantastic, but if you're too busy to hear it, I'll go ahead and air it without your approval."

"Without my approval? What kind of story is it?"

Mason waved the folder. "Did you catch my segment last week with Captain Tanner?"

"The Marine from Afghanistan?"

"From the U.S., he fought in Afghanistan."

"Whatever."

"Did you hear the segment?"

"Missed it."

"Well, then, you missed a good one."

Elliot wrinkled his nose, plucked a hair from his nostril, then looked back at Mason. "What's the connection to your pitch?"

"Let me tell you Tanner's story."

"I know his story."

"You said you didn't hear the segment."

Elliot swiped a picture frame from his desktop and angled up the glass to use as a sort of a mirror. He cocked back his head and inspected his nose.

Mason said, "Why do I get the feeling you're not giving me your full attention?"

Elliot looked past the frame. "What's that?"

"I asked how you knew Tanner's story, seeing as you didn't hear the segment."

"Andrea gave me the highlights. Wasn't it part of the broadcast where Rick dished you a helping of crow? It's the talk around the station."

"Whatever," Mason said. The nickel and dime banter was beginning to piss him off. He decided to take control of the conversation, pitch Elliot his piece and insist on approval to run with it in the morning. "Here it is in a nutshell—"

"I'm considering having the bridge of my nose shaved down, just a tad. What do you think? In consultation, Dr. Hasham told me an incision here, and one here, and I'd have a perfect Tom Cruise nose."

Mason felt himself go hot in the ears. "You've got to be frickin kidding me, Elliot. I'm here to pitch a monster of a segment, and you're worried about plastic surgery?"

Elliot straightened up in his chair. "It's just an idea I've been tossing around."

"Well, toss it out the goddamn window and leave it there until we're done. You're pushing sixty and your face is as shriveled as a frozen pecker. Nothing you can do to your nose is gonna improve that. Deal with it and move on."

Through Elliot's thin silver hair, Mason could see his scalp reddening. The Irishman looked as if he wanted to scream. But to his credit, he simply took a deep breath. "Alright, Valentino, what do you have?"

Mason ignored the Valentino comment. "I believe Captain Tanner and his team were unwitting participants in a Defense Department experiment. And I want Americans to know about it."

Elliot raised an eyebrow.

"Tanner's men were killed as a result of U.S. negligence, and now the Defense Department has been going to great lengths to cover up their mess. It stinks to high heaven and I want to be the one to expose it."

Elliot scratched his head. "Wait a second. I've heard enough of your broadcasts to know you don't like questioning U.S. motivations. Your position on the Patriot Act, the invasion of Afghanistan, it's all red, white and blue."

"Christ, Elliot. I'm a radio talk show host. My opinions reflect my majority audience. And my gut tells me most Americans are going to be appalled when they hear that the government's been sacrificing the welfare of our troops to conduct secret experiments. My listeners will love me for bringing the story out of the shadows. There's nothing more patriotic than looking out for our own men and women in uniform."

"Gotcha," Elliot said.

"Plus," Mason quickly added, "a story like this will give the Lefties more reason to hate the U.S., and I think I can pull in listeners from competing stations, increase our market share. As far as I'm concerned, it's a win-win proposition."

"Yes, it could be," Elliot said, training his sight hard on Mason. "Assuming, that is, you have proof of a cover-up. Can you defend your assertions?"

"Of course."

"Let's hear it," Elliot said. "Because you know damn good and well I won't allow you to level charges like this over the airwaves without solid evidence. I'll remind you the government runs the FCC, and if you're going to trash them without evidence, there'll be a strong backlash."

"It's all right here." Mason lifted the folder.

"What is it?"

"An investigation report. A source I have inside the military dug up details on Tanner's operation."

"Alright, let's hear it."

"According to this," Mason waved the folder, "Captain Tanner was part of a Marine Expeditionary Unit that got whacked neutralizing al Qaeda cells in Afghanistan. The circumstances surrounding the incident are suspicious, to say the least. Tanner, who was the only surviving member of the MEU, couldn't remember much about the night his team was slaughtered in that cave, just a few shrieks and the death throes of his men. Later, while he was recovering in a military hospital in Germany, a couple suits came in and questioned him about the operation. When Tanner asked them for details about how his men were killed, these Bozos refused to tell him."

Elliot was listening intently, bobbing his head and staring absently at his office wall.

"Now get a load of this," Mason continued. "A few days after our radio broadcast, Tanner turned up dead in his home, his face swollen like a grilled tomato."

"Swollen?"

"Yeah, you know, like he'd been chewed up by a rattler or something."

"You're kidding me," Elliot said. "I had no idea."

"And I bet you have no idea what I found in this report, either. In fact, no one does, outside of a few folks at DARPA with top-secret military clearance."

From across the desk, Elliot eyed the folder. "This is all quite intriguing, but what makes you think Tanner and his team were dupes in a government experiment?"

"It's all right here, an investigative report with findings by the MRMC. It details Operation Cold Strike."

"Cold Strike?"

"The codename given to Tanner's mission."

"What does it say?"

Mason tossed the file on the desk in front of Elliot. "See for yourself."

Elliot lifted the file, flipped through its pages.

"Scan down past the military gobbledygook bullshit to the Summary of Findings."

Elliot slid his fingertips to the bottom of the page, turned it, scanned down further, then stopped to read.

Mason said, "The bodies of Tanner's men were later recovered and the cave where they were killed was scoured clean."

"I see," Elliot said.

"Look at the Forensic Toxicology Summary. All the men suffered an acute failure of the central nervous system, the result of extreme dosages of what the report calls batrachotoxin, a neurotoxic steroidal alkaloid. It induced a severe pharmacological reaction. It says there the source of the neurotoxin is as of yet *undetermined*."

Elliot's eyes raced back and forth over the paper, and Mason could tell from the intensity of his expression that he was hooked, just like his listeners would soon be.

Mason added, "The report also says both physical and chemical spot tests were performed as a screening protocol, with confirmation of the results produced by Mass Spectrometry analysis. You see, Elliot, there's no doubt, the men were wiped out by some kind of a venomous creature."

"This is good," Elliot said. Then he stared up with a puzzled look. "But why go with a cover-up angle. There's no indication the government was conducting an experiment. In fact, they're investigating it themselves."

"The MRMC is investigating it. They're not involved in the cover-up."

"Then where's your proof?"

Mason began to feel a swell of irritation. He hated having to explain himself, especially to people half as smart as he was. "For crying out loud, Elliot, put two and two together."

"The report says nothing about a cover-up."

"Of course not," Mason said. "The MRMC is not an oversight committee. They're just trying to figure out what happened, why Cold Strike failed, the cause of death."

"Then what makes you think this has been whitewashed?"

"It says right there the bodies were removed from the cave and the site was swept for evidence."

"Yeah, so?"

"Christ, Elliot, you need to me to sing it in a song for you? Look right there, it says the cave was clean, nothing found. If they'd turned up a nest of scorpions or a den of snakes, wouldn't you expect to find mention of it in the report? These men were slaughtered by venomous creatures, yet no venomous creatures were found... at least not the kind you'd think."

"What do you mean?"

"There's a reference to insects alright, well, kinda. It'll blow your mind. Take a look at the bottom of the report, to where it was forwarded. And read why. That's the connection. That's the cover-up."

Elliot turned to the last page and scanned to the bottom. His eyes bulged.

"That's right," Mason said. "Now you got it."

"Is this for real?"

"Oh yeah, baby, as real as the pimples on your ass."

"Un-fucking-believable," Elliot said, then he read aloud, "MRMC requests immediate response from DARPA's Defense Sciences Office (DSO), Division of War Technologies, Hybrid Biosystems Unit: Project Sunflower (Cyborg Bee and Scorpion Armament Testing)—Wow, cyborg bees and scorpions?"

"Yeah, can you believe it?"

Elliot continued to read. "MRMC requests classified access to Project Sunflower to reconcile and close out investigation into the failure of Operation Cold Strike. Please respond through proper TS channels."

Elliot closed the folder. Mason could see beads of sweat forming under his flop of thin silver hair. The effect of the report was staggering, and Mason knew he'd just dropped a bombshell. He'd taken what appeared to be nothing more than the failure of a routine military operation, and he'd exposed it for what it really was—a dangerous biotech experiment gone bad.

Mason said, "And the matter of Tanner being found dead, I think it's the boys at DARPA doing some housecleaning. I'll bet someone was sent to finish him off, probably using the same toxins that killed his team in Afghanistan. You know, to make it look like he brought back a disease or something."

"Why would they do that?"

"To silence him," Mason said. "Tanner was becoming a big mouth, making radio show appearances, bringing too much attention to Cold Strike."

"So they eliminated him?"

"Yeah, Rick's ex-girlfriend found the body."

There was a drawn silence, then Elliot blinked and peered down at his desk. "This is legit, right? I mean, you're not bullshitting me just to run the story?"

"Nope, this is legit," Mason said. "Have a buddy in the military who's got connections, but I can say no more."

"Okay, I'll take your word for it," Elliot said, his voice suddenly intense. "But if this turns out to be a fairy tale, and you end up bringing down heat from the FCC on this station, I'll have your balls in a jar."

# 22

RICK STOOD OUTSIDE the hotel room door, his back to the hot sun and a sack from the Goodwill hanging in his hand. He knocked on the door and waited. A car with a broken muffler roared past on the street behind him. It was late Sunday morning and the traffic was light, the streets deserted of people. The Desert Rock Inn was a decent enough hotel, out of the way, with towering palms that offered plenty of shade, a newly stuccoed exterior, and rooms with enough amenities to make staying comfortable. Rick could see himself here a few days. And with Beth to keep him company, it might actually turn out to be pleasant.

He knocked again.

The door opened the length of a gold security chain, and a pair of startling green eyes peered out from within. Then the door closed, and Rick could hear the rattle of the chain sliding off its track. A second later, Beth swung open the door, smothering herself in the light of day. A white terrycloth towel wound snuggly around her body from chest to mid-thigh. A pink toothbrush protruded from the corner of her mouth, and a lather of thick white paste spilled over the bottom of her lip.

Rick stepped inside, shut and locked the door. The AC rumbled on high, filling the room with icy air. He stood a moment, savoring the chill temperature, whispering a thank you to the technology gods.

Dropping the sack on the bed, Rick said, "Only place open was a thrift store. They didn't have much, some shorts and a T-shirt. I think I got the size right."

"Thank you," she mumbled with a mouthful of toothpaste.

"Call the university yet?" Rick asked.

Beth shook her head no and hurried to the sink, catching a drip of toothpaste in her hand. She finished brushing, rinsed her mouth. "I've been finding excuses not to call."

Rick picked up her cell phone from the nightstand and handed it to her. "You're gonna have to suck it up and get it over with."

"But it's Sunday, offices are closed."

"After what happened last night," Rick said. "You can bet someone will be there."

After a slight hesitation, Beth took the cell, flipped it open and dialed. A sharp look and Rick understood she wanted privacy. Reluctantly, he stepped back outside into the heat. Flipping open his own cell, he dialed the station. With a little luck, Mason would be in his office working on material for next week's broadcast. Maybe he'd know where to find Eckerman.

Elliot's secretary answered. Her voice crackled from the poor reception.

"This is Rick. Did Mason make it in this morning?"

"Yes, unfortunately."

"Could you connect me, please?"

"Alright, but talk to him at your own risk. He's irritable today, I mean, more so than usual."

"I'll chance it."

Rick listened to a few minutes of station music, then heard the click of a receiver being lifted. "Mason here. It had better be fast, and it had better be good."

"This is Rick."

There was a pause. "Oh, hell, sorry, Rick. Didn't know it was you. How's it hanging?"

Ignoring Mason's half-assed apology, Rick said, "Do you have any idea how to get in touch with Eckerman? Did he mention where he was staying?"

"At a hotel here in Phoenix. But he's not there anymore."

"You sure?"

"Positive."

Rick paced the concrete walk in front of the hotel room. "Did he mention when he was flying back to Europe?"

"No, but if you want, I could ask him for a copy of his itinerary."

Rick stopped pacing and cupped the cell phone closer to his ear. "Did I hear you right? Did you say you could ask him?"

"Yep, he's here at the station. In the guest lounge, I think."

"What's he doing there?"

"Getting me a box of Ding Dongs from the fridge."

"No, I mean, why is he still at the station?"

"We're scripting a few of his stories for the broadcast. I've come up with a great new angle for working the talisman into the Cold Strike segment."

"You said Eckerman checked out of his hotel, where's he staying?"

"At my place, in the guest house."

"You're kidding me."

"No, why?" Mason said. "You jealous?"

Rick wiped his sweat from the receiver, switched ears. "Something's come up, and Eckerman has information I need."

"I wouldn't doubt it," Mason said. "The guy's like a sage. You should hear some of his alternative histories and esoteric stories. Pretty amazing stuff, really. And he's been telling me more about the Brotherhood. These are bad folks, Rick, and from what I gather, they're hell-bent on getting back that talisman. You know, I think Beth needs to seriously consider getting rid of the thing."

"That's why I'm looking for Eckerman. I need to get more information on the Brotherhood."

"I can tell you all you need to know. They're nuts. I mean, seriously, you have to figure an organization willing to chase a rock over the span of two thousand years has to be made up of people a little off in the head." Mason paused. "I'm serious, Rick. Beth shouldn't be screwing around with these people."

Strangely, hearing Mason echoing his own worries made the danger seem all the more imminent. Rick wondered just how much the old man had told him. "Sounds like Eckerman opened up the dossier on these people."

"Let's just say if Beth doesn't get rid of the talisman, she might consider hiring a bum or somebody to start her car for her in the mornings."

Rick could feel hot beads of sweat running down his temples. He was still shaken from the incident at the lab and being reminded of these people's ruthlessness wasn't helping to make him feel any better. But clearly Eckerman had confided in Mason, and Rick hoped to exploit that relationship, learn anything he could. He needed information if he wanted to stay a step ahead of these people. "What specifically did the old man tell you?"

"Look, Rick," Mason said. "I'm working on next week's material. I don't have time to get into details. Suffice to say, these are bad men and Eckerman warned you."

"You don't need to remind me," Rick said. "I'm well aware of what he told me. Listen, I need for you to do something for me."

"Whoa, hold on a second there, buddy, I don't swing that way."

"Cut the crap, Mason. This is important. I need you to stay at the station, and be sure to keep Eckerman with you. I'm on my way over."

"Sounds serious."

"It is," Rick said. "I'll fill you in on the details when I get there. Just make sure Eckerman doesn't leave, and don't tell him I'm coming either—that's critical. Got it?"

There was a pause, then Mason spoke again, this time with greater smugness. "Alright, I'll keep him here, but I'm considering this a favor, which means you owe me one."

"If Eckerman gives me anything useful," Rick said, "I'll owe you two." He slapped shut the cell phone and wiped the sweat from his brow. Fortunately, Eckerman was still around. But of course it made sense that he would be. If Beth's gut feeling was right, and the old man was an antiquities collector, he stood to make millions if he got his hands on the talisman.

The hotel room door eased open and Beth emerged dressed in sandy shorts and a white T-shirt. The look on her face was grave. She squinted against the sun, then tented a hand over her eyes. "I just talked to Doris. She tells me there's been a lot of buzz about last night's fire, and Chendekar's been in a closed-door meeting all morning."

Rick could see Beth's hand trembling.

"They're going to want to see me today," She said. "I'll probably be asked to clear out my office."

Rick took a deep breath, fighting back the guilt welling up inside him. He was responsible for Beth's predicament. He never should have involved her. He stepped forward, throwing Beth into shadow. Reaching out, he weaved his fingertips through her silky hair, tucking stray tangles behind her ears. He wanted to kiss her, to let her know that no matter what came of this, he cared and he still loved her. But he knew it was an awful time to throw their relationship troubles into the mix. She was worried and vulnerable and—

Beth pulled herself close to him and pressed her lips to his. For a brief moment, they stood locked together in a tight embrace, the heat of their bodies humbling the sun's swelter. Her lips were as sweet as juice, and, like a drug, their taste numbed his mind, reducing his feelings to a single primeval urge. He wanted desperately to carry her into the room, to know her again. Rick fought the desire.

When they parted, Beth stared into his eyes, a fierce look of determination suddenly taking form. "I'm going to fight for my career," she said. "If I'm guilty of anything, it's of doing my job. I won't allow the university to fire me for that. I'll explain to Chendekar everything. I still have the talisman and that gives me an edge." She breathed deeply, her jade eyes locked onto Rick's. "You give me strength," she said. "Did you know that?"

Still reeling from the passionate kiss, Rick was unable to reply.

She kissed him again, a peck this time.

Questions about their relationship rose up like a sandstorm in his mind, and he wasn't quite sure what to think, how to react. Was her affection the sign of a new start, or was it simply an emotional reaction to the stress she'd endured over the last few days? He stepped back, unsure. There were a lot of questions he needed to ask her.

Beth changed the subject. "Did you get in touch with Mason to find out if Eckerman's still around?"

For a moment, Rick didn't answer, his mind in another place. "Eckerman, oh yeah…." The reality of their troubles struck him again, and Rick forced himself to stow away questions about their relationship and to focus on the immediate problem. "Not only is Eckerman still around, he's staying at Mason's place."

"You're kidding me."

"It's true. I just talked to Mason, which reminds me, we'd better get moving. He promised to hold Eckerman at the station for us."

With her lip curled in a pout, it was clear Beth didn't relish the idea of meeting the old man. Rick knew what she thought of him, of his kind, of antiquities collectors and dealers who were out to make a buck at the expense of history and culture. But to get Eckerman talking, Beth would have to be respectful and diplomatic, nice even. Rick said to her, "Information is critical if we're going to weather this storm. What I mean is we can't risk angering the old man. I know what you think of his type, but be nice anyway."

Beth frowned. "Okay, but if he tries—"

"I'm serious," Rick said. "Don't anger him. What we learn about the Brotherhood could mean the difference between life and death."

## 23

IT WAS AN hour and a half later when Rick and Beth stepped from the elevator onto the third floor of the station building. A crew of three cleaning ladies worked the long hall running to Mason's office. One was feather-dusting the wall's promotional photos, the other two fussing in Spanish over a broken carpet cleaning machine. Rick and Beth hurried to the end of the hall, where Mason's door stood slightly ajar. Rick could hear the little shock jock inside, jabbering with Eckerman. The old man's thick German accent rang out with enthusiasm.

"Yes, yes, but you see, he was the last ruler of a once great empire, and in the eyes of an ancient king, it was better to burn a city than to have it fall into the hands of one's enemies."

"Hogwash," Mason said. "Sounds like a crock of shit to me."

Rick pushed open the door.

Mason sat behind his desk, perched high on a cushioned chair. Looming over him like a bear was a big muscular fellow Rick had never seen before, hair leveled short at the top and thin at the sides, a military cut if ever there was one. Eckerman sat in a chair positioned well away from the desk, his hands folded neatly on his lap. As Rick and Beth entered, all three men looked up in surprise.

The big guy shuffled some papers into a red folder, which Rick could see was labeled *Controlled Hybrid Biological Systems (CHiBS)*.

Mason caught him by the forearm. "Relax, it's just Rick, my

station engineer, and his woman, Beth. They're okay."

The big man released a stack of papers from his grasp and shot up erect. He smiled to Beth, then stared at Rick with bright, serious eyes. "I'm Jarred, a friend of Mason's."

Rick extended a hand, which Jarred promptly received and shook. He had a fierce grip and was clearly no stranger to the gym. Not wanting to waste time, Rick said to Mason, "Mind if Beth and I have a word with you and Mr. Eckerman?"

Jarred scooped up the folder. "I'll work on this in the lounge," he said to Mason under his breath. He hurried out, shutting the door behind him.

"Ah, Dr. Harper," Eckerman said, leaping to his feet, "I've been most eager to make your acquaintance. And you've come at a splendid time. I was just telling Mr. Manning here about the pitiful end to the once grand Hittite Empire."

"What you were saying was bullshit." Mason turned and eyed Beth. "Wow, honey, it's good to see you again, you're looking fine, I mean really fine, better than ever." He winked.

"Easy there, Mason," Rick said.

Eckerman clasped his hands and smiled. "Perhaps you could dispel Mr. Manning's doubt."

Mason said, "There's no way the king burned down his own city. I mean, seriously, was he crazy?"

"Not crazy," Beth said. "Rulers of the ancient world had a different mindset. What Mr. Eckerman tells you is true. The last king of the Hittite Empire organized a systematic evacuation of Hattusas, taking what things of value he could. He then set fire to the Acropolis, the royal buildings, and the temples."

Eckerman beamed. His white bushy hair quivered as he nodded approvingly. "Yes, the Scorched Earth Policy."

Mason's eyes showed interest. He opened a Pepsi. "Scorched Earth Policy? What's that?"

"A last resort," Beth said. "A contingency practiced by the ancients. The idea was to destroy one's own resources, so as to leave nothing of use to conquering armies."

"No shit? They destroyed their own cities?"

"Yes," Beth said. "In 478 B.C., in the face of an invading Persian force, the Athenians did just that. They burned their own crops and fouled their own cisterns. They considered it a better alternative than allowing Xerxes and his army to capture the city."

Mason slurped from his Pepsi, his eyes transfixed.

"The practice continued through the Middle Ages," Beth said. "For example, in 1167, when Cairo faced invasion by Frankish Crusaders, the Muslim ruler of the city commanded its destruction. Tens of thousands of naphtha and petroleum pots were used to ignite the buildings, engulfing the city in fire. It burned for fifty-four days."

Mason stared loose-jawed. His idiot expression was more than Rick could handle. They'd come for information about the Brotherhood. The small talk was over. "Mr. Eckerman," Rick said, "we need your help."

"My help?" he said. "You'll pardon me for asking, but why the change of heart?"

"We ran into a snag."

Everyone took a seat around Mason's desk.

"Last night we were at the university. Beth was analyzing the talisman, sourcing and dating the obsidian."

"How's that a problem?" Mason said.

"A man with a gun came inside and tried to kill us." Rick let his words hang in the air. He studied Eckerman's face, looking for the slightest tell, anything that might betray his involvement in the attack—an evasive glance, a nervous twitch, anything. But aside from the eternal sheen of sweat glistening from the old man's skin, his face was like stone. Rick couldn't imagine he was involved.

"I regret your misfortune," Eckerman said. "I take it you and Dr. Harper suffered no injuries?"

"Nothing serious."

"And the talisman, it is safe?"

"It's safe," Beth said, folding her arms across her chest.

Eckerman let out a sigh of relief.

Rick said, "It's important we learn as much as possible about the man who tried to kill us."

"You don't believe this was a random attack?"

"Not for a second," Rick said. "Do you?"

Eckerman removed a handkerchief from his satchel, dabbed it against his forehead. "Regrettably, no. Likely it was a cowardly attempt by the Brotherhood to retrieve the talisman."

Mason trained his eyes on Beth. "You're in over your head, babe. Time to give up the rock."

Beth's face flushed. "Don't call me babe, jerk."

Trying to avert an argument, Rick said, "This isn't about an artifact. It's about our lives. Someone tried to kill us last night, and I'd be a fool to think it has nothing to do with the talisman."

"Undoubtedly," Eckerman said.

"Tell me about this Brotherhood?" Rick said.

"There's a simpler way to resolve the matter," Eckerman said. "Relinquish to me the artifact, and I'll return to Europe. I can assure you, it will be safe in my charge."

Beth jumped from her chair. "Over my dead body!"

"Oh, I like it. Sexy *and* sassy," Mason said, grinning like a clown.

"Listen you little twerp—"

Rick stood and rested a hand on her shoulders. "Beth—"

She pulled away, admonishing him with furious eyes. "Whose side are you on?"

Mason leaned back in his chair, the grin still affixed to his face. "I think someone's undies are in a bunch."

Rick turned on him. "You're not making this easy."

Eckerman raised a finger. "If you'll just give me the talisman—"

"You'll get nothing from me." Beth fired back.

"Oh, and the claws come out." Relishing the moment, Mason rubbed his tiny hands.

The three continued to argue, their voices rising like the winds of a gathering storm.

Until Rick had had enough.

He slammed a fist to the desk, sending papers and pens flying in crazy directions. A polished picture frame flaunting Mason's promotional head-shot rattled to the edge and tipped over, crashing to the floor. The suddenness of it all ended the arguing, and Rick shot to his feet, glared at everyone in turn. All three had lost a little color in their faces. "Enough of this!" He peered at Eckerman. "The talisman will stay with us." He looked at Beth. "You'll quit arguing." Then he turned to Mason. "And you'll stop antagonizing my girl or I'll stuff you into one of those Pepsi cans."

No one said a word.

Rick turned back to Eckerman. "It's urgent I learn as much as possible about the Brotherhood. If you're as concerned about people's welfare as you claim to be, you can start with ours."

The old man stared at him, blue eyes wide open.

"Will you help us?"

"Certainly, certainly." Eckerman said. "Again, you must understand, giving me the talisman would be the easiest and surest way to eliminate your problem. However, since Dr. Harper is unwilling to do the right thing, I shall be the gracious one and assist you in any way I can."

Rick glanced at Beth, who was leaning forward and drumming a finger against her knee. He could see she was stewing inside, itching to respond to the old man's comment. She started to speak, but Rick gave her a stern look. She folded her arms and turned away.

The office intercom light blinked green, followed by a washed out voice. "Line two is for you, Mr. Manning."

"Tell whoever it is to get lost," Mason blurted out.

Rick scratched at the stubble sprouting from his chin, then said to Eckerman, "If you don't mind, I'd like you to tell me what you know."

Nodding, Eckerman twisted open an Evian bottle and poured water into a chipped cup. It slopped over the sides onto the desk. He lifted the cup and sipped down the level. "Yes, well, where to start."

"The beginning's a good place."

The old man mopped up the spill with his handkerchief then stared up into the shadows of the ceiling, searching his thoughts.

Rick sat patiently, giving him time.

"The danger you face is grave, certainly, and it comes in the form of a fraternal organization known as the Brotherhood. They're an ancient order dating back to the end of the Achaemenid dynasty, over twenty-three hundred years."

"Unbelievable," Beth said.

"Hey," Mason said. "If she gets to complain—"

"Stop it, the both of you," Rick said. He turned back to Eckerman. "Ignore them, please."

"Yes, well, I was saying that the founding of the Brotherhood harks back to days ancient, sometime after Alexander drove a stake through the heart of the Persian Empire. They are a Mithraic order whose goal is, and has always been, to recover the Talisman of Persepolis. They seek to fulfill the ancient Achaemenid kings' vision of a world governed by Mithra's Chosen, in this case—themselves."

"Funny," Beth said with a sardonic smile, "in all my years researching ancient Persia, I've never heard of the Brotherhood."

"And what would you expect, Dr. Harper, that kings would erect monuments to honor them? Oh no, the Brotherhood is a clandestine organization. For more than two thousand years they have operated in the shadows of history."

"I see, how very convenient," Beth said. "But there's another huge flaw in this little tale of yours. You claim the Achaemenids were worshippers of Mithra."

"Indeed."

"Nothing could be further from the truth. Granted, early in the empire Mithraism had a powerful following, but so too did many other mystery religions. With the coming of the prophet, Zoroaster, polytheism fell into decline, eventually succumbing to new beliefs. The Achaemenid kings were clearly Zoroastrians, a fact supported by all of the written and iconic evidence. They did not worship Mithra."

Eckerman's flush cheeks rose high with a smile. He wagged his finger. "How very quaint, Dr. Harper. Again, history is replete with lies and—"

"Never mind all of this," Rick interrupted. "The bottom line is the Brotherhood wants the talisman, right? You say it's their sacred stone."

"Precisely," Eckerman said. "According to prophecy, they will one day reclaim it and rise as Mithra's Chosen."

"Rick, this is all nonsense," Beth said. "We're wasting our time. I know the history, and I can assure you, the Brotherhood, this prophecy, it's all nonsense."

"After your experience last night, Dr. Harper, I would say the facts are quite settled on the Brotherhood. And as for the prophecy, the *Telesma* is clear: Once the stone is recovered, the Hidden Chambers will be revealed, the world's landscape forever changed."

Beth laughed. "Oh, now you're throwing legend into the mix."

Mason turned and eyeballed Eckerman. "Hey, Peter, you never mentioned anything about hidden chambers."

"Another legend," Beth said, "a warren of hidden rooms and passages lost beneath the ruins of Persepolis. According to the ancient historian, Plutarch, they contain the riches of the empire."

"Are they for real?" Mason asked.

"Of course not," Beth said. "The chambers are just part of a legend. It would seem Mr. Eckerman has thrown into his narrative everything but the kitchen sink. This has become so far-fetched I can no longer bear it."

Rick didn't buy it either, but he feared if Beth kept arguing with the old man, he might become angry and shut down, refuse to give them what they needed. "Look, believing all this ain't easy for me. But I believe you believe it, Mr. Eckerman, and I believe the Brotherhood believes it, too. That, along with getting shot at last night, is good enough to convince me something must be done."

"No doubt," Eckerman said.

"So what exactly can you tell me about the Brotherhood?"

"What do you mean?" Eckerman said. "I've told you—"

"I mean, other than its history. I need names, locations, resources."

The old man appeared confused. "I can offer you nothing like that."

"Nothing?"

"My dear boy, what were you expecting? A telephone number and the address to their headquarters in London? As I've said, they're a highly secretive organization."

Rick shrugged. "I was hoping for more than just a story."

"Mr. Lowell, there's plenty I could tell you regarding their origin, their hierarchical structure, or their religious beliefs, but concerning specific membership and where to find them, well, of those things I am woefully ignorant."

Rick stared at Eckerman, unsure how to respond. This was terrible news. He squeezed his fists, and closed his mouth for fear the next thing out of it might be a scream. Damn it, he needed to know who these people were, who had taken a shot at them last night. He didn't want to sit around and wait for a second attempt.

Abruptly, Beth's cell phone rang.

She pulled it from the pocket of her wrinkled shorts, flipped it open. "Hello."

Rick could hear a concerned woman rambling on the other end. After a few seconds, Beth broke in, a slight tremble in her voice. "I understand, okay, Doris, thank you. One hour. No, no, of course not, I won't be late."

"What is it?" Rick asked.

Beth snapped shut the cell phone, looked at him with worried eyes. "It looks like the lab fire just caught up with me. Chendekar, the Dean of the College of Humanities, just concluded an emergency meeting with the school's Board of Trustees. He's demanding to see me immediately." Beth paused. "And he told Doris there's going to be hell to pay."

## 24

BETH STOOD OUTSIDE the office of Dr. Denesh T. Chendekar, Dean of the College of Humanities at the University of Arizona. She shifted from one foot to the other, trying to ignore the dull ache that had begun pulsing through her back with annoying regularity. Her head throbbed and her joints protested the slightest movements. But the discomfort was no surprise. The stress of last night's attack, the lab fire, the career-ending meeting she was about to face, it was all hitting her hard, manifesting itself physically here on the 4th floor of the Emil W. Haury building. She took a deep breath and tried to focus her thoughts. Emphasize to Chendekar the talisman and the prestige it will bring to the university. Defend your actions, she reminded herself. Don't apologize for them.

A clicking noise, almost inaudible, sounded from somewhere behind her. She turned and glanced up one end of the hall, then turned and glanced down the other. "Doris, is that you?"

There was no answer.

It was Sunday afternoon, and except for Dr. Chendekar and Doris Heckel, who'd both been forced to come in on their day off, there was no one around—which was just as well. The last thing Beth needed was to have to play Twenty Questions about last night's incident with colleagues and department staff.

She turned back to Chendekar's office, straightened her posture, and tucked a stubborn tangle of hair behind her ear. Lifting a clenched fist to knock, she noticed her reflection in the door's polished placard. Oh, fantastic, her hair was a mess. She looked down and cringed at the sight of her clothes: wrinkled shorts, a T-shirt, and tennies. She was about to walk into the office of the most powerful man in her department, the man who in a few short moments would decide the fate of her career. And how did she look? Like she'd just crawled out of an excavation pit.

Beth teased her hair to give it body, brushed a few wrinkles from her shorts, then glanced back at the placard. The image hadn't improved much. She was still a mess. Oh well, there was no turning back. She took a deep breath, and with as much dignity as she could muster, knocked on the door.

Moments later she was seated inside, looking around the dean's office for anything new she might point out to compliment. Dr. Chendekar was a linguist, Oxford trained, and over the years he'd accumulated an impressive collection of documents from around the world—brightly colored illuminated manuscripts from England and France; papyrus scrolls of Egyptian hieroglyphs, many dating back as far as the 12th Dynasty; and fragments of tropical wood and bone, inscribed in the languages of pre-Columbian civilizations—all authentic and lovingly wall-displayed in glass cases, under the gentle glow of accent lighting. Beth's eyes turned like a magnet to her favorite piece, a hand-sized cuneiform tablet written in the language of the ancient Sumerians. With its yellow patina and crumbled corners, the clay tablets recounted the flood myth, complete with the Sumerian version of an antediluvian Noah. It predated the biblical account by over a millennium and was an incredible piece. But by far the most imposing object in the room was the scale replica of the Rosetta stone, a linguist's dream. Cast in resin and inscribed in the three scripts of the original, it was mounted conspicuously on the wall behind Chendekar's sprawling mahogany desk.

Beth turned her sight from the Rosetta stone and eyed Dr. Chendekar, a short, stocky man of Indian descent. Normally attired in the posh fabrics of Giorgio Armani, he'd settled this afternoon for navy-blue slacks and a sheer, white cotton dress shirt, sleeves rolled to the elbows. He stared at the floor, hands tented at his dark lips, meandering long circles around his desk. He stopped every now and then, when an idea seemed to flower, only to shake his head and continue the mysterious stroll. Chendekar's delay was making Beth sick. She considered interrupting his reverie to remind him of the meeting, but the break in his thoughts would probably only anger the man, who was already known to have a short fuse.

At length he returned to his desk, eased himself into a high-back leather chair, and with a heavy hand slapped a stack of crisp papers lying neatly in front of him.

"Have you any idea, Dr. Harper, what these papers are?"

Beth tried to discern the print. "I'm afraid I don't."

Chendekar's eyes took in her appearance, scrutinizing the casual clothing. "I see we're comfortable this afternoon?"

"It's a long story."

"One would think a person in your precarious position would make every effort to maintain a scholarly air, Dr. Harper. Your nonchalance disturbs me. If this is some kind of mockery, I don't find it particularly amusing."

"Believe me, mocking you was the last thing I intended to do."

"Then perhaps your plan was simply to complicate my life?" He drummed a perfectly manicured index finger on the mysterious stack of papers.

Beth could only imagine what they were, likely her walking papers, some kind of legal document she'd have to sign before clearing out her office and descending into academic obscurity. She tossed back a tangle of hair, leaned forward the best she could with her stiff back. "I know things look bad, Dr. Chendekar. But there's a perfectly good explanation for what happened last night."

"Yes, indeed, there ought to be." He lifted the papers and waved them in her face. "A police report, Dr. Harper. This is a police report." His face flushed, intensifying the shadow of whiskers covering his jaw.

"I can explain."

"You had better," Chendekar said, "and it had best be the mother of all explanations."

Beth clasped the edge of the desk and pulled herself close. "I've made an incredible discovery."

"A discovery? Splendid. And what exactly would that be? How to circumvent the laboratory submission policy, perhaps? Or maybe you've discovered how to disable the alarm system and conduct unauthorized research."

"But I—"

"Or perhaps you've discovered how to disregard safety procedures and utterly destroy two costly research stations in one of the most prestigious—and expensive—scientific laboratories in the United States."

Beth felt her throat go dry, tried to speak, heard herself choking for words.

"The lab manager, Mr. Edward Sorini, estimates damages to be well into the six figures."

"But the damages aren't my fault!" Beth straightened herself, surprised at how forcefully the words came out. She pointed at the police report. "Doesn't that say anything about the attack? We were almost killed."

"A very good point," Chendekar said. "In addition to all the other offenses, by virtue of your misdeeds, you gave a thief access to the laboratory and an opportunity to steal costly equipment."

"But that's not the way it happened."

"Oh, and the university had high expectations for you, Dr. Harper."

"The man who tried to kill us was no thief."

Chendekar ignored her objection and raised a sheet of paper. "This is an itemized list of the equipment destroyed or otherwise damaged. The good news is, since you're an authorized university employee, our insurance will cover your little adventure. The bad news is someone must still be held accountable."

"Someone?"

"You, Dr. Harper. You must still be held accountable, you must suffer the consequences." Chendekar's stare was intense. "I've already met with members of the Board of Trustees and university attorneys."

Beth lifted her hand, which had become numb, and tucked a tangle of hair behind her ear. All at once, the office lights seemed to dim around her. She felt ill. And she knew what was coming next.

"We expect your resignation," Chendekar said. "Effective immediately. We thought this best for everyone concerned. The university has no need for a rogue professor, nor does it want any unwelcome publicity."

Beth's thoughts became lost in a fog. "But I was on track for tenure."

"You can forget the tenure track, Dr. Harper. Consider yourself derailed."

"No, you mustn't do this, you see, I can explain."

"There is some good news, however."

Beth stared at the man, wondering what on earth it could be.

"In exchange for your resignation, the university will not pursue legal action."

Oh, terrific, if she tendered her resignation, she wouldn't end up sitting in the slammer. Great news. Tears welled up in her eyes. She forced them back, trying to think. Events of the past week suddenly became a blur, no longer important. She was losing her job, no, not her job, her career, her life. Everything she had worked so hard to build was collapsing around her. She swallowed, covered her face with trembling hands. She wanted Rick near her. She wanted his arms around her shoulders, his even voice telling her everything would be okay. She sat for a long moment, the reality settling in.

Chendekar said something, but Beth wasn't listening.

Then suddenly, as if a switch had been thrown, her thoughts became clear. She pulled her hands from her face, teeth clenched like a vice. *Unbelievable*. She had nearly accepted the dean's verdict. How could she have almost given up? There came a surge of defiance. She wouldn't surrender her career without a fight. She sprang to her feet and squared herself to Chendekar. "Your facts are correct, Dr. Chendekar, but you've put them together all wrong. Yes, I disregarded lab procedures, and yes, I conducted unauthorized research, but I did it all for a very, *very* good reason."

Chendekar sat still in his chair.

"Did Eddie happen to mention that I tried to book time in the OH lab, or did he happen to mention that I tried to reserve the QuanX? I needed to use them, urgently. I faced a deadline. I pleaded for a little understanding, but Eddie turned me down flat."

"That hardly justifies—"

"Breaking into the lab? It would seem so, until you factor in *why*." Beth pulled a bundle of folded paper from her back pocket and tossed it on the desk in front of Chendekar. "I conducted an obsidian hydration test. These are the lab results. Look at the sample's micron layers."

Chendekar seemed surprised at Beth's sudden aggressiveness. He peered down at the papers, unfolded them and leafed through the first few. Then he riffled to the end and read, mumbling the numbers. "Alright, Dr. Harper, so you've proven you're in possession of a twenty-five-centuries-old piece of obsidian. I'm not impressed."

"A piece of obsidian I had planned to present at the Symposium of Persian Archaeology in Chicago next week."

"It was my understanding you were to present a series of cuneiform transliterations from the Achaemenid period."

"Originally, yes, that was the plan. Until the discovery."

Chendekar rolled back slightly, assessing Beth with a penetrating stare. "Discovery? Enlighten me, Dr. Harper."

"The obsidian samples I tested," she said, pointing to the papers Chendekar clutched in his hands, "they come from the Talisman of Persepolis."

The dean's dark face showed no reaction. He sat for a long moment and stared into Beth's eyes, studying her as if trying to decipher an ancient manuscript. Then, at long last, he glanced down again at the papers, tossed them onto his desk. "Whoever sent you these samples, Dr. Harper, has clearly played you for a fool. What's worse, because of it, you've ruined your career."

"Dr. Chendekar—"

"There are plenty of artifacts these samples could have come from."

"Dr. Chendekar—"

"To be duped into believing their origin was the Talisman of Persepolis," he laughed, "well, that shows an incredible naivety on your part, not to mention a serious lack of professional judgment."

Beth threw up a hand. "Dr. Chendekar," she said, "it was *I* who removed the samples from the artifact."

He paused momentarily, then shook his head in disbelief. "You must be mistaken."

"No mistake," she said. "Not only did I personally remove the samples, I also conducted a thorough analysis of the relief. The scenes encircling the talisman match precisely with all known written and pictorial sources. In addition, the etchings were fabricated using ancient Persian carving techniques, no modern high-speed tools. OH tests prove the stone's age, and spectrometer analysis of the obsidian confirms its chemical fingerprint. Its source is Persian."

"That can't be."

"It is."

"Dr. Harper, if this is some kind of charade, a desperate attempt to salvage your career."

"I promise you it's not."

Chendekar stood from his chair and stared thoughtfully out the window. Beyond the tinted pane, a bright day beckoned. Beth had hardly noticed it, until now.

"Why didn't you bring this to my attention?" he said, back still turned. "If what you say is true, I would have guaranteed you full access to the lab."

Beth paused before answering. Explaining her concerns would be the hard part. The part she knew would make her look silly, perhaps even a little selfish. "Dr. Chendekar, I had two reasons for not coming to you," she said, "both of which seem petty now that I look back at them."

Chendekar turned. "Yes?"

"You see, I feared looking foolish in front of my colleagues. What if the talisman had proven to be a forgery?"

"Understandable."

"But worse, I feared if the artifact was genuine, it would be reassigned to a more senior scholar, taken from me in some kind of a political reshuffling." Beth paused. "You see, by some quirk of fate, the talisman found its way to me, and I felt responsible for seeing it through every step of the process, from its authentication to its revealing at the Symposium next week in Chicago."

Chendekar turned back to the window, removed the handkerchief tucked neatly into his breast pocket, and scrubbed a small spot from the glass. "I'll not lie to you, Dr. Harper," he said over the squeaking. "The events of last night, the trouble you've caused this university, it's quite serious. And although I'm pleased your intentions lacked malice, I must still tell you, the school's decision—my decision—it stands. I expect to see your resignation on my desk within the hour. If you refuse, the university's legal team is prepared to take immediate action against you."

## 25

THE UNIVERSITY OF Arizona was a sprawling campus that stretched nearly four hundred acres over a semi-barren swathe of land in the high Sonoran desert. Home to over two dozen schools and colleges, it housed some of the most prestigious academic research facilities in the world.

On the southern grounds of the campus, at the corner of Fourth Street and Park Drive, a black cargo van idled cool in the parking lot. Inside, Gus, an initiate of the Brotherhood, clutched at the steering wheel, his knuckles stretched tightly over the rubber grip. Sarth rested in the front passenger seat next to him, binoculars raised. Carefully, he scanned the perimeter of the Emil W. Haury building, a four-story, red-brick construction, striped with columns of shade-drawn windows. Surrounding the building, a scattering of beargrass and flowering yuccas struggled to survive, all awash in the muted browns, yellows, and greens of a lifeless desert.

Sarth had watched Harper enter the building half an hour earlier, dropped off curbside by the same man who'd been at her side last night in the laboratory.

He lowered the binoculars, dropped a hand to his calf, and tugged at the gauze bandage wrapped carefully over a patch of raw flesh.

*Curse the laboratory.*

Last night had been a failure, and the burn Sarth had suffered was clearly punishment, a sign of Mithra's displeasure. Harper had proven to be resilient, and the man, too, was an unexpected complication. Indeed, he'd shown remarkable bravery and impressive reflexes, saving the woman from a sure fatal bullet. In surviving the assault, they had demonstrated a shrewd resourcefulness, and Sarth would not underestimate them again. His revenge would be swift and decisive. Mithra's anger would soon be placated.

Sarth lifted the binoculars, sweeping its field of view to an SUV resting idly on South Campus Drive. Inside, Harper's man sat patiently, waiting no doubt for his woman to exit the building.

Sarth turned away the binoculars and surveyed the campus. It was summertime, the weather oppressively hot, and few people dared to venture outside their little air-conditioned sanctuaries. Now and then a man or a woman would brave the heat and make a trip between buildings, moving like slugs, burdened with some menial task. All things considered, Sarth was quite displeased with the conditions. Daylight, wide-open public spaces, potential witnesses, this was not how he preferred to operate. Still, Father had demanded possession of the talisman immediately, and Sarth had assured him delivery. Regardless of present circumstances, he would have to act now.

With the press of a button, the glove compartment dropped open, and Sarth removed a cell phone, dialed a number. A woman with an enthusiastic voice answered, "Anthropology department, this is Doris Heckel."

"Mrs. Heckel," Sarth said, "this is Professor Nehru. Forgive me for disturbing you again, but could you tell me, has Dr. Chendekar become available?"

"Sorry," she said, "still tied up in that meeting. It shouldn't be too much longer, though. Want to leave a message for him this time?"

"No, no, that will not be necessary, thank you."

Sarth shut the phone and returned it to the glove compartment. He peered down at the ivory-handled garrote resting neatly on his lap, then lifted it carefully and began winding the leather cord around his left hand, over and over again, pulling it tighter with each turn. His fingers paled to a cadaverous color. He wiggled them, noting with great pleasure their curious lack of sensation. Amazing, he thought, the power of blood. Though the sight of it was repulsive to most, Sarth considered the life-sustaining fluid to be a gift from Mithra, not only in its physiological function, but in its spiritual qualities, as well. Washing in the blood of a sacrifice was a pleasure few would ever experience. The ritual cleansing was like being reborn, a renewing of the soul. Sarth released the garrote and watched with interest as the color surged back into his fingers, spreading rapidly like rivers of pale red.

A thin shaft of sunlight broke over the van's windshield into the cabin. Sarth peered through the window and with averted vision glimpsed the powerful orb of Mithra. He lifted his hand to the light and turned it ever so slightly, spilling radiant energy over the blazing black sun inked into the flesh between his finger and thumb. Closing his eyes, he concentrated on a pattern of slow, rhythmic breathing. In his mind's eye, he constructed a meditation point, a scarlet orb against a background of brilliant white.

He focused on the orb, purging from his consciousness all mental and physical distractions. One by one he cast them away, until at length he could hear only the whooshing of his pulse—one beat, then another, then yet another, and from the beat's slowing frequency he could perceive his heart rate falling, dropping lower and lower, until his muscles freshened with energy, his body as tranquil as the darkness of space.

He opened his eyes, ending the meditation.

Soon, Harper would be leaving the Anthropology building, and his work would begin anew. Sarth nodded to Gus, slipped the garrote into a concealed pocket, then casually stepped from the van.

# 26

BETH SAT NUMBLY in Chendekar's office, having just been given the most sickening ultimatum of her life: resign her professorship at the university or face charges of professional misconduct. She was utterly stunned, unable to pull her mind away from the sudden barrage of questions: If she resigned her professorship, where would she go? What would become of her career? She had studied and trained all of her life to become an archaeologist. There was nothing else she knew, nothing else she loved. She'd devoted her time and passion to exploring and understanding the great civilizations of the past. And now it was all coming to an end, here, in Chendekar's miserable office.

Despite mounting her best defense, despite having dropped a bombshell with news of the Talisman of Persepolis, despite it all, Chendekar was still handing her walking papers. How could the man be so unreasonable?

He cleared his throat.

Beth blinked once, then everything came back into sharp focus—Chendekar's dark face, his narrow eyes, the collection of relics arrogantly displayed on the office walls, the Tucson sky burning brightly beyond the office window.

She pulled herself from the chair, preparing to leave with as much dignity as possible. She sighed, took a step toward the door, then stopped, unable to propel herself forward. It was if her foot had rooted itself to the floor. This was insane, Beth thought. She couldn't just walk away and let it end. Not like this she couldn't. She turned on her heel.

Chendekar raised a finger, as if to warn her against speaking. "We're finished here, Dr. Harper."

"I don't think so," she said. "Not by a long shot."

His eyes widened. "I beg your pardon?"

"I've just explained to you that I've discovered and authenticated the Talisman of Persepolis, the greatest artifact in all of Persian antiquity. And you act as if I'm speaking Greek. Have you heard nothing I've said?"

"For the record, Dr. Harper, I converse fluently in Greek, as well as seven other languages, and yes, I did hear you what you had to say, however—"

"The Rosetta Stone," Beth pointed to Chendekar's replica. "A priceless artifact, featured prominently in the British Museum. Every day, thousands of tourists flock to it, people from all walks of life who are enamored by its history. You know as well as I, the Talisman of Persepolis would be an equal draw, if not a greater attraction. And the university could claim credit. Are you willing to let that opportunity slip away?"

"I'm well aware of the talisman's value, Dr. Harper, both in terms of its historical significance and its popular appeal." Chendekar swung around the desk and inclined forward, stopping inches from her face, carrying with him the faint odor of an exotic cologne. "But you see, Dr. Harper. I simply don't believe you. What I mean is, you've given me only words, empty assurances, nothing tangible."

"But I have the talisman, I swear to you."

"You do, do you?"

"You'd better believe it."

Chendekar said nothing; he simply stared. A minute passed. Then another. Beth remained steadfast, unwilling to show any weakness, suffering the occasional waft of the dean's eye-watering cologne.

Then at last he backed away, retreating behind the desk and easing himself into his leather high-back. "If what you say is true, then you should have little trouble proving it. I want the artifact here." He reached out over his desk and rapped a fingernail against its lacquered finish. "Right here."

"Absolutely," Beth said, "but what assurances do I have that—"

"Save the negotiations, Dr. Harper," he said. "I want the talisman, now. That is, of course, if you honestly have it."

Beth felt a sudden swell of relief. Oh, she had it alright. And she'd show him. She'd wipe that smug little look right off his face.

He peered at her, a wry smile breaking the edge of his lips. "Bring to me the stone, Dr. Harper, and I'll accept it in lieu of your resignation."

At these words, Beth became energized, driven. The backache suddenly disappeared, and she felt a renewed sense of hope and possibility. "I'll have it on your desk right away."

"Within an hour, Dr. Harper."

"Alright, an hour." She turned and hurried to the door, taking long, eager strides.

"Dr. Harper," Chendekar called out, his tone suddenly menacing.

She turned back.

"If this is some kind of trick to save your skin, I'll see to it that you never work in this field again."

With a hard swallow, Beth nodded. This was no trick, she thought. She had the Talisman of Persepolis. Soon, Chendekar would see.

*       *       *

Outside the dean's office, the hall was empty and dimly lit, humming with the buzz of a dying fluorescent bulb. Beth hurried off in the direction of the elevator, feeling as if her legs wouldn't carry her fast enough. Inside the elevator, she tapped the ground floor button and watched as the doors began to close, painfully slow. Seconds later, the chime rang and the doors eased open. Beth bolted out. If she hurried, she'd have time to stop for some nicer clothes before retrieving the talisman. Chendekar would die when he saw it. Imagining a relic of its mythical stature was one thing, but holding it in your hands and tracing a finger along its subtle etchings, that was something else altogether.

A thrill fluttered through her body. With the proof of her discovery staring Chendekar in the face, the negotiations would begin. Beth snickered at the thought of his earlier chiding: *Consider yourself derailed, Dr. Harper.* The man thought he was being so clever. But, oh, how he was so wrong. Far from being derailed, with the talisman as a bargaining chip, Beth was once again on the fast track to tenure.

In the building's lobby, she stopped, flipped open her cell phone, and called Rick to have him pick her up in front. He'd wanted to escort her to Chendekar's office, as if she were some sort of a child. But she'd refused. She was a grown woman and had made her own mistakes. She had insisted on facing Chendekar alone.

Rick answered his phone. "How did it go?"

"Great news, sweetheart. Looks like the talisman's going to save the day, after all. If I can get it to Chendekar within the hour, I'll keep my job."

"Fantastic," Rick said, "now we're talking. One problem solved, just one more to go. I'm pulling up to the curb now."

Through the glass doors, Beth could see the Explorer rolling to a stop near the road that abutted the anthropology building. Rick lowered the passenger side window and gave her a wave.

She hurried through the doors, stepping into what had quickly become thick, soupy air. Instinctively she looked east, scanning the horizon for a storm. In the far distance, a dark band of clouds had risen up and was creeping its way westward, driving in front of it flashes of lightning and an ugly looking thunderhead. A seasonal monsoon, just what she needed right now.

Beth pulled her gaze from the storm and started for the car. There was little foot activity in the area, which was typical for a weekend during the summer session. This time of year, campus was the last place students wanted to be. And now with weather approaching...

Rick flashed the hazards, jumped out of the car, and like a gentleman hurried around to open the door for her. She smiled at his thoughtfulness, then felt a quick pang of guilt. How could she have ever walked out on such a good man?

From somewhere distant, a heavy engine rumbled, and there came the scream of spinning tires, slipping, then catching traction on the asphalt.

Beth wheeled around in the direction of the noise.

A black van broke from a lane of cars and veered straight for the Explorer. Rick spun around, startled by the sudden squeal, still gripping the door's handle, eyes wide with panic. The van was seconds away from impact with the Explorer, and still accelerating, a large shadowy figure hunched behind the wheel.

Beth leapt forward and opened her mouth to scream, but her voice was strangled away by a painful squeeze around her neck. Feet kicking up, she fell backward, her momentum stopped by a tremendous force.

A hazy blue sky flashed in front of her eyes, and she felt a strong, wiry arm entangle her own. The squeeze around her neck suddenly loosened, then instantly a callused hand slapped over her mouth.

As she struggled to make sense of it all, there came the sound of a horrific crash, a cacophony of twisting metal and shattering glass. She tried desperately to glimpse the Explorer, to see Rick, to make sure he was okay, but the strong arms fettering her body forced her in the opposite direction. She couldn't see. She couldn't tell what had happened. Frozen in her mind was the image of Rick standing paralyzed at the car, the van seconds away from collision. Beth's body went limp.

The rubber soles of her shoes skidded across concrete as she was half-carried, half-dragged backward toward the street.

The realization that she was being abducted stirred up a new-found energy, and Beth bucked her body and flailed her elbows, trying furiously to break free of the man's hold. But it was no use, he was as strong as an ox.

A voice thick with accent whispered in her ear. "Continue your struggle, Dr. Harper, and the consequences will not be pleasant."

The man knew her name! This was no random attack. She kicked and twisted, harder this time, fighting with every ounce of strength to turn her head, to get a glimpse of Rick. But it was no use, the man's lock was brutal, his hand and chest acting as a living vice, with her head caught between. All she could see were flashes of empty sky.

There came another powerful rev of an engine and more screeching tires, this time just feet away and painfully loud. A mingling of heavy exhaust and burning rubber hung in the air, stinging her nostrils as she struggled to take in a breath.

With a monstrous hand clasped to her mouth and her air supply constricted, Beth began to dizzy. Where was Rick? Why wasn't he helping her? Something was wrong, terribly wrong. He was hurt! Or worse! The crash, the awful meshing of steel and glass… Rick! The thought was too painful to bear.

The man dragged her harder across the pavement.

Beth's heels banged over the curb onto the road, scraping along sticky asphalt. He twisted her neck with a fierce yank. She winced in pain and in a knee-jerk reaction bit at the hand covering her mouth, but the man's grip held fast, and all she managed was to tear a piece of her own inner-lip. She tasted blood.

In the distance a horrified woman cried for help, but the sound of the shrill voice was quickly overcome by the sliding of a heavy metal door.

The disembodied scream was joined by another, and then yet another. Beth could feel her body lighten as she was hefted up by the waist.

Furiously, she kicked her legs to free herself, but it was no use.

All at once her body swung like a pendulum, and a crushing blow fell across her back as she landed heavily upon the corrugated bed of the van.

She drew in a sharp breath and expelled it with a moan. From her back she could see the man that had grabbed her, a towering figure concealed in black. With the skill of a hurdler he leapt into the van, and in one fluid motion he pinned her by the shoulder with his boot and slid shut the door. It closed with a sickening crash, killing the hazy light of the afternoon and the distant shouts of the Samaritans.

The engine roared, and in a final screech of rubber, the van tore away.

Bruised and curled in the shadows, Beth trembled. It seemed to her this was the end. The talisman had been a curse after all. But none of that mattered anymore, not the talisman, not her own life. All that really mattered now was Rick.

## 27

THE SERVER AT Java Joe's cleared her throat. "Excuse me, pipsqueak, my eyes are up here." She pointed to her face with one hand, while balancing a small, coffee-filled tray with the other.

Mason peeled his eyes from her breasts, irritated by her courage to confront him. "Who the hell are you calling a pipsqueak? I'll have you know, lady, I bring in more cash after an hour talking into a microphone than you do all year swinging them hips and serving that coffee. And a piece of advice: If you don't want guys eyeballing your knockers, stop squeezing them into T-shirts that are two sizes too small. Capiche, darling?"

The server, a busty brunette in her late twenties, hesitated, her cheeks flush with anger. For a second Mason thought she might actually hurl the coffee at him. But instead she just took a calming breath, composed herself, and served his drink, no doubt realizing she was butting heads with somebody way out of her league.

"The double-shot espresso is Peter's there." Mason pointed a finger at Eckerman. "The cappuccino's mine."

She dropped two tiny silver spoons onto the table with a clatter, then tossed down a couple packets of sugar. Before she had a chance to leave, Mason waived her away, figuring it best to remind her who was in control.

As she stormed off, her rear end swinging, Mason grinned, leaned forward, and pulled close the cappuccino. He winked at Eckerman, who was sitting across from him in a plush green armchair. "In the U.S., that's how men deal with chicks with attitude. Some women just don't know their place in the hierarchy, what can I say?"

"Yes, well, it's good to know that chivalry is still alive and flourishing in America." The old man brushed away the sugar packets and lifted the espresso cup in a salutation. "Sweetener only confuses the palette and destroys the rich flavor of the brew. It is for the non-connoisseur. Wouldn't you agree, Mr. Manning?"

Mason, whose hand was already en route to a packet of Equal, redirected and snatched up the coffee cup instead. He sipped, winced at the bitterness, then nodded reluctantly. The old man, after all, was European, and if there was one thing Europeans knew it was their coffee.

In one quick flick of the wrist Eckerman turned up the tiny cup, and the golden, froth-capped liquid instantly disappeared. He smiled and raised a bushy white brow, obviously pleased with the quality of the espresso. After playing his tongue around the front of his teeth, he dabbed a napkin at the corner of his lips and trained his sight on Mason. "You have been exceedingly kind these past few days, offering the lodgings, allowing me to become immersed in your world of talk radio. I hope to one day repay your generosity."

"Ah, forget about it, I think it's a hoot just having you around. Anyway, my listeners are going to love hearing your stories."

"Oh, nonsense," Eckerman said, swatting a hand in the air. "People aren't interested in an old man's babble."

"Let me be the judge of that." Mason leaned forward. "Here's what I'm thinking. Since the talisman is obviously an artifact of considerable intrigue, we'll push the secret society angle. We'll explain about the Brotherhood, say they were tipped off and told of its location in the cave."

"I find that highly unlikely," Eckerman said.

Mason waved away the old man's objection. "We'll then claim that the Brotherhood's assassins followed Tanner's team into the cave with the intention of slaughtering them like sacrificial lambs."

"But that ignores the facts."

"Facts?" Mason protested. "Screw the facts. If people wanted facts, they'd watch Judge Judy. They listen to me for fresh angles. For possibilities."

Eckerman sighed. "Alright, then, what is it you propose?"

"We'll start off by recapping Operation Cold Strike, remind everyone what happened to Tanner and his men. That's where the experimental technology comes in. We'll make a hero out of the poor kid. After the assassins murder his team, Tanner becomes desperate. He resorts to using DARPA's backup weapon and unleashes a swarm of cyborg bees on the bastards. When the dust settles, the assassins are dead, and the talisman's just lying there for the taking. It'll be great."

"I see."

"Is that what really happened?" Mason asked rhetorically. "Who's to say? I mean come on, what is reality, anyway?"

"Indeed."

"That's where you come in. I'll introduce you as an expert on the artifact. You'll recount a few background stories, definitely the one about the Persian king, and maybe the one about the assassin who killed your partner."

Eckerman nodded absently, staring through the café window.

Mason paused his spiel. "Peter, you listening to me?"

"I'm sorry," the old man said. "It's just that the talisman, and your friends, we can't ignore the danger."

"Hey, you explained things to them, even warned them about the Brotherhood. If they're not willing to listen to reason, what can we do?"

"Yes, indeed, what can we do?"

"Forget about it, that's what we can do."

"You don't understand."

"I do understand. The bottom line is you tried your best to convince Professor Princess. But things didn't work out. You're just gonna have to move on."

Eckerman slumped back into his chair, tented his fingers at his lips, and slipped into thought.

A minute passed while the old man stewed, his nostrils flaring with each deep breath. Mason slurped his cappuccino, and again he winced at the bitterness. If he was to be a connoisseur, like the Europeans, he'd have to suck it up and get used to the unsweetened taste.

"I've got it!" Eckerman shot up in his chair. "You and I, we'll team together and find the talisman."

"Forget about it," Mason said. "Like I told you, we gave it a shot. Time to move on."

"Nonsense. Now that Mr. Lowell and Dr. Harper have experienced firsthand the dangers involved, they have surely become leery. Indeed, they've probably hidden the stone in one of their homes. You know Mr. Lowell's address, do you not? We can go there and search for the relic. Together we'll succeed."

"No," Mason said. "Together we'll get our asses kicked. You notice the size of Rick's biceps?"

"I'm not afraid—"

"You'd better be. He was a Ranger in the special forces. He could come up with a hundred ways to twist off our nuts."

"We must try." The color in Eckerman's face intensified.

The old man was becoming unhinged. And over what? A stupid rock. Mason began to suspect maybe Eckerman was holding something back, something important, like a lost piece to an unfinished puzzle. "Is there something you're not telling me, Peter?"

The old man cocked his head, his blue eyes bewildered. "No, of course not," he said. "It's just that I fear harm will soon come to your friends. Perhaps we did not do enough to convince them." Eckerman leaned close, his voice an octave lower. "Mason, my good fellow, I know you're a noble man, and I understand that entering Mr. Lowell's premises without consent tugs at your moral conscience. However, let me assure you, our actions would be justified. Indeed, we'd be doing him a favor."

"A favor?"

"Why certainly, a favor. You heard Mr. Lowell himself describe the assassin's vicious attack. You mustn't forget, the Brotherhood has already struck, and with murderous intensity. They will strike again, and again, until your friends are dead." Slowly, Eckerman leaned back, peering intensely at Mason. "Is that really what you want?"

"Hey, don't be a douche bag, of course not." Mason didn't want anyone to get hurt, especially not Rick and Beth. But now, the way Peter had put it, someone getting killed seemed inevitable, just a matter of time. He groaned. Damn these moral decisions.

Mason leaned closer to Eckerman and whispered, so as not to be overheard by a group of hippies who'd taken a table next to them. "Okay, you and me, we'll steal the stone."

The old man shot up straight, his eyes bright, and his hands clasped in a tight knot. Amazingly, he looked twenty years younger.

"But there's one thing you gotta remember," Mason said. "If Rick catches us breaking into his place, it was all your idea."

Eckerman simply smiled, extended a hand, and said, "You have a deal."

The coffee house suddenly darkened. Mason and the old man turned to the window. Black clouds loomed on the horizon, blotting out the sun and drowning the cityscape in an ocean of gray shadow.

"That's odd," Eckerman said, "a storm, in the summertime?"

"A monsoon," Mason said. "They move in from time to time."

The old man's eyes were dark orbs of glass. He stared at the arcing thunderheads.

"They're pretty nasty," Mason added. "But fortunately they pass quickly."

"A terrible omen, perhaps?"

"Give me a break. It's just a change in the weather."

A strange hush fell over the coffee house as others, too, gazed solemnly through the window.

"Ah, forget the storm," Mason said. He worked down his cappuccino with noisy slurps, until all that remained was a brown froth swirling at the bottom of the cup. "We can use some rain. It'll cool the air."

Slowly, conversation around them began to pick up again.

Mason turned to the old man, rubbed together his hands. "What do you say we get moving, Peter? We've got a house to burglarize."

## 28

SHARDS OF SHATTERED mirror and fragments of twisted metal littered the street outside the Emil W. Haury building. Rick lay unconscious on the nearby walk, feet from the ruined Explorer and surrounded by half a dozen onlookers all clamoring over his injuries and details of the abduction.

Slowly Rick came to. He could hear the distant whine of a siren, growing more intense with each passing second. His mind sifting through a confusion of aches and pains, he felt the gentle touch of a woman's hand upon his shoulder.

"My God, mister, are you okay?"

Rick tried to shake the haze from his head and piece together what had happened, but his memory fell into a scatter.

*Squealing tires, a van.*

An awful heat registered against his skin and he yanked his forearms away from the scalding concrete. He struggled to sit up, then put a hand to his temple.

The woman's voice came again, "Sit still, mister, the ambulance is on its way."

From among the gathering crowd came a flurry of disembodied voices, "That was insane!"

"Anyone get the license plate?"

"No, but I got a pretty good look at the guy. He was tall, Middle Eastern I think, couldn't see the driver, though."

"Who was the woman?"

*The woman?* Rick thought. He was still unsure where he was, what had happened. He tried again to jog his memory. A sharp pain pulsed through his side, his arms were scratched up something awful, and he could see his own blood caked dry on the concrete in front of him.

*The woman.*

In a rush it all came back: the van, the crash, the scream. Beth's scream! He felt a sudden panic, and a surge of adrenaline coursed through his veins, awakening every nerve in his body. Like a doused flame the pain disappeared. Rick scrambled to his feet and took stock of his surroundings.

From under the Explorer's hood smoke drizzled upward, rising lazily into the soupy air. The van's impact had pinned the car curbside, buckling the wheels at a crazy angle, and through a shattered window, Rick could see the driver's side door cratered in, pinned against the steering wheel.

He needed a car. He needed to get to the hotel, to the talisman. Whoever grabbed Beth—the Brotherhood—that's where they would take her, and once they got her there, once they got what they wanted, they'd kill her. There was no doubt in his mind.

"Mister, you ought to sit down," the soft voice said again from behind him. "If something's broken, you'll only make it worse by moving around."

He turned and saw a young girl, blonde hair, face pale as cream, a flowered backpack slung over her shoulder. "I need your car," Rick pleaded.

"No, you need to sit down. You're hurt."

The sirens grew louder, seconds away.

From the street, a man's voice called out, "I'm a doctor, is anyone here injured?"

Rick looked back to see a car in the street, idling, window down, and inside a silver-haired man with glasses worn low on his nose. He seemed to be awaiting an answer. Rick sprinted into the street and around the sedan to the open window. "I need your car!"

"You're bleeding," the man said. "You need my help."

Rick had no time to explain. He needed to get to the hotel, he needed to get there fast. Beth. In one quick motion, he pulled open the door, leaned in, and punched loose the man's seatbelt.

"What are you doing?"

"No time to explain." He grabbed the man's wrist from the wheel and twisted his arm against its natural bend, forcing him out of the car in a squeal of pain. "Sorry about this, doc."

Rick leapt into the driver's seat, slammed shut the door, and threw the transmission into gear. The gas pedal dropped as he punched it with a heavy foot. The rear tires spun wildly, then grabbed the asphalt. Leaving behind a wake of gray smoke, the car tore off, heading westward.

In the rearview, Rick could see flashes of red light as an ambulance and fire truck rounded the corner, barreling toward the scene.

He scanned the road beyond the emergency vehicles, searching for police cars. He knew they'd arrive any second, and the doctor would be more than eager to have a chat with them.

The car sped away from the university, flying over surface streets. Rick searched ahead for an onramp to the freeway. Thoughts of Beth quickly returned as he shook away the remnant haze of the accident. He'd heard someone mention a tall, Middle-Eastern man, probably the same guy who'd shot at them in the lab. The son-of-a-bitch had already shown an eagerness to kill, and now with Beth in his clutches the only thing stopping him was possession of the talisman.

Rick prayed that Beth could stonewall the bastard, lead him in a roundabout way to the hotel. If he failed to beat them there, to get to the talisman first, Beth would surely be a goner.

The entrance to Interstate 10 lay ahead, and Rick decelerated, whipped around the wheel, and gunned it up the onramp, reaching nearly 80 mph before merging into the slow lane. He continued to accelerate. Startled drivers blasted their horns in a collective show of anger as he raced by them at a breakneck speed. Buildings and trees passed in flashes of brown and green.

Then a horrible thought occurred to him. No doubt Beth was frightened and in fear for her life. What if she didn't stall? What if she told the man right where to find the talisman? She might reason that if he knew its location he'd be satisfied and let her go. But Rick knew differently. If she told him where it was, and if he believed her, he'd kill her without hesitation and drop her body roadside. A panic descended over him, and his stomach churned. He gave the car more gas, ratcheting up the speed, topping 100 mph and weaving in and out of lanes as seamlessly as possible. The engine shuddered under the great strain, but Rick realized he'd have to push these insane speeds if he hoped to beat them to the hotel. What he needed was a bit of luck—a bit of luck and a plan.

He looked east through the rearview mirror, scanning for the Highway Patrol, but glimpsed instead a growing thunderstorm. What had begun as a distant band of grey had now grown into a menacing wall of darkness, swallowing the eastern horizon.

He turned his attention back to the road, veered slightly to miss a merging Lexus. With his eyes on the road and hands at ten and two, Rick forced his mind to construct a plan. He had to remove emotion from the equation, and as much as it pained him, he needed to see Beth as an objective, not as the woman he loved. He flipped open the glove compartment, hoping to find anything he could use as a weapon. A mess of papers fell onto the floorboard. With a quick hand, he swept under the seat, searching for a crowbar, anything at all.

Nothing.

But it probably wouldn't matter. Even if he was lucky enough to reach the hotel first, there was little he could do tactically. Confronting him would be two men, the assassin and the driver of the van. Given Rick's condition, it would be a tough fight. And if they had guns, which they surely did, overpowering them would be nearly impossible.

Rick fast approached a string of slower vehicles, with no lanes to pass. He swung the car onto the center shoulder of the highway, kicking up dust and loose rocks. High beams flashed behind him from angry motorists, and he merged back into the fast lane, continuing dead ahead.

The Brotherhood wanted the talisman—that much was clear. And if Eckerman's stories contained even a kernel of truth, they wanted it desperately. That would mean a willingness to negotiate, a willingness to trade for Beth.

As he drove, he reexamined the angles, but everything seemed to point to one conclusion: to save Beth he needed the talisman, and to get the talisman, he'd have to get to the hotel first. Rick stepped on the gas pedal, sending the sedan flying faster along Interstate 10, cutting northward away from Highway 77 toward the dark range of the Tortolita Mountains.

## 29

BETH LAY HUDDLED in a shadowed corner at the rear of the cargo van, suffering every bump in the road, sliding against its corrugated metal bed as it accelerated wildly out of turns. Though panicked by the reality of her abduction, she forced herself to make sense of it all, to assess the situation: This attack was no coincidence. It couldn't be. These men knew her name. They were after the talisman. And they were going to kill her to get it. Something in Beth's chest tightened. Her limbs became rigid. But still, she forced herself to think. No, no they wouldn't kill her. They wouldn't dare. They had no idea where the talisman was. If they did, they'd have had no need to kidnap her. They would've broken into the hotel room and simply taken it. She and Rick would be— oh, God, Rick!

In her mind flashed an image of Rick sprawled bloody on the concrete, and she felt a thick lump form in the middle of her throat. She hadn't actually seen the crash, but she'd seen the van careening toward him and witnessed the panic in his eyes. She'd heard the awful tearing of metal and the shattering of glass. And that had been enough. The image in her mind was real.

The van continued its flight from the university, racing at high speeds for what seemed an eternity. After gaining a great deal of distance, it finally slowed, the wild turns ceasing. Beth glanced to the front of the cab, where she could see the man who'd wrestled her inside. He was knelt to one knee and facing her, a menacing figure silhouetted by the glare of the sun. He stared at her for a time, his expression hidden in shadow. He didn't speak. He didn't even seem to be breathing.

The driver called back to the shadowed figure, his voice empty of emotion. "It was a clean break, no signs of the police."

"Understood," the silhouetted man answered. "You have done well, Gus."

"Damn straight," the driver said. "We nabbed this bitch good."

Beth struggled into a sitting position and huddled herself into the corner. She stared at the dark figure, feeling a vicious and intense hatred. Never in her life had she wanted so badly to hurt a person.

Never. Until now.

She glanced around for anything she could use to defend herself, but the cab was bare. There was nothing that would make an effective weapon. Beth had a sudden thought. Maybe she could throw open a door and wave for the attention of other drivers. Surely someone would see her in distress and call the police. But even as the idea took shape, Beth could see that the exits—both the double rear doors, and sliding track doors—were missing their handles.

Impossible to open.

The two men had been careful to prevent her escape.

As if sensing her thoughts, the silhouetted figure spoke. "Any attempt to escape would be futile, Dr. Harper. You will find no weapons, nor anything with which to improvise one, as you so cleverly did with the acid last night in the laboratory."

Beth steadied herself in the corner. "So you're the jerk who shot at us."

"You want me to duct tape the bitch's mouth shut?" the driver called back.

Beth said, "After everything you've done, if you think I'm going to give you the talisman, you're as stupid as you are ugly."

Abruptly the road became gravel and the cabin shuddered. But the silhouetted man did not move, his balance seemingly unaffected by the jostling of the van.

"Where are you taking me?"

"On the contrary, it is you who will be taking *us*—to the talisman. But first we must exchange vehicles. Undoubtedly the police have already begun to broadcast an APB, complete with the details of your abduction. Regrettably, that includes a description of this van."

"You'll never get away with this."

The dark figure waved a dismissive hand. "Let's not make this any more difficult than need be, Dr. Harper. Tell me, where is the talisman?"

"Drop dead," was Beth's answer. "After what you did to Rick I'll—" The sudden thought of Rick and the awful collision made Beth's heart tighten. Her eyes began to well, and she could feel the roll of a warm tear down her cheek. She swiped it away. "—I'll, I'll die before I give it to you."

"Your posturing does not impress me. When the time comes, I'm certain you will choose life over death."

"Think I'm bluffing? Try me, jerk."

There was a quick movement of the man's hand and a long knife appeared. Sunlight glinted off its razor-sharp edge. With terrifying speed and agility he shot forward, the knife leading his path.

Beth threw up her hands in a useless effort to protect herself, waiting for the horror she knew was coming. Then suddenly, from the far end of the cab, a radio crackled. The dark figure looming over her turned.

"The police are broadcasting a citywide," the driver called back. He cranked up the volume.

Words were lost in the static, then as the reception improved a woman's voice cleared: "...the suspect is a tall man with closely cropped black hair, medium build, possibly of Middle Eastern descent. Witnesses say he fled with the victim in a black van, no rear or side windows, a tinted windshield, possible damage to the grill. License plate and driver unidentified."

Another wash of static.

"A third man suffering injuries fled the scene shortly thereafter in a stolen 1998 silver Crown Victoria, four-door sedan, Arizona license plate number AX3 4BH."

Beth gasped, jolted by the sudden realization that the man mentioned had to be Rick. She couldn't believe it. With him standing frozen by the Explorer, and after such a devastating collision, she'd assumed the worst.

Without warning, the figure bearing over Beth grabbed her by the throat and pulled her close. Carefully he brought the edge of the knife under her chin, pressing it firmly to her jugular. A quick turn of the van or the slightest falter and Beth was sure he'd cut her.

"Your companion is still alive," he said. "It seems Gus erred in his efforts."

"Go to hell." Beth's words were strangled.

"My, a harsh reaction from such a lovely woman." The man pulled her closer and regarded her with dark, sinister eyes. "This man, he is your lover?"

Beth did not answer.

"Yes, clearly you harbor feelings for him. It would seem you have something to live for, after all, Dr. Harper."

Beth took a slow, steady breath, feeling droplets of sweat rolling down her temples. A strange weakness gripped her as she found herself overwhelmed by two powerfully conflicted emotions: relief knowing Rick had survived, and terror realizing she likely would not.

"Okay," she whispered, taking care not to jostle her head. "You want the talisman, you can have it. Let me go and I'll tell you where to find it."

"Oh no, Dr. Harper, that is not how it's to be done." He pulled the blade from her neck and slipped it into a hidden sheath.

The van skidded to a stop on the gravel road, and the man threw her against the cabin wall. In a matter of seconds he disappeared out the passenger side door, and Beth could hear movement to the rear of the van. The double-doors flung open and before she could react, two monstrous hands, knobby and scarred, seized her by the shoulders and dragged her into the light. She wriggled an arm free and was just about to swing wildly when she felt herself being whirled like a pinwheel bottom side up. Through a fog of gravel dust, she could see a white car, its trunk open, and without so much as a grunt, the man hefted her up and swung her over the bumper. She landed hard on her side, and with an ear-splitting pop the trunk slammed shut. At that instant, Beth found herself alone in what felt like a dark, silent tomb.

# 30

TRAPPED WITHIN THE cramped confines of the trunk, Beth found the air thick and suffocating. But as unsettled as the space made her feel, it also hid her from view of her abductors. She rolled from her left side onto her right, testing the metallic walls with her hands, trying to visualize the space. With knees bent and elbows tucked, she groped around as best she could, searching for an emergency release. She knew many of the new cars had them, and if she could find one, maybe at the right moment, she'd be able to throw open the trunk and make a dash for it.

She dragged her fingers along the lid, then down again near the latch, where she'd expect to find a release cord. But she could feel nothing more than a metal shell. She stopped and took a deep breath. It was only then she realized how oppressively hot it was, each breath of air like sucking in steam through a straw.

She heard the car doors open. There was a slight jostle as the men loaded themselves inside. Both doors slammed shut. The engine rumbled alive, and Beth could feel the car rolling slowly forward. After a long moment, it stopped, then began to back up, tires crunching over the loose gravel. It stopped. The engine cut off.

The brazen attack at the university and now switching cars to throw off the police, these men clearly had a plan, and they were following it to the letter. But Beth couldn't just lie there, waiting for them to make their next move. If she intended to survive, she'd have to rely upon herself. She needed a plan of her own.

She forced herself to think. Without a trunk release what were her options? Maybe she could pull out a taillight and break through the plastic casing, then tear off a portion of her T-shirt and use it to flag for someone's attention. The plan working seemed a long shot, but what else could she do?

She maneuvered onto her side, turned slightly to face where she guessed the taillight to be, and began to feel for it. Almost immediately she heard a metallic *click* behind her and the trunk abruptly flooded in a wash of gray light.

She rolled to face the rear of the trunk. At its center she could see a small portal, no larger than a handbag. It had been opened to reveal the interior of the sedan. From her vantage point, Beth could see the man with scarred knuckles sitting relaxed in the back seat, legs crossed, hands resting on his lap.

"I trust you are comfortable, Dr. Harper," the seated man said.

"Of course," Beth answered. "Top-notch accommodations you have here."

"That's the spirit, young lady. Maintain it, cooperate, and soon this will all be over."

"Why don't we just cut to the chase," Beth said. "I'll tell you where to find the talisman, and you let me go."

"Yes, a fine idea. However, I would like to insert a step, if you don't mind. First, you tell us where to find the talisman, we go as a group to retrieve it—'trust but verify' I believe your President Reagan was fond of saying—then we'll allow you to go. You'll be free to return to your pathetic little pursuits at the university."

"Your moral compass is way out of whack, mister. You're in the business of hurting and kidnapping people, and you call *my* pursuits pathetic?"

"Let's not quibble, shall we," the man said. "Tell me, where is the talisman?"

Beth hesitated, a thought occurring to her, a tactic that might actually work. "It seems I have no choice," she said. "Rick and I checked into a hotel room, the Holiday Inn on South Alvernon. The talisman's there."

As she spoke she could hear the sound of muffled tapping

emanating from the front seat, like the chatter of a keyboard. A minute later, the tapping stopped. "Nah, the bitch is lying to us, Sarth."

The seated man said, "Gus appears distressed, Dr. Harper. There is no Holiday Inn at that location. In fact, in the city of Tucson there are only two such hotels, one on Palo Verde, the other on Grant."

There was more rapping from the front seat, then a brief silence.

"Dr. Harper, you are playing games with me," he said in an even tone. "I will not tolerate it."

"I don't know what you mean."

"Is it coincidence that the Tucson Midtown Police Department is on South Alvernon?"

Beth's heart sank. Along with waving her T-shirt out the car's taillight, she'd had the idea to send these idiots driving past the police station. The plan had been a long shot, but under the circumstances, it was the best she could do. It seemed they'd come prepared with police scanners and laptops. They weren't going to be fooled easily.

"Are you familiar with Silverbell Lake, Dr. Harper?"

"I've heard of it," Beth said. "Never been there, though."

"You're there right now," the man said. "Our vehicle is backed three feet from the water's edge, on an incline. A nice remote spot on the shore, no one around, just you and I, and my fine associate here. Oh, of course, I can see a few fishermen far out on the lake, but they'll not bother us."

Beth tensed, understanding exactly where he was going with this. The threat was clear, and she didn't want to risk getting caught in another deception. She decided it was time to tell the truth. "Okay, let's not do anything drastic. I'll cooperate."

"Oh no, the time to cooperate has passed." A graveness previously absent filled the man's voice.

"Didn't you hear me? I'll take you to the talisman."

"You have proven that you cannot be trusted, Dr. Harper, and so I will now initiate an alternative plan, of which you are not a part. This is the end of your life's journey, I'm afraid."

At those words, Beth sickened. She could feel the muscles in her body convulse, and her mind flashed alive with haunting images of her struggling in the trunk, the car submerging into the murky lake, slowly filling with water.

The cabin doors swung open and the two men stepped out of the car. The one who'd been speaking leaned back inside and reached for the center armrest, which served as the hatch for the makeshift portal. As he slowly lifted it, he peered inside at Beth, a menacing smile turning up the edge of his lips. He called back to his partner, "Gus, reach through the window if you will, Brother, and disengage the emergency brake."

"No, don't!" Beth screamed through the opening.

"May Mithra take pity on your soul, Dr. Harper." And with those words, the man closed the portal, smothering the trunk in complete darkness.

# 31

RICK LOWELL'S TOWNHOUSE was located in a quiet Phoenix suburb, in an oasis-themed condominium complex situated a few miles east of Williams Field Road. Towering palms and green, perfectly manicured lawns surrounded the units, arranged in groups of small islands.

On the lane leading to Rick's unit, Mason babied his Jag over a series of speed bumps, then pulled into a parking space marked for guests. He cut the engine, turned and smiled at Eckerman. "Alright, Peter, let the games begin."

"A game?" the old man said grimly. "Oh, my dear boy, if only it were so."

They stepped out of the car and looked around at the dizzying arrangement of buildings. Mason scratched his head, held up a sheet of paper with Rick's address and compared it with the numbers painted on the curbs. "That one there," he said pointing to a corner unit.

Together, they hurried along a flagstone walk leading past a fountain and through a high gate into a fenced off courtyard. Rick had set it up as a sort of recreation area. To Mason's left sat a rack loaded with free weights and hanging dumbbells, and next to it, an exercise bike. To his right, a stainless steel propane grill sparkled under the midday sun. A low, umbrella-topped table and cushioned patio chairs obscured the unit's bay windows.

Mason walked directly to the door, tried the handle. It was locked. He turned to Eckerman. "The window."

Shielding their eyes, they peered through the glass. Inside, all was still and smothered under a pall of heavy shadow. On the drive over, Mason had called Rick's home telephone number a half a dozen times, never getting an answer. Now, satisfied that Rick wasn't home, Mason pulled off the screen, pressed his hands firmly against the glass, then tried to slide the panel. It, too, was locked.

"Gonna have to break it," he said.

"I'm afraid we've no choice," Eckerman agreed.

Mason turned away from the window and gave it a quick jab with his elbow. The pane rattled and gave a bit, kind of like a stiff trampoline, but it didn't break. He grinned sheepishly. "Don't have much experience doing this sort of thing." He lined up for another shot. "I'll see to it Rick gets a few extra bucks in his Christmas bonus this year." Mason swung his elbow, harder this time, feeling the glass give. There was a dissonant shatter, and Mason jerked back his arm. "Wow, that wasn't so tough," he said, feeling hugely triumphant. "Kind of fun, in fact. Wanna give it a whack, Peter?"

The old man raised his bushy eyebrows. "You'll forgive me if I decline. I believe we have more pressing matters to attend to."

"Yeah, of course," Mason said. "I'm just saying, it's kind of fun, that's all. I could really get into this cloak and dagger stuff."

Eckerman walked up to the break in the window and pulled away the hanging shards, which Mason thought looked remarkably like long daggers of ice. The old man reached inside, flipped up the locking lever, then pushed open the panel. With a great heave he swung himself over the sill, disappearing into the gray stillness. A moment later Mason heard the deadbolt disengage, and the front door creaked open.

The air in the living room was hot and stale, which confirmed Rick hadn't been home in a while to run the AC. Mason looked around. The townhouse was two-stories, with a modest kitchen and dining room downstairs, two bedrooms upstairs, one of which Mason remembered Rick saying he'd converted into an office. Figuring that Rick would've stored the talisman either in his bedroom or in the office, the two men padded upstairs. In the hall, Mason lagged behind, his attention grabbed by a collection of framed photographs hanging on the wall.

After watching Eckerman disappear into the office, Mason turned back to the photos, his eyes drawn immediately to one in particular. In it he saw a group of young men decked out in army fatigues, leaning into one another with their hands thrown out in peace signs and other goofy gestures. White smiles, every one of them. Not a care in the world. The center soldier, Mason now realized, was a young Rick Lowell, maybe twenty years old. He was lean and broad-shouldered, with forearms like steel cudgels. Pretty much his current physique. Mason swallowed, praying Rick wouldn't catch him inside the house, remembering the broken window downstairs, the one Eckerman had talked him into breaking. Mason continued his walk down the hall.

A bit further along, he noticed another series of photographs, these were themed around Rick and Beth's travels together. In one photo, the two stood atop the Eiffel Tower, Beth feigning danger at the rail, leaning over it in a precarious position, while Rick grasped her arms in a sort of mock rescue, both with huge smiles on their faces. In another photo, the two sat astride horses, posing for a shot in what appeared to be London's Hyde Park, Beth lying half pulled from her saddle, half draped over Rick's lap, his hand held high above her rear end about to deliver a spanking. And again the two of them were flashing their pearly whites. Christ, they were good-looking people, Mason thought, feeling a twinge of envy.

A few more careful steps and Mason stopped at the last picture. In all the others he'd seen, Rick and Beth had revealed themselves wild in spirit and loving life, the expressions on their faces making obvious their feelings for each other.

But this photograph was different.

Mason pulled it from the wall and studied it closely. The shot appeared to have been taken at Beth's graduation party. In it, she stood shoulder to shoulder with Rick, in the foreground of a large congratulations banner, her new Doctoral diploma leveled high at her chest. Both were showing smiles, but they lacked the same sincerity that had come across in the other photos. Here, their smiles seemed forced, fake, in fact. What had caused the tension? Mason wondered. Had they been arguing about something? It was impossible to tell for sure, but soon after Beth's graduation, Mason knew they'd ended their relationship.

Had this night marked the beginning of the end?

A strange feeling kicked up inside of Mason, and he was suddenly overcome by a foreign emotion, an emotion he'd spent the better part of his life learning to suppress—regret.

For months at work, he'd been taunting Rick and giving him a hard time over his breakup with Beth. But it was clear now that this woman had meant the world to him. Christ, the guy still kept her pictures on the wall. Mason rubbed the back of his neck, feeling the heat radiate from his skin. An intense pang of guilt jabbed in the pit of his stomach. And it really pissed him off. Guilt was a chick emotion, the kind of emotion felt by a woman who'd neglected to pick up her hubbie's dry cleaning, or by a timid little homemaker who'd burned the family's Wednesday night lasagna. It sure as hell wasn't the kind of emotion to settle inside Mason. But still, there it was, like a parasite, eating away at his gut. He recalled a few of his antics at the radio station, and he considered how he'd been treating Rick. Maybe, Mason thought, just maybe, he had been acting like an asshole.

A throat cleared, startling Mason out of his reverie. He tore his sight from the photograph and wheeled around to see Eckerman rooted under the office door jamb, staring at him curiously.

Mason returned the frame to the wall.

"Something wrong?" Eckerman asked.

Mason hesitated. "No," he said. "Why do you ask?"

"Well, my dear boy, you've been idling on the stairs for the past ten minutes."

"So I lost track of time, sue me."

Eckerman scratched his thick white mane, then nodded to the office. "I've searched it thoroughly. No sign of the talisman. Perhaps we should try the bedroom?"

"Right," Mason said. He got his legs working and hurried past Eckerman to the end of the hall. At the bedroom door, he paused, thinking. He waited for the old man to catch up. "Actually, there is something wrong."

"What is it?"

"I'm not so sure we should be doing this. I mean, this whole business with the talisman, maybe we ought to leave it alone, let Rick and Beth handle it. The fact is, my engineer's a capable guy, and Beth, she *is* the expert, after all."

Eckerman grumbled a few words in German, then leaned closer to Mason and said, "Mr. Manning, may I remind you of a very important fact: The talisman does not belong to your colleague, nor does it belong to Dr. Harper for that matter, regardless of their good intentions. Furthermore, the talisman has no place in a museum, catalogued and warehoused in some unsecured, god-forsaken basement, or worse yet, displayed prominently for the public, where it will surely become the target of thieves. No, Mr. Manning, the talisman must be safeguarded from the Brotherhood, hidden away for everyone's protection. And so we must endeavor to find it, my dear boy. Do you understand?"

Again becoming convinced, Mason began to nod. He couldn't argue with the old man's logic. Maybe what they were doing really was a good thing, even if the tactics seemed a little bit shady. "Alright," he said, "let's check out this bedroom and get it over with."

*     *     *

At the radio station, Rick's engineering philosophy was to maintain design simplicity and avoid unnecessary complexity. Mason looked around the bedroom. Given its Spartan furnishings, it was clear Rick maintained the same philosophy here, as well. The walls were bare—no fixtures or photos of any kind. And they lacked color, showcasing the same vanilla white that must've come standard when he bought the place. Mason noticed a gallon of blue paint, a tray, and a roller on the floor against the far wall. At least plans for improvement were in the works.

"Search there," Eckerman said, pointing to a bachelor's chest sitting next to the bed. "I'll start in the closet, and with a little luck, my dear boy, with a little luck...."

Mason went to work pulling open the drawers, pushing aside stacks of magazines, and rifling through papers and envelopes. "What's the plan if we don't find it?" he called out to Eckerman, who had already disappeared into the closet.

"We shall locate Dr. Harper's residence, continue our search there," came the muffled reply. "The talisman has not been attended to for quite some time. It must be found and placated."

Mason's hands stopped digging. "Placated?" he said. "Christ, you talk like the damned thing's got a heartbeat."

There was a long pause before the old man answered, "My English, Mr. Manning, forgive me. Perhaps *cared for* would be the appropriate phrase."

Mason shrugged, then went back to work. He pulled out the bottom drawer. Inside was a stack of sealed letters bound with a rubber band, each one addressed to Beth Harper. Next to the bundle of letters was a small felt-covered case. Mason plucked it up and opened it, surprised to find a platinum wedding band nestled inside. His eyes grew wide. The ring was set with a diamond the size of a compact car. *Holy cow!* It must've cost Rick a fortune. But he and Beth had broken up months ago. Why the hell was he still holding on to an engagement ring? It took Mason only a fraction of a second to decide if a chick ever had balls enough to dump him, he'd have the ring back to the jeweler and under the display case within the hour.

Quickly, Mason replaced it, arranging everything in the drawer to look as it was, then he turned to the closet, where he could still hear the old man rummaging around inside. "So," Mason called out, "how do you plan to go about it?"

"I beg your pardon?"

Mason pulled himself to his feet and sat on the edge of the bed. "Once we find the talisman, how do you plan to safeguard it?"

Eckerman was silent.

"I mean, think about it. The Brotherhood had no problem locating that manuscript of yours. They didn't have much problem taking it from you either. What makes you think you'll be able to do any better hiding the talisman?"

From inside the closet there came the muffled crash of fallen boxes. Mason watched as Eckerman emerged, holding a shoebox-sized case. "Honestly, my dear boy, your lack of faith in me is disturbing. When I possessed the *Telesma*, I was unaware of the Brotherhood's existence. It was the murder of my colleague and the theft of the tome that set me about on this journey of discovery. Now that I'm cognizant of this organization's history and their intentions, I shall endeavor to take every imaginable precaution. Indeed, I shall spare no expense in protecting the stone."

"I have a better idea," Mason said with a sudden ring of enthusiasm. "After we find it, let's bust the damn thing up into gravel. Send it to these screwballs in a million little pieces. They won't have much reason to go bothering people for it anymore."

Eckerman shook his head. "If only it were that simple." He tucked the small case under his arm, pulled a handkerchief from his pocket, and dabbed at the sweat beading upon his forehead. "I could no more destroy the talisman than I could raise a hand against my own children."

"What are you talking about?" Mason said. "It would be easy. Just pick up a hammer and let it drop."

"I think not."

"Come on, the talisman isn't flesh and blood, it's just a rock."

Eckerman's lips curled in disgust. "Botticelli's *La Primavera* is just canvas and paint. To foil thieves would you tear it to shreds?"

"Of course not," Mason said, even though he had no idea who the hell this Botticelli was.

"And the Mask of Tutankhamen, it is but jewels and gold. To discourage its theft shall we subject *it* to the furnace?"

Mason sat wordless, scratching his chin. Maybe the old man was right, again, maybe crushing up the talisman was overkill, but still, there had to be a way to stop the Brotherhood.

"Then there's the matter of the talisman's theological destiny," Eckerman continued. "The Brotherhood and others who have prized the stone believe quite simply that it's indestructible."

Mason narrowed his eyes. "You mean they think taking a hammer to it would be useless?"

"As useless as pounding a mountain into sand."

"Where on earth did they get such a cockamamie idea?"

"Why, from the *Telesma*, Mr. Manning. According to key passages, the talisman is the heart of Mithra Himself. And one day in the future, it is to be gifted to the Chosen, a symbol of their sovereignty and divine right to rule. That would be impossible if the stone were destroyed. Would it not? So you see, my dear boy, the relic is quite indestructible."

"But that's just religious mumbo jumbo, right? I mean, seriously, you don't believe it."

Eckerman hesitated, returning the handkerchief to his pocket. "I believe those who have cared for the stone believe it, which explains why the talisman has survived the centuries."

Mason looked up at the small metal case tucked under the crook of the old man's arm. "What do you have there?"

"Your persistent inquiries are distracting me. I've yet to find out."

Mason slapped the mattress. "Put it down, let's have a peek."

Eckerman set the box on the mattress and knelt at the edge of the bed. Mason regarded the small case. Primed metal and riddled with dings, it looked a lot like a small cash box, with the lid held shut by a silver clasp.

"Let's not gawk at it," Eckerman said. "Let's open it. We may have found the talisman."

Mason rubbed his hands, then unfastened the clasp and eased open the case. The hinges creaked. A flash of black, and his eyes grew large.

"What is it?" Eckerman demanded to know. "The talisman? Let me see."

Mason opened the case a little further, his anticipation suddenly plunging. "No, not the talisman."

"Then what?"

He turned the case for the old man to see. "Looks like we found where Rick hides his gun."

# 32

BETH ROLLED ONTO her back and with a swift and powerful kick punched through the small makeshift portal partitioning the car's cabin and trunk. A feeble light spilled inside, filling the space in a pool of gray. Beth knew at any moment her kidnappers would release the emergency brake and send the car rushing into the lake. And she was powerless to stop them. "For the love of God," she screamed through the tiny portal, "don't do this!"

Her mind reeled in a frenzy of scattered thoughts. What had she gotten herself into? She banged her fists and kicked her feet against the walls of her metallic coffin in a futile attempt to break free. "Let me out you jerk!"

Suddenly, in the midst of her rage, an idea seized hold. Show them your hotel room's keycard. What these men wanted was an assurance. The keycard would give it to them. No tricks, just the truth, the location of the talisman. They could have it. It sure as heck wasn't worth sinking into a watery grave.

"Wait, wait, my keycard! It's proof where I'm staying. The talisman, it's what you want, you can have it!"

She fumbled through her front pockets—empty. She patted her back pockets—the firm edge of plastic. The keycard! She yanked it out and thrust her arm through the portal, flailing the card to get their attention. Could they see her? Did they even care?

Abruptly, the trunk opened and Beth rolled around to see the dark-clothed man looming above her, tall against a background of swaying junipers.

She bolted upright, but before she could speak, the man snatched the keycard from her hand. She stared beyond him in disbelief at the scattering of trees that fell away in sparse copses. The car was parked on a slight incline, but it had been backed against a stand of trees, not a lake! In fact, there was no lake anywhere. The car appeared to be parked on some kind of a shoulder that adjoined one of the many service roads that led from the main highway into the desert.

"No lake," she said. "I can't believe it."

"Disappointed are you, Dr. Harper?"

"Of course not, but—"

"But you're alive," the man said, taking an insolent tone. "And if you wish to remain so, you'll offer no further resistance."

From inside the car came the crackle of the police scanner. He paused to listen, then added, "I will entertain no more of your tricks. You will sit with my companion in the front seat. I shall assume a position in the back seat behind you. If you move, in the slightest, I will put a bullet through your heart." He parted his black coat, revealing a gun with a long barrel, holstered in a shoulder sling. "Do you understand me, Dr. Harper?"

Face to face, in the light, Beth finally had a chance to study the man's features, the deep creases in his skin, the cold blackness reflected in his eyes, eyes devoid of feeling, like a pair of watery orbs that betrayed within him a sort of sick emptiness.

Beth shuddered.

"Do you understand me?" the man repeated.

"I understand you," she said. "Straight to the talisman, no more tricks."

*        *        *

The Desert Rock Inn, located on the northernmost outskirts of Tucson, was an unremarkable two-story that horseshoed an inner courtyard, with a gated pool and a stand of towering palms. Prickly pears and an assortment of desert succulents landscaped its perimeter. It was the kind of place that catered to travelers on a budget, or people who simply wanted freedom from the university hubbub found closer to the center of the city.

From the back seat, Sarth kept his eyes on Dr. Harper, while Gus rolled the car to a stop two hundred yards from the hotel next to a boarded up muffler repair shop. The vacant lot in front of the shop was mostly packed dirt and areas of high-growing weeds. Sarth lifted his binoculars and surveyed the hotel's surroundings for anything out of the ordinary. Satisfied that the authorities had not been alerted, he turned to the hotel's south-facing façade, where the woman had indicated the room to be. It, too, appeared innocuous. To Mr. Lowell's credit, he had not been foolish enough to involve the police.

Sarth reached across the front seat and touched Gus's shoulder. "I would like you to retrieve the talisman, if you'd be so kind, Brother. I'll take your position at the wheel and keep company with Dr. Harper." He handed Gus the room's keycard and turned to the woman. "Where, exactly, will the stone be found?"

Harper exhaled deeply. "In my pack. It's wrapped in cloth, bottom drawer."

"Your willingness to cooperate has improved considerably, Dr. Harper. You are to be commended. Soon Gus and I will have what we need, and you shall be free to go." It was a calculated line, Sarth knew, meant to ease the woman's fear and to eliminate any further resistance. Once Sarth recovered the talisman and returned to the service road, he would be compelled to tie up loose ends. And Dr. Harper, without question, was a loose end.

"If you will, Brother Gus, bring to me the talisman."

Without a word, the big man passed back the keys and exited the car, lumbering cautiously toward the hotel.

Sarth tucked his gun inside his jacket and moved to the front seat, where he again trained the barrel on Dr. Harper. "Worry not, my dear. Soon all of this will be over, a fading memory."

With his free hand he started the car, allowing it to idle as Gus neared the hotel room door. The thought of soon possessing the sacred relic brought Sarth a thrill. Tomorrow, Father would perform the Ascension Ceremony, of which the talisman was an integral part. And upon its completion, Mithra would again rise from the earth, and the Brotherhood, for all its devotion and sacrifice over the centuries, would ascend to its rightful place as spiritual leaders of the New World Order.

Sarth lifted the binoculars and watched as Brother Gus swiped the keycard through the door's electronic lock and slipped into the hotel room. Sarth turned back to Harper, who was sitting forward, staring blankly through the windshield. Her hands trembled slightly on her lap, and her chest rose and fell with measured breaths. In profile, Sarth could see she was a strikingly beautiful woman, with sharp cheekbones and smooth, lightly tanned skin. Perhaps within her veins coursed traces of Persian blood. He regretted what he would soon have to do. And sadly, there would be little time even to offer her life-giving essence to Mithra, and that, he thought, was truly unfortunate. "It is a shame that we meet under such trying circumstances, Dr. Harper. You appear to be a woman who, given the proper moment in time, could have offered me a great deal of pleasure."

Harper said nothing, drawing her hands closer to her breast.

Sarth turned his gaze back to the door of the hotel room. Moments later, Brother Gus reemerged, a small brown knapsack tucked under his arm. Sarth felt a sudden rise of anticipation, which he quickly suppressed. Not until the talisman was safely in Father's hands would he allow himself the pleasure of celebration.

Nearing the car, Brother Gus lifted the pack and smiled triumphantly. The talisman, Sarth thought. At long last, it has returned.

                        *         *         *

Rick Lowell stood watchfully under the shadow of a squat palm tree, leaning into it shoulder first, his cheek scratching against its hairy trunk. It was intensely uncomfortable, but he was thankful to have something solid to help keep him standing.

With every breath, it felt as if a rib would punch clean out of his gut. No doubt one was cracked, maybe even broken. He took in a lungful of air and forced back the pain.

He'd chosen a spot far from the hotel where he knew he would not be seen, a place with plenty of cover. The palm was surrounded by dry shrubs and crowded with snakeweed. The entire area seemed to be a late-night hangout of sorts, with cigarette butts, beer bottles, and open condom wrappers littered about.

But it worked well for what Rick needed.

From where he stood, he had a clear view of the hotel and of the white sedan parked a few hundred yards up the street. It was from that sedan a large man had emerged, a man who was now inside their hotel room, tearing it to pieces, no doubt. Rick watched the door, waiting for the bastard to leave again. He wanted nothing more than to kill the son-of-a-bitch, him and the other guy, for what they had done to Beth. But right now, mentally and physically, Rick was bad off, and in no condition to get into a fight.

He felt another needlelike stab at his side. He gritted his teeth and forced back the pain, concentrating. What he needed was to stall, to buy some time, to collect his thoughts and make a plan, bandage up a bit, if possible.

In the race to get to the hotel, he had considered calling the police, but quickly dismissed the idea. There was too much at stake. He'd stolen a car, which meant the police would spend time interrogating him. Precious time he couldn't afford to waste. If the Brotherhood recovered the talisman first, they would no longer have a need for Beth. No, calling the police was a bad idea. Rick knew he'd have to handle this on his own.

As expected, the man reemerged from the hotel room, carrying Beth's pack. He was a hulking man, not tall, but thick and barrel-chested. He had long, vein-laced arms, and wore a tightly fitted T-shirt, like many of the bodybuilders at the gym.

Rick watched as the guy strode confidently toward the car, grinning and holding up the knapsack as a gesture of triumph.

*Prick.*

Rick turned and focused on the car. Even from a distance, he could see a dark form sitting low in the front seat. He knew it had to be Beth. His shoulders sank, and he once again leaned into the tree. Sweat rolled down his face. His shirt clung to his chest. He pulled it away to cool his skin.

Flipping open his cell phone, he double-checked the life of the battery, then watched as the man with the knapsack swapped places with the driver: a slender man standing well over six feet tall, no doubt the guy who'd shot at them last night in the lab.

The tall man moved to the back seat, one hand tucked snuggly into his jacket. Clearly, he was armed.

Seconds later, the car pulled from the curb, U-turned, and sped away, Beth still inside.

Rick sank down to the dirt, aching, exhausted, worried about the woman he loved. He touched the talisman, then hung his head and prayed.

*          *          *

The brown buildings of Tucson flashed by in the window as the car raced westward toward the highway. Sarth hardly noticed. His gaze was fixed upon the small canvas knapsack resting on his lap. With a swift and eager hand he unbuckled its strap and removed the wrapped stone. Quickly he uncovered it, longing to touch its glassy black surface, to behold its divinely inspired etchings.

As the cloth fell away, Sarth stared in sick disbelief. A quiet rage built inside him. His hands cupped an ordinary piece of sandstone, gray and uninspiring, its cracks packed with soil. A slip of paper fell from the cloth. Furious, Sarth lifted the paper and read the hastily scrawled message: *Let's Make a Trade, Asshole!* On the backside was a telephone number.

Fists clenched and knuckles white, Sarth turned to Brother Gus and spoke in a calm and controlled voice, "It would appear, Brother, that our journey is not yet complete."

## 33

"HOW SHALL I proceed, Father?"

"You must wait to kill the woman." Jonathan Walter spoke into the receiver with cautious deliberation. "The talisman is priority one, and since this Mr. Lowell seems content with a trade, we'll use his beloved as bait. Once the talisman is securely in our possession, you'll be free to settle the matter, permanently."

"Understood."

"Call our good Mr. Lowell and arrange a meeting. I'll contact you shortly with details concerning the time and location."

"Very well, Father."

"Until then, Sarth, remain vigilant, and may Mithra shower you with His blessings." Walter replaced the receiver, turned and stared thoughtfully through the high-rise window overlooking the crowded San Francisco cityscape. Below, cars navigated the black thorough-fares, crisscrossing the endless city blocks that fell away in great stone lattices toward the bay. Crowds of men and women plodded over the streets and sidewalks, filing through the doors of the many apartment and office buildings, like cattle being herded through the gates of a corral. Walter smiled. There would be no limit to the degree of influ-ence he would soon have over the masses. And the prospect thrilled him. After a delightful moment of contemplation, he leaned forward across his desk, tapped the intercom button. "Helen, I will need an es-tate rental in northern Arizona, remote, secure, and well-furnished. It must be gated, preferably with forested grounds for privacy."

"Understood, Mr. Walter."

"And Helen, prepare the Gulfstream, I'll be leaving within the hour."

Walter reclined in his chair, folded his hands into a cradle behind his head, and began to calculate. A remote location in Arizona would be the perfect site. The desert would lend itself splendidly to the ceremony, with its open spaces and towering rock formations. Clearly, the events were unfolding by design. Mithra's design.

After a moment, Walter pulled himself from the chair and retrieved the *Telesma* from its safe behind the mascaron. Returning to his desk, he parted the tome's ancient vellum pages, turning them gently, one by one, passing first the *Histories,* then the *Initiations,* then the *Ceremonies*, stopping only when he reached the final chapter: the *Rites of the Talisman.* There, he began to read, slowly, carefully, as was his routine in the quiet evening hours.

Not since the time of the great Persian kings, since the talisman's disappearance some twenty-three centuries ago, had the rites been performed. But soon all that would change. Soon, the artifact would be in his possession, and through its employ—and by the grace of Mithra—the bridge of many centuries would be spanned, a destiny fulfilled. The Brotherhood would become heir to the throne of civilization.

With infinite care, Walter mouthed the ancient Greek text, then closed his eyes and repeated the lines, precisely, verse by verse. For Mithra to be pleased, perfection in the execution of the Ascension Ceremony was critical. There could be no mistake, not one word transposed or mispronounced.

Reflecting upon centuries past, Walter fell deeper into his reverie. The world of the twenty-first century was quite a different place than that of what the ancient's knew. To control his subjects and to strike fear into the hearts of his enemies, the great Persian king, Darius, needed only to conjure sandstorms or call forth deadly plagues, a simple task, given the limitless power of the talisman. Those were the tactics of the day, appropriate and sufficient to maintain control. But the modern world was a far different place. It was global, saturated with weapons of mass destruction and biological technologies of the sort capable of unleashing awesome devastation.

What was needed today was not direct population control, but rather influence over key political figures and heads of state, the men and women who already maintained a stranglehold over the masses. By the power of the talisman and by the will of Mithra, Walter would do as he pleased. And what he pleased was to take immediate action: establish authority over the Secretary-General of the U.N. and the Strategic Commanders of NATO; direct the presidents and prime ministers of half a dozen key western nations; manipulate the member-states of OPEC and the European Union. All of this, of course, just a beginning. There would be no limit to the possibilities.

Walter would rule from the top down, establish complete global control. Only then could Mithra's message be properly disseminated; only then could Mithra's glory be fully realized.

But first Walter would have to recover the talisman and fulfill the prophecy.

The intercom buzzed.

He tapped the button. "Yes."

"Jet's fuelled and waiting in the hanger, Mr. Walter."

"Thank you, Helen."

Gently, Walter closed the *Telesma* and centered it on the desktop. Now, all that remained was to lure this Mr. Lowell to the site of the Ascension Ceremony and to take possession of the sacred stone. Then, for the first time in over two millennia, Mithra would again be called upon to judge the worthy, and the Brotherhood's role as arbiter of mankind would be ordained.

Walter lifted the receiver, dialed rapidly. "Gather the Inner Circle," he said. "The time of the Ascension draws near."

## 34

THE RESTROOM IN which Rick Lowell found himself standing was in the lobby of a nice hotel, a mile down the street from the Desert Rock Inn. Everything around him was as clean as a surgeon's scalpel. Reeking of bleach, the white sink, the white toilet, and the white floor were all scrubbed to a brilliant sheen. Rick stared at himself in the mirror and winced as he tightened a bandage wrap around his chest and tucked off the ends, adding a generous strip of medical tape to ensure the hold. The oblique abdominal muscle on his right side had bruised to a deep, ugly purple, but Rick had dealt with injuries like this before back in his military days, and he could tell none of the bones had been displaced. A very good sign. There'd be no risk to his lungs, and the other ribs would act as a natural splint. The chest wrap constricted his breathing, but it made the pain more manageable. He pulled on his shirt and glanced at the cell phone he'd laid conspicuously on the rim of the sink. *Come on, call you son-of-a-bitch. Call!*

Despite his battered condition, Rick was convinced he now had the upper hand. No doubt these men were all well armed, but what he lacked in resources he more than made up for in leverage. It had become clear that the talisman wasn't just a stone to these people. It was a *sacred* stone. And Rick would use that to his advantage. When the call finally came, it would be *he* who set the terms of the exchange, *he* who picked the time and the location. Realistically, they'd refuse to meet anywhere public, would probably push to square things deep in the desert somewhere. But Rick wasn't that stupid. Meeting somewhere secluded meant increasing the risk of getting killed.

The cell phone rang and Rick's heart nearly leapt from his chest. With some difficulty, he swallowed, then snatched up the phone. It rang again, and he realized his thumb had frozen on the button. Christ, his nerves were beginning to fail. Don't lose sight of the stakes, he admonished himself. He had to get Beth back, at any cost. The phone rang a third time and Rick jabbed the button and spoke with determination. "Who am I talking to?"

There was a brief silence and then a voice, soft, yet deeply disturbing. "You have done well to keep your lady friend alive, Mr. Lowell. But if you wish to continue your good fortune, you will listen carefully and do precisely as you're told."

"First, there's something you and I need to get straight—"

"Let me warn you against making demands," the man said. "Quite simply, if you're interested in seeing Dr. Harper alive, you'll heed my directions."

Hearing the threat against Beth, Rick's first instinct was to assure the man he'd do whatever he wanted, to plead with him not to hurt her, but experience taught Rick something else altogether. He couldn't allow these bastards to dictate the terms. If he did, they'd interpret that as weakness, and when the time came for the exchange, showing weakness would be fatal. He decided to hold his ground. "You can't put a price on the talisman. That I know. This artifact is more than just a dollar sign to your organization. You need it and I have it. So don't go blowing smoke, you prick, it's just gonna piss me off."

There was a pause on the other end of the phone. Then the voice came again, calm like before. "You seem to have a rudimentary understanding of the relic, Mr. Lowell. And no doubt you've gained some insight concerning our organization. So you'll understand the truth in my words when I tell you we will simply bide our time, wait for events that we know are destined to occur. The talisman has been sleeping for many centuries. If need be, it will sleep for many more. I can kill your woman now, then pursue other avenues to acquire the stone. Is that what you want?"

The threat to Beth unnerved Rick, and a thick lump formed in his throat, but he kept his focus. "I don't believe it, not for a second. You wouldn't dare risk anything happening to your precious stone."

"Is that a gamble you're willing to take, Mr. Lowell?"

"Look, you don't want to gamble, I don't want to gamble, so why don't we just—"

"Then do as you're told," the man said. "Tomorrow at precisely 11:00 a.m. you will pull to the shoulder of the road along U.S. Highway 163, midway through Monument Pass, at the junction of a trail marked by a small wooden cross. You will tell no one of your plans and you will arrive unarmed. But most importantly, Mr. Lowell, you will bring the talisman."

"You're crazy," Rick said. "Highway 163 through Monument Pass? That's in the middle of nowhere. Better we meet at—"

"You've been given your instructions."

"Listen you shit, I'll take this rock of yours and bust it into a million pieces. What good will it be to you then?"

There came a slight guffaw, then the man spoke with mild amusement. "Your threat does not intimidate me, Mr. Lowell, simply because damaging the stone is impossible. Mithra would never allow it."

"You're a lunatic, a goddamn lunatic if you think—"

"Tomorrow at 11:00 a.m. the body of Dr. Harper will be at the location I indicated. Whether blood yet courses through your woman's veins or whether she's as lifeless as a fossil, the choice is entirely up to you."

"If you hurt her you son-of-a-bitch I'll—"

There was a click at the other end of the receiver. Rick was breathing heavy now. His chest wrap constricted his violent heaves. Fumes of bleach burned in his nostrils.

It was already early in the evening, and he would have to be at Monument Pass in less than twenty-four hours. That left him little time to prepare. He'd have to get hold of the essentials: a topographic map of the valley, a pair of binoculars, a firearm. But most importantly, Rick needed rest. Where could he go? Who could he rely on? He straddled the sink and dropped his head, repeating the questions to himself. Where could he go? Who could he rely on? A minute later, the answer came to him.

His head jerked up. Mason's house! It would be the last place the Brotherhood would check. Quickly, Rick collected his things and pocketed the cell phone, stuffing the talisman and bandages into a small pack he'd bought at a nearby Walgreens. In an instant he was out the door, inside the Crown Victoria, and off to Mason's house in Paradise Valley.

\*         \*         \*

By the time Rick reached the Phoenix area, the summer monsoon had finally unleashed itself in a fury of whipping wind and pelting rain. Large thunderheads hung over the city, piled together like herds of wildebeests, smothering the streets in a pall of eerie darkness.

Rick wound the sedan up a series of tree-lined drives, through the affluent Phoenix suburb of Paradise Valley, dotted with luxury homes and sprawling estates. He'd been to Mason's place only once before, nearly three years ago when the shock jock had hosted a station Super Bowl party, well before Rick discovered the abrasive side of the little guy's personality. Finding the right street was proving to be a difficult task.

The windshield wipers slapped away sheets of water as Rick drove through the darkness. He leaned forward, struggling through the deluge to read the tiny green signs that flashed by in the high beams. When at last he found Mason's street, he turned and followed the black, winding ribbon that was the road's slick asphalt. Soon, he turned into a brick-paved drive that looped up to a massive ranch house, aglow in a haze of yellow-orange light.

Rick pulled the sedan in front of the estate's detached, four-car garage, then cut the engine and hurried out, shielding his face from the wet, slashing wind. When he reached the front door, he pounded urgently.

A minute later, with the wind and rain thrashing the world around him, Rick watched the door swing open to reveal the diminutive form of Mason Manning. The shock jock stood stooped in the entryway, sporting a red tracksuit that was as bright as his thatch of strawberry hair. Seeing a familiar face, even Mason's, Rick felt an unexpected swell of relief. He rushed into the foyer.

Mason's eyes widened, and he stumbled back a step. "Christ, Rick, you okay? I mean, you look a mess."

Rick didn't answer. He pushed himself forward, swung shut the door, then turned the bolt. "You alone?"

"Well, uh…yeah, sure."

Rick looked around, surveying the house, which was just as he remembered it. The formal entry was rich in the color and flavor of the Southwest: hand-woven Navajo rugs and textured walls hidden behind a large display of original R.C. Gormans. To either side of Rick, dual sweeping staircases ascended toward a vaulted ceiling, meeting at a second story landing lavishly decorated with painted Native American statuary. Beyond the entryway was the living room, showing off miles of polished wood paneling and hand carved bookcases. No one was around.

"I need your help," Rick said.

"What kind of help?"

"Something bad has happened." He looked for a chair. "Where can we talk?"

Mason pointed through the foyer. "The Arizona room, I'll get some drinks." He began backing up, his eyes still wide. "You know, uh…I've been home all night, kickin' it and watching poker on the tube."

"Good for you," Rick said, heading for a place to sit down.

The Arizona room abutted a large open kitchen and was adjoined by an ornately carved wooden archway, crafted in the form of entwined branches that ran up one side of the opening and down the other. Rick stepped through the archway and made a beeline for the massive table that dominated the room. He melted into a chair, laid his pack in front of him, then leaned back, rubbing his eyes and feeling the wear of a disastrous day.

Moments later, Mason appeared again, a bottle of beer in one fist, a can of Pepsi in the other. He plopped himself down, two chairs away from Rick, and snapped open the soda. Three long swigs and it was gone. He slapped the empty can on the table. "Like I said, been watching poker all afternoon."

"Why you keep telling me that?" Rick said. "Sounds like an alibi."

Mason shrugged. "I'm just saying, that's all." He turned his gaze to the pack. "So what kind of help do you need?"

"It's this talisman. Things have gone from bad to worse." Rick could feel his voice beginning to break. "Beth's been kidnapped."

"Kidnapped?" Mason lurched forward. "Are you shitting me?"

"God, I wish I was." Rick stared unseeing at the beer bottle. "The fact is I'm in a world of trouble."

"Damn, Rick. What can I do?"

"I didn't know who else I could turn to, Mason. I'm relying on you here."

"Sure, sure, I'll help you out, just name it."

"That big guy I met at the station, your friend, Jarred. He's active military, right?"

"Yeah."

"There're a few things I need that he might be able to provide quickly. I have to get in touch with him, now."

"Now? In this weather? Let's wait until morning. I'll call him first thing."

"Tomorrow's no good. I need these things right away. These people have Beth and they're going to kill her unless I do something about it. I have to meet them in the morning by the buttes near Monument Pass."

Mason was staring at Rick's arms. "You're cut up. What happened?"

"Like I said, they kidnapped Beth." Rick took a drink from his bottle of beer. "I was in their way."

"You should call the police."

"Can't. I stole a car to get here, I'll be arrested."

"You stole a car?"

"Trust me, I had no choice."

Mason nodded. "What things do you need? Maybe I—"

"You have a handgun?"

Mason shook his head. "No, but we could go to your place and pick up the Glock."

"My place isn't secure. They could be waiting for me there." Rick cocked his head. "Wait a second, I never mentioned owning a gun. How'd you know I had a Glock?"

"Just assumed, that's all." Mason's eyes darted to the table. "I mean, you were an Army Ranger."

Rick nodded, drank from the bottle. When he looked again at Mason, he was surprised to see that a cell phone had appeared in his hand.

Mason dialed and put the phone to his ear. "Jarred, listen, I need your help. How do six free months of commercial spots for your mother sound?"

Rick listened to Mason work his magic. With all his faults, there was still one thing he was a master at—making things happen. And at the moment, making things happen was exactly what Rick needed.

"Good, good," Mason continued. "I'm going to hand you over to Rick, my engineer. I want you to collect the things he needs and get over here as soon as possible. Got it?"

A pause.

"Yeah, you pea-brain, in this weather!"

There was a moment of silence as Mason listened, then he handed Rick the phone. "Let Jarred know what you need. I'll be right back." With that, Mason stood from the table and hurried out of the room. Rick lifted the receiver to his ear.

*       *       *

The flagstone path that meandered toward the guesthouse was flooded with rainwater. Mason sloshed from one stone to the next, his umbrella whipping against the wind. Within the clouds' lower stratum, lightning flashed, illuminating the estate's thrashing trees. Ahead, a warm light glowed from the kitchen window, and Mason could make out the silhouetted figure of Peter Eckerman. Not bothering to knock, Mason pushed open the door and stomped inside, kicking off blades of grass that clung stubbornly to his shoes. He closed the umbrella and yelled for the old man.

Eckerman appeared at the kitchen threshold, a sandwich in his hand. "Mr. Manning, is something the matter?"

Mason brushed water off the sleeves of his tracksuit. "Rick's here, and I think he's got the talisman with him."

Eckerman's fingers went limp and he dropped the sandwich to the floor.

"I think this is our chance," Mason said. "At the moment, he's a bit distracted. I think I can snatch it."

"Wonderful." Eckerman's blue eyes beamed. "Shall I return with you? Perhaps I could create a diversion?"

"No, no," Mason said, "keep to the guesthouse. If Rick learns you're here, he'll protect that baby like it's... well, like it's a baby."

Hands clasped together, Eckerman nodded that he understood.

"The first chance I get, I'll swipe the stone and sneak it back to you. Keep the lights out and Rick won't suspect a thing."

The two men exchanged smiles, then Mason snatched up the umbrella and hurried back to the house.

## 35

BETH HARPER SHIFTED uncomfortably, sitting at the edge of a broad bed, in a room that was a clutter of Victorian furniture: pieces carved of rosewood and mahogany, many still partially draped in dusty white sheets. Floor lamps with tasseled shades stood in every corner, projecting wedges of light over a mismatch of frayed carpets.

Beth stared at the heavy oak door set into the opposite wall, the door the tall man they called Sarth had led her through two hours earlier, and the only door leading out of this god-forsaken room. Her nose wrinkled at the smell of food, and she turned again to look at the silver tray. On it rested a bottle of red wine and a hot meal: wine-braised brisket of beef with caramelized pearl onions and sliced medallion potatoes. The dinner baffled Beth. Did these people honestly expect her to eat after the hell they'd put her through? Did they honestly believe feeding her a fancy dinner would somehow work as a gesture of good will? Maybe they thought a nice meal would encourage her to call Rick and ask him to bring over the talisman. If that's what these people thought, well then, they were bigger fools than Beth ever could have imagined.

She stood from the bed and moved toward the near wall, where layers of heavy drapes hung from ceiling to floor. Parting them at the center, she stared at a plywood covering that had been affixed over a window. Thunder exploded from somewhere distant, startling Beth back a step.

The clanking of keys sounded from beyond the door, followed by the snapping of a lock and the whine of the hinges. Beth turned and braced for a confrontation.

Emerging from the darkness was an older man Beth had never seen before, slender and donning a well-tailored suit with an Italian silk tie. Cradled against his breast, held as though he were protecting a child, was a leather tome, its cover worn and deeply faded. The man stepped into the room, carefully closed the door behind him, then turned and studied her with wolfish eyes. His hair was a mane of thick auburn, coarse and neatly drawn back. His skin was dark and remarkably free of wrinkles. He exuded youth, yet Beth suspected he was much older, perhaps a man of sixty. After a long moment, he moved forward and spoke softly, "I trust the accommodations are to your satisfaction, Dr. Harper?"

Beth could hardly believe the nerve, another phony gesture of concern. "An accommodation to my satisfaction—whoever you are— would be my apartment back in Tucson, not this place. How dare you come in here pretending to be concerned about my well-being."

"My name is Jonathan Walter," the man said, ignoring her objection. "Please, you may call me Jonathan."

"How about if I call you a kidnapper and a scumbag? An expensive suit and a buttery voice doesn't change who you are or what you've done."

"You're anger is understandable."

"Understandable?" Beth said. "Just who the hell do you think you are?"

"I am many things, Dr. Harper, among them, a man of humble beginnings, a man of God, and thanks to you, a man who will soon exercise a great deal of power and influence."

"In other words, the mastermind behind this little charade," Beth said. "And that tall creep that kidnapped me, what's his name, Sarth, I suppose he's one of your goons?"

"He is a servant of the cause, a disciplined and highly valued member of the Brotherhood."

"Brotherhood, right," Beth said. "A nice euphemism for your little band of thieves. I know your type. You're a treasure hunter, plain and simple, an unscrupulous antiquities dealer, probably. Nothing but a common criminal."

"I expect you to believe nothing of what I say," Walter said. "It is unimportant. I have come here out of respect for your expertise and as a show of goodwill, to share with you the greatest hand-written manuscript of all time." He held up the tome.

Beth wanted to lunge forward and claw the guy's eyes out. Who the hell did he think he was kidnapping her and holding her against her will? But as she stared at the leather bound manuscript, her interest became piqued, and professional curiosity took hold. "What is it?" she asked tersely.

"May I present to you, Dr. Harper, the *Telesma,* the only sur-viving account of the true history of the Talisman of Persepolis."

Involuntarily, Beth stepped forward, reaching out with her hand, but she quickly caught herself and straightened her posture. The *Telesma* was the tome Eckerman had spoken of, the tome Beth doubted even existed. But the volume Walter held in front of him appeared in-credibly old, and Beth felt a sudden urge to examine it.

As if sensing her desire, Walter moved to the parlor table, where he unrolled a large cloth and set down the ancient manuscript. He parted the cover and stepped aside. "Be my guest, Dr. Harper."

Beth walked to the table and peered over the tome, illuminated under the room's golden light. It was a striking manuscript, written in Old Greek and amazingly preserved, with an odd, over-sized cylindri-cal spine, the likes of which Beth had never seen before. Gently, she stroked the pages, feeling the supple texture of the vellum. The condi-tion of the script itself was far better than any other she had examined, the lettering standing out as black as coal. She began to read and digest the substance of the text, which was clearly a treatise of sorts on the history of the talisman. It recounted—at odds with modern scholar-ship—a mythical origin of the artifact, identifying it as the heart pulled from the breast of the sun-god Mithra and given to the kings of Persia as the god's chosen people. Carefully, she turned the pages, noting the paleographic markers. The Old Greek script was grammatically correct and accurate for the time period Eckerman indicated, which greatly limited the number of people who could have forged such a document.

In her career, Beth had examined many such works, and the materials and script of this tome, well, it all seemed quite authentic.

She lifted her gaze and stared unseeing into the shadowed corners of the room. Appearances, she knew, could be deceiving. Without undergoing a battery of tests: radiocarbon dating, ink analysis, and multi-spectral imaging, there was no telling for sure whether or not this manuscript was a forgery.

She turned to Walter. "A very interesting book," she said. "Either a significant historical document, one that would generate a whole new perspective on the history of the talisman. Or simply a well-crafted forgery."

A smile turned up the edge of Walter's lips. "A forgery? My dear, what makes you think—"

"On the surface, with the exception of its odd, cylindrical spine, there's no question this manuscript appears authentic. But appearances are only part of the equation. Though the vellum is well aged and though the script is without question of the time, there are certain red flags I can't ignore."

"Dr. Harper—"

"First, the history recounted here," Beth pointed at the tome, "is a complete departure from scholarly consensus. It incorporates the talisman into the rites of a Mithraic cult, an ancient and ultimately failed mystery religion."

With those words, she could see the veins in Walter's temples begin to blue and expand.

"Also," Beth continued, "there's the matter of the tome's context. The book rests in your hands, not in the hands of a reputable museum or university. There's no telling where it came from. And frankly, Mr. Walter, you're a man who cannot be trusted."

Walter held up a hand. "Dr. Harper, before you go any further, may I ask you a question?"

"If you must."

"You have personally handled the talisman. Is that not correct?"

"That's correct."

"And you have examined the entire band of relief that encircles it. Is that not also correct?"

"That's correct."

"Well, since the only surviving images of the talisman are those found on the monuments at Persepolis, and since those same images depict the stone from but a single angle, then it's fair to say you are the first expert since the days of the ancient kings to have actually studied the relief in its entirety—all the way around the stone?"

"That's right," Beth said. "Where are you going with this?"

"If you would, Dr. Harper, please gently turn to the page just before the *Histories* and tell me what it is you see."

Beth stared at Walter, who now appeared eager, standing erect with his hands clasped firmly together. She turned her attention back to the manuscript and carefully lifted over the pages. At the location Walter indicated, she saw a series of wonderfully inked illustrations that had been sketched below a passage of ancient Greek. She began to read aloud, "*Τοῦ δ' ἑρμηνεύειν τὰ φυλακτηρίου αἰνίγματα ἔνδον εὑρετέα ἡ ἀρχή.* Of interpreting the Talisman's enigmas, within is to be found the first step."

"Your translation is impeccable, Dr. Harper."

"A riddle?"

"Nothing of the sort," Walter said. "The passage means only that the *Telesma* is the key to understanding our place in the cosmos, Mithra's divine plan."

Beth's gaze fell below the text to the ancient illustrations. And she was stunned by what she saw there. Each of the talisman's relief scenes was depicted, every one of them, exactly as she remembered: the amassing army, the defiant charioteer, the talisman and the blazing sun, the winged beasts, they were all perfectly rendered, as were the scenes on the reverse of the talisman, the scenes undiscovered by modern archaeologists.

"Perhaps you could explain to me, Dr. Harper, how those scenes," Walter lightly brushed the vellum page, "unknown to all but yourself, could have been included in a forgery?"

Beth was at a loss for words. It suddenly seemed to her that Walter was right, that the tome was authentic. She stepped back, whispering involuntarily, "It's amazing."

"Yes, it is," he said, closing the tome with a gentle touch. And as he did, Beth noticed a strange marking upon his hand, one she recognized as—"

"The marking on your hand," she said, "the black sun, it's the same marking bared by the other man, Sarth."

Walter peered at his hand. "Yes, the sign of the Brotherhood. It signifies our devotion to Mithra."

"Then you really aren't treasure hunters…" Her voice trailed off.

"Of course not."

"A cult," Beth blurted out, horrified. "I'm dealing with a cult." Suddenly, she recalled what she knew of the Mithraic rituals, and her body became rigid, images of human sacrifice forming in her mind.

"Allow me to put you at ease, Dr. Harper. It is clear to me you were chosen to be a part of Mithra's greater plan, and for that I am grateful. I can assure you, you will not be unnecessarily harmed. We only demand that which is rightfully ours—the talisman. I understand Sarth's tactics may have appeared extreme, but let me assure you, a compromise has now been reached. You will be happy to know Mr. Lowell has been contacted and arrangements for your return have been made. Tomorrow, this shall all be over."

At the mention of Rick's name, Beth felt an immediate sense of relief. Because of Rick's efforts to reach the talisman, he had saved their lives. She was sure of it. She released a deep breath.

"Now if you'll excuse me, Dr. Harper. I have important matters to attend to. Eat the meal we have provided and rest comfortably. By this time tomorrow, all shall be well." He smiled, carefully lifted the *Telesma* from the table, and left the room.

Again, Beth heard the jangle of keys, followed by the scratching of metal as the lock engaged. In a near daze, she shuffled across the room and dropped herself into a cushioned armchair. This was all too much to fathom: A Mithraic cult, a priceless manuscript, and the most extraordinary artifact of Persian antiquity—the Talisman of Persepolis.

After some time, she shook away her dismay and refocused on the positive. Tomorrow she'd be free, and the nightmare would be over.

She couldn't wait to see Rick again, to hug him and fold herself into his arms. She had made so many mistakes in their relationship, and now she was determined to set about fixing things. There was so much she needed to tell him.

\*      \*      \*

In the darkness of the hall outside Harper's chambers, a figure stood waiting. As Walter approached, Sarth revealed himself and walked alongside. "All is well, Father?"

"All is well," Walter answered. "I have eased the woman's fears, which should ensure her cooperation."

Walter stopped before the softly lit drawing-room, his form split between shadow and light. "Tomorrow, after the arrival of Mr. Lowell, when the talisman is securely in our possession, you are to kill them both."

# 36

RICK STARED THROUGH the panoramic windows of the Arizona room, counting the seconds between thunder and lightning. The winds of the monsoon had become ornery, thrashing the trees and hedges of Mason's estate. Matching the fury outside, a storm of thoughts raged in Rick's mind. He found himself worried sick about Beth, wondering whether these bastards were allowing her any comforts. He wanted desperately to get his hands around their necks and—

Rick heard a heavy knock, followed by footsteps into the foyer, a door opening, and Mason's agitated voice greeting Jarred and complaining that he'd taken too long to arrive. Rick stood to his feet and hurried to the living room, where he saw the big man soaked, but in good cheer, his red face bearing a broad smile. In both hands, clutched against his barrel chest, was a plastic storage container. Upon meeting Rick's gaze, Jarred nodded.

The three men gathered around a large coffee table in the center of the living room, settling onto a wraparound leather sofa. Rick eased himself down gingerly, his ribs still intensely sore. Jarred rested the box on the floor in front of him.

"Were you able to get everything?" Rick asked.

The big man nodded.

Rick worked up a smile, feeling a great sense of relief. "I owe you, big time."

"Mason says you were special forces, a Ranger."

"That's right, back in the day."

"Then we're brothers," Jarred said. "Bringing you these things, it's the least I could do."

Mason sat quietly, watching the exchange, looking a little glum. Rick turned his attention to the box at Jarred's feet. "You mind?"

"You're why I brought it."

Rick pulled off the lid and examined the contents. He'd asked for half a dozen things, and they were all here, carefully packed. He leaned forward and pulled the handgun from its foam mould. It was a Beretta 92, a solid, semi-automatic firearm, no obvious dents or holster wear. He examined the stock, which was in good shape, then looked down the sight. Nothing bent. A quick turn in his hand and he was staring down the barrel, searching for bulges or pitting. He flipped it, slid in the magazine, and pulled back the slide. The feel was smooth and tight. He peered up at Jarred. "Nice gun."

"Thanks."

"A collector?"

The big man smiled.

"Don't worry," Rick said. "I'm good for any damages."

"I believe it."

"You'll forgive me if I don't elaborate too much on my troubles. The fewer people caught up in this mess the better." Rick held up the Beretta. "I can assure you, though, the gun is just for protection."

"Understood." There was a brief silence before Jarred began to speak, making small talk. "So, Rick, when were you active?"

"In '89, part of the 3rd Ranger Battalion."

"Panama?"

"Yeah, I was there in December of that year, securing the Rio Hato Military Airfield. My team later moved into Panama City and took the military headquarters of the PDF. Not a pretty time. How about you?"

"Pushing papers now," Jarred said. "But before my ass started polishing chairs, I did two tours in the Gulf War."

"And now you're a career man?"

"With each passing year it seems more likely."

"Nothing wrong with that," Rick said. "It's an honorable profession."

"Yeah, well, they keep sucking me in with incentives." Jarred grinned. "I re-upped last month with a big bonus."

"What's your M.O.S.?"

"Information Technology Specialist."

Rick glanced over at Mason, who was squirming in his seat. The glum look was gone. He was all smiles. "You military guys have a natural bond, you stick together, huh?"

Jarred and Rick both shrugged.

Mason's grin widened. "Hey, you think if I had been in the Army and the three of us were in the same unit together, we'd have all been buddies?" He stretched his neck and waited, eager for their response. "Do you think?"

Jarred laughed. "I don't know, Mason. You and I, we're different people. I can't see you and Rick having much in common either."

Mason's smile dissolved away. "Yeah, well, I just thought maybe…"

Rick turned over the gun in his hand, gave it one last look, then popped out the clip and returned it to the mould.

"I'd best get out of your way now," Jarred said. There was a brief hesitation, then all three men stood and walked to the front door, where Rick extended a hand. The big man took it and shook hard.

"Good luck with your troubles," he said. "Call me when things are smoothed over. We'll get a beer, you can return everything then."

"Deal," Rick said. "You've been a big help."

Minutes later, Jarred's car pulled from the drive, disappearing into the watery darkness.

Back on the sofa, Rick stuffed his pack into the container and snapped tight the lid. "I couldn't have gotten my hands on these things without your help," he told Mason.

"So, that's it?" the little guy said, scratching his thatch of red hair. "You're just going to drive to Monument Pass and have a gunfight?"

"Hell no," Rick said. "That's the last thing I want to do."

"Then how do you plan to get Beth back?"

"A trade," Rick said. "Beth for the talisman."

Mason's face lit up. "You're taking them the talisman?"

"That's what they're demanding, it's what they expect, but it's not what I'm going to do." Rick looked toward the window and stared out, unseeing. "If I take them the talisman, in a place like Monument Pass, the desert, no one around, they'll kill Beth and me both."

"Then what are you going to do?"

"Meet as planned and convince them to let Beth go. Afterward, I'll take them to the artifact personally, hand it over on better terms in safer surroundings."

"What safer surroundings?"

"A bus station or an airport terminal, somewhere with lots of people and security cameras, somewhere the Brotherhood wouldn't dare try anything stupid."

Mason was nodding. "How do I fit in?"

"Once I see that Beth is okay and the Brotherhood releases her, I'll call you with a specific location. You'll bring the talisman."

"You mean you're just going to give it to them?"

"If everything goes as planned and Beth is safe and secure, these assholes can have it. Damn stone's brought everybody nothing but trouble."

"Christ, Rick, this all sounds risky."

"Can't get the police involved and I don't have time to recruit a special ops team." Rick chuckled nervously. "No other way."

There was a brief silence before Mason said, "Do you have the talisman here?"

Rick nodded to the container.

"Shouldn't I put it in the safe?"

"Not a bad idea," Rick said. "One thing, though. Is Eckerman still in town?"

Mason's answer was quick. "No, no, he took off early this morning, before the storm rolled in. Said since he couldn't reason with you, there was no sense sticking around."

"Good. I wouldn't want him anywhere near the artifact."

"Right," Mason said. "No problem there."

Rick removed the pack from the box, pulled out the wrap with the talisman. Holding it up, he said, "Here's the rock that's caused all this trouble." He passed it to Mason, who took it with both hands, unwrapped it, then held it high against the lighted ceiling. He gawked at it in much the same way he had days earlier at the studio.

Rick said, "It has to stay in the safe until I call you, okay?"

"Sure, of course." Mason re-wrapped the stone and started for the stairway. Rick reached out and touched him on the arm. It was critical Mason understood the magnitude. "I'm relying on you. Beth's relying on you. We can't make a mistake."

"I understand, Rick. You can count on me." He turned away and hurried upstairs, the talisman in hand.

*       *       *

Early the next morning, Rick sat at the table in the Arizona room, staring out the window, surprised at the brightness of the morning. The winds had died and the thunderheads dispersed, leaving in their wake a bright turquoise sky. The only sign of yesterday's storm was the scattered puddles that spotted the grounds, and even they had already begun to evaporate under the warming sun.

Mason walked into the room, his hair a bush of red tangles. The freckled skin around his eyes was furrowed and swollen, and Rick wondered whether he had gotten any sleep.

"You okay?" Rick asked.

Mason's thick lips were curled in a frown. He shrugged. "Yeah, I'm fine, just bad sleep. Got a lot in the old noggin that I'm wrestling with."

With a million worries of his own, Rick had no time to play therapist. "Look, I've written a few things down for you." He pointed to a folded sheet of paper lying on the table. "This afternoon, when I call your cell, I'll need you to drive the talisman to the location on that paper. You've got to be quick and you've got to be available."

Mason nodded.

"I also wrote down some instructions, should things go wrong and I don't make it back."

"Don't talk like that."

"It's a possibility."

Mason nodded, then stared at Rick. "My jacket fits you real nice. It's way too baggy on me. When you get back, you can keep it, a gift."

Rick stood from the chair, lifted the Beretta from the table and tucked it in his jeans. Then he grabbed the topographic map, slid it into a back pocket. He stepped forward and reached out to Mason, gripped him on the shoulder. "It's because of your help Beth and I stand a chance," he said. "I want you to know I appreciate you."

Mason's frown turned into a smile. "I'll see the two of you later, right?"

"You bet."

They walked to the foyer, Mason handed him a key. "The Jeep's in the second bay. I woulda given you the Jag, but my loyalty only goes so far." His grin deepened.

Rick opened the large maple door, stepped onto the porch and stared out over Mason's estate. The sun, resting low on the horizon, cast long shadows from the trees. Birds sang a cheerful melody, excited by the passing of the weather. Rick took a deep breath and turned to Mason. "Remember last night, when you asked Jarred and I whether we would've all been buddies, had we served in the same unit together?"

Mason peered up. "Yeah, I remember."

"You and I, we may not always see eye to eye at work," Rick said. "But when the going gets tough you come through. That's a hell of a quality in a man, one I always admired in a fellow soldier. So yeah, I think you and I, had we been in the same unit together, we would've been buddies."

Mason smiled and said, "Be safe, I'll wait for your call."

## 37

LIKE A LONG, black needle, Highway 163 pierced the vast, red-stained desert that was Arizona's Monument Pass. Sitting atop the crest of a broad anticline, the valley was in fact a cemented plateau, over five thousand feet above sea level, a geological wonder in the heart of the Navajo Reservation. Its rocky landscape teamed with clusters of green cliffrose and bright yellow blossoms of rabbitbrush. The rains had passed here, darkening the loose soil and reviving the leafy covering of the occasional juniper.

It was 10:36 a.m. as Rick Lowell raced down the highway, peering at the great stone mesas underscoring the distant horizon. Quickly approaching the pass, he stared ahead, awed by the massive buttes and spires that rose like titans from the crumbling mounds of shale.

Shadows swallowed the Jeep as Rick flew into the pass, searching for the white cross he'd been told would mark the trail. Half a mile ahead a white Range Rover sat idle on the shoulder. A dark-skinned man with a cowboy hat squeezed between his fists leaned casually against the rear hatch. Rick eased off the accelerator and slowed to sixty. As he approached, he strained to see the man's face, nearly missing the crooked white cross that jutted up from the soil fifty yards ahead. This had to be it. And the man was probably his contact, some grunt sent to escort him or to give him further instructions.

Rick slowed to a stop ten yards from the turnoff, adjusted the gun tucked hidden at his waistband, then cut the jeep's engine. After stepping from the car, he smoothed over his jacket and took in a lungful of air, heavy with the syrupy scent of purple sage. Rick stared appraisingly at the man leaning against the Rover. His face was dark and weathered, an Indian, clearly. He bore the expression of a man expecting someone.

Rick waited, standing near the Jeep, eyeing him suspiciously. At length, the Indian wedged the cowboy hat over his head, slapped it snug, then began kicking away clods of soil packed between the tread of his boots. Finished, he started forward in an easy gate, making no threatening gestures, just ambling ahead, hands swinging at his sides. A shimmer of sunlight flashed from something pinned at his chest, and immediately Rick could discern the form of a silver star, a badge.

*The man was a cop.*

Rick walked forward, ready to lay it on thick if necessary. He could say he was lost and needed directions, the way to the Tribal Park Visitor Center.

A few more feet and Rick smiled, holding up his folded map. "Darn thing's topographic, got the wrong kind of map. Shows contours and elevations, that sort of thing, useless for finding the Visitor Center. Maybe you could help me out?"

The officer stopped, eyed him suspiciously. "You Lowell?"

Rick hesitated. "That's right."

"Then come with me," the officer said, gesturing to his SUV.

"How about I follow you in the Jeep?"

The officer shook his head no. "I was told to drive you out personally, leave if you refused." He turned and walked toward the Rover, not waiting for an answer.

Rick followed the officer cautiously, noticing an old-style holster and pistol strapped to his side. It had been twisted around to fit almost at the hamstring, which was why Rick hadn't it seen earlier. The officer motioned for him to get in at the passenger side. Rick rounded the car, observing that it was covered in dust and emblazoned with the words *Navajo Nation Police*. He peered over the cab. "Who sent you?"

The man stared back and turned a crooked smile, eyes hidden in the shadow of his hat. He rubbed together his thumb and forefinger.

"Ben Franklin and his nine brothers." He opened the door and eased himself inside.

The Rover bumped east along the rocky trail, dipping into the shadow of Merrick Butte. The massive formation, with its layers of burning sandstone, loomed high in the distance, framed by an ugly, ever darkening sky. Though the weather had improved, it seemed another storm was in the works.

Rick sat quietly in the cab, pushing back the pain in his side and preparing mentally for what was to come. These people wouldn't be happy when they learned he'd left the talisman behind. Still, he had no choice. Bringing the stone was suicide. His only chance was to convince these people to free Beth and take him instead. Afterward, he'd lead them to the airport, complete the trade, and be done with the whole damn thing.

Sidelong, he glanced at the officer, who seemed overly relaxed, palm resting atop the wheel. He hummed tunelessly to himself, uninterested in who he was driving deep into the desert, or why. His radio squawked and he adjusted the tuning. The reception cleared enough to resolve a washed-out voice. "Dispatch to Officer Sani, you read me?"

He lifted the mike. "Officer Sani here."

"Got a complaint," said the female voice. "Mosi says her old man's drunk and locked her out of the trailer again, third time this week. She says if he does it again she'll poison his whiskey with snakeroot. You wanna drive by and smooth things over?"

"Can't now, sugar, I'm on my way to Lady Finger. Got word of rock climbers trying to hump her again. Send Yiska. Mosi has an eye for him, she'll listen." Officer Sani replaced the mike.

There was a long silence as the Rover drove deeper into the desert, nearing another towering butte. Rick decided to probe for information. "Mind if I ask who paid you?"

"Don't know."

"Aren't you a little curious?"

"Ain't curious."

"A thousand dollars, just to drive me out into the desert?"

"And ignore the helicopters."

"Helicopters?"

"That's what I said."

Rick turned away, puzzled. Why in the hell would the Brotherhood need helicopters? Then a thought occurred to him: Maybe they planned to fly in, make the exchange, then fly out again. It made sense, minimizing risk. By air, they'd be able to see for miles, verify that Rick had come alone. Any sign of trouble or the authorities and escape would be a cinch.

The Rover bounced onto another trail, one that skirted the base of a massive butte. This close to the formation, Rick felt like a grain of sand. It was monstrous, jutting up from the ground like a giant molar. The car skidded to a stop in a clearing of rocky soil. Officer Sani turned to him. "Whatever it is you and your friends are up to, good luck, but don't involve the locals. Understand me? Now, if you don't mind, I'd like you to get the hell out of my car."

Rick turned from the officer and looked out the window. Aside from the imposing presence of the butte and the vast number of shrubs that blanketed the soil, the surrounding desert was empty. Nobody around. "You want me to get out? Here?"

"That's right."

Rick looked around again, then pushed open the door and stepped out onto the hot soil. He shut the door.

Wasting no time, Sani gassed the accelerator and skidded off, bouncing back down the trail toward the highway.

Rick waved away the cloud of dust kicked up by the tires and watched as the Rover rounded the butte and disappeared into the shadows. For a moment, Rick stood there, thinking, his hand scratching at the stubble on his chin. He turned to the east, toward the gray horizon, watching as the storm's second front rolled westward.

# 38

MASON SAT NESTLED on the living room couch, his eyes fixed upon the glassy surface of the talisman. Cupped between both hands, the obsidian artifact hummed with an unseen energy. He could almost feel it. The relief images cut around the talisman's center were as impressive as any piece of art he'd ever laid his eyes upon. Each scene depicted an event in a much broader story, and the craftsman who'd fashioned the stone, Mason thought, had done a remarkable job etching it in fine detail. Close inspection of the battle scene revealed an army whose mass of individual soldiers bore shields and brandished spears. The charioteer who defied them, too, was carved with striking precision: his beard in curls, his robes covered with Persian symbols, fluttering against an unseen wind. No wonder the thing was worth a million bucks.

But what impressed Mason most wasn't the incredible craftsmanship, but the enormity of the stone's two thousand year history. It was an artifact possessed by some of the greatest heavyweights of Western civilization: the brave and cunning Cyrus II; the rough-and-tumble Darius I; and the biggest bad boy of them all, Alexander the Great. And now here *he* was, Mason Manning, just like the rest of them, gripping the stone in his hand, feeling its power. The thought of having something in common with Alexander the Great sent a jolt of excitement up Mason's spine.

He turned the talisman over to examine more of the relief. A creature caught his eye, winged and hideous. Mason stared at it closely.

It was an odd beast. Without its wings it could've easily been mistaken for—

There was a rap against the French doors that opened to the guesthouse, and Mason looked up to see Eckerman and his blue eyes peering inside. Mason covered the talisman and hurried to the door, opened it.

"Ah, can you smell the clean air?" Eckerman asked with a bright smile. He inhaled deeply, then stepped inside. "You were right, my dear boy. The storm has brought a much-needed change."

"Yeah," Mason said, shutting the door, "but have you seen the horizon? We're in for another round."

"Who cares?" Eckerman waved a dismissive hand. "I'm much too elated to fret over something as trivial as the weather."

"Have you had breakfast?"

"No, no, I have no hunger, thank you." Eckerman caressed his hands as if applying a lotion. His gaze fed upon the room. "I see Mr. Lowell has departed the premises."

"Yeah, he's gone."

"Splendid." Eckerman turned up his palms. "Well?"

"Well what?"

"Well, were you successful? Did you secure the talisman?"

"Oh, the talisman. Yeah, I got it."

"Wonderful!" Eckerman beamed. "Absolutely, positively wonderful!"

"Now hold on a second."

"Right, of course. For a man of my years, such a display must appear unseemly."

"There's a problem."

"A problem?"

Mason scratched his head. "We can't keep it."

"I beg your pardon?"

"The talisman, we can't keep it."

"I don't understand," Eckerman said. "Did you not recover it?"

"Yeah, I did, but we can't keep it," Mason repeated, a bit more firmly this time. "I'm gonna have to put it in the safe."

"No, no, it will be more secure with me."

"No, it's going into the safe."

Eckerman's smile disappeared. His shoulders slacked. "But what of the Brotherhood, if somehow they find it? Have you forgotten the danger that the stone carries?"

"Come on, Peter, the talisman having powers? Those were nothing but stories. Fun to listen to, but in the end, just entertainment."

"Have you gone mad?"

"No, but I'll get there if you keep pushing me."

"Mr. Manning, Mason, my dear boy, think about what you're saying."

"I *have* been," Mason said. "A lot, in fact. And I've begun to realize what's happening to Rick is real, not a game. Him and Beth are in serious trouble, and I'm not gonna let them down." Mason picked up the relic. "This is going in the safe. And that's that."

Eckerman rushed forward. "Please, you must reconsider. I...we are so close to success. And as for Mr. Lowell, you owe him nothing. You mustn't forget, deep down inside, the man loathes you."

"Are you kidding me?" Mason snapped back. "Rick and I, we're as thick as thieves. And you know, had we been in the Army together, the two of us would have been good friends."

The old man's voice suddenly changed, filling with rage. "Give me the talisman, damn it!"

"Whoa, buddy. I think you're forgetting whose spread you're standing in."

"Give it to me, you bloody fool!"

Mason's jaw nearly dropped. He felt his ears go hot. "Pack your things and get the hell out of here, you old kook. Beth was right about you all along."

Mason twisted the wrap tighter around the talisman and marched toward the stairs, Eckerman howling in tow.

"You must not!" the old man was now screaming, over and over again.

Mason ignored him, hurrying up the stairs as fast as his short legs would carry him. Atop the landing, he turned, but Eckerman was still behind him, red-faced and sucking wind.

"I told you to pack your things, old man. You're not welcome here anymore." Mason turned back for the office.

Then the old man's voice changed, becoming deep and throaty, like the cry of an injured grizzly. "Damn it! I said give it to me, now!" There came an awful scraping sound, stone against marble.

Mason spun on his heel and caught a glimpse of the pedestal that displayed the statuette of a Hopi Kachina. But the statuette was missing. In a flash he saw Eckerman's face: skin as red as a burn, eyes wild with fury. The old man swung recklessly. There came a blur of brightly painted stone, and Mason felt a sudden crush against his temple. His knees buckled. An oily warmth oozed over his face. Then all went dark.

# 39

RICK LOWELL HESITATED, looking high to the east where the afternoon sun lingered in the sky. Near the horizon, storm clouds continued to gather, dark and foreboding, sweeping a wide swath across distant mesas. Rick closed his eyes and breathed deeply. *Beth, stay strong. I'm coming for you.* He opened his eyes and turned his gaze to the massive buttes and spires rising up around him. He searched their crumbled bases for any sign of activity: people or cars. He saw neither.

Then from the north came a hum, faint, distant. Rick strained to discern its type. Within seconds the sound intensified, and he could tell it was the low, rhythmic thwack of a helicopter rotor. He turned and scanned the sky. Against the graying blue, a dark speck appeared. He lifted his binoculars, bringing the object clearly into focus. It was a helicopter, all right, a small four-seater, black and shaped like a teardrop. Sunlight glistened from its surface as it dipped slightly, banked, then made a beeline for his position. Rick stuffed the binoculars back in his shoulder pack and waited. Absently, his fingertips fell to the butt of his gun, and he braced himself for a confrontation.

Moments later, the helicopter swooped from the sky, steadying itself into a hover ten yards away, then slowly touched down. The main rotor whipped furiously, its backwash scattering brush and stirring up clouds of dust. The rear door swung open and a brawny man emerged, the same son-of-a-bitch who'd been searching for the talisman in their hotel room. The muscles in Rick's body tensed, sending a needle-like pain pulsing down the side of his ribcage. He winced, took a slow, deep breath, then forced himself to think back to his military days. During operations, mission success always hinged upon conditioning—physical and psychological. Control of each was critical. Today could be no different. Rick would have to eliminate his attachment to Beth. He'd have to remove her from the equation, completely. He had to see her as the objective, nothing more.

He watched as the big guy lumbered toward him, crouching slightly and shielding his eyes from the billowing dust. A few feet away, he stopped, tucked his shirt into his jeans, and stared at Rick appraisingly. "Okay, douche bag, the stone, let's have it."

Rick had prepared for this possibility, being met by a goon, a nobody, someone who'd demand the talisman, with Beth nowhere to be seen.

"You hard of hearing," the man said. "Give me the rock."

"I don't think so," Rick said, forcing himself to control his anger. "First, I want to see Beth." Glancing at the guy's heavy hands, Rick could see his movements were slow and without grace. If he went for a gun, Rick would kill him where he stood.

"Give me the talisman, *then* you can see the bitch."

The way this gorilla was referring to Beth, Rick wanted to kick out his knee and break his skull. Instead, Rick opted to keep his cool. "First, I see Beth. On this point, there will be no compromise."

The man studied Rick, as if measuring his resolve. "Okay, have it your way." He motioned to the chopper. "Get in."

Mindful of sudden surprises, Rick took a seat in the rear cabin. The big guy settled next to him. The pilot, who was wearing sunglasses and a baseball cap, adjusted a few instruments, preparing to lift off. Rick wondered whether he was part of the Brotherhood's organization or just a hired hand. After some thought, he decided it really didn't matter. If the pilot interfered in any way, hindered Rick's fight to save Beth, he'd be signing his own death warrant.

The chopper lifted off, then quickly banked south, penetrating deeper into the rocky expanse of desert, skimming over shale-capped mesas and slender pinnacles of sandstone. The rotors thumped rapidly, roaring like a beast, generating a steady vibration.

The pilot worked the lever and nudged the stick gently, urging the chopper skyward. He picked up a transmission on his headset. "Didn't copy that. Say again, Mr. Walter." There was a long pause as the pilot listened, hand touched to his ear. "Roger that. I'll get on it, sir, right after the drop."

Rick glanced out the window as the chopper tore across the landscape. Below, patches of low-growing shrubs blurred by, flashes of muted green. Fast approaching the face of a massive butte, the pilot suddenly pulled up, swinging the chopper high, rapidly gaining altitude and breaking over the butte's weathered capstone.

Atop the summit, human activity caught Rick's attention. At the western end he observed a large transport helicopter, parked and powered down, its cargo doors wide open. Working nearby were six men Rick had never seen before. Two, he assumed were pilots, given their green jumpsuits and dark-visored helmets. The other four men could have been anyone, but seeing how they were big and stupid looking, most likely they were hired muscle. All in all, there were far too many for Rick to handle on his own. He shifted in his seat, thanking God for having been first to reach the talisman, his one ace in the hole.

At the eastern edge of the butte, over a rectangular section of level stone, Rick could see a temple of sorts that had been erected: Parallel stone benches running ten feet apart, ending at a raised dais, upon which had been built an altar. On the altar was a large, lumpy object draped in a sheet of golden silk. Surrounding the entire makeshift temple, a dozen copper braziers threw up long flames, flickering against a steady wind. Ten figures in scarlet robes, with faces hidden behind hideous animal masks, stood next to the benches, facing each other, rocking from side to side. Their robes fluttered violently. In the center of the spectacle, Rick could make out an eleventh figure—also masked, but garbed in a contrasting white robe. He sat slumped and motionless on a stone chair. What in the hell were these people up to? Suddenly, Rick remembered what Beth had told him. The Brotherhood was a cult, a bunch of fanatics, lunatics really, and by the look of things here on the butte, they were off in the head more than Rick ever would have imagined.

The pilot leveled the chopper, coming quickly to a hover.

Slowly, he glided toward the western end of the summit, heading for a landing spot marked by a circle of flares.

Eagerly, Rick searched for Beth, praying to see her alive and healthy. But there was no sign of her.

None.

He turned to the big guy. "Where the hell is Beth?"

"Take it easy, will you? There's the bitch." He lifted his heavy arm, pointed below to the parked helicopter.

Rick spun back and looked. He spotted a thin woman stepping out cautiously from one of the helicopter's rear transport doors, waves of short black hair whipping in the wind.

*Beth!*

Rick's chopper was still in flight, approaching slowly, yet he felt the urge to leap from its doors, to run to her and take her in his arms. He caught himself getting overly emotional. A mistake. Keep it together, damn it. You're not out of the woods yet.

"Happy now?" the big man said. "Hey, if things don't work out for you today, you can be sure I'll take real good care of your woman. Real good care, if you know what I mean."

Rick's feeling of joy suddenly disappeared, replaced by a fierce sense of outrage. He had an answer for this son-of-a-bitch. He'd kick him out of the goddamn chopper.

"Hell if your fists aren't balled up tight," the man said. "Bet you'd like to take a swing at me. Am I right?"

Rick took another deep breath. The guy's goading you, he reminded himself. He's trying to get you to do something stupid. Rick had come this far and was so close to getting Beth back. He had to keep his cool. Soon, all of this would be over, nothing but a shitty memory, a story to tell Jarred over that beer he owed him. "Why would I want to swing at you?" Rick said. "You're such a pleasant person to be around. Let's just wrap things up. What do you say?"

A heavy gust buffeted the chopper, and the pilot fought to keep it under control, easing it slowly off-kilter to the landing spot. Once grounded, he turned and motioned for Rick and the big guy to get out. Rick did as he was told, eager to make the exchange and put all this behind him.

As Rick ducked out of the chopper, he heard Beth cry out his name, her voice carrying over a steady wind. He peered up, careful to keep a crouch under the spinning rotor. From across a stretch of uneven rock he saw her, worried eyes and a nervous smile. His pulse quickened. He broke into a sprint, watching his feet as he ran.

Seconds later she was in his arms, her hands clutching his face. She kissed him hard, then pulled away and peered up at him with startling jade eyes. "Outside of Chendekar's office, I thought they'd killed you," she said, "the worst feeling I've ever experienced, a living nightmare. But you're alive! Oh, thank God!" She planted another kiss on his lips. "I'm sorry, Rick, I'm so sorry. It's a fine mess I've gotten us into."

"Never mind that," he told her, "what's done is done. I'm going to get us out of here."

"You mustn't be in such a haste to leave," came an unfamiliar voice.

From behind an open cargo door stepped a man garbed in the same scarlet robes as the weirdoes at the other end of the butte. Rick suspected the man was middle-aged, maybe sixty, but he appeared unnaturally young, with thick brown hair and a sharp jaw-line, under which was conspicuously absent the sagging gullet present in most men his age.

"Undoubtedly, you are the intrepid Mr. Lowell. I've heard a great deal about you."

"And who the hell are you?" Rick demanded.

"Jonathan Walter," the man answered without hesitation. "Pater Patrum of the Brotherhood. Mithra's Chosen."

The chopper powered up its rotor blades to an ear-splitting RPM, then in a roar it lifted off and raced eastward toward the darkening sky.

Rick released Beth from his grasp and assessed his surroundings. The thugs in the Windbreakers he'd seen from the chopper had sprung into action, circling them at a distance, hands tucked high in their jackets. Rick assumed they were well-armed and ready to draw out. At this point, going for his own gun would be suicide. He realized the only thing keeping them alive was the talisman. He turned to Walter. "About this artifact of yours—"

"Yes, of course, in good time," Walter interrupted. "First, I have something for you, a gift you may consider it. The Call to Mithra has begun, and I shall allow you to bear witness." He gestured in the direction of the temple, where the masked figures continued to sway and chant. "You'll excuse me, but I must preside over the opening liturgy." Without delay, Walter turned and marched off, carefully traversing the butte's capstone, the hem of his robe snapping in the wind.

Feeling a sudden presence, Rick turned to see an astoundingly tall, dark-skinned man looming behind him—the same man who'd shot at them in the laboratory, and who'd abducted Beth and forced her to the hotel. On the phone he'd called himself Sarth. He tipped his head slightly, as if to say he was pleased to finally meet up close and personal.

Rick turned his attention back to Walter, who had taken up position at the base of the dais, between it and the seated man. Walter now donned a golden Phrygian cap and in both hands clutched an old and weathered book. From it, he began to chant indiscernible phrases.

"If you would be so kind," Sarth whispered from behind them. "Advance to the perimeter of the Mithraeum."

Rick turned to Beth, nodded that it would be okay. The two walked slowly toward the temple. Sarth followed closely behind. As they neared, Rick could make out detail that was impossible from the chopper. The ten figures gently rocking on their feet were all men; this he determined from their height and weight. The eleventh man, seated on the stone chair, had his arms draped behind him, his feet and knees closed. He appeared bound under the loose-fitting robes.

"Strange," Beth said. She had become wide-eyed, staring almost academically at the perverse scene.

"What is it?" Rick said.

"Aside from Walter, who's clearly the ceremony's Pater Patrum, Father of all Fathers, there should be a twelfth man in the sanctum."

"A twelfth man? How do you know?"

"This is a Mithraic ceremony," Beth said, "by Walter's own admission. Notice they've constructed the temple from stone and at a high elevation. This is tradition, to be closer to Mithra, the sun-god, who Himself, according to myth, was born from the rock. It all fits, except the twelfth man. He's missing."

Rick turned back and scrutinized the ceremony.

"You see," Beth continued. "Each of the masked men represents a figure of the zodiac. Twelve signs, twelve men. Yet here there are only eleven."

"There's the reason," Rick said, pointing. "Look there, on the bench." Between two men rested a folded robe. And upon it was a mask.

Beth's eyes followed the line traced by Rick's finger. "Yes, I see now, the final man has yet to arrive."

One by one, members of the cult moved to the perimeter of the temple, each approaching a waist-high brazier, urged on by Walter's fervent chanting. At the braziers, they stopped and sprinkled a powdery substance over the blaze, enraging the flames and sending smoke roiling high into the air. The scent of mint hung strong for a moment, then quickly dissipated, carried away by the shifting winds.

As smoke cleared from around one of the nearby figures, Rick studied his hideous mask. It was fashioned of wood, carved in a manner reminiscent of Munch's Scream—stretched long and warped. It depicted an arachnid of sorts, with a pair of protruding mandibles, and eyes that were slits of darkness. Two jointed stalks projected from its sides, ending in sharp, open pincers. Immediately, Rick realized he was staring at the scorpion, one of the twelve signs of the zodiac.

Walter's chanting grew louder, and in unison the robed figures joined in, their low, maniacal droning mingling with the howl of the wind. The sun had climbed to its peak overhead, but fingers of the approaching storm had now touched it, eclipsing it in part, illuminating the butte under a ghostly half-light. With the book closed and held high over his head, Walter cried aloud what sounded like the script of a demonic spell. Behind him, further intensifying the scene, a knot of thunderheads gathered, piling forward like exhaust from an army of smokestacks.

Then, all at once, Walter ceased his crazed chanting, spun on his heel and in one swift motion reached over the altar and yanked away the golden spread covering the massive lump. There, Rick could see the dark, severed head of a bull, its horns sheathed in silver, a thick gray tongue protruding from its mouth. Open eyes stared lifelessly toward the sky.

Beth gasped and Rick took her by the arm. He could feel her body trembling.

"What's happening?" he said.

"This is the Tauroctony." Beth's voice was barely audible. "The ritual slaying of the bull."

"I don't understand. Why would they kill a bull?"

"To acknowledge Mithra's power and supremacy," she said. "The ancients believed the god to be responsible for the movement of the spring equinox out of the constellation Taurus the bull and into the constellation Aries the Ram. For reasons of planting and harvesting, this was a date of great importance, and thus its change in the heavens was a remarkable event, instilling awe and confusion. The slaying of the bull represents this shift. You see, if Mithra could move the entire universe, then He could in fact control everything within it."

Rick shook his head. "It's all so bizarre."

"To us, yes. But to Walter and the others, it's fundamental to their faith. They truly believe that by performing this ceremony, they will appease Mithra and somehow curry His favor."

The masked figures had returned to their original positions and resumed the gentle sway, which now made sense to Rick. It was a movement to represent the shift in the equinox. Walter, too, had changed position, standing at the base of the altar, his back turned. He leaned bear-like over the bull's severed head. When he finally turned, Rick could see in his hand the glint of steel, a long, silver dagger, polished to a brilliant luster. Slowly, Walter stalked toward the seated figure, moving ceremoniously forward as the other worshippers chanted wildly. Rick's eyes were drawn to the white-cloaked man, to the mask covering his face: a stubbed snout, two hollowed eyes, and horns like wooden tongs. It was the face of a bull.

Suddenly, Rick realized what was happening, and a feeling of indescribable horror washed over him. Now standing behind the stone chair, Walter ripped off the man's mask, revealing a face bruised and bloodied beyond recognition. Over the wind, Rick heard a painful groan escape the man's swollen lips. This was no participant. Like the bull, this guy was to be the sacrifice. And Rick couldn't just stand by and watch. He had to do something, anything, but whatever it was, he had to do it now.

# 40

MASON AWOKE TO an explosion of thunder, a rumble so loud the house seemed to shake to its very foundation. He opened his eyes and tried to lift his head. A dull, throbbing ache pulsed through the back of his brain. With a Herculean effort, he sat up and braced his back against the landing's banister. Still a bit groggy, he tried to remember what had happened. He looked around, saw where he was sitting. Behind him, his beautiful Indian Kochina lay in pieces on the marble floor, its feathered headdress stained with something red. He reached a hand to his temple, felt a flaky substance, rubbed some off, stared.

Dried blood.

His broken Kochina—in a rush it all came back to him. The old man had cold-cocked him, done quite a number on his head.

Eckerman, you prick.

Then, as if slapped in the face, Mason felt a sudden wave of panic.

*The talisman!*

He searched around the landing, didn't see it, slid himself against the banister and peered down the stairs, nothing. It was gone. That son-of-a-bitch Eckerman had taken it.

Amidst another crash of thunder, Mason struggled to his feet. Through a transom window, he saw a flash of lightning, followed by another deafening boom. The second front of the summer monsoon had hit, and he could hear the rain coming down in a fury.

Then more panic. How long had he been unconscious? Had

Rick already called? Weak-kneed, Mason descended the stairs, using the railing for support. Every footfall was like a landmine exploding inside his head. At the foyer, he stopped and looked at the clock. He'd been unconscious for nearly two hours. He staggered to the kitchen, checked the phone.

The message light flashed zero.

Rick hadn't called, thank God.

He felt a sense of relief.

At the refrigerator, he pulled out a can of Pepsi and walked to the breakfast bar, rolling the cold aluminum back and forth across his forehead. Christ, it felt good. He perched himself atop a stool and moved the can to the back of his neck, continuing the therapeutic roll. Damn if the old man hadn't double-crossed him. The prick. Mason let out a heavy sigh, then jerked up his head, relief quickly fading.

It had been his responsibility to safeguard the talisman. Rick was relying on him. It was their only bargaining chip. Without it, Rick and Beth were dead. A sickness settled in the pit of Mason's stomach.

He had to get the talisman back.

But how?

Simple. He'd have to find the old man.

But where?

He thought hard.

The airport. Of course! It was a no-brainer. Eckerman was probably beating feet back to Germany.

Mason's first instinct was to run the Jag to Sky Harbor, check departing international flights, but then he realized he'd need help. He'd have to nab the old man before he boarded, and Mason knew he couldn't do it alone.

Jarred. He'd call his buddy, have him hurry his ass over. With a little luck they'd find Eckerman lounging in the airport cafe gloating over his little shenanigan, sipping espressos while he waited for the next flight to Munich. Together Mason and Jarred would be able to nab the son-of-a-bitch and get the talisman back.

Mason slammed down the Pepsi can, picked up the telephone, and dialed the big man's number. "Jarred, Mason here. Listen, I'm in a world of trouble, and here's how you're gonna help me fix it."

## 41

WHITE ROBES FLUTTERING in the wind, the seated man whimpered and groaned, his badly beaten face lolling over his chest. He'd been wearing the mask of the sacrificial bull, which Rick now realized meant certain death. The crimson-cloaked figures continued their advance, moving wraith-like toward the stone chair, heads cocked, ghostly hands reaching outward. Walter followed closely behind them, the dagger tightly in his grip.

Beth drew in a sharp breath and turned away.

It was an unholy scene, and Rick knew it had to be stopped. He reached to his waistband, going for the Beretta, but as quickly as he drew it, Sarth was upon him, the barrel of his own gun pressing into the base of Rick's skull.

"You can't let this happen," Rick said.

"But it has already begun," was Sarth's cold reply. "Lift your weapon where I can reach it."

Rick hesitated.

"Must I pull the trigger?"

"Do that and you'll never see the talisman."

"I will not ask again."

Rick sensed it was no bluff. Slowly, he lifted the gun within reach of the assassin. Sarth drove out a hand, as quickly as a cobra strike, and snatched it from his grasp.

"Please, you can't allow this to happen."

"It is an offering to Mithra."

"It's murder."

"Murder?" Sarth said. "Hardly. The pathetic Mr. Stewart has betrayed Father, and he will now suffer the consequences. Observe. The manner in which he meets his end will be quite fitting."

"Beth doesn't need to be here. Let her go, take her back to the chopper."

"I think not. She, too, shall bear witness."

Rick saw Beth turn away from the awful scene, hunched with her hands clasped over her ears. Rick, too, wanted to turn away, but as he did, Sarth drove the gun harder against his head. "Face forward. I wouldn't want you to miss a thing."

Reluctantly, Rick did as he was told and turned back.

The figures had now fully encircled the man, shaking their bodies violently, working themselves into a bloodied frenzy while lashing winds buffeted their robes. And over it all, a wavering light from the braziers cast the orgy in a fiendish glow.

From within the confines of the human circle, the silver dagger lifted, and then fell. There came a scream, high and blood-curdling. Rick's stomach turned as he saw a black pool spreading over the naked stone. Then, seconds later, the man's gargling cries stopped and Rick, utterly mortified, hung his head.

For a long moment, he could not move, paralyzed by hatred and anger. How could they have done this? How could they have murdered an innocent man? Then from somewhere in the distance Rick heard a chopper, its rotors faintly humming. He lifted his head and spotted a speck of black against the gray northern sky. He reached out for Beth, touched her arm. Still, she trembled.

Rick knew he had to get her off this damn butte and home to safety. He turned to Sarth. "Alright, you've had your sick fun. We've seen how your deranged organization works. But we'll have no more of it. Beth leaves now, or so help me God you'll never see the talisman again. If you think I'm bluffing, just kill me now and find out, you son-of-a-bitch."

The chopper's roar intensified, and Rick looked to see it carefully touching ground at the western end of the butte. "I want her on that helicopter. Right now. Did you actually think I'd be foolish enough to bring the talisman along? You can keep me with you as insurance. After Beth's called me with word she's somewhere safe, I'll take you to the stone."

Sarth smiled, and for a second Rick thought the assassin might actually laugh. His cold, muddy eyes turned and observed the chopper, now parked and powered down. The passenger door swung open and out stepped a heavy man in a cardigan sweater, his white bushy hair blowing frantically in the wind. Rick and Beth looked at each other in amazement.

"The old man," Beth said. "They've captured Eckerman."

Rick watched as Eckerman glided across the capstone, satchel bouncing against his waist, his movements deft and fluid. He advanced unescorted, with wide blue eyes fixed upon the temple proper. His look betrayed a certain excitement. Clearly, he was not a man in distress.

He moved past Rick and Beth, refusing to meet their gaze, continuing toward the others who, after their murderous orgy, were now standing motionless beside the benches. Eckerman stepped up to the folded robe that lay between the two men and quickly slipped it on. Then, he placed the mask upon his head and carefully lowered it. Rick could see two faces carved into its twisted façade, both alike in every feature save one—the mouth. The first image bared a smile, the second a frown. Gemini—the twins.

Slowly, Eckerman made his way toward Walter, who stood on the dais, powerfully erect, hands bloodied. Upon reaching him, Ecker-man produced a small object from under his robes, then he knelt with his head lowered in deference, offering the object with solemn grace.

"The old man hasn't been captured," Beth said, astounded. "He's one of them. Eckerman's the twelfth man."

Rick wanted to say something, but he couldn't find the words, his concentration fixed upon the object Eckerman had given to Walter. Rick tried hard to discern it; he had an awful feeling.

Sarth jabbed the gun against the base of Rick's skull and in a near whisper said, "It seems your insurance just expired, Mr. Lowell."

Rick watched in sick disbelief as Eckerman threw himself prostrate before Walter, who now stood against a backdrop of amassing thunderheads alive with intermittent flashes of electrical energy. Walter's eyes bulged as if by strangulation, and his mouth was frozen in a demonic smile. Then abruptly, he thrust his hands high up into the air and proclaimed in a thunderous tone, "I present to the Inner Circle, after more than two thousand years in painful obscurity, the Talisman of Persepolis!"

## 42

RICK AND BETH remained frozen, standing shoulder to shoulder atop a dizzying thousand-foot-high butte overlooking the northern Arizona desert. Wind swept across its jagged capstone and lashed at their faces. But only scarcely did Rick feel it. And only slightly did his senses register the rumbling and electrical flashes of the approaching storm. Beth leaned into him, locked her arm around his, staring in near shock at the remnants of the scene that had just unfolded.

The murder, Rick thought, had been a ghoulish act, perpetrated under the guise of a Mithraic sacrifice. It was chilling and sickening and made all the more horrific by the cultists' frenzied screams. Eckerman, who'd warned them of the Brotherhood's threat, turned out to be one of them, and Rick was having a hard time believing it.

"Is the serpent part of the zodiac?" he asked Beth.

"No."

"Well, it ought to be," he said. "And Eckerman should wear its mask. I'd like to arrange it for him, as a permanent implant."

Beth was quiet, still staring at the blood-smeared floor of the temple. Scattered puddles of red rippled in the wind. In a whisper she said, "They have the guns, they have the talisman. There's no reason for them to keep us alive. What are we going to do?"

"I'm working on it."

"Those thunderheads are minutes from sweeping this butte. Soon, this stone will be as slick as ice."

"Then perhaps," came Sarth's hissing voice from behind them, "we should get started."

"Do with me what you will," Rick said, "but leave Beth out of this, please."

"No," Beth answered harshly. "We stick together."

"Your bond is touching," Sarth said. "Really it is." He jammed his gun against the back of Rick's head. "Face forward and step away from Dr. Harper. Stretch out your arms, as did your Christ when He was nailed to the cross."

Rick sidestepped to the right and held out his arms. "That storm's gonna hit any minute. We all need to get off this rock, or it'll be hell up here."

"Do not concern yourself with hell, not just yet anyway. Do as you're told."

Like apparitions, three of the robed figures glided toward Beth. From behind their masks they studied her as if puzzling over a cipher. Then all at once they converged around her, grabbed at her arms and legs, their hands ivory against crimson sleeves. Beth flailed her elbows, trying to shake them off, but as a group, they easily overpowered her, pulling her kicking and biting to the ground. Immediately, they began dragging her in the direction of the stone chair.

Horrified, Rick leapt forward to help her, but was stopped instantly by the deafening report of a gun. He felt a bullet pass inches from his ear.

"The next round will strike true," Sarth warned.

"Let her go!" Rick screamed. "She's done nothing to you."

"Nothing?" Sarth said. "You're mistaken, Mr. Lowell. She is guilty, you are both guilty of handling our sacred relic. The talisman has been touched by hands unclean, and the Inner Circle must now do what is necessary to purify it."

Rick stood with his arms outstretched at the western perimeter of the temple. He peered straight down the aisle between the benches, at the sacrificial stone chair. It was awash in blood. Beth struggled as they pulled her near.

Walter stood motionless at the foot of the altar, his head lowered, the strange book clutched in his hands. The other cultists, including Eckerman, took their positions alongside the benches, and once again they began their demonic sway. Over the howling wind, Rick could hear the chanting grow louder.

A tangle of robed arms forced Beth onto the chair, while two figures remained standing at her side, preventing her escape. As if on queue the braziers flared, throwing up long flames and immersing the temple in a haunting glow. Rick's mind raced, running through tactical maneuvers. But there was nothing that engendered hope. Given the circumstances, each option seemed useless. Rick's breathing quickened and his heart drummed rapidly in his chest.

Then Walter, with his head still lowered, gently turned a page in the book and began reading aloud, still in a language unfamiliar to Rick. Each word, it seemed, was spoken in slow motion, as if careful enunciation was critical to the success of the ceremony. After minutes of droning on, reciting passage after passage, he lifted his head and glared over the temple with maniacal eyes. He shifted the book into one arm, then trumpeted on without its aid, still speaking in tongues.

Rick looked beyond Walter, where a billowing mass of thunderheads, water-saturated and crackling with arcs of electrical energy, had now fully smothered the sun and surrounded the butte's eastern edge. Wind came intermittently, striking with the anger of a whip. Crashes of thunder, seconds apart, eclipsed Walter's oration, yet he continued on, until at last, reaching into his robe, he produced the talisman. Without missing a beat, he thrust the stone high into the swirling air.

And what Rick saw next horrified him.

The talisman lurched in his hand, surprising even Walter, whose eyes bulged. He began shaking it furiously, as if to dislodge some hidden power. Then suddenly, from the black stone, a rush of negative energy issued forth, pouring away in a stream of darkness. It moved as if carried on the crest of a wave, spreading out in a cloud over the temple, toward Beth, toward the swaying figures, toward Rick himself. A piercing cry seemed to emanate from the heart of the thing as it flowed like a river of blackness, swirling around one robed figure, and then another. Quickly, it dropped and surged across the ground, coalescing into a thick mass around the body of the murdered man, where it swelled and contracted, then abruptly vanished, sucked away by the corpse. There came a sudden twisting and writhing as the body seemed to respond to Walter's insane verse. Then the black cloud burst free again, as if from every pore of the dead man's skin. Still, Walter scowled, crying what sounded like words of anguish. Moments later, the swarm made a turn for the altar, narrowed, and in a vile stream of blackness, siphoned itself back into the glassy stone.

Rick nearly dropped to a knee, overcome by a sick feeling of dread. He righted himself, taking conscious control of his body, his breathing, which now came in sharp, spasmodic gulps.

As he mastered himself, he peered across the temple at Beth, whose face was a canvass of white. He saw Walter advancing behind her, rain pelting furiously around them. Walter moved with the stealth of a cat stalking its prey, silver dagger in hand, raising it slowly above his head.

Beth was to be his next victim.

There was no thought, no fear, just instinct as Rick shifted his head to the left, bringing up his hands to grapple away Sarth's gun. He clasped the barrel and the assassin's hand, while simultaneously pulling him forward. Sarth resisted with tremendous strength, but Rick managed to sidestep and slip an arm under his elbow to gain leverage. In the struggle for the gun, there came a powerful blast. A round discharged in the direction of the temple. There was a muffled cry and a masked figure lurched, the bullet punching into his chest. The figure clawed at the wet, gaping wound and fell backward, collapsing over the bench. Rick continued to wrestle with every bit of strength he could muster, throwing up a knee while at the same time driving down Sarth's arm. He connected with the assassin's huge, bony fist, popping the gun free and sending it skidding over the capstone to a jagged crevice, where it dropped inside and disappeared with a clatter.

Rick pivoted and swung with a tightly balled fist, landing a solid backhand against Sarth's jaw. The blow sent him howling to the ground. Rick turned to see Beth struggling in the clutches of her captors. Behind her, Walter had quickened his pace, raising the knife in preparation to punch a mortal wound. Rick launched himself forward, screaming and waving a hand to warn Beth. Two of the cultists managed to lock her arms, fighting to drive her back onto the bloody chair.

As Rick sprinted across a field of broken stone, he could see Beth pleading to him with frightened eyes, eyes that suddenly widened, turning to sheer panic. She screamed, her words barely audible over a smash of thunder, "Rick, behind you!"

A gunshot rang out and he felt the focused impact of a bullet striking his back. He tried to turn but lost purchase on the fractured ground. His momentum carried him forward, even as he twisted in mid-air and landed with a crash onto his backside.

*     *     *

"No!" Beth screamed, horrified by the sight of Rick being shot. The suddenness of it all forced something in her chest to seize, an intense pressure squeezing against her lungs. Breathing became labored, while her heart pained with grief. Now, hyperaware of her surroundings, Beth suddenly felt the rain, carried by waves of heavy wind, slapping against her back, drenching her clothes. Everything seemed to be happening as if in a nightmare. Against the clawing hands of her captors, she fought uselessly to free herself, to run to Rick's aid. She glimpsed Walter approaching fast, lit for an instant by a brilliant flash of lightning. Tucked under one arm and shielded from the rain was the *Telesma,* in his other hand, cocked murderously above his head, the ceremonial dagger. In a fit of panic, she resumed her struggle with every ounce of fight in her body, screaming, kicking her legs, flailing her arms at the elbows. But dammit, the cultists were too strong. Inside her, fear and panic rose to insane proportions.

To discourage Beth's resistance, one of the figures grabbed a fist full of her hair and tried yanking her steady. Furious, Beth craned her head and sunk her teeth deep into his wrist, tasting the salt of his skin. He shrieked and pulled away his arm. And as he did, Beth's body, heavily soaked in a solution of water and blood, slipped free of the restraining hands and slid off the chair as easily as soap slipping from a tight grip.

*Rick was hurt. She needed to reach him, to help him.*

Beth bolted up straight on the slick stone, but as she did, Walter maneuvered around her, an insane sight to behold. Drenched from the storm, his crimson robes and golden Phrygian cap hung heavy over his body, the *Telesma* clutched tightly to his chest. And still he brandished the silver dagger, lifting it skyward against a backdrop of arcing thunderheads. His eyes were dark, wicked orbs.

Just as Walter delivered the strike, Beth lunged forward and wrested the tome from his grasp, thrusting it high over her head as a shield. The dagger plunged downward through the thick air. She felt a tremendous blow, the blade slicing with little resistance through the center of the ancient vellum.

Then there came a scrape, like metal against stone, and the manuscript flew from her hands, the dagger wedged against something in its spine. Walter let out a cry of anguish, which became mingled with the sudden boom of thunder.

Beth leapt up from her crouched position and sprinted toward Rick, who remained on the ground, pelted by rain, his body shifting ever so slightly. Upon reaching him, she dropped at his side. If they were to die, she thought, they would die in each other's arms. Rain spattered over his face and hair, and a watery pool of blood gathered behind his head where he'd struck the stone. Concerned more about the bullet wound to his back, Beth reached for the zipper of his jacket, bracing herself for what she was about to see. But as she touched his chest, she felt a hard plate, like the shell of a turtle. Rick spoke faintly, "The bullet didn't... I'm wearing a vest." He lifted his head, wincing.

"Oh, thank God," Beth said. She cradled him in her arms.

But her relief quickly vanished as she felt the jab of a gun barrel against her neck. Sarth's voice hissed from behind. "I shall tolerate no more of this charade," he said. "The two of you are infidels, and I intend to put an end to the both of you, once and for all!"

## 43

"STAY YOUR WEAPON!" Walter called out over the din of the passing storm.

Sarth's jaw tightened, and in a fit of disgust he pulled away his pistol.

Rick struggled to brace himself up by the elbows, staring at Walter, who stood with the posture of a younger man, tall against fast moving clouds. In each hand, he grasped two halves of what was once the *Telesma*, holding up each half as if in exhibition.

"Dr. Harper is a godsend," he continued to bellow, "a messenger of Mithra. Look here." He shook the ruined tome, its soggy pages separating into individual leaves and blowing to the ground. From the book's damaged spine, Walter pulled away a long, cylindrical object, its color a brilliant swirl of blue, dusted with flecks of gold.

"Amazing," Beth said, "a cylinder seal, hidden in the spine of the *Telesma*."

"What is it?" Rick asked.

"The ancient equivalent of a notary stamp. Look closely, you can see words and pictures engraved upon its surface. Scribes used them to roll over wet clay to transfer impressions."

Rick struggled to sit up. Beth helped him to his feet. He reached to the back of his head, touching his scalp, exploring the wound. He turned to Beth and saw concern in her expression. "It's nothing, really. A minor cut, I'll be okay."

Her jade eyes softened with relief.

Walter approached, glaring at the object held in his hands.

The thunderheads continued their roll westward, and with their gradual passing, the rain began to ease.

Sidelong, Rick observed Sarth, who remained vigilant, his gun at the ready.

"Indeed, it is true," Walter said. "All along you've been part of Mithra's divine plan. I understand that now. 'The key is hidden within.' Did you not speak those words last night, words written in the *Telesma*, the very words my tired mind contemplated a thousand times, yet never understood? And now you have opened the book, truly opened it, and revealed to me the next step in Mithra's glorious design." He held up the seal. "Behold, the key hidden within."

Beth's bright eyes regarded it. "It's fashioned of lapis lazuli, an indication of its value. And the scenes are Persian, not Greek. All of this is amazing, a message, concealed in the tome for over two thousand years."

"Indeed, a message," Walter said. "We must examine it."

Rick saw this as a chance. He needed to reinforce Walter's insane belief that Beth was a messenger of his god, Mithra. He had to make him believe she'd become indispensable. Walter wouldn't harm her if he believed he needed her. "To make sense of the message you'll need an expert, someone like Beth. She's been instrumental thus far. You've admitted as much yourself."

Walter stared at the seal, nodding as if considering Rick's words.

Far to the west, the thunderheads rolled on, bolts of lightning flashing in their blackened interiors. Only a gentle mist hung over the butte, as the tail end of the storm passed overhead.

Walter knelt to the ground and smoothed out a puddle of mud left by the storm. He settled the lapis cylinder over its surface and gently rolled it out, until it completed a full revolution. Then he removed it and studied the impression.

Rick saw there what looked like an alien script.

"It's Ancient Persian," Beth said, as if somehow sensing his confusion. She mouthed a few strange words and then stopped, inhaling sharply.

Walter peered up, his eyes wild with excitement.

Beth, too, seemed deeply affected, having lost much of the color in her face. With a nervous hand, she swept a wet tangle of hair behind her ear. "The message, it reveals the location of the Hidden Chambers."

"The Hidden Chambers?" Rick said. "You mentioned something about them to Mason."

"Yes, they're a warren of subterranean rooms and passages that lie hidden beneath the ruins of Persepolis."

"Another legend?"

Beth turned and beheld him with piercing green eyes. "Had you asked me a week ago, I would have told you of course it's only a legend. But now, with everything that's happened, I'm not so sure anymore."

Walter nodded to Sarth, who seized Beth by the arm and pulled her in the direction of the helicopters.

Rick lunged forward to stop him but was wrestled back by two of the thugs in Windbreakers.

"Stop!" Beth cried out. "Get your hands off me!"

"You're coming with us, my dear, as Mithra planned."

"But Rick—"

"Mr. Lowell will be escorted from the butte, allowed to return home safely."

Beth tried to yank her arm free, but in Sarth's powerful grip, she had little success. "Dammit, where are you taking me!"

"To where we have been summoned, my dear. Persepolis."

"No, you can't take me, let me go!"

In the great distance, a low rumble exploded from the heart of a thunderhead.

Solemnly, the crimson-robed figures, Eckerman among them, began their procession toward the large transport helicopter, which was now powering up, its massive rotor blades cutting violently into the thick air.

Rick remained standing, two gun-toting thugs rooted behind him. He watched with a sick feeling of hopelessness as Beth was led away to the chopper.

With little regard for the body of the man Walter had murdered, or for even the body of their own companion, the robed figures began loading into the helicopter, one by one, followed by the men in Windbreakers. Finally, Rick watched as Sarth forced Beth through a rear transport door, then disappeared inside behind her.

Walter was last to enter. Crouched under the whipping rotors, he turned, gazed at Rick and the two thugs who remained behind. With a wry smile Walter drew a hand across his neck, a grim signal to his men.

Son-of-a-bitch, Rick thought. Walter had no intention of letting him go.

The crazed cult leader ducked into the helicopter and pulled shut the door. Without delay, it lifted from the butte, hovering briefly before accelerating eastward over the desert, away from the storm. Rick watched in tense silence as the helicopter banked south, then disappeared into the horizon.

Walter was a crafty bastard. He knew in order to ensure Beth's cooperation he needed to convince her that he planned to set Rick free. Nothing but a lie. The plan was to kill him. And once Beth outlived her usefulness, she would be next. Rick couldn't let that happen.

He took a deep breath and stared the forty yards to the edge of the butte, where the smaller chopper remained parked, its black metal shell framed in gray by the receding thunderheads. Sitting in the cockpit, the pilot glanced in their direction, then he nodded and began to power-up.

This was it, Rick realized, two against one, both men armed and standing behind him in a dominant tactical position. As dismal as the odds were, Rick knew they'd never get any better.

Abruptly, one of the thugs lifted his leg, brought it against Rick's lower back, then kicked him forward, sending him tumbling onto the wet capstone. Rick rolled and jumped to his feet, turned.

Both men stood shoulder to shoulder, ten feet away, their guns drawn and aimed directly at him.

"Got a riddle for you, Doug," the one said to the other, his long, brown hair blowing in the wind.

"Let's hear it."

"What do you call a man filled with bullet holes, falling from the top of a thousand-foot butte?"

Doug opened his tiny mouth, chuckled. "I don't know, what?"

"Ah, hell, why bother *telling* you, when I can just show you."

Both men raised their guns, fingers tensed on the triggers.

*Shit, they were gonna fire!* Rick bolted forward, praying for the best, but he'd only covered half the distance when the shots rang out.

Two rounds struck him dead center in the chest. The impact forced him to stiffen, but he kept his momentum and drove forward.

He could see the men's faces registering surprise, dark eyes widening as they suddenly recalled his protective vest. The idiots had forgotten!

Refusing to make the same mistake twice, they raised their guns higher, aiming for Rick's head. But not before he'd reached Doug, dodging to the left of his outstretched arm. Rick grabbed the gun, jamming its hammer with his thumb.

"Muthafucker!" Doug screamed, trying to pull the gun free, but Rick had already stepped into him and twisted it from his hand.

"I've got a shot," cried the other man.

Rick pivoted and swung Doug around, his boots scraping over the capstone.

Doug's companion fired two rounds in quick succession, ear-splittingly loud despite the scream of the chopper's rotors.

But Rick had finished his turn, maneuvering Doug between them. Both rounds punched into Doug's back, and he drew in a sharp breath, then hiccupped a bubbling stream of blood. Rick pushed him forward, into his friend, who tried quickly to sidestep away.

Rick's firing grip on Doug's gun was instant, and he raised it high, aimed for the second man's head. "Drop it!"

But the man had become frenzied, his veins bulging from his neck. He refused to listen, throwing up his own gun in response.

Rick didn't hesitate. He fired two rapid shots, striking the man's head, dropping him to the ground. Blood pooled quickly in a rocky depression below his skull.

Spinning away from the carnage, Rick looked toward the chopper. He could see the pilot, who'd been watching the struggle from the cockpit. For a quick moment they locked eyes, then the pilot turned away and in a panic began throwing switches on the instrument panel.

Hurriedly, Rick yanked out his cell phone, flipped it open. The screen was gray and cracked down the center, broken from his earlier fall. Damn! If the chopper escaped the butte without him, he'd be trapped, no way down, no way to call for help. His isolation here would be a death sentence.

Rick peered back at the pilot.

*He was lifting off.*

Rick stuffed the gun in his waistband and sprinted full-force toward the chopper, covering great lengths of rock with each stride.

*Thirty yards away.*

An agonizing spasm pulsed through Rick's injured ribs, but he suppressed the pain and continued his sprint. The chopper slowly lifted from the ground.

*Twenty yards.*

The pilot glared at Rick from behind the bubbled window, pulled the chopper's stick, then slowly started to skim the capstone toward the edge of the butte.

Rick fought hard to increase his speed, refusing to acknowledge the stab in his side. The muscles in his legs seared.

*Ten yards.*

The chopper was breaking away from the top of the butte, moving out over its sheer vertical face.

Rick screamed in defiance of the pain.

*Five yards.*

From a great distance, thunder exploded. Rick willed his body faster.

By the length of a car, the helicopter had cleared the capstone, hovering hundreds of feet over the rocky Arizona desert.

Barreling forward, Rick was now inches from a fatal drop and still a dozen feet away from the withdrawing chopper.

The sun broke through the thinning clouds, and a stray beam of light glistened from the chopper's skid. *The skid!* It was his only chance.

One final stride and Rick propelled himself from the butte, hurtling recklessly through the air, arms outstretched, the desert floor a thousand feet below him.

# 44

MASON RECLINED IN his leather swivel chair, feet up on the mahogany desk that monopolized the corner of his home office. He shifted an ice pack from one side of his head to the other and stared through a picture window, watching the back end of a storm that had just finished soaking the city of Phoenix. Ribbons of gray clouds followed the thick, billowing thunderheads like shredded tails of a tuxedo.

Moments ago, Mason ended a phone call with Jarred, who'd promised to hurry over and help track down that old fool, Eckerman. But before he left, Jarred said he needed to send Mason an important email, an attachment of the summary reply from DARPA. It was the official response to MRMC's investigation into the failure of Operation Cold Strike, and Jarred had intercepted a copy just minutes ago.

A new message dinged. Mason pulled his eyes from the brightening sky and peered at his inbox. He moused over and right clicked the new message, then opened the attachment.

The document was long and wordy and appeared to be mostly a bureaucratic tap dance prettied up with a lot of military jargon. Mason thought about Tanner and his mission and those poor Marines, how they'd bought the farm in that shitty cave in Afghanistan. No soldier deserved to die like that. He scanned down, searching for what was sure to be confirmation of DARPA's involvement in the whole affair.

In their initial investigative report, MRMC had made a direct request to DARPA's Hybrid Biosystems unit, to the brass in charge of

Project Sunflower. They'd had questions concerning the testing of an experimental war technology. No, not questions. They'd practically pointed their suspicious little fingers at them. Our own government's investigation suspected the DARPA people, and it made perfect sense. They were a bunch of crack-brained military scientists who'd been screwing around for years with cyborg bees and scorpions. Didn't these people realize that eventually something bad was gonna come back and bite them in the balls?

Mason continued to read. *Confirmation of DARPA's involvement in Cold Strike had to be here somewhere.*

But scanning down, line after line, Mason found nothing.

He scratched his head, reached for another Ding Dong. Damn box was empty. He slapped it to the floor. Then, in a paragraph at the end of the summary, his eyes fell upon something startling. Mason leaned closer to the screen, carefully reading, then paused and sat back in his chair, perplexed. The DARPA people were denying involvement. Completely. They were claiming that the failure of Operation Cold Strike was not a result of their ventures. In fact, their response went so far as to say during the time in question the War Technologies Division had been conducting absolutely no field tests of any kind in the Afghan region.

Troubled by DARPA's denial, Mason re-read the paragraph. Damned if that's not what it said. *No involvement.*

He dropped his ice pack to the floor, rocked furiously in his swivel chair. *No Involvement.*

The recovery team who'd gone into the cave to remove the bodies said clearly they'd found no evidence of foul play, nothing that could account for the massacre. They'd seen the bodies, the welts on the men's skin, the festering sores. Heck, even toxicology from MRMC said definitively that the cause of death was an unknown insect toxin. It would have taken a whole lot of snakes and scorpions to do the job, yet the clean-up team found nothing. Zip.

Something just didn't sit right with Mason, but he couldn't quite put his finger on it. If eventually he wanted to work this into a high-impact radio piece, he needed to be able to connect the dots, draw some undeniable conclusions.

There had to be something he was missing. Run through it again, he told himself. MRMC's toxicology report was conclusive, the men were poisoned, but the recovery team found nothing lethal in the cave. And DARPA's hands were clean. What could have caused the slaughter? The only things to come out of the cave were the bodies, Tanner himself, and the talisman—

The office phone rang.

Mason jumped up in his chair. Rick's call! Oh shit, what was Mason gonna tell him?

He checked the caller I.D., then relaxed when he saw the name of his travel agent, Daniel Spitzer. He lifted the receiver. "What do you have for me, Danny?"

"The flight information you requested out of Sky Harbor." Danny was over the age of fifty, but he'd been cursed with an unnaturally high voice. Over the line he sounded like a child.

"I've gotta ask," Danny said. "Are you making travel plans?"

"No, no, nothing like that."

"Come on, M, this is Danny Boy you're talking to. You know I work on commission."

"Look, I told you I'm not making any plans."

"So they've already been made, huh?" Danny said, his voice rising to a higher octave. "Are you flying out on business or pleasure?"

"Neither."

"Right, right, listen M, business is slow for me. I can't just let you change travel agents without a fight."

"I'm not changing—"

"Who was it last year that refunded those non-refundables to Cancun, when those two blondes you asked to the Ritz busted a gut laughing, then told you to go stick it in your ear?"

Mason didn't answer.

"It was me, Danny Boy."

"Who was it that—"

"Listen, you dimwit, I'm not changing travel agents, so give your pubescent little voice box a rest, would you. What I am doing is going after an old German prick who clubbed me on the head and stole a priceless artifact, which I have to get back before a buddy of mine ends up with a dead girlfriend. So give me the fucking flight schedule dammit, I've got a life to save."

There was a pause, then Danny's high voice. "Gee, M, all you had to do was reassure me that I'm your man. You didn't have to go making up a whopper of a story."

Carefully, Mason listened to the flight schedule and scribbled the information onto a notepad. "Sorry for the outburst, Danny. I owe you one." He hung up the phone, staring down at what he'd just written. A few leads. It was somewhere to start. But he needed Jarred. Come on you big dope, hurry it up. Where was he? It seemed to be taking him forever. Mason glanced at the clock. Christ, he'd talked to him only fifteen minutes ago. Seemed like hours. It was the pressure of waiting for Rick's call. At any moment the phone would ring, and Mason would be sitting there with his pecker in his hand. What would he tell him? What could he possibly say? I know you were depending on me, buddy. I know your life's hanging in the balance, but you're just gonna have to come up with another plan. You see, Eckerman knocked me one good on the head and stole the talisman. Sorry, Rick, you're shit out of luck.

The prospect of having to admit such an embarrassing failure made Mason sick to his stomach. He thought back to this morning, to what Rick had told him before leaving for Monument Pass: *Yeah, if we were in the same unit together, you and I, we would have been buddies.* Mason never took the military route, but the fact was he loved his country. Had he been in the Army he was sure he could've handled it, could've fought right alongside Rick in Panama. And Rick knew it, too. That's why he'd entrusted him with the talisman.

Goddamn it, Mason thought, he had to redeem himself. He had to get the stone back. Whatever the cost.

His breathing became labored. He tugged at the collar of his shirt, drew in a deep breath. He needed a frickin Ding Dong, and he needed one bad. He stood from his chair, picked up the ice pack, and headed downstairs to the pantry.

## 45

Rick hurtled himself from the edge of the butte, and was soaring unleashed a thousand feet over the rocky landscape. With arms outstretched and hands opened wide, he felt like an acrobat being launched from a trapeze. His eyes were fixed upon the helicopter as it slowed its retreat, steadying against a powerful wind gust. Rick felt his fingertips strike something solid, something cylindrical.

*The landing skid.*

He clasped on hard, as if trying to squeeze water from a stone. But even with both fists locked tightly, his momentum swung him wildly upward in an arc, his grip slipping from the dampness of the bar.

His hands broke free, and he was falling, overcome by a sick sensation of weightlessness.

The main rotor spun furiously, his body whirling downward under the backwash.

Then suddenly, he jerked to a stop, hanging by the crook of his leg. His momentum had upended him, throwing his leg over the skid.

The helicopter dipped and turned, the pilot adjusting for the sudden weight.

Rick flexed himself up, his gut wrenched with pain. The helicopter pitched and yawed, and streaks of red desert flashed at the edge of his vision.

Quickly, the pilot steadied the chopper.

Rick sucked in a long draft of air, oxygenating his muscles. Then with a tremendous effort, he kicked up his second leg, wrapping it around the other, entwining his body in a horizontal position around the skid.

The pilot pulled further from the butte, clearing into the open sky.

The roar of the main rotor made it difficult for Rick to think. *Now what? How would he survive this?*

Eager to shake Rick off, the pilot put the bird into a spin. Blood rushed into Rick's head as he was twirled like a pinwheel. He tightened his hold, fearing he would be thrown free. He knew he'd have to act immediately or else lose his grip on the bar and plummet to the earth.

Rick narrowed his eyes, shielding them from the stinging backwash. Above, he glimpsed the belly of the chopper, the door and its handle hopelessly out of reach. In the midst of the chopper's reckless spin, he had no chance to climb up to reach it. But there was a second bar two feet above him, parallel to the skid. If he could get to it, he might be able to pull himself up into a sitting position.

The pilot slowed his spin and steadied the chopper, likely considering a new tactic to shake him.

It was a chance for Rick to act.

Keeping one hand tight on the skid, he reached up with the other and caught the bar. It was narrow, easy to handle.

Suddenly, the pilot accelerated, tearing across the open desert. In a crazy move, he dropped the chopper from the sky, swooping downward at an insane arc. Rick's gut lurched into his throat, and he nearly slipped from the skid. The chopper drove earthward, faster and faster. Rick could feel the roots of his hair pulling violently in his scalp. Faster he dropped.

Then, in an instant, the chopper swung level, its speed slowing as it began a second climb. Doubting he could handle another plunge, Rick threw up his other hand and grabbed hold of the parallel brace, praying the pilot wouldn't begin another dive. He adjusted his grip and hoisted himself up, then swung his legs over the bar and came to rest in a sitting position. The rotor's backwash slapped him with greater force.

Now, the bottom of the door was only a foot above his head, giving him an idea. He could pull his gun and bang it against the glass, get the pilot's attention. Unless the idiot wanted Rick to start shooting into the cockpit, he'd be forced to bring the helicopter down. But just as Rick reached for the gun, the pilot began a second dive.

Rick's hand lurched back to the brace and he ducked his head, squeezing his eyes shut. In the darkness, under the scream of the rotors, he felt as though he were in free fall. Time slowed to a crawl. He held his breath and wrung the bar with every ounce of strength he could muster. When at last the chopper leveled and began another climb, Rick made his move.

First, he slapped his palm to the handle of his gun, made sure he had a firm grip before pulling it. Then in one quick motion, he yanked it from his waistband and swung it up to the glass door of the cockpit, cracking its barrel hard against the glass. He struck it a few more times to make sure he had the pilot's attention, but the chopper didn't level out. Instead, he continued to climb. Bastard was going to dive again.

Rick had no choice.

He angled the gun, pointing it into the cockpit—and fired. A bullet split through the glass, but with the noise of the main rotor, Rick couldn't hear the pilot's reaction.

Finger tensed on the trigger, ready to fire another round, Rick felt the helicopter level, then slow its speed. Gradually it began to descend, dropping in gentle arcs.

Rick looked down to see the desert floor just a few hundred feet below him, its rocky soil dark from the summer showers. Moments later, the chopper came to a hover about ten feet from the ground. And there it remained. Clearly, the pilot wanted him off. Rick's plan had worked.

With one hand holding the bar, Rick stuffed the gun back into his waistband and jumped from the skid, landing with bent knees. He tumbled into a roll to absorb the shock of the impact. A maneuver he'd practiced many times in jump school.

Springing to his feet, he pulled the gun and turned to face the chopper. But already, the pilot had rocketed skyward, refusing to stick around for an encore.

Rick held the shot.

He took a deep breath and looked around to establish his position. It was critical he get to the Jeep before fatigue set in. He did a three-sixty, searching for the highway. To the southwest, maybe a hundred yards away, Rick spotted a Volkswagen van, parked in what at first appeared to be the open desert, but he soon realized it was the highway, shielded by a slight rise in the terrain. Against the van leaned two men, gaping in his direction.

Rick began a jog toward them. As he neared, he could better make out their appearance. They stood shoulder to shoulder, both smoking cigarettes and nodding their heads in trance-like satisfaction. They had long hair tucked messily under red, white, and blue bandanas, and they wore Rolling Stones concert T-shirts that dropped well below their waists. "Unbelievable, man," one called out. "Un-fucking-believable!"

Rick was huffing with some difficulty and could feel the pain returning to his ribs. "I need a favor," he shouted as he neared.

"Sure thing," the taller one answered. He flicked his cigarette to the ground and crushed it with his tennis shoe. "Need a lift back to your crew?"

Rick stopped a few feet away and hunched over with his hands to his knees, breathless. "Crew?"

"Yeah, you know, your film crew, for the movie."

For a second Rick thought the guy must've been on drugs. But then suddenly, he understood.

"So tell me," the other guy said, "are you like the actual star, or just some kind of, you know, stunt double." He took a long drag from his cigarette.

Rick straightened up. Incredibly, these guys had witnessed his struggle on the chopper and assumed he was filming a movie. They'd even pulled off onto the shoulder of the highway to watch. He didn't have the heart, nor the energy to explain. "I'm just the stunt double. I have my own car, the Jeep, back along the Interstate. Can you take me to it?"

"You bet we can," the tall one said. "Hop in." He yanked open the side door to the van. "So what's the name of the flick gonna be, and do you mind if we get a couple of autographs?"

# 46

THE JEEP WAS parked three miles to the south. When the van pulled up, Rick threw open the side door and ducked out, thanking the two star-struck men for their help. Without hesitation, Rick jumped into the Jeep, started the engine, and swung the car in the direction of Phoenix.

Minutes later, gunning down the highway, he felt his adrenaline rush dissolving away. Around him, the cabin hummed gently, filled with the steady vibration of a gritty road and a purring engine. And in this calm, Rick began to think—about Beth, about himself, about their past. He thought about his marriage proposal, about the mistakes he had made.

In the three years before their separation, the two of them had lived and traveled together, had become inseparable, a team. Their love had grown intensely. And so last summer he'd resolved to make the ultimate commitment. It seemed natural to him that on their vacation to Paris, in the City of Lovers, he should ask for Beth's hand in marriage.

Painfully, he recalled that August night as if it were yesterday, the two of them standing alone together on the Pont de la Tournelle, overlooking the dark waters of the Seine, the Parisian lights hiding all but the brightest stars. It was there Rick had reaffirmed his love and asked her to become his wife.

But it wasn't to be. As he uttered his heartfelt words, Rick could sense her unease. Beth loved him, he had no doubt about it, but given the time in her life, marriage and children were too big a step for her. Having just completed a Ph.D., she had accomplished a major milestone, but it was only one of many she felt she needed to reach before settling down and starting a family.

Looking back, Rick could see she was right. She wasn't ready. With her studies and her career, she was still carving out a space in the world, and he'd threatened to ruin it. And to make matters worse, over ensuing months he began pressing her for a commitment, angry at what he saw as a rejection of his love. Little by little he pushed her away, only realizing his mistake after their split, when it was too late. He should have given her time. He'd asked for too much, too quickly.

Now, Beth's world had become a disaster. And he was responsible, involving her with the talisman, drawing her into something neither one of them could control. She would have been better off unaware of the artifact, safe if nothing else. Now instead, she was in the hands of Walter, a psychopath, and at the mercy of some sick, demented cult.

Rick's painful reverie was broken by the sight of a crystal blue sky. The sun had burned away remnants of the storm and reestablished its reign over the desert. Already the highway was bone dry, and piñon trees baked in scattered isolation. If not for the existence of black pools that lay dotted across the landscape, it would've been impossible to tell a storm had ever passed through.

But one had.

And from the top of that hellish butte, Rick had experienced its fury first hand. He'd experienced a lot of things. Things he'd much rather forget. His thoughts narrowed on the Brotherhood's ceremony and the ghoulish human sacrifice. He thought of the talisman, too, the river of evil that had emerged from it. A hallucination—it had to be. An exhausted mind. There was no other explanation. With rain-soaked thunderheads crowding over Walter, and flashes of incessant lightning, it could have easily been a trick of the weather, a figment of his imagination.

Whatever the cause, Rick had no time to figure it out.

More important was Beth. After Eckerman's arrival on the butte, Rick's plan to save her had collapsed like a house of cards. The old man who'd professed so much concern for the world, who'd warned them about the danger of the Brotherhood, he'd been a part of their organization all along. And what's worse, Rick had made the betrayal possible by trusting Mason.

Rick stared at his hands on the wheel and saw them shaking. Whether the cause was physical exhaustion or the stress of his worry for Beth, he wasn't sure. Maybe a little of both. He needed a new plan. He couldn't leave Beth at the mercy of the Brotherhood. These madmen had shown what they were capable of, the lengths to which they were willing to go to get hold of the talisman. Beth's expertise and this nonsense about her being some kind of divine messenger would keep her safe for a while, but Walter was unstable and could very well change his mind on a whim. Once she outlived her usefulness, Rick had no doubt he would kill her.

He needed to get to Mason's house quickly, shake the little bastard until he spilled what he knew. Mason had a way of nosing around other people's business and gathering information. Maybe he'd picked up something useful from Eckerman, a lead of some kind. If Rick was to have any chance saving Beth, finding her before these people dragged her away to Persepolis was critical. Rick laid his foot heavy on the accelerator, rocketing down the highway.

By the time he reached Phoenix, his body had nearly buckled under the pain. Knotted arm and shoulder muscles burned, and his ribs throbbed with an ache so fierce it felt as if they had pulled themselves free of the cage. He fought back the pain and focused on his plan.

When Rick finally pulled into the long, looping driveway of Mason's estate, he stared intensely. The sight of Mason's house stirred a newfound rage. Rick slid the Jeep to a stop in front of the sprawling four-car garage, jumped out and made a beeline to the porch. Not bothering to knock, he threw open the heavy front door, slamming it into the wall. From across the large foyer, he could see the little red-headed prick in the living room, snacking on a Ding Dong. His round, freckled face jerked up from the sudden bang, his eyes bulging with fright. Jarred was there, too, hunched like a grizzly on the couch.

"Mason, I'm gonna strangle you." Rick bolted through the foyer, nearly toppling a marble statue.

Scrambling, Mason dropped the Ding Dong and retreated

backward over the sofa, falling clumsily to the other side.

"You gave Eckerman the talisman," Rick said. "You ruined everything. I trusted you!"

Mason tried to stand, but in his awkward haste, he lost his footing, falling back to the floor. His short legs pumped and skidded repeatedly over the carpet. "No, Rick, no, you don't understand."

Jarred jumped to his feet, sidestepping between them.

"Watch out, Jarred, the little shit's got it coming."

The big man put his hands on Rick's shoulders. Even with an open grip, his strength was intense. "Hold on a second," he said. "Hear what happened before you go and do something you're gonna regret."

Rick glared past Jarred at Mason, noticing a long gash spread across his forehead. It was red and swollen, nearly the same color as his shock of messy hair.

"Where's Beth?" Jarred asked.

Rick's shoulders slumped. He stepped back, exhausted.

"I take it things didn't go well," Jarred said. "I'm sorry."

Mason climbed to his feet, breathing like a panicked rabbit. Carefully, he maneuvered around the sofa, picked up an ice pack from the coffee table, and laid it over the knot on his forehead. He dropped himself onto a cushion, staring with an expression of emotion Rick had never seen in him before. His eyes were wide and pain-filled. But it didn't appear to be physical pain. It was emotional. "I let you down," Mason said, his voice deeply earnest.

Rick felt his nerves beginning to calm.

"I screwed up, I know," Mason continued to say, shifting the ice pack.

"What happened?"

"Plenty, and some of it's gonna piss you off. But you have a right to know anyway."

Rick looked at Jarred.

The big man shrugged.

"I didn't give Eckerman the talisman, you gotta believe me. He begged me for it, he pleaded, he even demanded it, but I told him no. I went upstairs to put it in the safe. I was waiting for you to call with instructions, just like you told me. I knew how important it was.

But the old geezer followed me upstairs and cold-cocked me with one of my own statues. The Kochina, of all things, broke it into a hundred pieces. Can you believe it? The thing cost me fifteen grand."

Rick's gaze fell on the ice pack. "You okay?"

Mason shook his head. "No, I'm not. I let you down, and I'm sorry."

Rick took a deep breath. "I guess I had it figured all wrong."

"It was a sucker punch," Mason said. "Had I seen it coming, I would've shown the old man my footwork, dodged or something. I can kick his ass, you know that, right?"

"I'm sure you can," Rick said.

"When I woke up, Eckerman was gone, I called Jarred."

The big man tipped his head. "The two of us just returned from scouring the terminals at Sky Harbor. We couldn't find—"

"Eckerman," Rick finished his thought. "I know. He showed up at the butte."

Mason jumped to his feet. "What?"

"Eckerman's one of them, he's part of the Brotherhood, and from what I saw today, the whole lot of these people are dangerously insane." For an instant, Rick recalled images of the temple scene—the bull's severed head; the pools of blood; the madmen hidden under ceremonial robes, swaying to the rhythm of Walter's chant. Rick shuddered.

"The old man's one of them," Mason repeated, as if suddenly convinced. "I should have known."

Jarred frowned. "Eckerman must've screwed up your plans."

"That's an understatement," Rick said. "Without the talisman, I had no bargaining chip. They took Beth, then tried to kill me."

Jarred pointed to the bullet holes in Rick's jacket. "I see the vest made a difference."

"It saved my life, I owe you."

"Where did they take Beth?" Mason asked.

"I was hoping you could tell me. I figured since you gave Eckerman the talisman, you'd become friends. Thought maybe I could shake a lead out of you. I should have known with Beth's life on the line you wouldn't stab me in the back. I'm sorry for doubting you."

Mason dropped his head. "No, I'm the one who ought to be sorry."

"The old man snuck in a lucky shot," Jarred said. "You did what you could."

"No, there's something else I need to tell you."

Rick and Jarred exchanged glances.

"Mind you," Mason quickly added, "this was before I understood the magnitude of all this, before I truly realized the danger." He stopped as if unable to bring himself to say it.

"Spit it out," Jarred said.

"I was convinced some of Eckerman's stories would make good radio. I imagined my ratings rocketing through the roof, so in return for his promise to go on the show, I teamed up with the old man."

"What do you mean *teamed up*?"

Mason scratched his head, winced as he inadvertently touched his cut. "We kind of, well, you know, broke into your townhouse."

"You did what?" Rick said.

"Broke into your place, searching for the talisman."

"Are you nuts?"

"Look, Rick, I'm sorry."

"So that's how you knew I had a Glock."

Mason nodded.

"Him breaking into your house," Jarred said. "I had no idea." The big man stepped back. "If you wanna ring his neck now, be my guest."

Mason glared. "Dammit Jarred, this is hard enough."

Rick said, "What in the hell were you thinking?"

"You have to believe me. All this I did imagining it was some kind of a game, you know, cloak and dagger stuff. Had I known what was gonna happen, I never would have—"

"What other trouble have you caused?"

"That's it," Mason said. "I swear." He looked up at Rick, paused. "If you're gonna kill me, do you mind if I eat a Ding Dong first?"

Rick turned away and dropped into an armchair, lowering his

head between his hands. "Forget about it, what's done is done. I have to move forward, I have to find Beth."

Mason bolted up straight on the sofa. "Jarred and I can help."

"You bet we can," the big man said.

"I don't know," Rick said. "Mason's been enough help already."

"You gotta give me a second chance," Mason said. "There must be something I can do."

"You can tell me if Eckerman ever mentioned a man named Walter."

"Don't think so, who is he?"

"A member of the Brotherhood, the one pulling the strings. I need to find him."

"Eckerman never mentioned him."

"Are you sure? Think. Anything he may have said inadvertently or in passing?"

Rick could see the struggle in Mason's eyes as he searched his memory. "No, nothing."

"Dammit, I can't catch a break." Rick stood up and paced the living room floor, thinking. After a minute, he stopped, staring at the columns of afternoon sunlight lancing in through the windows. "That leaves Persepolis."

"Persepolis?" Jarred said. "What's that?"

"A ruined city, ancient, once the capital of the Persian Empire."

"I don't understand. What does it have to do with Beth?"

"It's where they're taking her. They discovered something called a cylinder seal in the spine of an old manuscript. On it was a message revealing the location of some hidden chambers beneath the ruins."

Mason's eyes widened. "You mean like tombs?"

"I don't know, possibly. I really don't care what the hell they are. I just want to get Beth back."

"You sure they're taking her there?"

"Walter said so himself, he's got it in his head she's a messenger of his god, Mithra. Plus, ancient Persia is her specialty. It makes sense they would bring her along as an expert."

"That's great," Mason said. "If they need her, they won't hurt her."

"Maybe," Rick said. "But what happens when she's no longer needed?"

Mason stared at the holes in Rick's jacket and cringed. "Right."

"But there's a bigger problem. Persepolis is half a world away, in Iran of all places. That'll require travel visas, it'll take weeks. And by that time…" Rick could feel sweat running down his temples. He was beginning to suffocate. He pulled off his jacket and fumbled to remove the vest, clawing at the straps until they loosened. He pulled it off and flung it to the ground. "I don't know what I'm gonna do."

"What *we're* gonna do," Mason said. "We're going to save Beth. Just you wait and see."

"Don't you understand? By the time we get the needed documents, this'll all be over. She'll be dead."

"Not gonna happen." Mason jumped to his feet, pulled a cell phone from his pocket and dialed. "Andrea, this is Mason, I need you to check the AP and Reuters for any important conferences scheduled to take place in Iran."

Rick could hear Andrea's garbled voice. "You heard me right," Mason said. "Iran." Now hurry and check it out, I'll wait."

Holding music spilled from the receiver. Mason paced the floor, stepping in time to the beat. A minute later Andrea's voice returned to the line. "You don't say, that's perfect," Mason said.

He ended the call and dialed another number, then he turned to Rick. "You're right, tourist visas take weeks." He grinned. "Thing is, we're not tourists."

A man's voice sounded over the line. "Afternoon, name is Mason Manning, and I'm the foreign affairs news correspondent at KSND in Phoenix, Arizona. I need to arrange three press visas for an emergency OIC summit in Tehran. This is a big news story and my program director's sitting here with his checkbook open, if you know what I mean. Got to have the visas in twenty-four hours. So tell me, who do I need to impress to make that happen?"

Rick could hear the man speaking excitedly.

"Thank you, sir," Mason said. "You bet I'll hold." He slapped a hand over the receiver, peered at Jarred, then at Rick. "Pack your bags, gentlemen. We're going to Persepolis."

# PART TWO

*Ancient Persia*
*Fall, 331 B.C.*

*AMIR SLOWED TO a gallop, a solitary speck of black moving across the great windswept expanse of the Marv Dasht basin. Fatigued, the king's attendant reined in his stallion, then slowly turned in the saddle, his weary eyes gazing out over the rising peaks of the Zagros Mountains. Darkened by early morning shadows, the chain's deep brown folds dipped and rippled in a curious pattern, reminding Amir of the furrowed skin of an old and wicked man. Amir was thankful to have finally traversed the mountains, to have traded the menace of their crumbling slopes for the security of the grassy plains. The journey from the battlefield had been a long and difficult one, bringing his steed near the brink of exhaustion. Yet, despite its weakened state, Amir snapped the reins and urged the beast forward, resuming a gallop toward the city of Persepolis, the capital of the great Persian Empire, home to untold numbers of men, women, and children. And, regrettably, the very city to which he would soon lay waste.*

\*　　　\*　　　\*

*Nearing the city's perimeter, Amir ignored the scatter of outlying farms and pastures, instead fixing his eyes in the distance, upon the city's bazaar: an immense sprawl of tents and mud-brick buildings that rose from the earth like a jumble of tiny blocks. Minutes later, reaching a cluster of stalls, Amir dismounted and stroked the stallion's* neck, its black, glistening coat awash in heat and sweat. It had served him well and, and if nothing else, deserved a few final hours of comfort.

A stranger in filthy white robes emerged from a knot of laborers. "For a small price, I'll provide your mount excellent care, my good fellow."

Amir handed him the reins and opened his purse, removing a gold dinar.

The man accepted the coin with a toothless grin, then, assessing the stallion's miserable condition, patted its steaming neck and led it away to a nearby paddock.

Turning east, Amir peered in the direction of the royal palace, his final destination. In the distance, he could see its crenellated walls towering high above the tents, stretching north and south beyond his vision, crowned by the light of the saffron sun. He leveled his gaze and searched for a route through the bazaar's shifting crowds. Men and women of every stripe swarmed between the countless stalls and mud-brick pavilions, throngs of citizens going about their business, examining goods and arguing prices with remarkable skill. Still, there were others in the bazaar, Amir knew. Others not so benign. The market teemed with pickpockets and charlatans of the worst kind.

But it was not for the loss of his purse that Amir feared. With a subtle hand, he reached to his breast pocket and felt the reassuring bulk of the scroll—his king's urgent, and perhaps final, communiqué. For a moment, one so very fleeting, Amir imagined destroying the scroll, shredding its fateful pages and setting it to flame. But as consoling a thought as it was, it also sickened Amir. The act would be one of great defiance and dishonor, an act too treacherous to commit. For above all, Amir was a loyalist, a humble and obedient servant to King Codomannus. And Amir would do as commanded, even if it meant—he hesitated, the thought gruesome and unsettling—even if it meant....

Amir refused to consider it any longer. He had orders, and he would carry them out, immediately. He tightened his robe and stepped into the bustle of the bazaar. Quickly, yet gracefully, he navigated its interior, marveling at the enormous array of goods. Persepolis was a grand hub of economic activity, attracting merchants from the farthest reaches of the empire. Every ware produced within its vast borders could be bartered here: clothing and jewelry, tools and weapons, pottery and bronzes, hardwoods and cedar, food and livestock, all things the mind could imagine, and many things the mind could not. It was a great tragedy, Amir lamented, that it would all soon come to an end—no man, woman, or child warned of the impending ruin, no one spared. Amir wiped the sweat from his forehead and continued his walk toward the palace.

After a long series of bends and turns, the bazaar abruptly ended. Amir paused, looking ahead, gaping at the edifice looming above him, a magnificent palace framed by a brilliant blue sky. Though the city was surrounded by a thousand farms, and though its center boasted an equal number of artisan dwellings, its heart was this, the royal fortress, solid and imposing. It was from within these walls Codomannus governed the empire, and as the king's chief attendant, Amir was intimately familiar with its opulent grounds: its broad, relief-carved staircases; its sweeping courtyards and tranquil gardens; its columned vestibules and richly decorated halls. Beyond these walls was a sight unlike any other, and each time Amir returned from his travels, he couldn't help but feel humbled by the palace's size and splendor.

He marched toward the staircase that led to the Gate of All Nations, feeling a growing sense of unease, a peculiar chill, as if suddenly he'd been laid bare before the world, his grim mission revealed for all to see. Remain steadfast, he scolded himself. Focus on your duty, your responsibility. The king's instructions had been explicit, and Amir was honor-bound to carry them out, regardless of the ultimate consequence. With these thoughts, Amir took solace and began his climb up the sweeping staircase toward the entrance.

The Gate of All Nations was an imposing vestibule with squat, decorative columns supporting a ceiling that rose some fifty feet above the polished floor. Flanking the entrance was a pair of colossal statues: two kneeling bulls carved from black Persian marble, with gilded horns and bejeweled hooves. Orange flames leapt from an arrangement of braziers encircling them.

As Amir approached the entryway, two guards marched to the center. With exaggerated movement, they crossed their spears and lifted their round shields. Amir produced his credentials. The guards bowed ceremoniously, then stepped aside.

The great vestibule echoed hollow with Amir's footsteps as he hurried across the marble floor, his eyes searching beyond the opposite portal to the gardens and the eastern walls of the palace. Quickly, he turned south and passed into the courtyard surrounding the brightly painted Apadana. He took long strides past an arrangement of bubbling fountains, toward the enormous audience hall built nearly two hundred years ago by Darius the Great, the most honored of all Persian kings. As Amir neared, he glanced at the building's façade, embossed with dark images of the king's elite guard—the Immortals.

The beat of his heart quickened as he climbed the steps to the veranda and crossed the colonnade, where he entered through a set of ornate double doors. Inside, he paused, his eyes feasting upon the lavish interior. The hall was a marvel of Persian engineering, erected on a ten thousand square foot foundation. Seventy-two towering columns and a lattice of oak and cedar beams supported the high ceiling, itself adorned with gilded tiles and exquisitely carved sapphire cornices.

Arranged midway down the central aisle was a square parasol trimmed with black ostrich feathers. Under it rested the king's throne, currently occupied by the man Amir had been sent to brief, Regent Xavier, a portly aristocrat with a clean-shaven head and an impossible number of silver rings that pierced his nostrils and lips. The purple gown signifying his authority fell loosely over his bloated frame, while two fair-skinned eunuchs stood obediently askew, one bearing a plate laden with cheese and dates, the other a large decanter of wine. At the sight of Amir, the regent struggled to erect himself. "For what trifle am I disturbed?"

Amir approached, producing the king's communiqué.

With black, curious eyes, the regent regarded the scroll. "You bring news of Codomannus?"

"I do."

The regent motioned a eunuch to retrieve the scroll, then, once in his possession, he examined it closely, turning it over with plump fingers. "The seal, it has not been broken."

"Naturally," Amir said. "The king's communiqué is official."

*The regent split the seal and slowly unrolled the crisp papyrus, reading carefully. His milky face colored. "Codomannus failed in his campaign against Alexander?"*

*"Regrettably, it is so."*

*"Where is the king now?"*

*"Withdrawn to Ecbatana, where he plans to amass another army. With the blessing of Mithra, he will recapture the empire."*

*"And Alexander?"*

*"He has savaged Babylon and is en route here to Persepolis, as we speak. His army is considerable, and crossing the mountains will take time. Even still, we must act on the king's orders now—without delay."*

*"But his demand is outrageous," the regent said, eyes bulging wide. He turned and thrust out a silver goblet. "Wine!" A eunuch tipped a decanter, filling the cup. The regent brought it to his lips and drank with the thirst of a camel.*

*"True, the king's orders are distressing," Amir said. "And I, too, am disturbed by what ultimately will come of Persepolis. Still, the command must be executed."*

*"Certainly not. What the king demands is insane. Do you not understand? If carried out, the sky will blacken with plague. Crops will wither. The people of our great nation will die." The regent waved a dismissive hand. "I refuse to do it."*

*Amir hesitated before speaking again. He'd suspected the regent might be stubborn, even resistant. But blatant refusal to carry out a royal decree amounted to treason, and Amir could not allow it. "With all due respect, Regent Xavier, the choice in the matter is not yours. The king still lives. And until the moment when he draws his final breath, his decrees must stand."*

*"No, no, the king has lost the empire to Alexander. You have said as much yourself." He gestured to the scroll. "I declare these orders rescinded."*

*Amir gasped, unable to fathom the man's arrogance. What right did he have? "You'll forgive me for being blunt, Regent Xavier, but you overstep your authority. You haven't the power to rescind the king's decree."*

*Face darkening, the regent leapt to his feet, surprising Amir with his speed and agility. "How dare you speak to me as if I was a common peasant. I refuse to destroy Persepolis and murder its people. And for showing such kindness and mercy you dare say I overstep my authority?"*

*"Execute the king's orders and by the divine grace of Mithra our people will die quickly and painlessly." Amir hesitated, searching for more convincing words. "If you allow Alexander to capture the city, death will be slow and tortuous. Our men will be slaughtered by the sword, our women ravaged by soldiers, our children carried off into slavery. The king's way... it is better."*

*"I'll not permit it," Xavier said. "I will reason with the Greek. Alexander is said to be a charitable man. Perhaps I can negotiate a—"*

*"You can negotiate nothing with Alexander. By his very hand he will slay you and carry away the riches of the empire."*

*"No, he will listen. I can be very persuasive." Xavier lapsed into silence, sweating, moaning at the edge of audibility. After a moment, the plump man spoke again, his tone suddenly official. "Codomannus has been defeated on the battlefield, the people are without a king, and so as Regent of the glorious Persian Empire, I hereby assume royal command." Xavier extended a robed arm. "Kiss my hand, Amir. Acknowledge my authority."*

*Amir stepped back, stunned. What he was hearing was treason. He'd expected a severe reaction from the regent, perhaps even a moment of disbelief, but outright refusal to honor the king's decree? Amir realized he would now have to resort to a threat. Tightening his robe, he stepped forward, head held high. "As you are aware, Regent Xavier, a company of the king's Immortals reside here in the city. I shall go to them personally and present his orders. They are deeply loyal to Codomannus and will not tolerate your sedition."*

*"You would involve the Immortals?" Xavier glared, and for a long moment he stood, his large frame wavering, his chest rising and falling. When at last he spoke again, his voice had changed dramatically, becoming soft and kind. "Amir, my good fellow, be reasonable. Don't you see? I am simply doing what's in the best interest of our glorious city, of our people."*

"*Slaughter at the hands of the Greeks is not in their best interest,*" *Amir said.* "*The outlook is bleak, certainly, but by the king's decree it is mercy we offer. The people's end will come quickly and without suffering. Mithra will cradle them in His benevolent arms, and they will ascend into the realm of eternal bliss.*"

*Regent Xavier eased his heavy frame back onto the throne, considering Amir's words.* "*Perhaps I was hasty in my decision.*" *He lifted his goblet and gulped down the remainder of his wine. After a heavy sigh, he said,* "*Very well, Amir, your argument is persuasive. Let us take action, together. Let us descend into the Sacred Chambers and initiate the Call to Mithra.*" *He gestured to a distant servant, who immediately scrambled to the base of the stoop.* "*You will dress attendant Amir as required for his presence in the Mithraeum.*" *Xavier looked back at Amir.* "*Prepare yourself and meet me in the Royal Treasury.*" *The regent labored to his feet, and with his two eunuchs in tow, descended the throne's marble stoop. With great pomp and ceremony they paraded down the aisle and disappeared through the eastern portal of the Apadana.*

*Amir blinked, scarcely able to believe his success. He had done it. He had convinced the regent that loyalty to the king was necessary, a virtue greater than all others, greater even than life itself. Amir smiled, satisfied with how he had managed to quash Xavier's defiance. Invigorated, Amir turned to the servant, a gaunt man in teal robes.* "*Let us prepare, my friend. Our destiny awaits.*"

*The servant bowed and led him away to a small antechamber, where Amir stood patiently while the man sized him and searched through a cabinet of silks. From a cedar drawer, the servant's thin hands produced a pair of sandals and a bundle of purple robes with silver embroidery.*

*Amir donned the ceremonial garment, pleased with its fit, then stood for a moment, breathing slowly and deeply, bracing himself for what was to come. He caressed the soft silk, thinking it was fitting he should be garbed in such splendid attire. For in addition to fulfilling the king's orders, Amir knew painfully well he was preparing to meet his own death. Soon, the Mithraeum would become his tomb.*

*Outside on the veranda, Amir squinted under the afternoon sun. Lifting a hand to shield his eyes, he peered south, to the Gate of Kings. Walking briskly, he crossed the gate's threshold and followed the long, narrow causeway past the Hall of Columns to the Royal Treasury, a large building adorned with superbly executed bas-relief that depicted King Darius and a group of colorfully clothed dignitaries.*

*Inside the Royal Treasury, Amir greeted Regent Xavier, who seemed in much better spirits, his eyes bright and his cheeks flush with color. Clearly, he had come to see the virtue in the king's decree. He had accepted the inevitable.*

*"This way, Amir," Regent Xavier said, motioning to a dark, distant alcove. He turned and hurried off, robes fluttering as he walked.*

*Amir followed, the two eunuchs trailing closely behind him. In the alcove, the eunuchs took the lead, walking a short distance to the dead-end, where they stopped, their fair skin appearing ghostly in the shadows. Carefully, they felt along the dressed stone, searching. A moment later, they rotated and lifted something Amir could not see, a lever perhaps, then together they pushed against the wall, until it slowly began to pivot, exposing a low, narrow opening. Pale light spilled out from somewhere beyond. Amir's eyes resolved a set of stairs descending steeply into the gray.*

*The eunuchs moved aside, and the regent strode forward, confident. Amir followed, and the two men ducked through the portal and descended the marble steps, their sandals clapping in the empty stairwell.*

*As he neared the gallery, Amir was gripped by a feeling of overwhelming despair. Never again—he realized, taking each step slowly—would he see the light of day, nor would he feel the brush of a cool wind against his flesh. It was a bitter thought, of course, but a thought tempered by the knowledge he was dutifully obeying the wishes of his king.*

*With a hideous grating sound, the hidden portal closed behind him.*

*Reaching the gallery floor, Amir focused his eyes. The space around him glowed dimly from the light of burning braziers, as it had continuously for the past two hundred years, in accordance with Mith-*

*raic law and tradition. Smoke rose from copper pans, and the scent of mint hung heavy in the air. Amir studied the room. Though great in dimension, it felt small and stifling. An illusion created by its huge obsidian walls. At the far end of the gallery, faint light revealed the cavernous opening to the Mithraeum, the sacred hollow where he and Xavier would soon perform the Ceremony and unleash the Mercy of Mithra.*

*"Amir, you fool," the regent's voice came in a whisper behind him, "did you really think I would allow you to inflict ruin upon my city?"*

*Startled by the wicked words, Amir turned.*

*Xavier had pressed up close, his hot, fetid breath and the stench of wine filling the air. "You're a fool to value honor above survival."*

*Amir backed away, realizing he'd been tricked.*

*Suddenly, a dagger appeared in the regent's hand.*

*Amir tensed.*

*The large man sprung forward, and there came a silvery flash.*

*Amir felt something cold sting across his chest, followed by an intense burning sensation. He looked down to see his silken robes spreading dark with blood. Amir stumbled back, pained by the wound. He turned to flee, but the door, he now recalled, had been shut. There was nowhere to run, nothing he could do. No, wait, there was something. He could honor his king's decree. He could bring about a merciful end to Persepolis!*

*But before Amir could act, the regent's blade plunged into his back. An intense pain seized his body, a pain unlike any other he'd ever felt—deep and searing. There came a coppery taste, and then warm blood erupted from his mouth, down his chin. He fell to his knees, then onto his chest. His king, Amir thought with an increasing sense of dizziness, he could not fail his king. Unable to breathe, he clawed forward, closer to the wall, his eyes seeing little more than hazy impressions. But there, there it was, a glimmer! If he could just reach it! Scorch the Earth!*

*Amir lifted an arm, reaching, reaching. But abruptly, a great weakness overcame him, and with a horrible sense of dread, everything fell into complete and quiet darkness.*

*             *             *

*Regent Xavier stared down at the pitiful corpse. A deserving end to a miserable servant. Amir had been an idealist, not a practical man. Execute the king's orders? How utterly foolish! Why would Xavier destroy a prosperous city and commit suicide when he could live splendidly and rule an empire? Alexander was said to be a wise man, a charitable man. Surely, the two would come to a peaceable agreement. Even if that meant relinquishing the talisman in exchange for a prominent position in Alexander's circle.*

*Xavier looked to the Mithraeum, where shadows danced upon the cavernous walls. There, he spied the black stone, divine and infinitely powerful, resting upon the sacred altar. Codomannus had been a fool not to carry it into battle. The king's forces were overwhelming, outnumbering the Greeks six to one. And so Codomannus had marched overconfidently. But despite greater Persian numbers, it was Alexander who triumphed. The Macedonian was indeed a gifted general. Xavier realized that now.*

*He walked to the altar and gently lifted the precious stone. Nestling it within the pocket of his robes, he returned to the gallery and glanced once more upon Amir's bloodied corpse. Pathetic. How truly pathetic. After turning away and climbing the steps to the concealed portal, Regent Xavier tapped and waited. When the door finally opened, he stepped into the dark alcove, excited and full of thirst for good wine. He peered at his loyal eunuchs and spoke with a renewed sense of authority. "Alexander's army approaches," he said. "Summon the royal stonemasons and seal this portal. The treasures that lie within will be our little secret." Xavier smiled crookedly. "Come now, there's much to do, and little time to do it! Let us prepare a warm welcome for our Greek brethren."*

# 1

THROUGH THE JET'S cabin window, Dr. Beth Harper stared below at thick fields of moonlit clouds, thoughts of recent events crowding her mind. At the moment, the talisman had simply lost its appeal, and Beth found herself questioning her priorities of recent months. She'd turned down a marriage proposal from the most caring and courageous man she'd ever known, a man who had just risked his life to save her from a cult of lunatics. And all he'd ever asked was for her love and commitment, for a chance to build a life together, and for a family. It was an opportunity any sensible woman would have jumped at. But selfishly she'd rejected him, too blind and career-focused to understand what was truly important. But now it had become clear. She'd made a huge mistake choosing the university over the man she loved. It was a mistake she'd have to work hard to fix, if ever she got out of this mess.

Which, under the present circumstances, wasn't going to be easy. Over the past twenty-four hours Beth had come to learn three things about Walter that would make her escape risky and very difficult. The first was that he was a wealthy and resourceful man, having been able to arrange an immediate and unquestionably expensive expedition to Persepolis. The second was that he had a great many people willing to do his bidding, fanatics—clearly—eager to please and willing to do anything asked of them, no matter the cost. And the third thing Beth had come to realize about Jonathan Walter was that he was dangerously insane.

A failed attempt to escape, Beth knew, would mean certain death.

But escape was her only choice. Carefully, she considered the possibilities: the plane would likely land in Shiraz, where Walter no doubt had arranged transportation to the ruins. Shiraz was near to the site, only sixty kilometers, and so it made sense. Fortunately, it was also the university town where Beth had spent a semester living during her post-graduate days, excavating a nearby archaeological site. If she could escape into the city, she'd be able to contact old friends, find shelter and safety.

The question was when and how she could manage it. Walter was a careful man and would likely have his lackeys shadowing her, especially after landing in Shiraz, and en route to Persepolis. Escape, Beth knew, would have to come during the moment of greatest distraction—upon finding the entrance to the Hidden Chambers. In the ensuing chaos and excitement, she could slip away, sneak back to the safety of the city.

But when the time came to actually do it, Beth wondered, would she be ready? Would she have the nerve? For someone traveling by foot, Shiraz was still a great distance away, and if she failed in her attempt to escape….

There came a soft rap on the cabin door, and Beth pulled her gaze from the window. The door opened and in the threshold stood two men encased in shadow. First to step into the light was Jonathan Walter, who'd shed the ceremonial robes of the Mithraeum and cleansed himself of the sacrificial blood. He now wore a pressed suit and a red silk tie. His hair was neatly combed back, his expression emotionless. Behind him followed the old man, Peter Eckerman, wearing the same blue rumpled cardigan, his mane of thick white hair flowing in waves.

Beth's stomach sickened at the sight of them both, standing there like gentlemen, calm and collected, when in reality they were nothing but monsters—monsters hidden beneath a human veneer. It was this Dr. Jekyll and Mr. Hyde dichotomy that struck her with an intense sense of fear.

Walter said, "I trust the apparel is to your satisfaction, Dr. Harper?" He was referring to the clothes he'd arranged for her to wear:

a denim shirt, khaki pants and boots. Attire he figured she would soon need.

Beth did not answer.

The two men stepped deeper into the compartment and Eckerman closed the door. Though filled with expensive furnishings—rich cherry paneling and plush leather chairs—the cabin had been Beth's prison for the past ten hours, and so it seemed to her cold and bleak, and now with the two of them looming in front of her, it felt overwhelmingly oppressive.

Walter took a seat next to her, while Eckerman lingered at a table laden with cuts of meats and cheeses and dishes filled with fruit. He began picking through a bowl of dates until he found one to his liking.

Walter removed a folded paper from his breast pocket. "A copy of the inscription on the cylinder seal, my dear."

The talisman no longer interested her, nor did the inscription. But Beth knew she'd have to cooperate and help Walter find the entrance to the Hidden Chambers. It was her only ticket out of this mess. If he sensed her reluctance, he might very well kill her before she could effect an escape.

Walter handed her the paper. "It troubles me."

She unfolded it and read aloud the translation. "Under the watchful eye of the great king is to be found the wealth of the empire."

"Thoughts, Dr. Harper?"

Beth considered the ancient message. Given what she'd come to learn over the past week, its words made perfect sense. "What troubles you?" she asked.

"The great king."

"Surely, it must refer to Darius," she said.

"Agreed, but that is not what troubles me."

Beth watched as Eckerman sunk his teeth into a date, ignoring the juices running down his fingers. After finishing, he took a cloth napkin from the table and wiped his hands clean, then dabbed at his chin whiskers.

"There must be a thousand depictions of King Darius scattered across Persia," Walter continued. "Finding the one referred to on the seal could be problematic."

"I don't think so."

Walter raised his dark eyebrows. "Explain."

"What you say is true, Persia is far too great an area to search, but it'll hardly be necessary. The legends surrounding the Hidden Chambers speak of only two entrances. The first was said to be permanently sealed shortly before Alexander the Great took the city in 330 B.C., probably to prevent the Greek from plundering its wealth. This entrance was known to be located somewhere in Persepolis proper, likely the king's palace, but the Iranian government has been reluctant to allow archaeologists to excavate an already fragile site, all in pursuit of a legend."

"Sensible," Walter said, "but that still leaves a vast area to search for the second entrance."

"The Hidden Chambers were said to be built by Darius contemporaneously with Persepolis itself. So tell me, if you were the king and decided to include another entrance to these subterranean chambers, where would you put it?"

Walter thought for a moment, then turned up his smooth hands. "I cannot say."

"Well I can," Beth said. "You'd put it somewhere outside of the city, somewhere secure yet within close proximity."

"That still leaves dozens of possibilities."

"Yes, but there's a site that stands out, an oddity among all the rest."

A faint knock at the cabin door preceded its opening. A suited man holding a satellite phone stepped inside. He was clearly of Persian descent, with dark eyes and a black goatee.

Walter peered up at him. "Any news, Aref?"

"Yes, Father. Sending Sarth ahead was a wise decision. His venture was successful. The minister awaits your call."

"Excellent," Walter said. "May I?" He gestured to the phone, which Aref brought forth without hesitation.

Walter turned back to Beth. "One moment, my dear." He dialed a number and brought the receiver to his ear. A few seconds later he said, "Am I to understand that I'm speaking with the Minister of

Culture of the Islamic Republic of Iran, Dr. Jafar Hazhir?"

Beth could hear garbled speech at the other end. Though the words were hurried and incomprehensible, she could detect panic in the tone.

"Understand," Walter went on, "I will say this one time and one time only. If in the future you ever again wish to hear the voice of your lovely daughter, or feel the warmth of your wife's caress, you will cooperate fully and do precisely as you're told."

*Wife and daughter?* A sick feeling settled in the pit of Beth's stomach.

"Effective immediately," Walter said, "you will suspend all activity at the site of Persepolis. You will forbid the presence of tourists, researchers, and the authorities. You will enforce this closure until I instruct you to do otherwise. Have I made myself clear?"

A shrill and panicked response.

"Very well," Walter said. "Your cooperation is appreciated. Especially, no doubt, by your daughter Sara and your lovely wife Nashva. Of course, I need not mention the consequences if you were to ignore any of these demands."

Another quick response.

"Splendid, then we have an understanding. I shall contact you later with further requests, if need be. And Dr. Hazhir, though this is undoubtedly a stressful time for you, please do not allow your recent misfortunes to damper an otherwise cheerful day." Walter ended the call and handed the phone back to Aref, who promptly turned and left the cabin.

Walter peered back at Beth. "I apologize for the interruption, Dr. Harper. You have my full attention."

Beth tried to speak but found it difficult to come up with the words. Right here in front of her, this monster had just threatened the lives of an innocent woman and child, and all to satisfy a sick lust to find the Hidden Chambers.

"Dr. Harper," he said, "your thoughts on the location of the second entrance, if you please."

Beth forced herself to stay focused, to bury her feelings. She said to Walter, "Eckerman is a part of your—" she stopped short of using the word *cult*, cautioning herself to appear indifferent, to avoid angering them. "—a part of your organization. Is that not correct?"

Upon hearing his name, the old man turned with a fistful of grapes, bushy white eyebrows raised.

"Peter is one of our honored Brothers, yes."

Honored Brothers, Beth thought. It was all she could do to contain herself, to stop from telling him what she really thought of his cult and his *honored Brothers*. They were really nothing more than a bunch of psychopaths. Her heart began to drum wildly as she recalled the horrific scene on the butte, the ceremony—she stopped, and with a tremendous effort, she pushed away the thoughts. *Stay in control.*

Beth took a deep breath and continued, "I assume the members of your order share the same unique interpretation of Persian history."

Walter smiled thinly. "If by 'unique interpretation,' Dr. Harper, you mean its true history, then yes, we do. You see, over the past two thousand years, from the time of the first Achaemenid kings, events of import have been dutifully passed on to us by our progenitors. As the current Inner Circle of the Brotherhood, we are the latest link in an unbroken chain that extends back over the centuries, connecting us with our glorious origin."

Beth paused, wondering just how much of what Walter had learned from these so-called progenitors was truth and how much of it was fiction. She decided not to pursue the question. She said, "When I first met Mr. Eckerman, he cautioned me to beware of your organization, a warning I now see in retrospect was meant to scare me into relinquishing the talisman."

Walter did not respond.

"Mr. Eckerman also told me something which at the time I dismissed as utterly foolish. He said Darius and the other Achaemenid kings were not in fact Zoroastrians, as history paints them, but rather they worshipped Ahuramazda as a façade to appease and gain the acceptance of Persia's dominant religious population."

"What Peter told you is true," Walter said. "And now surely you must agree. You have seen the iconic depictions of Darius wielding the talisman. Since the artifact draws its power from the will of Mithra,

Darius would have had little use for it, had he not worshipped the deity."

"Your view is not the consensus among scholars. In fact, it's a historical position I've never heard postulated."

"Yes, well you see, we've had little incentive to set the matter straight."

Beth said, "Nearly all the evidence suggests the Achaemenid kings were Zoroastrians. Herodotus tells us this, and we've had little reason to doubt him. Darius himself justifies his kingship in the Behistun Inscriptions, stating: 'By the grace of Ahuramazda am I king.'"

"As Peter told you, none of it is true, all a façade to gain popular acceptance."

"As much as I hate to admit it," Beth said. "I now believe you may be right."

"And that troubles you?"

"I'm surprised," Beth said, "but not troubled. It's the truth archaeologists seek, regardless of whether or not that truth enjoys popular support."

"A sensible philosophy, my dear."

Eckerman snorted. "I'm curious, Dr. Harper," his voice thick with German accent, "why have you changed your mind? I doubt you've much faith in the things we tell you. Did you not say moments ago that all of the evidence proves the kings worshipped Ahuramazda?"

"I said *nearly* all the evidence. There's one bit that's puzzled archaeologists for years, a contradiction it would seem that has now been resolved."

"Contradiction?"

"Yes, Darius built himself an impressive tomb at Naqsh-e Rustam, very near to Persepolis."

Eckerman frowned. "Your history lessons are beginning to bore me."

Beth stared at the old man, trying her best to conceal her loathing. "Are you familiar with Zoroastrian burial practices?"

"I am."

"Then perhaps you can tell me how common are their tombs?"

"Tombs?" Eckerman said. He popped a grape into his mouth

and began to chew. "Not common, at all. In fact, they have no tombs."

"Precisely," Beth said. "It's a clear violation of their faith. Zoroastrians did not bury their dead. They exposed the deceased to vultures in a long-standing and elaborate ritual that was meant to return the body to nature. And it was a religious practice strictly adhered to, whether the dead were rich or poor, a king or a peasant. So if Darius was a Zoroastrian, why then did he build himself a tomb? That's the contradiction of which I speak."

"Now you have the answer," Walter said. "He built it in truth because he was not a Zoroastrian, he did not worship Ahuramazda. He praised the one true God, Mithra."

"But that still leaves a point sorely in need of resolution." Beth swiped back a tangle of hair from her forehead. "You maintain that in order to gain acceptance among the populace the Persian kings did their best to demonstrate a commitment to Ahuramazda, a commitment that you say was nothing but a façade."

"That's correct."

"Then why would Darius pre-build his own tomb, an act that would threaten the very legitimacy of his rule?"

"Details," Eckerman said, waving a dismissive hand. "Who is to say why, and what on earth does any of this have to do with the location of the second entrance?"

"Think about it," Beth said. "If to build his own tomb Darius was willing to risk anger and revolt among the people, he must have had a great incentive to do so."

Eckerman popped another grape into his mouth. "What sort of incentive?"

"To conceal something of extreme value."

The old man stopped chewing.

Suddenly, Walter's eyes grew large, then just as quickly they narrowed, maniacally, sending chills through Beth's body. "*Under the watchful eye of the great king*… yes, I understand," he said. "The tomb built by Darius at Naqsh-e Rustam was meant to serve as more than just the king's final resting place."

"That's right," Beth said. "There can be no question. Darius's tomb must conceal the second entrance to the Hidden Chambers."

\*     \*     \*

Hours later, alone in the cabin, Beth gazed through the window. The jet was nearing Shiraz, descending in gradual stages. Below, the glowing lights of the city danced and flickered under the warm sky. Yet despite the danger that lay ahead, Beth couldn't help but feel a sudden thrill of anticipation. A secret entrance to the chambers beneath Persepolis, forgotten relics, treasures of immeasurable value, it was all quite unbelievable, and yet with everything that had happened in recent days, she knew it to be true. As the cabin lights dimmed in preparation for landing, Beth began to wonder just what kinds of unforeseeable challenges lay ahead of her.

# 2

THE GLOBAL EXPRESS Ultra Long-Range Business Jet had just reached cruising altitude when Mason stepped from the rear lavatory and walked into the main cabin. His thatch of red hair listed to one side under the circulation airflow. Rick had never seen the man more serious. His face was a mask of stoicism. Mason stopped, rested his hands on his hips, and surveyed the cabin. When his eyes came to rest on Rick, he tipped his head and marched over. "Mind if I sit?"

"It's your jet," Rick said. "What you must've paid to contract it, you can sit anywhere you like."

"Chump change," Mason said, lowering himself into one of four leather-upholstered armchairs arranged around a small table.

Rick said, "I can't tell you how much I appreciate the help."

"Don't want to hear another word about it. I'm responsible for Beth's predicament, and I'm gonna help get her back."

"Securing our visas and footing the bill for this charter is a hell of a start."

"No other way to beat customs. Because of the unmentionables you and Jarred brought along I had the hold loaded with all sorts of broadcasting equipment, to make everything look kosher when we land."

"About that," Rick said. "Jarred and I were thinking."

"Oh shit, stop the presses."

"Seriously, Mason." Rick looked over his shoulder for Jarred, who was staked out at the galley, looking over a tray of sandwiches. "Jarred, join us a second, would you?"

Disappointed by the interruption, the big man sighed, then lumbered over and took a seat.

"I was just telling Mason about the equipment we brought along."

"So everything's cool," Jarred said. "He didn't mind?"

"Mind what?" Mason said, narrowing his eyes suspiciously.

Rick said, "We were thinking it would be a good idea if you didn't handle any of the weapons that we brought along."

Jarred nodded agreement.

"What the hell are you talking about? I'm part of the team. We save Beth together, the three of us. And I'll need protection same as you guys."

"There's no telling what to expect," Jarred said. "We don't know what sort of improvising we might have to do."

"And without weapons and firearm experience," Rick added, "you'd only end up hurting yourself."

"Bullshit, I have plenty of experience."

"Watching *Cops* on the Fox channel don't count," Jarred said. "Look, Mason, we're only telling you this because we don't want you to get hurt."

"Ah, you can blow me. It's the military camaraderie you guys got going. You've been sucking each others' asses since the day I introduced you. You both served, and so you consider me an outsider. Well, I ain't gonna accept it. I'm part of this team and what one of us does, we all do. And that includes arming ourselves if necessary."

"There'll be no room for error," Rick said. "Everything we do, we have to do right the first time. People's lives could depend upon it."

"I'm arming up, nothing more need be said about it."

"Alright then," Rick said, growing irritated with Mason's stubbornness. He stood up and walked to the end of the cabin. "Jarred," he said, "remove the clip from your Beretta, set it on the table in front of Mason."

Jarred raised an eyebrow.

"Just do it."

"If you say so." He pulled his gun from its shoulder holster, popped out the clip and made sure the chamber was clear, then he slapped it on the table.

"Pick it up and make it hot," Rick told Mason. "You'd better get it pointed at me before I reach you, or I'm gonna show you the hard way why you're not touching any of the weapons."

Mason's eyes grew wide, and his hands began to fidget. "This is ridiculous, I have nothing to prove—"

"Make it hot, now," Rick said, charging across the cabin.

Mason jumped to his feet and fumbled for the gun, his grip uncertain around the barrel. Once in his hand, he snatched up the clip and brought both pieces eye level, puzzling over them, his hands shaking wildly.

Rick reached Mason, grabbed him by the shoulders, and pivoted around, flipping him across his waist. Mason landed hard on his back, his breath expelling with a burst. For a second, the little guy stared up numbly, face flushed. Rick helped him to his feet, then picked up the gun and clip he'd dropped in a panic.

Rick said, "That's why you're not touching anything you have no experience with."

Jarred grinned. "Christ, Mason, you didn't even know where to stick the clip. Hope you're better rehearsed with the ladies."

"And you picked up the gun with your left hand," Rick said. "Since you're a righty, you would've had to switch, time that would have cost you. Every second counts when your life's being threatened."

"Not to mention you buckled under the pressure. That was just Rick coming at you, and you were shaking like a wet dog. What would you have done if it were someone trying to kill you? Remember the holes in Rick's Kevlar, don't you? Those were made with real bullets."

Quietly, Mason sat back down, then stared off through the window.

Rick took a seat next to him. "We're not trying to humiliate you here, we're just trying to convince you it's best to leave the weapons to us."

"You made your point," Mason said, still staring through the window.

Rick said, "You mentioned this was about camaraderie, and I think you're right. But it's the three of us, not just Jarred and me. What I said yesterday about us being friends in the Army, I meant it. Had we served together, there's no doubt we would've had each other's back."

Mason turned from the window, looked at him.

Rick said, "Thing is, in the service, everyone has a function, a specific purpose, like one part of a greater machine. That's what makes the U.S. military so effective. Jarred and I, we have what we're good at, and you have what you're good at. In fact, without the logistics end of it, like arranging the travel visas and contracting this jet, we'd be nowhere right now. We're in this together all right, the three of us, and each one of us doing what we do best."

Mason turned a faint smile. "I guess you're right. Never looked at it that way before."

"Good, then it's settled," Jarred said. "I'm getting another sandwich." He stood up and hurried back to the galley.

For several minutes, Rick and Mason sat in amicable silence. Rick listened to the hum of the Rolls-Royce turbofans, watching faint circles of light projected from the windows slide along the cabin walls. The jet banked west and climbed. Rick thought of Beth.

Mason got up and walked to the galley, grabbed some snacks and returned. He snapped open a Pepsi and tried to make conversation. "Never met a woman quite like your Beth," he said. "She's more than a gorgeous face and a brilliant mind, she's feisty. I like that. She'll have no problems taking care of herself till we can get there to help."

"You're right," Rick said. "She's tough and resourceful. We'll probably get there and find she's taken care of these idiots herself." He forced himself to laugh, something it seemed he'd forgotten how to do.

Mason laughed along with him.

"You know," Rick said after a minute. "There's something else on my mind."

"What's that?"

"Something I saw on top of the butte that I haven't been able to shake from my memory."

Mason unwrapped a Ding Dong. "What did you see?"

"Remember the stories Eckerman told us about the talisman,

how the Brotherhood regarded it as some kind of a supernatural artifact?"

"Yeah?"

"Well, I saw something I can't explain."

Mason leaned forward in his chair, eyes narrowing with attention. "What kind of something?"

"I don't know how to describe it, really. It was during the ceremony. Walter lifted the talisman and flailed it around, all the while chanting in some kind of a strange language. The whole thing was unsettling, surreal."

"These people are nuts, we know that now."

"Yeah, well maybe I'm nuts right along with them," Rick said, "because what I saw come out of the talisman is beyond rational."

"Come out of the talisman?" Mason repeated back as if he hadn't heard him right.

Rick nodded. "Best I could say it was a stream of negative energy, like a river of… a river of evil."

Mason's eyes were transfixed. "Maybe there's truth to Eckerman's claim. Maybe the talisman is beyond human comprehension."

The comment hung in the air.

A moment later, Mason said, "I've been wrestling with a puzzle of my own, trying to figure out how Tanner's men were killed. Jarred did a little digging and we learned from an MMRC's toxicology report that they died from an unidentified toxin."

Rick straightened up in his chair. An unidentified toxin? Mason's words jolted his mind. Tanner's men were poisoned? Mentally, something clicked.

*Of course, Tanner's men were poisoned.*

Rick felt a sudden rush of adrenaline as his mind began to make sense of things.

"Problem is," Mason said, "there was nothing in the cave that could have poisoned them. Nothing. It's beginning to make me believe Eckerman's stories of supernatural plagues have some truth behind them. Maybe the talisman really is possessed."

"Not possessed," Rick said in a moment of clarity. "Infested."

"Infested? What do you mean?"

"That river of darkness I saw, maybe it wasn't a river after all. Maybe it was a swarm."

"A swarm? You mean like insects?"

"Exactly." Rick was beginning to see things clearly now. It made perfect sense. "After the monsoon hit, things got pretty twisted up there on the butte. What looked like a flowing river could just as easily have been a thick swarm of some kind."

"No, no," Mason said, shaking his head. "We've all seen the talisman. I've examined it myself, up close. If there were bugs on it, I'd have noticed."

"Not on it," Rick said. "In it."

"It's a rock for crying out loud. It's solid. There ain't nothing in it."

"I wouldn't be so sure about that."

"How do insects nest themselves inside solid rock?"

"I don't know how, but they have." Rick scratched the stubble on his chin, thinking back to the night he and Beth broke into the lab. "A few nights ago Beth analyzed the stone to verify its authenticity. I remember her sliding a sample under the microscope. Something she saw surprised her."

Mason stared at Rick.

"Holes, lots of microscopic holes."

"You sure about that?"

"Absolutely, I remember it baffled her. She made a note to ask a colleague about it."

Mason quickly unwrapped another Ding Dong, swallowed down half of it in one bite. He stared past Rick, unseeing, and spoke quietly, "A toxin, and DARPA wasn't involved, nothing found in the cave, there's no other explanation." He looked back at Rick, his eyes suddenly in focus. "You're right. The talisman's a frickin nest!"

"Beth found Tanner dead in his house, welts and pustules covering his body. He had the talisman. It all fits."

"Wait a second," Mason said. "We've handled it, too. Why haven't we been attacked?"

"I don't know. Maybe the insects are like wasps and bees, attack only when they're threatened or agitated."

"You said Walter shook them up, had them pouring out like a river."

"You're right," Rick said, perplexed. "But they were harmless. No one was attacked."

Jarred had noticed the excitement in their conversation and walked over with another plate of sandwiches. He sat in an armchair, listening.

Mason said, "Were you wearing protection of some kind, maybe a repellent?"

"No, nothing, and I doubt Walter and his cronies were either. They haven't the slightest clue what they're dealing with. They're convinced the talisman's some kind of a divine relic. They were going through the motions of a ceremony—wait a second," Rick said abruptly. "They were burning something. I remember the temple. They'd assembled a number of braziers. Fires were flaring up out of them, smoke drifting everywhere. It was sweet and minty smelling."

"Sweet and minty?" Mason said.

"Thyme," Jarred said with a mouthful of food. "They were burning thyme. It smells sweet, and a little like mint."

"It must have repelled the insects," Rick said.

Mason nodded. "It makes sense. Burning lemon eucalyptus leaves repels all sorts of nasty bugs. Maybe thyme has a similar property?"

Rick said, "Remember your radio broadcast with Tanner?"

"Yeah."

"What was it he said about the old hermit?"

"That he was crazy," Mason said. "No surprise there. You'd have to be to live alone in a cave with a nest of deadly insects."

"I remember Tanner saying the old guy was burning something. After they shot him, they panicked and tried CPR. Tanner said even though the guy was dying, all he seemed concerned about was the time."

"Like Tanner said, he was crazy."

"Not crazy," Rick said, "worried. He was the only man alive who knew the danger of the talisman. For chrissake, he was hiding it away from the world. When he pleaded to Tanner for the time, he wasn't worried about *chronological* time. He was worried about thyme—*the plant*. He knew what would happen if they stopped burning it."

"Jesus, you're right," Mason said. "We got it all figured out. This is great."

"Not so great," Jarred said. He set down the plate of food and brushed off his big hands.

Mason turned to him, smiling. "What do you mean? We've been fussing over this for days. What Rick says makes perfect sense."

"Yeah, you've discovered that the talisman is a nest, home to thousands of microscopic insects, with toxin potent enough to kill a man in seconds."

"Yeah, so?" Mason said. "It's not our problem anymore."

Rick jumped to his feet. "It's not our problem, it's Walter's. And Beth is with him."

Jarred nodded grimly. "That's right, Beth is with him, and the rock's a living time bomb, ready to explode."

Mason's smile dissolved away.

Something inside Rick tightened and in his mind he repeated Jarred's words: *The rock's a living time bomb ready to explode.*

## 3

"BY THE WILL of Mithra we have brought home the talisman." Jonathan Walter stared high over the dark peaks of the Husain Kuh Mountains in southern Iran. In one hand he held the talisman and with the other he caressed its glassy-smooth surface. "The night skies of Persia are by far the most beautiful. Wouldn't you agree, Dr. Harper?"

Beth beheld the starlit sky, her eyes following the trail of the Milky Way that swept in a great arc above her. It was beautiful, no doubt, like sugar spilt across black velvet, but without Rick at her side to share in its splendor, the moment seemed somehow hollow to her. "I prefer nights in the Arizona desert," she answered pointedly.

Walter turned to Beth, his lips stretched in a deep, mysterious smile. He continued stroking the talisman, holding his gaze upon her as if contemplating her ultimate fate. After a moment, he roused himself, then swaddled the stone with a cloth and returned it to a small shoulder pack.

A flood of bright lights exploded from behind them, and the multitude of stars suddenly disappeared. Beth turned to see an arrangement of klieg lights erected a short distance away, all angled skyward, illuminating the tomb of King Darius, cut deep into the cliff face over twenty-five centuries ago. Situated high above the earth and hollowed in the form of a Greek cross, the tomb was massive—nearly seventy feet in height and sixty feet in breadth. Its façade consisted of exquisitely carved bas relief: a series of bull-headed columns and an entablature topped with pedestals, upon which stood loyal subjects of the empire's vassal nations. In ceremony above them stood Darius himself, looking down upon a tiny recessed doorway. The entrance to the mortuary chamber. Under the king's watchful eye, Beth thought. Somewhere inside was concealed the entrance to the Hidden Chambers. Beth was sure of it.

At the tomb's base, Walter's men had constructed a scaffold, a towering skeleton of aluminum that did little to hide the impressive monument. The scaffold climbed fifty feet to the intersection of the cross, where the tomb's original stone landing fronted the entrance.

"If you are right, my dear, we now stand before one of the ancient world's greatest mysteries."

Beth spotted Eckerman milling about at the base of the scaffold. He wore the same old slacks, the same old blue cardigan, and at his side he even lugged the same old leather satchel, apparently undeterred by the prospect of exploration. His bushy white hair lifted in the breeze as he stepped up to the aluminum ladder, which rose through circular openings in each of the scaffold's five metal platforms. Eckerman began to climb.

Walter said, "It seems Peter has decided he can wait no longer. Shall we follow his lead, Dr. Harper?"

Beth did not answer. She simply took a deep breath and headed for the scaffold. At its base stood six men, two of whom she immediately recognized: Gus, unmistakable with his grotesquely thick arms and barreled chest; and Aref, another of Walter's cronies she'd seen earlier in her cabin on the flight to Shiraz. Both men were clothed for adventuring, and each had resting at his side a tightly-filled backpack.

Beth's eyes turned to the other four men, whom she had never seen before. All appeared Persian and worked to maintain deep scowls across their faces. The tallest of the four eyed Beth suspiciously as she approached, the other three, cradling rifles, stared watchfully beyond the perimeter of light, into the bleakness of the Iranian desert.

Walter stopped next to Beth at the ladder. His dark eyes scrutinized the frame, which had taken his men the better part of a day to transport and assemble. Walter, too, had spent the time in preparation, among other things abandoning his suit and wingtips in favor of more sensible khakis and boots. Finishing his inspection, he motioned for Beth to climb. "It would be best if you go first, my dear." He slung a small pack over his shoulder and prepared to follow.

Beth grasped the cold vertical bars of the aluminum ladder and began to climb, covering three rungs with each step. As she ascended from one level to the next, she again considered the possibility of an escape: in Walter's jet, she'd figured the ideal time would be during a moment of great excitement—the discovery and opening of the secret entrance. However, she'd failed to account for the tomb's height and the guards posted at the base of the scaffold. To flee from the tomb she would have to descend, but given the shrill noise she now made climbing and the openness of the frame's design, she wondered whether or not it would be possible.

She slowed her pace and climbed more carefully, testing the ladder to see if she could manage it quietly. But before taking the next rung, the entire scaffolding shuddered, and a German voice called down from high above, "This is an outrage, Dr. Harper! I would think you have some explaining to do."

Beth peered up through the openings in the platforms to see Eckerman standing at the handrail, glaring down at her. His face was contorted and awash in the powerful light of the kliegs. She quickened her pace. Reaching the top, she stepped onto the platform and moved across a long gangplank to the stone landing, where she could see recessed into the cliff face the small entrance to King Darius's mortuary chamber. Up close, the tomb's façade felt overwhelming. She'd visited the site before, but even as an archaeologist she had never been privileged to examine it so intimately. The top of the cross with its spectacular bas relief towered high above her.

Staring wild-eyed, Eckerman crowded close to her, his face red and swollen with anger. "Nothing," he said. "Inside the tomb, there is absolutely nothing! Explain yourself."

Beth ignored the old man, pushed past him, and ducked into the mortuary chamber.

*        *        *

Peter Eckerman couldn't believe this woman, arrogant and so full of herself. The entrance to the Hidden Chambers will be found in the tomb, she had earlier proclaimed. I'm sure of it. But clearly she was wrong. The mortuary chamber was empty! Far from an asset, in his estimation, Harper had become a terrible liability. A messenger of Mithra... poppycock. In fact, from the beginning she had proven to be nothing but a nuisance, refusing to relinquish the talisman when told to do so and speaking to him as though he were some kind of senile old fool. Her arrogance enraged him. He tried to relax, removed a bottle of Evian from his satchel, and took long, slow sips. At length, a calmness settled over him, and he felt a modicum of satisfaction imagining the horror he knew would soon befall this insufferable woman. He smiled and followed her inside.

The tomb was roughly twelve by twelve feet, hewn from the rock of the mountainside and completely bare of furnishings. A work lamp affixed to a tripod rested at its center, casting eerie shadows against the dusty walls and the web-filled corners of the chamber. Here, the klieg lights from below could not penetrate. "As you can see, Dr. Harper, the chamber is empty. You promised us the entrance, but in fact you have led us astray."

Harper did not answer. She moved from one end of the chamber to the other, regarding the walls and the ceiling, arms folded at her midriff.

Walter stepped into the chamber. "What is it, Peter?"

"Is it not obvious," Eckerman said. He indicated the room with a sweeping hand. "It's Empty."

Walter looked around, then peered at Harper. "Can you explain this?"

"Yes, explain this," Eckerman added snidely.

Harper maintained her pace around the chamber, purposefully ignoring their questions. She had moved beyond insufferable—she was taunting them!

"Dr. Harper," Walter said. "I was anticipating a sarcophagus or something under which we might find the concealed entrance. This room is completely empty."

Still the American said nothing. She knelt down on the floor and wiped away years of accumulated dust. Then she stood and walked to the wall, swiped away dust there, as well. "Marmo Graco Duro Antico," she said.

Greek? Eckerman thought. He may not have understood the language, but what he did understand was that Harper was deliberately speaking in riddles and making a mockery of the Brotherhood's endeavor. It was about time something was done. He turned to Walter. "I object to this woman's presence. She is a heretic and she has been an obstacle from the beginning. May I suggest—"

"Marble of Olympia," Walter said. He stared carefully at the surface cleared away by Harper's hand. "Indeed, the tomb is made of marble. Still, where shall we find the entrance?"

"The Persians were expert stonemasons," she said. "What appear to be solid walls could be deceiving. May I borrow your knife?" She nodded to the blade sheathed at Walter's side.

"Give you a weapon?" Eckerman said. "You must be kidding."

Harper said, "My interest is only in finding the entrance."

"I'm sorry, my dear," Walter said. "Perhaps another way?"

"Very well." Harper lifted her hands to her hips and looked around the chamber. "I doubt a search of the floor or ceiling will be necessary."

"And why is that," Eckerman asked impatiently.

"Because what we've been referring to as a hidden entrance is more appropriately called a hidden exit. Think about it, if it were an entrance to the Hidden Chambers, how would the king have made it up here? Your men had to build a fifty foot high scaffold and even that was quite a chore."

"It's not so hard to imagine," Eckerman said. "Perhaps in Darius's day there existed something permanent, something similar to our scaffold."

"Then so much for the entrance being hidden," she said. "No, I think it's far more likely the tomb served as an escape route, a way to flee Persepolis in the event of an emergency. A city under siege, for example."

Eckerman frowned. An escape route? Obviously, Harper had

not thought this through carefully enough. "Coming or going, I should think the problem of the tomb's height remains." Eckerman turned to Walter and grinned, having clearly outwitted the woman.

"Your reasoning is flawed," Harper said. "To descend the cliff face, a mechanism as simple as a knotted rope would have done the job nicely. It's far simpler to lower a body down than it is to hoist one up, gravity you know."

Harper was twisting things, trying to make him appear foolish in front of Father. Eckerman began to feel a constriction around his chest. It was as if his cardigan was shrinking with each passing moment. Quickly, he unbuttoned it. "Anyway, what does any of this have to do with the entrance not being hidden in the ceiling?"

"I believe the ashlars in the ceiling were permanently fitted. Ideally, the entrance—or exit I would prefer to say—would have to be easily reset. Difficult to do with ceiling blocks weighing thousands of pounds."

"I agree," Walter said.

"Alright then, why not the floor?" Eckerman said. "Quite accessible I should think."

"Because the floor is the final resting place of King Darius. You're standing above his remains."

Eckerman stared down at his feet.

"That's right," Harper said. "A cavity hewn deep in the rock contains his bones. After burial the cavity was overlaid with blocks of marble."

"Then it's the walls we must search," Walter said, suddenly invigorated.

Harper walked to the corner of the chamber and along a horizontal path began scraping her fingernails across the surface. Every few feet she stopped and marked a point in the dust. She continued around the room, completely encircling it, then she turned back to Walter. Sweat glistened from her sharp cheekbones. She swept a tangle of loose hair behind her ear and said, "Alright, have at it."

"I beg your pardon," Walter said.

"The knife," she said. "Since you refuse to give it to me, the two of you will have to check the masonry."

Eckerman found his temperature continuing to rise: his body, his neck, his face, everywhere hot. The tomb felt every bit as suffocating as the proverb suggested, and this woman only made it worse with her dismissive air and her flippant attitude.

Walter unclipped a walkie-talkie from his belt and switched it on. "Send up a guard, over."

"Copy that," came the quick, crackled reply.

Minutes later, a man armed with a pistol appeared at the door.

"Very well, my dear," Walter said. "A knife, as you requested." He unsheathed his blade and handed it over to her.

Blade in hand, Harper walked to the first spot she'd earlier marked with an X. There, she pried the tip of the blade into the wall, testing it. She moved to the next mark, repeating the procedure, but each time she probed, the blade met with resistance. "As I said, the builders of these tombs were expert craftsman. The stonecutters who dressed and set these masonry walls did so with millimeter precision." She continued around the room.

Moments later, reaching a wall in the far corner of the chamber, Harper stopped. "Interesting." She forced the blade between two quarried blocks, left it wedged in the stone, then knelt to her knee, grabbing for something at her boot.

Eckerman noticed the guard's grip tighten around the handle of his gun.

Casually, Harper untied and removed her boot. Then, clutching it in her hand, she stood to her feet, cocked it back, and slammed its thick rubber tread against the knife's hilt. With a scraping crack, the blade plunged deeper into the marble. Suddenly, Harper turned, and Eckerman saw reflected in her green eyes an intense look of excitement.

Walter rushed to the shadowed corner. "You have discovered something?"

"Yes, this cornerstone is not firmly set." With some effort she yanked the blade from the wall, wheeling around with it still in her hand.

Alarmed, Walter stepped back.

"Drop the knife," the guard yelled out, moving into a firing stance and leveling his pistol at Harper.

Eckerman watched with delicious anticipation. One step forward, Dr. Harper, he thought. Please, take just one step. But Harper didn't move, nor did a muscle of her tanned body even twitch. Slowly, she opened her hand and dropped the knife to the floor. It struck the marble with an echoing clank.

"I was simply going to examine the bottom of the wall," she said. "Would you mind lowering the gun?"

Walter nodded to the guard, who carefully eased his stance. "Step back, if you would, my dear," Walter said. "I shall do the examining." He picked up the knife and knelt beside the block, scrutinizing its base. "Yes, I see." He dragged the blade along the line between the wall and floor. "You're right, it would appear this stone is not completely set. Very hard to detect."

"Then let's not waste anymore time," Eckerman said, bounding forward. He stopped to size up the wall. "How does it open?"

"My best guess," Harper said, "is that the slab rests on some kind of a revolving cylinder system just below the level of the floor. We push it." She stepped next to Eckerman, flattened her hands against the wall, and drove herself forward. Eckerman positioned himself and pushed as well. There came a weak noise from below, a faint crumble.

"Something," Eckerman grunted, "something is happening." He pushed harder, with all his strength.

Then Walter stood and joined them, and together the three heaved forward. Under the strain, Eckerman could feel his head dizzy, the veins in his temples bulge.

Then the crumbling sound intensified, turning suddenly to a grind, and the wall began to slide. The dark crack of the corner grew in depth as the marble receded along a series of ancient stone rollers. The sound and vibration of the grinding spread in waves through the chamber's thick air.

Eckerman was first to stop pushing, followed at once by Walter, then Harper. Standing slumped and taking in long, labored breaths, Eckerman beheld the entrance: an eight-foot high rectangle of black leading somewhere into the darkness.

Then Eckerman felt a firm grip on his shoulder. From behind,

Walter leaned close and in a whisper said, "Mithra be praised, Peter. We have found the entrance to the Hidden Chambers."

# 4

THE GLOBAL EXPRESS jet had already reached Iranian airspace when Rick Lowell finally awoke. Over the past ten hours, on a bunk in a small cabin, he'd slept like the dead. And all things considered, physically, he felt pretty damn good. His muscles were tight and his joints a little stiff, but it was no more a nuisance than the ache he would experience after a vigorous workout. Even the throb in his side had eased significantly. A good start to the day, he thought, and if all went as expected and he found Beth safe at Persepolis, it would end even better.

Rick considered his prospects. Unlike at the butte, where Eckerman had double-crossed him, Rick now had two things going for him: he was showing up unexpected, and he was much better prepared. In short, he now had an edge.

There was just one more hurdle to overcome—Iranian customs. For that, Mason had brought along dozens of cases of satellite broadcasting equipment—props, essentially—all part of the show, and since radio was their business, talking the talk to customs officials would be a breeze.

But still, Rick worried.

The jet's hold was also filled with cases of contraband: automatic rifles, handguns, ammunition, communication headsets, thermal imaging goggles, the works. If agents did a thorough inspection and discovered the cargo, there'd be no explaining it away. The three of them would end up rotting in some hellish Iranian prison. When he took the time to put it all into perspective, Rick realized they were running a huge risk. He shook the thought from his mind, stood up from the bunk, and began a series of breathing and stretching exercises.

A short time later, after Rick finished dressing, there came a knock at the cabin door. Before he could answer, Mason pushed his way through, his doughy arms wrapped around a serving tray. He followed in the wake of a mouth-watering aroma. Rick eyed what the little guy was carrying, feeling a sudden, overwhelming hunger.

"Breakfast," Mason said, setting down the tray. On it were bowls and plates loaded with food: scrambled eggs and grilled ham steaks; a leaning stack of buttered toast; quartered strawberries and cantaloupe drizzled with cream; and cups slopping over with orange juice and steaming coffee.

Mason dropped onto a chair and began working a toothpick between his teeth, having presumably already eaten. He nodded to the food. "The reason Jarred's such a monster. That's his idea of a continental breakfast."

Rick didn't wait for an invitation; he dug right in.

"Pilot says we'll be starting our descent into Shiraz soon."

"How about customs?" Rick said. He forked a pile of eggs into his mouth.

"Not to worry. I've been told they'll send their agents onto the tarmac to do a quick outer inspection of the cargo and ask a few routine questions, then they'll clear us. No problems, so long as we cooperate and don't flaunt any violations." Mason scanned the tray of food. "Speaking of which, you'd best finish off those ham steaks. Iran is a Muslim theocracy. No pork allowed here."

Rick speared the steaks and laid them on a plate in front of him. He'd eat them next. A sudden lightness blossomed in his gut as the jet slowly dropped elevation.

Looks like we're on approach," Mason said.

Rick nodded, still a little concerned about their cargo. "And the weapons?"

"All packed up and buried at the center of a bunch of heavy broadcasting equipment. Customs people would have to be highly motivated to want to go digging through everything. It'd be a real pain in the neck."

"Let's hope you're right."

Mason's eyes narrowed. "When am I not?"

Rick sliced off a thick piece of ham and took a bite, leaving the question unanswered.

*        *        *

A short time later, the jet landed and taxied to its designated area. Rick, Jarred, and Mason followed the pilot's instructions and remained in the cabin. The wait was excruciating.

Rick was full, rested, and anxious to find Beth. He wanted to clear customs and get on with the task at hand. He peered out of the window into the pre-dawn morning. A haze hung over the airport, and the hangar's bright lights flooded the tarmac. A knot of men in greasy overalls went about unloading the hold.

Minutes later, a mountain of trunks and cases lay on pallets next to a truck.

Rick turned from the window and stared up the aisle to the cockpit door, which hung open to reveal a cramped, instrument-filled space. The pilot sat in his seat, a clipboard resting on his knees, shuffling papers and scribbling on what Rick figured were probably arrival reports and declaration forms. He answered a call on his headset and a moment later stood and hobbled down the aisle. Paled complexion, chapped lips, and folds of red skin under his eyes, the poor guy looked like a walking stiff. He forced a smile as he approached the cabin. "Okay, gentlemen," he said, "paperwork is complete. Customs agents are on the tarmac and will be here in just a minute. Have your passports, visas, and immigration cards ready." He turned away and began the process of opening the fuselage door.

Moments later, Rick watched with growing unease as a white Peugeot crowned with a single blue siren skidded up to the airplane. Two Iranian customs agents wearing olive uniforms and tightly fitted military caps stepped out from the car.

The pilot descended the steps and presented them with a stack of papers. After a few minutes of discussion, they waved him along. The pilot turned back to the jet and gave them a thumbs-up, then headed off toward the terminal.

"Alright," Rick said. "Everyone knows the plan. The weapons we carried on stay here. We'll arm up near the ruins with equipment from the cases."

Jarred and Mason both nodded, and together the three of them stepped out onto the landing.

The morning air was cool and slightly breezy, carrying with it the smell of an exotic spice. Rick wrinkled his nose as he descended the steps.

The taller agent, a man with deep creases around his eyes and a black, brushy mustache, stepped forward to intercept them. "Welcome to the Islamic Republic of Iran," he said in a rehearsed voice. "Your papers, please."

Rick collected everyone's passports, visas, and immigration cards, then handed everything over to the agent, who began a careful inspection. "The purpose of your visit?"

"We're journalists, here to cover the emergency OIC Summit."

"Expected length of stay?"

"Only a few days."

The agent's gaze remained fixed downward, his fingers expertly shuffling through the documents. Then he examined the photos in the passports, looked up and compared each to the faces before him. When he finished, he lifted the papers. "The packing list for these containers is missing."

"Got it warming up for you right here," Mason said, patting his rear end. He grinned devilishly and pulled a folded paper from his back pocket.

Straight-faced, the agent took the list and started reading from the top.

Rick watched as the man's partner casually circled the pallets, examining them with only mild interest—a good sign.

Mason called out to him, "Nothing there but a bunch of techno-junk for us radio geeks."

*For the love of God, Mason, keep your mouth shut.*

The agent halted at a large case, then lifted it slightly, gauging its weight. He pulled off his cap, scratched his head, then turned and gaped at their small truck.

"No problem," Mason yelled out. "We'll make 'em all fit, even if I have to clear room in the cab. I can always hogtie Jarred here and strap him across the hood."

Rick lowered his eyes and stared at the tarmac, praying that Mason would shut his mouth. Then at last, the agent handed back their papers. "It would appear all is in order. I can see no further reason to delay your—"

His partner suddenly interrupted him, speaking loudly in Farsi.

The agent turned, said something incomprehensible, then walked over to the pallets. Together they began circling them, touching the corners of each of the trunks, speaking excitedly.

Something had caught their eye.

"I don't get it," Mason whispered. "What's wrong?"

"Just keep your mouth shut," Rick said.

Jarred took a step closer and stared. "Oh, shit," he said. "Look what's on the containers."

"Not a thing," Mason said. "They're as bare as a baby's ass."

"Not so bare, dummy. Look at the corners."

Mason looked again. "Okay, so they have placards, so what? It's just the manufacturer's name and logo."

"The logo," Jarred said.

Mason narrowed his eyes. "Yeah, two bars with a little circle in the middle, whoopty-do."

"You idiot," Jarred said, his jaw tightening. "That's no circle. That's a six-pointed star."

"Okay, a circle, a star, big deal."

Rick fixed his sight on the logo, and his heart began to drum wildly. "My God, Mason," he said. "What have you done?"

"What do you mean what have I done?"

The agents were now speaking to each other rapid-fire. The short one unclipped his walkie-talkie and barked something into it. The man with the thick mustache turned and glared at them, the lines of his face deepening. Even from a distance, Rick could see the fury in his eyes.

"TeleComm, Ltd. is an Israeli manufacturer," Rick said. "And that's no logo, you dummy, that's the Israeli flag. Given these two nations' long-standing conflict, customs is gonna comb through those cases like forensics at a crime scene. We're screwed."

Together, the two agents hefted aside a large case and stared at some of the others behind it. There was a silence as Rick, Jarred, and Mason all watched in sick disbelief. Then at last Jarred leaned in slightly to Rick, and in a whisper he said, "What do you say I take out the tall one, you handle the other?"

## 5

BETH HARPER STARED into the black void with a mixture of excitement and disbelief. Somewhere in the darkness beyond lay a vast repository of history and culture. She recalled the legends of the Hidden Chambers and the rumors of its ancient treasure hoards. Consisting of a massive assemblage of jewels, precious metals, and fine works of art, the chambers were said to be a spectacular storehouse of tribute from each of the Achaemenid Empire's twenty-eight vassal nations. To archaeology alone, the magnitude of such a discovery would be incalculable. The possibilities stretched the limits of her imagination.

And yet, despite having reached this point, Beth Harper could still hardly believe it. In Walter's jet, and en route to the tomb, it had all been just a possibility—a fantasy. In the back of her mind, she'd expected the cylinder seal to be proven a fraud, to be nothing more than a cruel hoax meant to torture and confound would-be treasure hunters. But the entrance laying bare before her changed all of that.

A powerful beam of light suddenly stabbed into the darkness. Walter stepped next to her, holding a flashlight. Then a second beam lanced across the first as Eckerman, too, readied his own.

Beth said, "I'll need a light source, as well."

"I'm afraid not," Walter said, maintaining his stare beyond the hidden entrance. "Insurance to keep you close, my dear."

Frustrated, Beth turned to the void, watching as the yellow beams fought against the blackness. Walter was a clever man, no doubt.

He realized that the darkness would be a restraint more effective than anything he could ever devise. Without a light source, if Beth managed to slip away or somehow evade the group, she'd have to fight and grope for every foot. Escape would be nearly impossible.

"What can we expect ahead?" Eckerman asked.

"At some point an elevation drop," Beth said. "The chambers are deep under Persepolis. And we're three miles away from the ruins. I would expect a long walk. Beyond that, I cannot say."

Walter lifted his walkie-talkie. "Aref, my dear boy, Mithra be praised, we have found the entrance. I would like you and Gus to bring up the supplies. The others are to remain vigilant at the base of the scaffold, over." He turned to the guard. "You will return and assist the others. See to it we are not disturbed."

The man acknowledged Walter's instructions with a nod, then turned and ducked through the entrance of the tomb.

A short time later, Aref and Gus arrived, shouldering bulky packs loaded with supplies. Beth's eyes were immediately drawn to the pistols holstered at their sides. No light source and now two more armed guards, things were getting worse by the minute.

"Let's proceed, shall we?" Eckerman said. He angled his beam into the void. Walter followed his lead, and one by one they stepped through the narrow opening.

Beyond the mortuary chamber Beth found herself standing at the edge of a stone terrace. As in the tomb, the air here was warm and heavy with moisture. She breathed in deeply, tasting the ancient dust that still stirred from the movement of the sliding wall. The flashlights' beams swept high and low, then crossed each other left and right as Walter and Eckerman surveyed the enormous space. It wasn't a room. It was a massive cavern of some sort with a high, rocky ceiling that curved upward like a jagged bowl. The wall on the far side was distant and lost in the darkness.

Walter turned the beam to the ground. The terrace was long and narrow, maybe fifteen feet wide, and beyond it the floor dropped off into oblivion. Beth turned and examined the inside of the sliding wall. It wasn't a quarried block as she had expected, but rather a half block fashioned into the shape of a triangular prism, probably to reduce its mass and make movement along the rollers easier. Protruding from its side was a series of metal rods, each spaced a few feet apart. "See here," Beth said. "With those handles, the wall can be reset."

"Yes," Walter agreed. "And look there." He directed his beam behind them at the cavernous wall, to where a long rope hung in a thick coil around a stone hook. Heavy knots bulged along its length. "I would say Dr. Harper was correct, Peter. In an emergency, there was the king's escape."

"And you'll notice only one rope," Beth said. "After descending, it could be easily removed to prevent pursuit."

"Curse this stifling air," was Eckerman's only reply. He snorted and turned away.

"Aref, see what's beyond the terrace," Walter said.

The Persian man turned on his flashlight and eased his way to the edge. Carefully, he leaned over and peered down with the light. "A sheer drop, Father," he said in accented English, "Perhaps a hundred feet."

"Then how did the king ascend?" Eckerman said. "And more importantly, how will we descend?"

Walter moved his beam to the far end of the terrace, where it dead-ended at a rough-hewn wall nearly fifty feet distant. "I haven't an answer, I'm afraid."

"Wait a second," Beth said. "Hold your light against that wall." Slowly, carefully, she walked the fifty feet to the other end of the terrace. There, she saw a stone staircase cut into the cavern wall. It descended at a steep right angle into the darkness. "Stairs," she called out to the others. Her voice echoed in the black hollow.

With measured steps, the four men proceeded over, lances of light bouncing in front them. As they neared, Beth could hear Eckerman drawing labored breaths through his nose. They'd barely begun their exploration and already he was fatigued. She made a mental note of his condition. Perhaps if the opportunity presented itself, she could suggest pairing up to explore. One on one, she was sure she could handle the old man.

At the edge of the terrace, Walter lowered his beam. In the golden glow, Beth could see a series of switchback staircases, each descending steeply toward a landing before cutting back. There were five switchbacks in all, each running about twenty feet. Aref had been right; the ground was a hundred feet below them.

"Gus," Walter said. "You and Brother Aref take the lead. Mind your footing. These stairs may be stone, but they're also very old. There's no telling what sort of damage they've sustained over the centuries."

Gus and Aref maneuvered to the front of the group and paused, first glancing to each other, then gaping at the steps that fell away sharply into the gloom. After a moment, they adjusted their packs and slowly began to descend.

"If you please, my dear." Walter motioned for her to follow.

The stairs had no railing of any kind, and so as Beth approached the first step, instinctively she reached out with her left arm, bracing a hand against the rough-hewn wall. Although the width of each step spanned nearly three feet, given the pressing darkness and the nerve-racking height above the cavern floor, each step felt more like three inches. She took a deep breath, exhaled evenly, and carefully followed the two guards.

After centuries of neglect, the stairs had accumulated a healthy layer of grit, and with each step Beth could feel the coarse, unsettling texture beneath her feet. Everyone was quiet as they descended, concentrating on their footing, knowing the slightest misstep could be fatal.

Beams of yellow light played against the walls and pierced into the darkness as they moved. The sound of scratching boots and heavy breathing filled the air.

Soon, they reached the first landing and carefully reversed their direction, continuing their descent. With each step, the darkness seemed to enclose more thickly around them, swallowing the narrow beams of light. Then Gus's radio crackled. He stopped to listen. In a wash of static Beth could hear: "Brother... has arrived... in position... over." Gus lowered the volume and continued the painstaking descent.

Minutes later, they passed the second switchback, and they had nearly reached the third when Gus's weight jarred loose the edge of a crumbling stone. His foot slipped and he lost purchase, spinning violently in an effort to grab hold of anything anchored. The flashlight dropped from his hand and went banging down the steps, its beam flashing crazily in every direction. As he snatched helplessly into the air, Beth could see his face, mouth opened wide and lips twisted, his skin ghostly pale against the blackness behind him. The weight of his pack shifted him backward and he began toppling over the edge.

In an instant, Aref lurched forward, his hands shooting out like a spring, catching Gus by the straps of his pack. But the big man's weight was overwhelming, and Beth could see them both tilting toward the edge. Without thinking, she leapt forward and grabbed Aref by his dampened shirt. With all her strength, she pulled opposite their direction of momentum. It was just enough for Aref to regain his balance, and together they heaved Gus back to safety. As the big man came tipping onto the stairs, he threw himself at the wall and slumped down into a sitting position, his eyes wide with fear. His chest rose and fell with heavy breaths.

"You clumsy fool," Eckerman said. "You nearly destroyed our supplies."

Aref turned to Eckerman, his eyes narrowed with anger. "Maybe you would like to shoulder some of the weight yourself, old man?"

Eckerman shrunk back into the darkness.

"Come now," Walter said. "Let us focus our efforts on getting to the bottom. Shall we?"

There was a brief silence, then with some reluctance, Gus stood to his feet, took Walter's flashlight, and continued his descent. Aref glanced at Beth and tipped his head, leaving her with an odd, conflicting feeling. On the one hand, these were the men holding her captive, preventing her from returning home to Rick; but on the other hand, they were also human beings. She couldn't just stand by and watch a man plummet to his death. The moral dilemma left her with an unsettled feeling.

At length the group reached the floor of the cavern. Gus and Aref dropped their packs and began rolling the ache from their shoulders. Beth's eyes followed Walter's light as he swept it in wide arcs. With the exception of the terrace and the staircase, the cavern appeared to be completely natural: massive and with few deposit features, approximately two hundred feet in circumference, the result of millions of years of erosion and tectonic activity.

Beth was still marveling over the size of the cave when from behind her Gus said, "I'm no archaeologist, doc. But I'll be damned if that corpse there is two thousand years old."

# 6

RICK STARED ACROSS the tarmac at the airfield's cold and gray terminal building, a sprawling low-rise of steel and brick that stood like a prison in the morning twilight. Beyond it, and in every other direction he turned, a high chain-link fence topped with coiled razor wire encircled the grounds. Out of sight, but undoubtedly present in force, were the Iranian authorities. He and Jarred could incapacitate the two agents in front of them, but what would be their next move?

Rick turned to the big man. "Sit tight, let's see how things play out."

With a nod, Jarred reluctantly agreed.

The tall agent with the brushy mustache marched back over. "The contents of these cases," he said pointing a finger behind him, "they are the product of Israel, yes?"

Rick knew there was no sense lying. If he denied it, they'd just spill out everything onto the tarmac to verify. "I never gave it much thought," he said. "But now that you point it out."

"Hold on just a minute." Mason stepped forward and waved a pudgy little hand into the air, his red mop fluttering in the breeze. "We're Americans, you know. We have rights."

The agent's eyes darkened.

Rick maneuvered behind Mason and laid a hand on his shoulder, squeezing his deltoid like he would a wet sponge.

Mason groaned, then shrank back.

"What my friend means is that we apologize for any misunderstanding. We never stopped to consider the origin of our equipment. The station sent it along without consulting us. Clearly, had we known—"

"This is just like you Americans," the agent said, "flaunting your ignorance and disrespecting the sovereignty of other nations. It's an insult to my country."

"What insult?" Mason said. "It's just a bunch of electronics from Israel."

The agent spun on Mason, towering nearly a foot above him. "Israel? Here in the Islamic Republic of Iran, we do not recognize such a state. And for that reason, all of its imports are strictly prohibited."

"Okay," Mason said. "I can see where this is going." He pulled a checkbook from his pocket. "A shakedown, but I'll play along. How much do you want?"

"What!" the agent bellowed.

"Obviously I haven't been in your twisted little country long enough to exchange dollars for pesos, or whatever the hell kind of currency you people use."

"This is an outrage!"

"What's wrong, you can't cash an American check?"

The agent, now sweating with rage, yanked his walkie-talkie from his belt.

Rick had prayed Mason would keep his mouth shut, but it just wasn't in his nature. He was going to end up getting them all thrown into jail.

Speaking Farsi, the agent yelled into the walkie-talkie, spittle flying everywhere.

Rick had to take immediate control, calm the guy before he had the tarmac crawling with additional agents. In one swift motion, Rick snatched the checkbook from Mason's grasp, then backhanded him hard across the face.

Mason went sprawling to the ground.

"You insult this man by offering him money?" Rick said.

The agent lowered his walkie-talkie, the shock from what he'd just witnessed plastered across his face.

Rick knelt down and with both hands grabbed Mason by the shirt collar and hefted him to his feet. He shook him wildly on the way up for effect. "There's such a thing as honor and dignity, you little twerp! You may not have any yourself, but that doesn't mean others don't." Rick slapped Mason across the face with the checkbook. "Now take this and go sit in the cab of the truck. Open your mouth again and I'll knock your teeth out."

Mason wobbled on his feet, bleeding from the corner of his mouth. "I—I—"

The agent spoke a few quick words into the walkie-talkie, then clipped it back onto his belt. He smiled with great satisfaction.

Mason did as he was told and staggered toward the truck, while Jarred stood planted, nodding approval, obviously in tune with Rick's tactic.

"I hope you'll forgive Mason," Rick said. "He has a big mouth."

"Yes, a very big mouth." The deep creases around the agent's eyes began to soften. "He is fortunate to have a friend who knows when to shut it for him."

In the distance, speeding toward them, came a dark Mercedes van.

The agent straightened his posture. "As a representative of the Zone Authority responsible for the enforcement of all import regulations, I hereby confiscate these goods in violation of Article Two of the Free Trade Industrial Zone Regulations."

Rick felt a sinking feeling in his gut. He needed the supplies. They were critical for the fight ahead. "Look, I understand your position, these are your laws, after all, and I respect that, but I'm pleading with you, I've got to cover that OIC summit and broadcast a detailed news report. Without that equipment, I've got nothing."

"With this equipment you are in violation of Islamic law."

"Maybe you'd let me put together a bare-bones system, just pick out a case or two?"

"Purchase new equipment in Shiraz if you must," the agent said with a tone of finality. "But with our laws there can be no negotiating." He turned and waved an arm at the approaching vehicle, then pointed to the pallets.

The van backed up to the pile of equipment, and two men in dirty-white overalls jumped out. One pulled open the rear door, while the other tugged on a pair of work gloves. With practiced efficiency, they began loading cases and trunks into the back.

Hope quickly fading, Rick struggled to come up with an idea, but his mind drew a blank.

Then the tall agent turned to him, smoothing his mustache with an index finger. "Of course you may, if you wish, argue the matter with one of our magistrates." He paused and narrowed his dark eyes. "But that would require I take you into custody. The choice, my friend, is entirely yours."

## 7

THE CEILING OF the ancient cavern went black as Walter and Eckerman redirected their flashlights. Beth turned from the darkness, her eyes following the narrow yellow beams to where Gus stood hulking over the shadowed form of a corpse. "They didn't use kerosene lanterns back in Darius's days, did they, doc?"

"No, they didn't," Beth said, walking forward to examine the body. What she saw shocked her.

Lying face up on the jagged ground was the skeletal remains of a man. His flesh and organs had fully decayed, leaving a leather waistcoat and tattered undershirt collapsed around the ribcage. Bony hands laid palms up, drawn closely against the chest, giving the haunting impression the man had died fighting off something dreadful. With his face turned to the side, Beth could see the mouth open in a frozen scream. Judging by the style of the waistcoat, the leather trousers, and the button-up boots, she estimated the remains to be that of a man from the late nineteenth century. A Victorian explorer of some kind.

Gus lifted the lantern and with his flashlight peered through its dusty globe. "Thing looks to be in pretty good shape, at least better than its owner." He chuckled at his own wit, then walked to the edge of the light's illumination, where he picked up a large lumpy bulk. "Hey, the stiff's pack, now we're talking. Let's see what kind of junk this dude had." He plodded back over, fiddling with the straps.

"It would seem," Walter said, "that we are not the first to have rediscovered the chambers."

"I pray the parallels end there," Aref said, stepping from the darkness. He stared pitifully at the corpse. "Unlike our friend here, at some point in the future I should like to walk out of this place."

Gus unbuckled the leather strap, opened the pack, and spilled out its contents. An assortment of nineteenth-century exploring equipment went clanking onto the stone floor. Most of the objects, though very old, were quite ordinary: an oaken canteen and a small tin cup, a box of matchsticks and candles, tarnished scissors and forceps, a tangle of sewing twine and buttons. There was even a notebook and a scattering of dull-tipped pencils.

"What kind of crap is this," Gus said. "I can understand the canteen, but who the hell brings buttons and pencils to explore a tomb? Most of this shit is worthless."

Not really, Beth thought, most of *that shit* would've come in quite handy. Extra buttons, thread, and scissors to mend clothing; forceps to remove splinters and thorns; a notebook to record locations and important travel events.

From among the assortment, Gus lifted out an object Beth had never seen before. It looked like an iron nutcracker with a long rectangular head. "Okay," he said. "Now we're talking. This would've been useful."

"What is it?" Beth said.

Gus ignored the question and searched around the body. "Anyone see the guy's gun?"

Suddenly Beth understood. Gus was holding a bullet mold, another necessary tool in the arsenal of a nineteenth-century explorer.

She picked up the notebook and cracked it open. The pages were foxed and brittle to the touch. In the dim light, she skimmed the text, which appeared to be a detailed account of a small party's Near Eastern explorations. Reading further, it became apparent that the group's search was focused here, on the chambers beneath Persepolis. It was clear, too, that what the group sought was the site's rumored treasure hoards. Beth flipped a few more pages, stopped when she came across a chapter of detailed sketches. Whoever this man was, he was a fantastic artist. Beth stared at a few of his illustrations, which seemed to confirm much of what she had hoped to find here: an abundance of Persian art and architecture, all surprisingly well preserved. Also depicted in the sketches were rooms and tunnels of ornately designed walls and masonry work, some revealing many of the Achaemenid's well-known military triumphs, along with peoples and customs from the far reaches of the empire. And of course, shown as well were the hoard chambers—twenty-six in all, one for each satrapy of the empire. When Beth came to the final sketch, she stopped cold. What she saw made her skin crawl. The notebook shook in her hands.

Unnerved, she slapped it closed.

But it was too late. The image in the notebook had become seared into her mind, forcing her to recall the horror she'd experienced on the butte. Rendered clearly on the page was the likeness of a man, a companion of the artist perhaps. An unfortunate companion, pressed to the ground, scratching and clawing his way from the entrance of a dark chamber. He had become enshrouded in a fog of living haze, black yet strangely ethereal. It was the same entity Beth had seen on the butte enveloping the body of Walter's murder victim. Taking deep breaths, she forced herself back into the now. To escape the Brotherhood she knew she would have to be strong-willed. Fear and uncertainty would have to be mastered.

Eckerman stepped forward, gaining everyone's attention with a dramatic gesture. "In all the excitement over this poor man's supplies, has anyone stopped to ask themselves how, exactly, did he die?"

Gus regarded Eckerman with squinty eyes. "Maybe he fell from the stairs, like I almost did." There was resentment in his voice.

"Doubtful," Eckerman said. "The body's positioned too far from the edge. In addition, there's no trauma to the bones. Everything, including the cranium, appears to be fully intact."

"Okay, so maybe the guy had a partner, a no-good scoundrel who swiped his gun and shot him." Gus pointed two fingers at the old man. "Bam!" His voice echoed in the cavern. "That would also explain why he's got a bullet mold, but no revolver."

"Again, Brother Gus, you miss the mark," Eckerman said. Had this man been shot, you would expect to see a hole of some sort in his clothing. Yet, I see none."

Beth stared down at the remains. Though old and layered with fine dust, the leather waistcoat and breeches were completely intact.

Gus knelt and looked over the skeleton, then he rolled it onto its side. Pieces of bone dislodged and fell away to the ground. "You're right, no holes of any kind. Okay, old man, so I'm stumped, how did he die?"

"I haven't a clue," Eckerman said, shrugging his shoulders. "I simply pose the question."

"Maybe the body's a warning from Mithra," Gus said. "Maybe we shouldn't be messing around down here. Maybe we should leave."

Walter spun on the hulking man, his face suddenly twisted with rage. "Leave? We'll do nothing of the sort. Speak such nonsense again, and I'll have your tongue."

Gus shrank back.

"Let there be no doubt," Aref interrupted. "The corpse is not a warning. On the contrary, Mithra invites us to join Him." Aref swept his flashlight back and forth, marveling at something in the distance.

Beth followed his gaze to a clean, rectangular opening in the cavern wall, roughly eight by ten feet in dimension.

"A passage, of course," Walter said. "Our journey was never meant to end here in this bleak cavern."

"No doubt, Father," Aref said. "However, I speak not of the tunnel, but of that." He traced his beam over the ground in a path from the corpse to the tunnel entrance.

And for a moment, Beth felt as if she were gazing into the heavens. Stars of brilliant yellow glistened over the cavern floor as the light played off a great multitude of particles—gold dust, scattered everywhere. The sight of it was beautiful, it was unexpected. And it was just the distraction Beth needed to begin her escape.

# 8

FOR MASON MANNING, the quiet, early morning drive through the surrounding mountains of Shiraz proved to be both a journey of reflection and regret. How could he have let Eckerman play him for a fool? The old man had duped him into believing they were a team, then added injury to insult by knocking him a good one on the head. Mason prided himself on reading people, on spotting their motives, then anticipating their moves. But the old man had one-upped him, and as a result, Rick's girl was paying a heavy price. Damn if he was going to let Eckerman get away with this. Mason gazed out the window at the miserable landscape. All around him the earth was dead. Brittle, low-growing shrubs and gravelly soil seemed to smother the sinuous highway, stirring up feelings of anxiety and hopelessness. It seemed a hell of an awful place to be stuck without a Ding Dong.

Sandwiched in the cabin of the Mercedes flatbed between his two pain-in-the-ass buddies, Mason squirmed irritably, twisting and elbowing for a little breathing room. With his fingertips, he gently probed the small laceration at the corner of his mouth. It no longer bled, but it still stung like a son-of-a-bitch. "Christ almighty, Rick, what did you have to go and slap me for?"

There was a long pause, and then Jarred burst out in sardonic laughter. "What kind of fool question is that? You were a step away from getting us thrown into the clink."

"You kidding me? I had everything under control."

Jarred laughed again. "You're delusional."

"Okay, genius, take a look and tell me what you see in the back of the truck?"

Jarred turned and peered out the rear window. "Same as what was in it when we left the airfield. Nothing."

"That's right, nothing, and it's all because of you two idiots. You botched everything."

Jarred's eyes narrowed. "*We* botched everything?"

"Truth hurts, don't it?" Mason waved a dismissive hand. "You should have let me continue my negotiations."

Rick jammed the gearshift into third, picking up speed along the desolate highway. "Had we let you continue negotiating, right now we'd each be locked in a cinderblock room, cooking under an interrogation lamp."

"Bullshit, I was just getting started." Mason folded his arms and stared out the window, at nothing in particular. It was just like these two jerk-offs, refusing to trust him, refusing to let him follow his instincts. He may not have been an expert with guns and knives, but he sure as hell could handle people. It was how he'd risen to the top of his profession. It was how he'd made his fortune in radio. Rick and Jarred still had a pie in the sky notion of human nature, which Mason had been smart enough to dispense with a long time ago. When you stripped away all the pretense, people were animals. But for their lack of fur and feathers, they were really just wolves and vultures, all looking out for themselves, willing to tear out the next guy's throat if it served their purpose. Hell, most people would whore out their own sister for a cut to the front of a Starbucks line. What Rick and Jarred didn't seem to understand was that everyone, including those two customs agents, had a price, and eventually everyone sold out, it was just a matter of finding the right figure. And had Mason been given time to work on those agents, the flatbed would be loaded up right now. "Yeah, you two really screwed the pooch on this one. How you expect me to rescue Beth without any weapons or equipment?"

The question went unanswered.

Soon, the mountains gave way to a flat and fertile plain. At last, Mason thought, signs of life. Before him, spread out in a great open expanse were trees, trees everywhere, thick stands of birch and alder, and they were all lush and green and bursting with leaves the shape of giant teardrops.

Without a word, Rick pushed on, driving through a nameless town and eventually to a highway exit with a sign that indicated the route to Persepolis. At a three-way roundabout, he guided the truck northeast along a narrow, tree-lined road.

Still, none of the three men spoke, and like an acid, the silence was beginning to eat away at Mason's gut. Rick had to be working on a plan, and it was killing Mason not knowing what it was. "In case you didn't hear me when I asked the first time, I'd like to know what the plan is."

Not a peep.

"Christ, do I have to beg? What are we going to do?"

The Mercedes skidded to a halt, the smell of scorched brakes and burning rubber wrinkling Mason's nose. "What is it, what's happening?" Rick's steely expression sent a chill pulsing down Mason's spine. Following Rick's gaze, he spied a Y-intersection twenty yards ahead. One road branched right, continuing unobstructed. The other ran toward the foothills of a distant mountain range. It was blocked by a series of orange and white striped barriers. Posted in Farsi and in English was a warning sign: ROAD CLOSED BY ORDER OF THE MINISTRY OF CULTURE. PERSEPOLIS AND NAQSH-E RUSTAM UNDER CURRENT RESTORATION. ENTRY STRICTLY PROHIBITED.

"Beth's nearby," Rick said under his breath. "I can feel her."

"Okay," Jarred said. "Then what's the plan?"

Rick pulled to the shoulder of the road and cut the truck's engine. "Ideally, we'd move in close and recon the site at night."

Mason nodded. It made perfect sense. Darkness would act as a natural cover.

"But that's ideally," Rick quickly added, "and that's not what we're going to do now. We can't afford to waste any more time. We're already a day behind these people. Any more delay and we're jeopardizing Beth's chances of survival."

"Agreed," Jarred said.

"So we go in now?" Mason asked, hoping they wouldn't detect the nervousness in his voice.

"My map shows Persepolis about a mile beyond that barrier. It's still early and the sun hasn't broken over the mountains yet, so we'll have plenty of long shadows to move through. I say we park the truck under that copse over there, hoof it to the ruins, and do a quick perimeter check. My bet is they'll have positioned a watch. Armed, no doubt. With a little luck we can take them by surprise. If things go our way, we'll have pinched a few weapons. From there, we move in for a closer inspection, execute a spontaneous action."

Eyes widening, Mason said, "A spontaneous action?"

"In other words," Jarred said. "We wing it."

*Wing it?* That didn't sound very reassuring. Mason could feel his bladder beginning to tighten, and he had the sudden urge to relieve himself. "I know this ain't the best time, guys, but I really got to take a piss."

*        *        *

It was the work of thirty minutes for Rick, Jarred, and Mason to move to the perimeter of the ruins. By the end of the mile, Mason's lungs were burning.

Rick stopped and turned. "The ruins should be just beyond that stand of birch, but frankly, I'm surprised we haven't seen any of Walter's men. If the perimeter of the site is unobstructed, they might be positioned closer in. We'll move to the trees and observe." Rick looked at Mason. "Keep to the shadows."

Mason nodded. Shadows were good. Shadows were his friends.

Rick turned and raced away, Jarred following closely at his side. Mason kicked it into gear, as well, and hurried behind them, but despite his best effort, he found himself beginning to lag behind. Christ, couldn't these two slow down a bit, keep together in a group? Mason worked his legs in long strides. His heart drummed wildly, to the point he was sure it was gonna burst out of his chest. He gasped for air. Was running this fast really necessary? Or was it just Rick and Jarred's way of reminding him he was out of shape, not really part of the team. Determined more than ever to prove himself, Mason pushed harder, until his thighs felt as if they were awash in scalding oil. He ignored the pain and willed his legs to move faster.

Moments later, Rick and Jarred slipped into the shade of a birch tree. After a few seconds, with some relief, Mason followed them inside, parting his way past a low-hanging branch. He took a moment to master his breathing, to slow the gasps that were coming in quick-fire succession.

A minute later, calmed, he edged himself closer to Rick and whispered, "Maybe the two of you should slow it down a bit. You know, pace yourselves. You get winded, I don't want to have to pick up your slack."

Rick didn't seem to hear him. He and Jarred were staring spellbound through a break in the gnarled branches.

Mason turned to see what had caught their attention, and what he observed nearly knocked him to the ground.

The ruins of Persepolis.

In the hours before the flight, he'd read all about them on the Internet: the construction, the history, but nothing in print could have prepared him for this.

Rising some forty feet above the sterile landscape and cut partially into the heart of what the locals called the Mountain of Mercy, the ancient fortress loomed massive atop a 125,000 square meter terrace of perfectly dressed limestone. Built by King Darius I over the birthplace of the Achaemenid dynasty, the ancient city was intended to be a ceremonial capital, a symbol of the transcendency of the Persian Empire. Mason's eyes dropped from the marble capitals of the ribbed columns to the sweeping façade of the main staircase. Sculpted in exquisite stone relief, it depicted a twenty-three-nation tribute delegation, each representative wearing native costumes and bearing precious gifts. Centuries ago, these were the subject- states responsible for filling the vast Persian treasury. As splendid a sight as the ruins were, Mason knew Persepolis was just a ghost of its former self. Where once there stood fortified towers and brightly painted palaces, now rested only crumbled blocks and weathered columns.

He took a deep, excited breath. At first, like Beth, Mason had not wholly believed the legend of the hidden treasure hoards. It was an exhilarating thought, but a little too far-fetched for even him to accept. But now, face to face with the ruins of Persepolis, with this goliath of ancient history, Mason had no doubt every word of it was true. Somewhere beneath these crumbling stones were riches beyond his wildest imagination.

"I can't believe it," Rick said in a low, monotone voice.

Mason nodded. "I know, the ruins are fantastic, aren't they?"

Jarred stepped back from the branches, into the shadow. "I'm not sure that's what Rick meant."

"What do you mean?"

"The ruins," Jarred said.

"I know, they're beautiful."

"Yes... but didn't you notice? They're also deserted."

# 9

AS WALTER AND the others stared spellbound at the century-old trail of gold dust, Dr. Beth Harper knelt quietly among the litter of odds and ends that Gus had dumped from the corpse's pack. Slowly, she closed her hand around the scissors and slipped them into the heel of her boot. Then, she plucked up a candle, a small yellow rock, and a bundle of sticks. "It looks like," she said after standing and discreetly pocketing the items, "our Victorian adventurer here has discovered the wealth of the Hidden Chambers."

Walter turned and regarded her strangely. "Discovered its wealth, Dr. Harper?" His voice was laced with contempt. "This man may have discovered its gold and its jewels. But its wealth...? Certainly not."

Beth found Walter's reaction peculiar. If not to locate the hidden hoards of treasure, then for what reason was he here? What, exactly, was he after? Given her current crises, she decided not to dwell upon the question. Escape, she reminded herself, had to remain foremost on her mind.

Swiping back a tangle of loose hair, Beth exhaled nervously. *Escape.* She considered again the possibilities. When would be the opportune time? And how would she manage it? Even if she could create a big enough diversion, within seconds someone would be sure to notice her missing. And if they caught her... She looked down again at the hideous corpse and shuddered.

"We must end this delay," Eckerman said, interrupting her thoughts. "There is much to be discovered." He and Walter exchanged conspiratorial glances, then turned toward the dark tunnel, to where the trail of gold dust disappeared.

Aref directed the beam of light into the blackness, and Beth was immediately awestruck by what her eyes beheld.

Though the shape of the tunnel itself was architecturally non-descript—a simple rectangular shaft cut deep into the base of the cavern—its walls were something altogether different. Set from ceiling to floor as far as the eye could see were fire-glazed, polychromatic bricks arranged in a magnificent frieze of gold, green, and black.

Slowly entering the passageway, Beth stared from her left to her right, marveling at the brickwork's stunning depiction: a seemingly endless procession of royal guards—the king's Immortals. Each figure was molded and painted in fine detail: geometrically patterned robes of gold and emerald green; black, cascading beards styled with thick Persian curls. The warrior's faces were hardened, yet dignified, and they stood with timeless poise, bearing long spears and short bows, each prepared to forfeit his life in defense of his master—the king. Given the vividness of the frieze, Beth could almost hear the procession's thunderous march. And she was stunned by the tunnel's degree of preservation. Hidden for centuries deep in the cavern, it had been spared the brutal effects of weathering and human desecration.

"It's quite beautiful," Aref said.

Beth's eyes remained fixed upon the Immortals. "The level of craftsmanship exceeds that of the Ishtar Gate found in Babylon. Amazing."

Gus scratched his head. "It must've been something, putting this place together."

"It was something, alright," Beth said. "Ancient artisans had to carve and stencil out each brick, until their dimensions were exact. The bricks were then fired in a kiln, painted and set. What we see here is the final product. And if these bricks extend all the way to Persepolis, there has to be over a million of them. The expense in time and manpower must have been staggering."

Walter turned his gaze upon the group. "Yes, indeed, however, we must proceed."

The group collected their supplies, and with Gus in the lead, they began to advance, slowly, their collective footsteps echoing hollow in the narrow corridor, which seemed to run forever into the gloom. On the ground ahead of them, where the trail of gold dust ended, Beth could see a large, tattered pack and a scattering of objects around it.

Gus took a step forward, rubbing his square chin. "This looks like the spot that fool explorer started hemorrhaging gold."

"Curious," Eckerman said. There came a long, thoughtful pause. "Why would a man journey all this way in search of gold, only to carelessly spill it? Why did he not take the time to mend his sack?"

"I don't know," Gus said. "But whatever the reason, the dude was in a helluva hurry to leave."

"Leave?" Beth said. "Or escape?"

There was a long, uncomfortable silence before Walter said, "Enough of this useless speculation. We must move on."

Gus swiped away sweat from his forehead, then peered down the tunnel and continued his slow lead. Over the next thirty minutes, the group covered nearly three kilometers, the direction of the corridor never wavering from its arrow-like precision. Then, from somewhere ahead, beyond Beth's vision, there came a sound, faint, yet distinctly grating in its quality, like a handsaw cutting slowly and deeply into wood.

Everyone stopped to listen.

*Ksssaw, ksssaw, ksssaw.*

"What the hell's that noise?" Gus's hand reached to his pistol.

"We are not alone," Eckerman answered, shrinking back.

Then, as abruptly as it began, the grating suddenly stopped.

Aref's light played down the tunnel. "Look there, in the distance."

Beth strained her eyes to see through the dimness. About fifty yards ahead, it appeared that the corridor came to a sudden end.

"Gus, Aref." Walter motioned with a hand. "I'd like you to investigate."

"Indeed," Eckerman said, his large blue eyes staring worriedly down the tunnel. "And be sure to locate the source of that dreadful sound."

Aref pulled his handgun and began a measured advance. Gus, after a slight hesitation, followed his lead. Beth watched as the two men cautiously trailed the beam of their lights.

Moments later, they were shadowed forms, visible only as silhouettes against a soft, incandescent glow. Beth considered the opportunity. With the two guards at the end of the tunnel, was this her chance to escape? She glanced sidelong at Walter, then back at Eckerman. With faces of stone, their attention seemed fixed on the activity ahead. She could snatch the flashlight from Eckerman's grasp. The old man's grip would be relaxed; he wouldn't be expecting it. And with the light, she could make a wild dash down the tunnel, back to the tomb's entrance. Given Walter and Eckerman's age, no doubt she was capable of outrunning them, and with Gus and Aref at the far end of the corridor, she might actually be able to pull it off.

Her confidence swelled.

She clenched, then relaxed her fists, limbering her fingers, ready to make the snatch for the flashlight. Taking a slow, steady breath, she dropped her gaze to Eckerman's hand. She could do this. She could—

Suddenly, the three of them were awash in light. Gus and Aref had turned back, redirecting their beams. "Come forward," Aref called out. "The tunnel, there's been a collapse."

Without hesitation, Walter grabbed Beth by the elbow and urged her forward. "If you don't mind, Dr. Harper."

Beth did mind, but she knew better than to complain.

After a short walk, she found herself standing before a massive rockslide of stone and crumbled brick. The collapse, it seemed, had come mostly from above, very little from the sides. "The ceiling blocks must've given out under the weight of the mountainside."

"An earthquake?" Walter asked.

"That would be my guess," Beth said. "The Persians were expert stonemasons. Anything less than intentional demolition or an act of God and the ceiling would never have collapsed."

"We can dig through," Aref said. "The slide is like a pyramid.

If we climb to the top and clear away the debris, we should be able to squeeze through and continue our exploration."

Eckerman's plump frame began turning circles. His wide eyes stared curiously at the brick frieze. "No other doors, no other passages. It seems the only way to continue is ahead of us, through this, this mess." He squared himself to the rockslide and pulled from his pocket a linen kerchief, which he then used to dab at the sweat beading across his forehead. "Something puzzles me, however," he said in a worried tone. "The grating sound, from where could it have come? The tunnel ends here."

"From the debris," was Aref's quick answer.

"That's right," Gus said. "Probably just the settling of rocks."

"Fine, fine," Walter said, "I want the upper stratum cleared immediately. We proceed as planned."

Working in the glow of the group's collective light, Gus crawled his way to the top of the mound, sending cracked rocks and soil fragments skittering to the bottom. There, he began picking at the smaller stones, tossing them aside, until all that remained were the larger, more stubbornly wedged pieces. Each of these he then pushed with a heavy grunt, and one by one they tumbled to the far side of the tunnel. Within a few minutes, after some careful smoothing, he'd created a space nearly two feet wide, just large enough for a person to squeeze through. He turned, peered down at the group. "Alright," he said, sweat glistening from his face. "Who's first?"

"That, of course, would be you," Walter said.

"Of course," Gus said. With his brawny forearm he wiped his brow, then positioned himself at the front of the opening. Flashlight in hand, he belly crawled through, disappearing into the blackness.

Walter turned to Beth, staring at her with dark, emotionless eyes. "You, my dear, will be next."

She wasn't surprised by his decision. From the beginning, to prevent her escape, it had been his plan to keep her between two parts of the group. Walter may have been insane, but the man was no idiot.

She rubbed her hands, tested for a secure stone, then started the careful climb. Fortunately, most of the debris had already settled from Gus's efforts, and the larger stones that remained were packed tightly together. As she ascended, nothing stirred, save the occasional bit of sand that streamed down in tiny rivulets to the tunnel floor.

Beth pulled herself to the crest and peeked over to the other side. Gus was slowly descending, his massive frame half scooting, half sliding over the rocks. The yellow beam from his flashlight began to flicker and dim.

She squeezed herself through and followed in his path, using much the same technique, and doing her best to avoid the knife-like edges of splintered stones.

At the bottom, Gus stood to his feet and banged the casing of the flashlight. "Damn thing's on the blink." He shook it violently.

Beth reached the ground and brushed off her pants, stirring up a cloud of dust.

Gus's light wavered. "Cheap battery," he mumbled to himself. Then he looked up at the dark wedge above the rockslide. "Hope one of you guys brought an extra 6-volt."

The muffled sound of scraping and clattering arose from the other side as the others began to climb, Eckerman cursing each of the stones.

Then, in a moment of silence, Beth heard that strange noise again. *Ksssaw, ksssaw, ksssaw.* It was loud and it was moving. And it was directly behind her.

## 10

CONCEALED WITHIN THE shadows of the birch trees, Rick turned from the empty ruins of Persepolis and beheld his two friends, their faces drawn and pale. They stared at him with defeated eyes.

"I'm at a loss," Rick said. "This is the place Walter said he was coming." Rick's side began aching again, and his head throbbed. It was as if despair had awakened every one of his nerve impulses.

"Maybe they're all hiding," Mason said, trying to put a positive spin on their predicament. "Or maybe they found a way inside. They could be exploring the place as we speak. Sure. That's it. They're under the ruins. It's why we don't see them."

"Wishful thinking," Rick said. "If that were the case, Walter would've posted guards as a precaution. Beth's not here. Simple as that."

"Okay," Jarred said, "so let's say you're right. What's our next move?"

Rick swallowed, shaking his head. "I don't have one."

There came a long, drawn-out silence while each man pondered the problem. Rick's mind worked to make sense of the empty ruins. If, as Mason suggested, Walter and his men had found the entrance to the chambers, they wouldn't tolerate tourists or anyone else slipping past the road barriers and nosing around in their business. Guards would be posted to prevent that from happening. Was it possible Walter had remained in the states, making more detailed preparations? It seemed unlikely to Rick. On the butte, the man had been so insistent, almost obsessed in his desire to come here. Pained by the thought of having miscalculated Walter's move, Rick rubbed his fore-head and moaned.

Abruptly, Mason's eyes lit up, and in a flare of great theatrics, the little guy smoothed down his shock of red hair and proclaimed, "I guess we'll just have to head over to the other site, then. If they're not here, they must be there."

"What other site?" Jarred asked.

"Yeah, what other site?" Rick asked. Walter had mentioned Persepolis. That was it. Nothing else."

"Naqsh-e Rustam," Mason said.

Jarred's eyes narrowed. "What are you talking about?"

"Am I the only one of us three who can read?" Mason said. "The sign on the road barrier, remember? It said Persepolis and *Naqsh-e Rustam* were both closed for restoration. If Beth's not here, she must be there."

Instantly, Rick felt a stir of hope, a renewed energy. Mason was right. The sign had mentioned *two* sites, and it would make sense that if they weren't here, they'd be there. Rick pulled out his map and scoured it for the other location. "The place is close by," he said, "just a few kilometers. We can be there in twenty minutes."

With that, Rick folded the map, gave Mason a congratulatory slap on the back, and bolted from the shadows of the birch trees.

## 11

BETH FROZE. *KSSSAW, ksssaw, ksssaw.* The unsettling noise came again, moving swiftly in the darkness behind her. The image in the sketch of the doomed man flashed in her mind.

Gus spun on his heel, his flickering light pirouetting and throwing distorted shadows against the tunnel wall. For a fraction of a second there appeared a beast, huge and grotesque, with two beetle-like heads and limbs that ended in twisted claws. From the creature's sides sprouted a pair of sickly-red wings, outstretched as if in posture to attack.

The flashlight dropped from Gus's hands, cracking against the stone floor. Amidst the horror, the hulking man threw up an arm in defense, falling backward and tumbling to the ground.

Beth stumbled back, too, bumping against the opposite wall. Then, in a moment of clarity, her mind registered the sight. The beast, she realized, was a superbly-rendered carving, a vividly-colored relief of the mythical monster the Persian kings were famous for battling. She'd seen many just like it on ancient tablets and engravings.

With a sleeve, she wiped the sweat from her forehead. Apparently, Gus had also realized the illusion. His lips turned slightly in a grin, and with a look of relief, he calmly sat up and reached for the flashlight.

*Ksssaw, ksssaw, ksssaw.* Movement appeared in the corner of Beth's eye. She turned to the debris.

Inches from Gus, concealed among the rocks, a coiled viper bared its yellow fangs.

She watched in stunned disbelief as the snake lashed out like a whip, striking Gus in the neck. Then as quickly as it attacked, it jerked back, rubbing together its scales in that awful sawing sound. *Ksssaw, ksssaw, ksssaw.*

Gus screamed and slapped a hand over his bleeding wound, while the snake hissed and writhed.

"Damn, son-of-a-bitch I'm gonna kill—" Gus yanked the gun from his holster and fired repeatedly into the rocks.

Beth turned to shield her face, cringing as the shots echoed painfully in the narrow corridor.

Then the firing stopped—and so too did the sawing.

"What's happening over there?" Eckerman's voice carried from the other side.

Beth glanced back and saw the snake, which now lay in wet pieces over the rock. Gus, with the gun shaking in his hand, was breathing like a rabbit, his neck already blistered and swollen from the venom.

"Jesus, help me!" he cried out. Still hunched on the ground, he scratched his way to the wall, leaned against the sculpted monster.

Beth watched as his head lolled from side to side. The corridor gurgled with the sound of his shallow breaths.

Gus gazed at her with weak eyes. The flashlight dimmed. "Don't just stand there you stupid bitch, do something. Help me."

Beth would help, alright. This time, she'd help herself. The murder of the man on the butte, her kidnapping, these were evil acts, and these men responsible were evil people. And what had just happened to Gus, he'd brought it upon himself.

And now, Beth knew, it was time to make her escape. She scurried across the tunnel and snatched up the flashlight that Gus had dropped at his side. Without a pause, she turned and sprang down the corridor, deeper into the ruins.

"Hey, where you going?" Gus's voice was feeble. "Get back here, bitch. You hear me? I said get back here."

Beth pushed herself faster.

Ahead, the tunnel broke into a four-way intersection: one path continuing straight, the other two branching left and right.

A gunshot rang out. And then another. A bullet whizzed past her head, skipping off the wall and sending fragments of stone spraying in front of her.

She could faintly hear Gus in the distance. "I'm gonna kill you, bitch."

At the intersection, the flashlight dimmed to near darkness. She shut it off to mask her direction, then ducked left and felt her way along the wall, twenty, thirty feet.

Gus's cries slowly began to fade.

Beth had counted nearly a hundred steps when the tunnel wall abruptly ended, and she stepped forward with the sense she was entering a great void. Beth stopped. She needed to see, to assess her surroundings. Soon enough, Walter and the others would traverse the rockslide and come after her. She had to move ahead, hide herself deeper into the ruins. But first she needed her bearing. Risking detection, Beth flipped on the flashlight.

At once, its flickering glow revealed something astounding. Beth's heartbeat quickened. Her senses had been right. She'd entered a vast area, alright. A chamber. And what a chamber it was, an eighty-foot diameter hollow with walls of dressed stone and a ceiling lost to the darkness. Incredibly, it was filled with treasures of every sort, remnants of a dead civilization. But what her eyes feasted upon was not Persian, Beth quickly realized. It was Assyrian. Her attention was drawn like a magnet to the far wall, where erected from floor to ceiling was a relief replica of the great Assyrian palace at Nineveh. Expertly sculpted walls rose all around a courtyard dominated by the statue of a massive hybrid creature: a beast with the body of a lion, the wings of an eagle, and the head of a man, what the Assyrians had called a lamassu. Surrounding the palace in striking blues and greens were beautiful gardens, interlaced with flowing streams. Before Beth could fully admire the palace, her eyes were pulled away to a deep recess in the wall. From a distance, she stared closely and observed. In the alcove were shelves filled with tablets, hundreds of them, perhaps thousands, a magnificent library, complete and undisturbed. Eager to examine its contents, Beth stepped her way between a storehouse of incredible arti-facts, past gilded couches of ivory, past tables laden with golden ves-sels and ivory figurines, past bronze vases and silver vessels, past racks filled with weapons and woven fabrics. This chamber alone was the find of a lifetime, and yet, Beth knew, it was simply one of dozens that hid the riches of the Persian Empire.

Upon reaching the library, Beth stopped and marveled. The alcove ran deeper than she first realized. Much deeper. Shelved every-where were tablets the color of Saharan sand. Tens of thousands of them. And all intact. It was a discovery that would rival the unearthing of the Archives of Ashurbanipal.

Carefully, she removed one of the tablets, blew away its thin layer of dust, and brought it under the soft glow of the light. She began to read. The inscription, written in Old Persian, was a message from an Assyrian governor, paying homage to King Xerxes, wishing him good health and a long life and asking if the gifts sent had been pleasing and to Xerxes's satisfaction.

Beth scanned the cuneiform, her fingers trembling with ex-citement. She shelved the tablet and pulled away another, which ap-peared to be a letter to King Darius, laced with the requisite humility of the day. But as Beth read further, something in the text gave her pause.

She read it again: *I give praise to Ahura-Mazda, the god of your people, but more importantly I throw myself prostrate before Mithra, God and Protector of the great King Darius...*

Beth was shocked, for what she was reading altered the very foundation of ancient Persian history. And incredibly, it corroborated everything Walter and Eckerman had claimed: that the Achaemenid kings did in fact worship the sun-god Mithra. In her hands was physical proof.

As Beth considered the impact of the find, the tunnel crooned with the sound of muffled speech. The others had already traversed the slide and were approaching. Beth quickly replaced the tablet and stepped from the library. Turning circles, she searched for another way out.

Set into the opposite wall was a second tunnel. She took a step toward it, but then she stopped, looked around. The chamber was huge and packed with artifacts, many of them large and crowded together. If she could conceal herself among them, Walter and the others might pass through, giving her a chance to retreat back to the main corridor and on to the mortuary chamber. From there she could escape.

Suddenly, a distant light lanced into the chamber. They'd guessed her direction, or maybe they'd split up at the intersection, each taking a different route. Regardless of which, someone was coming and would be in the chamber within seconds.

Hide, or flee the tunnel? Beth knew she had to make a decision, and she had to make one fast.

# 12

FEIGNING A BREAKDOWN along the shoulder of the highway, a safe distance from the site of Naqsh-e Rustam, Rick stared out from under the hood of the Mercedes flatbed. His eyes traced a line of low-growing shrub to a field of rocks and boulders. Beyond the field, in an arc surrounding the tombs of the Persian kings lay an enormous clearing. There, a knot of armed guards stood idle, chatting and smoking cigarettes. Each appeared relaxed, except the smallest of the four, who was busy emphasizing his words with wild hand gestures. Behind the guards at the base of one of the tombs rose a metal scaffold, its aluminum bars winking in the sunlight.

Beth had to be here, somewhere. It made perfect sense. Walter needed her alive. He needed to exploit her historical expertise. But there was now the X-factor to worry about: the talisman. Whatever it was that infested the stone, it couldn't care less about historical expertise. Insects operated on a level of instinct. If disturbed, they'd attack anyone to protect their nest. And anyone included Beth.

Rick studied the face of the mountainside and the tombs cut deep into it. It was like staring at a series of tiny Greek crosses stamped into the side of a sheer cliff. But in reality, these crosses' miniature appearances were an illusion of distance. Each one of them, Rick estimated, towered a good fifty feet above the ground.

He circled the truck and climbed back into the cabin.

"She's here, isn't she?" Jarred said.

"Bet your petunias she's here," Mason answered. "And we're gonna get her out." He turned to Rick. "So what's the plan?"

The plan, Rick thought, was for Jarred and himself to get past the guards and into the tomb. From there they would assess and improvise, looking to acquire weapons and eliminating threats as necessary, without hesitation. The trick was going to be to convince Mason to stay behind and keep his duff planted in the car. It was clear he had been trying to fit in lately, ratcheting up his tough guy image and doing his best to be a part of the team. But the fact remained, Mason was a wimp. His weapons of proficiency were a checkbook and a national radio show, not a fist and an automatic assault rifle. Still, Mason wasn't going to tolerate being left behind.

Rick glanced at the little guy, whose face was alive with anticipation. Over the past few days, Rick had come to think differently about him, had come to realize that he wasn't the prick he pretended to be. Sure, Mason was a loner and maybe the most insecure human being on the face of the planet, but behind the macho, womanizing façade, the man harbored genuine feelings. He wasn't such a bad guy, and Rick didn't want to see him get hurt.

"We're in a bind." Rick sighed heavily. "Fact is, we need the muscle of all three us inside there. Jarred, me, and you, too, Mason."

"Okay, so what's the problem?" Mason asked.

"The problem is, an op like this has to have a point man, it's critical for success."

Jarred raised an eyebrow.

"You know what I'm talking about, right, Jarred? A point man, textbook military procedure."

Seeing the expression on Rick's face, the big man's eyes widened. He slapped a palm to his forehead. "Oh, that's right. We gotta have a point man."

Mason looked to Jarred, then to Rick. "What the hell's a point man?"

"Don't tell me you don't know what a point man is," Rick said.

Mason paused, his thatch of red hair fluttering under a cross breeze. "Of course I know, I uh, I just meant how does a point man fit into this particular operation?"

"Gotta have a point man," Jarred repeated.

"The point man," Rick said, "is the guy who runs the show. Normally, he controls alpha station with a comm, but since we don't have walkie-talkies or wireless headsets, we'll just have to use the car's headlights. You know, to flash signals if someone unexpected arrives, or if there's a serious change in the tactical environment. Without a point man observing from afar, we could very well run into an ambush. In this op, the point man will have to remain in the car and warn the other two of impending threats, anything unanticipated."

"With the headlights?" Mason said. "Wouldn't that be complicated and, well, inefficient?"

"Not really, we'll work out a few pre-determined signals. You know, like Morse code, but something simpler. Better than having no point man at all."

"That's right," Jarred said. "Better than running into an ambush."

Mason nodded, giving it some thought. "I see what you guys mean." He turned to Jarred, rested a hand on the big man's heavy shoulder. "Sorry, bud. You're the point man."

Jarred's eyes grew wide. "What?"

"It's the logical choice. Rick has to go. It's his woman we're saving, after all. That leaves just you and me, and there's no question I'm better suited for the job."

"How exactly are you better suited?"

"I'm smarter than you are."

Jarred opened his mouth to object.

"No time to argue," Rick said. "You're both equally qualified, so we'll have to do it the fair way."

"What's the fair way?" Mason asked.

"Like you said, Beth's my girl, I have to go. That leaves just the two of you." Rick leaned over and yanked open the glove box. He pulled out a paper and pencil. "I'll write a number between one and ten. The one of you who comes closest goes with me."

"Alright," Mason said, confident he'd win the pick.

Jarred said, "Rick, you sure you wanna do it this way?"

"Trust me, it's only fair. Now the two of you turn around while I write down the number." Rick tore off paper, scribbled. When he finished, he said, "Okay, let's do this."

Jarred and Mason turned back.

"You pick first," Mason demanded.

Jarred looked at Rick with an unsettled expression.

"No time to argue," Rick said. "Pick first, Jarred."

"Nine."

Mason grinned. "You idiot, that's what I'm talking about. I'm smarter than you are. I pick eight, that gives me a huge statistical edge. Eighty percent versus your twenty percent. One to eight and I win, nine or ten, you win. Looks like you're gonna be the point man, buddy."

"The number's ten," Rick said. "It's settled. Jarred you're with me. Mason, let's work out some signals."

Mason shot up straight. "Bullshit, let me see the number."

Rick un-balled his fist and let the little guy snatch the crumbled paper.

Quickly, Mason opened it, and just as fast his freckled face went white. "No shit, you wrote down ten." He swallowed hard, like he was taking down a golf ball. "I can't believe it. I'm the point man."

"No shame in that," Rick said. "And fair is fair. Now here are the signals."

# 13

IN THE DARKNESS of the Assyrian Chamber, Beth crouched motionless behind a toppled parasol. Its ancient fabric reeked with the stale of a thousand years. The light she saw bobbing into the room steadied. Then slowly it began to sweep a careful arc. Muscles tense, she concentrated on taking slow, deep breaths, fearful that a careless gasp would give her away. She strained to listen, but could hear nothing.

A moment later, there came the clap of heavy boots. Beth held her breath as the footsteps drew nearer. It was the sound of one man; she was sure of it. But then where were the other two? She tilted her head from behind the parasol and stole a glance at the tunnel entrance. Nothing but shadows. The three men must have split up, each taking a different direction. It made sense. They would cover more area in a shorter time. This, Beth thought, might actually work to her advantage. Split into three, their search would be faster, but far less effective. Whoever was here now would quickly move on, assume she fled down the opposite tunnel.

Near the center of the chamber, ten, maybe fifteen feet from the parasol, the movement stopped. Beth hunched lower, taking in a quick breath and sucking up dust from the floor. She fought back the urge to cough, holding her position for what seemed like an eternity. Then, the footsteps started again, echoing louder, closer. From under the woolen hood, she could see boots—five feet away, pointed in her direction. Her heart drummed with panic. Had she been seen when she looked to the entrance? Was he toying with her?

Suddenly, the light shifted to the far wall, to the tunnel opening. The boots pivoted. Beth closed her eyes and listened as they clapped away, their echo growing fainter. Choked with dust, she raised her head slightly from the floor and held her crouch until the footsteps reached the far end of the chamber. Seconds later, the flashlight dimmed.

Beth let out a deep breath and swallowed away what tasted like a mouthful of mud. Fear was nudging her to stand, to run in the opposite direction, but she fought away the urge and forced herself to think. She should wait. She should give whoever had followed her time to build up distance.

Still crouched, she counted off sixty seconds. Was that enough time? Beth wasn't sure. She counted off sixty more, slower this time, then, carefully, she peeked around the parasol and studied the tunnel opening. A soft glow emanated from somewhere deep within. She turned to the opposite opening, from where she'd originally entered. It was obscured in heavy shadow. No one was coming. Now was the time to make her move.

She stood up in the darkness, afraid to use her own light, and shuffled forward, holding out her hands and letting her fingertips do the exploring. She cautioned ahead, making contact with dozens of ancient objects, some familiar, some unknown, until at last she reached the path at the center of the chamber. She turned to the hazy glow, to see who had followed her, but the tunnel curved, and her pursuer was out of sight.

The other two men, Beth was sure, had taken different paths. All she had to do now was return to the main corridor. From there she could escape to the tomb. The thought of freedom energized her.

Careful to avoid toppling anything, she shuffled toward the opening. Halfway there, she paused and looked over her shoulder. Funny, the light hadn't dimmed. It was as if whoever had followed her stopped.

She decided to pick up her pace.

She took another step.

Movement caught her eye. She froze. Suddenly, a dark figure

appeared on the path, bounding toward her quickly. She barely had time to react before a hand reached from the blackness and grabbed her by the crook of the arm.

Beth tried to pull free and run, but she was held fast.

"It was a risky move, fleeing the group," said a man in a whisper.

Beth recognized the voice. It was Aref.

A gun barrel jabbed into her back, and the grip around her arm tightened. "Move to the light."

Sickened by her capture, Beth did as she was told, turning and walking slowly toward the opposite tunnel. As she moved, a feeling of tremendous angst settled into the pit of her stomach. She glanced sidelong at the countless artifacts cloaked in the darkness. How cruel it was, she thought, to be given a taste of a great discovery, only to have it torn away before getting the chance to savor it. It was as if the fates had conspired against her, and all that remained was for her to accept the inevitable.

Full of despair, Beth considered a final confrontation. And why not? She could simply turn and take her best swing, let the cards fall where they may. It was time for this nightmare to end, for better or worse.

As Beth entered the tunnel, the light grew brighter. She walked the tunnel's curve, still following Aref's orders. Ahead, she could see the flashlight. It lay on the ground next to a pair of boots. He had tricked her by leaving behind the light, silencing his movement, and backtracking in the darkness.

"Okay," Aref said. "We've come far enough."

Beth stopped and turned to face the man, stared into his dark eyes. She squeezed her fists. Go for the eyes, she thought. That's what Rick had always taught her, in case she was ever assaulted—the eyes.

"It's time to end this," Aref said, slowly raising the barrel of his gun.

## 14

"WE CAN FORGET taking them by surprise," Jarred said, observing the guards from behind the fallen boulders. "There's too much clearing to cover. We'd be shot dead before twenty feet."

Rick didn't like the assessment, but Jarred was right. The scaffold and tomb were surrounded by a wide sweep of open land. He and the big man would be sighted and shot well before getting close enough to engage. Yet the fact remained, there was no other way inside, short of repelling down the cliff face directly to the tomb entrance. The problem with that was their equipment was now sitting useless somewhere in an Iranian customs warehouse.

Two of the guards near the scaffold broke out in an argument. Their shouts carried over the field, but Rick was too far away to hear anything clearly. A third man stepped between them, and with the back of his hand, knocked the shorter one on the head. Rick didn't recognize any of the guards, but he was pleased to see they were at each other's throats. Their preoccupation and disunity might somehow work to his advantage.

"The day's just begun," Jarred said. "Sun's only been up a couple hours, but we can't wait till nightfall. There's too much at stake. Whatever we do, we have to do it soon, and we have to do it in daylight."

The two sunk low within the confines of the boulders, Rick considering their options. Maybe they could create a diversion of some kind, draw the guards away, then sneak up the scaffold into the tomb. It was doable, but Rick hated the idea of leaving behind four men, all armed and functional. It was something that could come back later to bite him in the rear. He ditched the idea.

A flash of reflected light caught Rick in the eye. He turned to see an approaching sedan. It pulled off into a gravel parking area. For a long while, the occupants remained inside. The guards had ceased their conversation and were observing.

Soon, the driver's side door swung open, followed by the passenger's side, then the two doors in back. Four figures emerged: two couples, one older, maybe sixty-something, the other younger, in their thirties. Rick watched as they donned colorful caps and hung cameras and video equipment from their shoulders. Laughing and talking away the time, they ambled toward the scaffold.

One lifted a camera and took a snapshot.

That's when the guards went into action.

"Can't park there!" shouted the smaller one, waving his rifle.

The two couples, who Rick figured were nothing more than tourists, suddenly took notice. They stopped. The older man pulled off his cap and scratched his head. Then he pointed at the tombs and yelled something in French.

When the guards caught up, they quickly surrounded the couples, brandishing their rifles.

It appeared to Rick there was a language barrier, for every time the guards yelled, the older man would lift his camera and point to the tombs. This went on for about five minutes. His patience at an end, the guard in charge grabbed the old man by the shoulder and spun him in the direction of the car. With a swift kick, he booted the Frenchman in the haunches and sent him hurrying away. But this only angered the younger man, who balled his fists and began screaming what Rick figured were French obscenities. The guards leveled their rifles and the Frenchman shrunk back, turned, then fled to the car, along with the others.

Jarred said, "Those guards are real pieces of work."

Rick wasn't paying much attention. An idea was beginning to form.

Laughing, the guards meandered back to their position near the scaffold and lit up another round of cigarettes.

Jarred said, "So tell me, Rick. What would you have done had I picked the number three?"

Rick looked at the big man. "What do you mean the number three?"

"You know, three. What would you have done had I picked it instead of ten? Right now you would have Mason here jabbering at you, instead of me."

"Oh." Rick's mind was back in the conversation. "Well, had you picked three, I would have said the number was one. Either way, you were coming along."

Jarred scratched his head. "But you showed Mason a ten. I saw the paper."

"You saw the piece in my right hand, not the piece in my left. A ten and a one. No matter what number you picked, you were gonna be at my side."

Jarred's eyes brightened. "Ah, you wrote down two numbers, a sly move."

Rick smiled and went back to his idea, giving it some more thought. "Wait here. Give me about twenty minutes. I'm gonna circle around to the highway." He turned and bolted off.

*       *       *

When Rick returned to the boulder field, he carried with him two cameras, a Panama hat, and a button-down shirt patterned with large red and yellow fishes.

Jarred stared at him like Rick had just stepped off an alien spacecraft. "Those tourists. You didn't—"

"Sure did," Rick said. "I cut across that field and flagged them down on the highway."

"And they handed over their cameras, just like that?"

"It took a few promises and a lot of persuading, not to mention all the cash I had in my pocket." Rick lifted the fish shirt. "Look what they had in the trunk."

"It's awful, and it screams tourist."

"Yeah, I know, it'll look great on you."

"Me? Why don't you wear it? I'll take the Panama."

"Sorry, I'll need it. I don't recall those men from the butte, but I can't be sure. One might recognize me." Rick turned the hat over in his hands, studying it. "I'll cock it low and keep the camera at my face, taking snapshots."

"Sly," Jarred said. He looked like he was thinking. "Let's see them try kicking me in the ass, like they did that poor old French guy."

"Alright, here's how we'll work it," Rick said.

They both knelt to the ground.

"We'll backtrack to the highway, walk to the entrance road, and come from that direction. They'll see us halfway up the road, but with our cameras they'll assume we're more tourists trying to photograph the ruins." In the dirt he traced the highway and the access road, marked the tombs and scaffold with an X. "My guess is they'll meet us about here, like they did the French couples. I'll feign interest in the tomb, keep the camera at my face. It won't take long for them to get pissy, so once they surround us…" Rick paused. "You know what to do."

Jarred nodded.

"Anything you wanna add?"

"No, I think it's the best option we have."

"Then let's do it." Rick gripped Jarred's thick shoulder. "I want to say beforehand, no matter what happens, I appreciate your help. More than you know."

"Forget about it," Jarred said. "When this is all over, you can add a steak dinner to the beer you already owe me."

Both men strung a camera around their neck. Rick snugged on the Panama, tipped it low. Jarred slipped into the shirt, which was too small to button close, so he left it hanging open.

Minutes later on the entrance road, within visual range of the guards, the show began. Rick lifted the camera and started snapping off photographs. Jarred walked with a pronounced limp, trying to appear less threatening.

With the soil crunching beneath their feet and the sun throwing bright rays over the earth, they strolled toward the tomb. It wasn't long before the guards noticed them. And as predicted they stomped out their cigarettes and quickly approached.

"Nothing to see here," one called out.

Rick and Jarred kept walking.

"Said we're closed," the smaller guard yelled. "In the middle of restoration. No tourists allowed, so beat it."

Jarred lifted his hand to his ear, like he couldn't understand what was said. Rick kept snapping.

Ten yards away, the guards lifted their rifles. "Stop right there. Said we're closed. No tourists today."

Jarred and Rick continued to walk, then stopped about five yards away. The guards marched closer. Two broke from the group and circled behind them.

Rick kept his head low.

"What's that you were saying?" Jarred asked.

"So you speak English, after all. We said get the hell out of here. You hard of hearing or something?"

"As a matter of fact, I am," Jarred said. "One too many metal concerts."

The guards crowded closer, all four gripping their rifles. Rick noticed that two of them had pistols tucked at their waistband.

The leader of the group, the one who'd earlier knocked the other on the head, stepped forward. He looked older than the rest with splotched, deeply furrowed skin.

Jarred said, "Hey man, we're just trying to see the site."

"Buy a postcard."

Rick snapped off a few more photos.

"Put the camera down."

Rick ignored him, kept snapping.

Angered by Rick's disobedience, the guard slapped at the camera, trying to knock it away. Rick twisted slightly, causing him to miss.

"Look, we don't want any trouble," Jarred said. "Just let us take our pictures."

"Trouble's what you got, boy," the smaller guard said.

Jarred sighed. "You know, I woke up this morning feeling great. Finished my S's, and was pumped about coming to see the tombs. Now this."

"What are you talking about, you finished your S's?" the smaller guard said.

"You know, I shaved, showered, and shit. And afterwards, I felt damn good about it, too. What's the matter, cupcake, you haven't shit today? Constipation soured your mood?"

"Oh a funny guy," the older guard said. "The problem is, I ain't got a sense of humor." He raised the butt of his rifle to strike Jarred.

But before he could swing, Rick dropped his camera and drove his foot into the guard's kneecap. There was a snap and the man yelped. He dropped his weapon and fell to the ground, curling and clutching his knee.

Jarred took care of the smaller guard, lunging forward and landing a heavy fist against his face. There came a crack as the guard's jawbone split in two. White teeth and a rope of bloody spittle exploded from his mouth. He dropped like a brick. "Take that, cupcake!"

Rick and Jarred spun to face the other two guards, whose expressions had become raw with surprise.

Rick charged at the one in front of him, grabbed a fistful of shirt, and fell backward, rolling the guard to the ground and onto his back. The rifle skittered away.

Rick leapt to his feet and lifted a boot. The guard's eyes registered panic just as Rick drove his leg down violently, crushing the side of the man's head. When Rick turned again, Jarred had already dropped the last one.

Quickly the two assessed. All four guards lay incapacitated, moaning and writhing on the ground.

"Collect the weapons," Rick said. He knelt by the older guard, pulled the gun from his waist. "Who's in the tomb?"

The guard moaned.

"I asked who's in the tomb?"

Gritting his nicotine-stained teeth, the man looked up at him, his eyes registering shock. "Hey, it's *you*, from the butte."

"Answer my question."

"Fuck you."

Rick leaned his full weight onto the man's broken knee. The guard howled in pain.

"Try again, asshole."

"Walter, Walter's in the tomb."

"Who else?"

"Eckerman, Gus, and Aref." He cried louder. "Look, that's it, I told you everyone, now get off my knee."

Rick eased up his weight.

The guard moaned.

"Beth, what about Beth?"

"The woman? Yeah, she's there, too."

"Is she okay? They haven't hurt her, have they?"

The man probed his knee. "Damn, it's busted up good."

"I said is she okay?"

"Yeah, yeah, she's fine, at least she was when they took her in."

Jarred hurried over, the four rifles slung over his shoulders. He had a gun tucked at his waist.

"Beth's in the tomb," Rick told him. "She's alive."

Jarred could scarcely hold back a grin. "You see, Rick. Walter's obsession with this divine messenger nonsense has kept her safe. He wouldn't dare hurt her."

The guard laughed in pain.

"What's so funny?" Rick said.

"Yeah, Walter's convinced she's a godsend, alright." He laughed again, then moaned, still clutching his knee. "But if you think he won't hurt her, you're as dumb as dog shit. He'll keep your woman only until the whim passes. Then he'll do with her what he always does with his undesirables."

Rick pulled the man up by his shirt collar, shook him hard. "What will Walter do?"

The guard looked Rick soberly in the eyes. "He'll offer her back to Mithra."

# 15

GUS WATCHED THROUGH dim eyes as Walter knelt at his side, speaking slowly and softly. "The woman has escaped. You failed me and you failed Mithra, my dear boy."

Gus couldn't believe what he was hearing. Failed Mithra? Who gave a shit about Mithra? That was Walter's deity, not his. From the beginning Gus had hired himself out to the Brotherhood for the money. Green was his God. He winced. The toxin burned through his body. Gus could feel it roasting his neck and his chest. "I feel weak, can barely move. Please, you've got to radio for help."

Walter pulled the walkie-talkie from his belt clip and shook it as if it was useless. "I'm afraid we're too deep into the tunnels. Communication is impossible."

"Then help me out of here, get me to a hospital."

"I'm afraid that won't be necessary."

"Won't be necessary? What the hell are you talking about?" Gus swallowed in pain. His breathing seemed to offer him little air. He dizzied.

Walter dug through his pack and removed a small mirror, then held it up.

Gus stared at the reflection, his mind in a fog. In the tunnel's pale light, he saw the image of a man. A man he didn't recognize. The poor bastard's neck and face had swollen up in nasty lumps. His skin had peeled away, revealing a wet mass of bloody flesh.

"The venom coursing through your body appears to be a hemotoxin," Walter said casually. "You see there Gus, where your skin has been badly flayed? That's the result of the toxin destroying organ tissue and red blood cells. Likely, you're hemorrhaging inside, as well. It must have been a deep and dreadful bite."

A few feet away, Eckerman paced the tunnel. "We must continue. Gus is of no use to us now. Anyway, he deserves to die for his incompetence."

Gus tried to scream at the old man, but his voice came only in a whisper. "When I get better I'm gonna—"

"I'm afraid you will not be getting better," Walter said. "In fact, you are already dead, my dear boy, rotting away in this tunnel like that unfortunate fellow back in the cave." Walter pulled his pistol, then slowly unsheathed a knife.

Gus stared in horror. Every nerve in his body screamed in pain. Light glistened off the blade, stinging his eyes. No, I'm not dead, he told himself, even as darkness began folding around him.

"I am not without compassion," Walter said, "which is why I shall let you choose." He raised the gun, then the knife.

Gus tried to spit at him, but could manage nothing more than a bloody drool.

"I understand," Walter said, grinning darkly. "You wish *me* to be the arbiter. Splendid."

He paused a moment, thinking. Then, with his eyes locked coldly on Gus's, he leveled the gun.

# 16

IT FELT TO Beth as if it was all happening in slow motion. With cool deliberation, Aref lifted his gun. But Beth wasn't about to die without a fight. Adrenaline driving her forward, she lashed out with both hands, lunging for the creep's eyes.

Aref leapt to his side.

Beth hurled past him, nicking his cheek with her fingernails and tumbling to the ground. She scrambled onto her backside.

Aref wheeled around, gun in hand, gaping down at her.

Beth closed her eyes and prepared for the worst.

A shot rang out.

She flinched, anticipating the bullet's impact.

But nothing happened. She felt no pain.

She opened her eyes, forcing herself to look.

Aref still stood over her, clutching the gun. He lifted it again, but this time jammed it into his holster.

She was confused. The shot?

Aref stepped forward with an outstretched hand. "Allow me to help you up, Dr. Harper."

Beth hesitated.

"Please, I will not harm you."

She ignored his hand and stood on her own.

"Listen to me, Dr. Harper."

Suspicious, Beth backed away.

"You could flee now, if you like, but your chances of escape will be much improved if you accept my assistance."

"But the shot," Beth said.

"It came from down the tunnel. Walter's cure for Gus, no doubt."

"I don't understand. Why would you—"

"Help you escape?" Aref finished her thought.

"Yes."

"You saved my life. On the stairs in the cavern. Do you not recall?"

Beth nodded.

"You could have easily allowed Gus and me to topple to our deaths." Aref's gaze grew distant. "Since that time, I've been struggling with a great dilemma: loyalty to Father, or…"

"Or what?" Beth said.

"I have decided I am honor bound to return your selfless deed."

Still suspicious, Beth said, "If it's your intention to help me escape, then tell me, are my fears real? Does Walter intend to kill me?"

"I'm afraid so. You are to be the first sacrifice in the re-consecration of the Mithraeum."

"A Mithraeum?" Beth said, surprised. "Here, under the ruins of Persepolis?"

"Not *a* Mithraeum, Dr. Harper. *The* Mithraeum."

"I don't understand."

"Where Mithra Himself was born from the rock and where He later slew the primal bull."

Beth stared off into the shadows. "And from its wound poured the blood that created all living things."

"Yes." Aref sat on the ground and began tugging his boots back onto his feet.

"I don't believe it," Beth said.

"It's not by accident Persepolis was built here, doctor. Darius chose the site because of the Sacred Cave."

"You're telling me—"

"Yes. We're standing just feet away from the birthplace of

humanity."

Beth felt a strange sense of conflict. What she was hearing sounded like the ramblings of the insane. Had Aref told her this a week ago, she would have said he was delusional. But now, with all that'd happened, all that she'd seen and experienced, who was to say? It was as if her scholarly convictions had been turned upside down. "Okay," she said, "let's assume there *is* a Mithraeum under these ruins. What makes you think it's the original?"

"It is written in the *Telesma*."

*The Telesma*. Suddenly, Beth understood Walter's lack of interest in gold. It wasn't money he was after. Of course not, Walter was already a wealthy man. The Mithraeum was his ultimate prize. He thinks he's found the Mithraic equivalent of Shangri-La. She asked Aref, "How does the talisman fit in?"

"I'm not sure what you mean?"

"What does it have to do with this Mithraeum?"

Aref finished knotting his boots. "The Mithraeum is where the spirit of our God is strongest. It is there the talisman will draw its greatest power."

Beth sighed. Once again she'd come full circle and was listening to religious fanaticism. "I'm sorry," she said, "I find it difficult to believe—"

"Do you wish to engage in debate, Dr. Harper?" Aref picked up the flashlight and stood to his feet. "Or do you wish to go home?"

She stared down the tunnel and thought longingly of Rick. *Home. Yes, she wanted desperately to go home.*

"If you choose life, Dr. Harper, you will do as I say."

Beth paused with a sudden thought. Was Aref being truthful in his willingness to help, or was this simply a trick? Was his true intention to lead her back to the others without a struggle? The thought of being recaptured by Walter, and the uncertainty of Aref's motives threw her mind into sudden turmoil.

"Dr. Harper, you must make a decision."

Beth's mind raced. Should she stand and fight while there was still only one man to contend with? Or should she trust Aref and risk being led back to the other's, where she would have to deal with three?

No, why would Aref go to all this trouble gaining her confidence and offering explanations of the Mithraeum? Moments ago, he could have easily killed her. There was no need to put on this charade. His intention had to be to help.

Beth decided to trust Aref, decided not to argue. She peered into the man's dark eyes and saw something that reassured her. "Okay," she said. "Let's go."

Aref probed his light down the hall and rushed back toward the Assyrian Chamber. After carefully threading past the artifacts, they stopped at the tunnel leading to the main artery.

"I'll move ahead," Aref whispered. "Follow quietly in my footsteps. When you hear me speak, stop. I'll explain to Walter and Eckerman that the room is clear, direct them along another path."

Beth nodded.

Aref turned and hurried off, making no attempt to move quietly.

Beth watched as his form darkened into the black. Then she began following the light's hazy glow.

Soon, the clap of Aref's boots stopped, and so too did Beth. She strained to listen.

"It's a chamber," she could hear Aref saying, nearly out of breath. "I searched it thoroughly, Father. She must have fled another way."

"Very well," Walter said.

There was a long pause.

"Peter and I will search ahead in the main tunnel. You take that one there. I'm confident, we shall find her."

Beth heard more activity, the clattering of boots. Minutes seemed like hours as she waited, full of fear, her hands trembling. Then the sounds began to fade into silence.

She crept along the wall toward the main tunnel, her hands brushing over raised portions of relief. As she rounded the curve, she could see a faint glow emanating from the opposite tunnel where Aref had been sent to search. The main artery lay just ahead. Left was Persepolis, and presumably the direction of Walter and Eckerman. Right, Beth knew, was the direction of freedom. Home.

A step before the intersection, she stopped and listened.

All was quiet.

Abruptly, as Beth took another step, a hand reached from around the corner and grabbed her shoulder.

She jumped.

"It's me, Aref. Forgive me, I did not mean to startle you."

"The light in the tunnel," Beth said. "I thought…"

"Dropped further down as a decoy. We'll use yours."

"The battery's low. I don't know how much longer it'll last."

"Long enough," Aref said. "Walkie-talkie's are useless this deep underground. Walter will not be able to call ahead. We'll traverse the slide and return to the tomb. From there, I'll draw away the others and allow you to escape. At that point, Dr. Harper, my debt to you is repaid. You'll be on your own."

Beth shook her head. "Fair enough." She stared into the darkness, toward the rockslide. This was the break she needed. Once on the other side, there'd be no stopping her. She was confident she could manage her way to Shiraz.

For a moment, her thoughts turned to her career, to the university. There was much she needed to explain, problems she needed to smooth over. But with recent discoveries, Beth was confident an agreement could be reached. Still, more important than any of that, she had to return to Rick. She realized how much she loved him, how much she still needed him, and she prayed he would take her back, care about her the way he used to.

"We mustn't delay," Aref said. "Give me your flashlight."

Beth passed it over.

He switched it on. Its glow was weak, but strong enough to reveal the gray surroundings. They moved in the direction of the rockslide. As they neared, Aref warned her, "Do not look at the body." He shifted the light away, into the cobwebbed ceiling.

But it was too late. Beth had already spotted the dark form lying slumped against the wall, directly under the winged beast.

*Gus.*

His head hung to the side, and all around him a dark pool gathered. Pieces of skull and brain matter plastered the wall behind him, giving the abhorrent impression the creature was feeding.

She looked away.

"Focus ahead, Dr. Harper."

With some effort, Beth continued to move forward, Aref at her side, until she found herself standing at the base of the collapse.

"You should go first," Aref said. "I'll keep watch behind us."

Beth needed no coaxing. She leaned forward and tested for a secure stone, then began to climb. To ease the task, Aref directed the light above her.

As she ascended, she took extra care to prevent toppling bricks and loose rocks. Noise, however slight, might alert Walter and Eckerman.

Her hands reached for the larger stones, the ones anchored and free of sharp edges. It was the work of five minutes, and she reached the top of the mound, peering through the opening into absolute darkness.

After a series of deep breaths, she leveled her body and squeezed through, feeling an immediate sense of relief. The main threat, she realized, was now behind her, on the other side of the rockslide. All she had to do was descend and run for the tomb. She maneuvered onto her backside, suffering quietly the scrapes of small, splintered stones. Oddly enough, the pain worked to keep her alert, to keep her senses alive.

She peered back through the opening and saw Aref beginning to climb. Forced to hold the flashlight, his ascent was far less rapid. He, too, seemed to take each step with great care.

Time passed excruciatingly slow. Though there was no sign of Walter and Eckerman, Beth feared they would return at any moment. Hurry, she silently pleaded. For God's sake, Aref, hurry.

When finally he moved within reach, she stretched out her arm and took the flashlight, then turned quickly, crawling down the jagged mound. A few smaller stones shifted and cascaded to the floor, but Beth maintained her speed, eager to reach the bottom. Midway down, a stone dislodged under her, causing her to slide uncontrollably. She threw out her hands, desperate to stop herself.

The flashlight flew from her grasp and went banging down the rocks, cracking against the tunnel floor. The light flickered, then died.

And as Beth slid in the darkness, a boot became lodged between a pile of heavy stones. Momentum drove her downward, while the torque of her body twisted her trapped ankle.

She jerked to a stop, feeling a sudden snap and a current of burning pain.

A cry escaped her mouth.

She forced her lips together.

"What's happened, are you injured?" Aref's voice carried through the opening.

For a time, Beth could do nothing but writhe in agony, her left ankle searing and throbbing. Eyes closed tightly, she tried her best to master the pain.

"What is it?" Aref repeated in an urgent whisper.

Beth parted her lips, forced herself to speak, "My ankle. It's lodged between the rocks. I think it's broken."

Aref didn't hesitate. She heard him struggle through the opening and pick his way down. "Where are you," he said.

"Here," Beth answered, helping to direct him with her voice.

Moments later, he was at her side, probing her calf. "Is this the leg?"

Beth winced. "Yes. It's stuck between the rocks."

She heard Aref feel around, then he grunted. A large stone shifted. A tremendous pressure eased from her ankle, and she pulled out her foot. Body rigid, she whispered, "I'm free." Her ankle pulsed with a fiery pain.

"Wait here," he said. "I'll descend and locate the flashlight."

The rocks slipped and crunched as he crawled down to the tunnel floor. Then there came the sound of brushing as he whisked the floor in great arcs with his hands. Beth heard a clatter. "The light, I found it," Aref said.

Beth waited in the darkness. She heard a metallic rattle.

"It's not working."

She couldn't bear to wait any longer. Injured or not, she needed to get off these rocks, to move down the tunnel toward the entrance. Though her ankle throbbed, Beth was sure she could manage it. She would crawl her way to freedom if she had to.

Carefully, she scooted down over the rough and jagged stones. When she reached the base of the mound she tried to stand, but the weight on her ankle forced her back onto her bottom.

Aref continued to shake the flashlight, switching it on and off repeatedly.

"I'm not sure I can stand up," she said.

"I will help you. Just allow me to—"

There was more rattling.

"It's no use," Beth said. "The flashlight's broken."

"Yes, I'm afraid you're right, and without a light to guide us, we'll never make it to the tomb."

"Wait, I have an idea." Beth felt into her pocket and removed the candle she'd taken from the explorer's effects. "Aref, come close to me, hold this."

"Where are you?"

"Follow my voice." She held out the candle.

Aref probed with his hands, found her arm, and took the candle. "Where did you get this?"

"Back in the cave, from the explorer's pack."

"Ah, you are resourceful." There was a pause. "However, I haven't the means to light it."

"I do," Beth said. From her other pocket, she removed the rock and the box of sticks, then she laid them on the ground in front of her. In her mind's eye she tried to image the process. She opened the box and removed a stick. With a fingernail she pressed a cleft into one end.

"I cannot see," Aref said. "What are you doing?"

Beth didn't answer, concentrating instead on the task in front of her. She held the stick between her lips so as not to lose it, then felt for the rock. After finding it, she crumbled off a small sliver.

"Did you hear something?" Aref said.

"Yes, it's me, I'm putting together—"

"No, I think it came from behind us, in the direction of the entrance."

Beth paused and strained to listen.

Silence.

"Walter and Eckerman are on the other side of the rockslide," she said. "We'll be okay for now, but I have to get this working before they return."

"Get what working?" Aref whispered.

With her fingertips guiding her, she wedged the sliver of rock between the cleft of the stick. It fit snuggly. "Okay," she said. "Let's hope this works."

"I don't understand, I can't see you. Explain."

"Bring the candle close to me. Make sure the wick is upright."

Carefully, Aref leaned near.

Still sitting, Beth reached out, felt for the candle. Satisfied that the wick was exposed, she touched the end of the stick to the ground and quickly scratched it against the stone.

There was a sudden flare and a greenish light.

Beth cupped the flame and brought it close to the candle. Touching it to the wick, she watched as the wax burned alive.

"How did you...?" Aref whispered.

Beth lifted the materials. "What Gus believed to be a collection of worthless rocks was nothing of the sort. They were nuggets of sulfur. Spalled and pressed into the cleft end of these sticks, they create the perfect match, a staple supply of every Victorian adventurer."

"Truly ingenious, doctor." Aref straightened himself, then held up the candle chest high. The light wavered with golden hues, highlighting his face in a pale orb. "Now, let's have a look at that ankle, shall we?"

Behind him Beth saw movement.

A dark form approached swiftly.

"Aref—!" she called out.

But before her words were fully formed, a towering figure grew behind him. A flash of steel pained her eyes.

Her hands flew to her mouth, to muffle a scream.

Aref tried to turn, but before he could manage more than a flinch, a blade swiped across his neck, leaving behind a streak of crimson gore. A rush of blood oozed over his chest, and he dropped to his knees, his face a canvass of death. The candle hit the ground and flickered, struggling to stay alight. Beth watched in terror as the figure threw aside the body and stalked toward her.

In the gloom of the tunnel, she resolved the face. Dark, emotionless eyes.

*Sarth.*

The assassin lifted the blade above her.

This can't be happening, she thought, horrified. She had come so close... *Rick...* The butt of the knife struck downward. There came a crushing blow across the side of her head, and darkness descended.

## 17

"YOU CAN RELAX," Jarred called back to Rick, who had begun loping down the ancient staircase, flashlight in hand. "The body ain't Beth's. In fact, it ain't anybody who lived in *this* century."

Breathless, Rick caught up to the big man and turned the hazy yellow beam to the ground. Jarred was right. What lay before them was a skeleton in vintage clothing. "It looks like some sort of explorer."

"Yeah, and this shitty place must've been his last hurrah."

Rick breathed a sigh of relief.

At the top of the stairs, they had decided to make Jarred the rabbit, have him move down alone. Rick stayed high, concealed in the darkness, a rifle trained downward to take care of any hidden surprise. When Jarred's light fell upon the body, Rick nearly lost it, convinced Beth had been killed and left to rot in this shit-hole of a cave.

Rick's fears were getting the better of him. He knew it; he just couldn't control it.

"I think it's safe to say they've moved on," Jarred said, "through that tunnel there, I bet."

The two men hurried to the threshold and probed the inside walls with their flashlights.

"Wow, look at the artwork," Jarred said. "Beth studies this stuff?"

Rick nodded, his mind still thinking of the corpse.

"You have to relax," Jarred said, regarding him carefully. "I know this hits close to the heart, but you have to keep telling yourself she's alive. Can you do that, Rick? Can you tell yourself she's alive?"

Rick didn't like dwelling upon his fears. What he needed was to move, to feel like he was making progress. "Let's get going."

Side by side, pistols leveled, they advanced down the tunnel, the pale beams of their flashlights sweeping a path ahead of them. Gold dust glittered on the floor. "Where do you suppose all this came from?" Jarred asked.

"I don't know," Rick said. "And I don't care. I just want to find Beth."

For what seemed an eternity they continued their march. All the while, Rick maintained extreme vigilance, ignoring the artwork on the walls and searching the shadows lying just beyond the range of his light. Jarred turned every few minutes, observing the emptiness behind them.

"There, in the distance," Jarred said at last.

On the ground lay a body. Rick's heart lurched. He rushed forward. As he neared, he realized with some relief the body was a man. A thick ring of blood pooled around him. A few feet beyond the corpse, a massive ceiling collapse blocked the tunnel.

Jarred stared at the body, then knelt down and felt its wrist. "Still warm, hasn't been dead long. Throat's been cut. He's young, looks Persian. One of Walter's men, maybe?"

"Maybe. But who killed him?"

Jarred shrugged.

Rick examined the rockslide. "The top's been cleared away."

The big man stood to his feet. "Then let's crawl through and keep moving."

Rick went first, climbing with little effort and working himself through the opening. Jarred followed, but from the sound of his moans and grunts, Rick knew he was having a hard time of it.

Once on the other side, Rick called back to him, "Got another corpse here. This one's bad."

Jarred squeezed through the opening and picked his way to the ground, then dusted himself off and stared where the body lay at the edge of the light.

"I know this one," Rick said. "They called him Gus. He

picked me up in the chopper. Definitely Walter's man."

"A sorry-looking bastard," Jarred said. "The guy on the other side was knifed. This one took a slug to the head. Christ, look at that, his brains are all over the wall—holy shit, what's that?" Jarred raised his flashlight.

Rick stared, too. The wall was overlaid with the image of some kind of creature. It loomed above the dead man, looking like it had just begun to feast.

"These people are sick," Jarred said.

Rick turned away, leaned against the tunnel wall.

"What's wrong? You've seen this kind of carnage before."

Rick stared into the cobwebbed ceiling, breathing rapidly.

Jarred approached him. "You okay?"

"Walter killed his own men. Why else would this corridor be littered with them? There's no other explanation."

"Don't sweat it, makes our job easier."

Rick turned his gaze and stared at the big man. "Don't you see? If Walter has no qualms murdering his own men—his hired help— then what kind of chance does Beth stand?"

"You're getting ahead of yourself. We don't know—"

"Driving to the butte, I had no doubt Beth was alive. I had the talisman. Walter wanted it. It was my bargaining chip. But now…" Rick lowered his head. "He's going to kill her, if he hasn't already. I know it."

Jarred grabbed a fistful of Rick's shirt. "Goddamn it." He slammed him into the wall. "You're breaking down. She's alive, I'm telling you. What kind of help you gonna be to her curled up fetal and crying like a pussy. If I hear you say she's dead one more time, I'm gonna split your skull and make brain boy over there look like a fashion model. Do you understand me?"

Jarred's anger jerked Rick out of his stupor. He looked up and glanced down the tunnel. "Christ, what am I saying? You're right, I can't fall apart."

Jarred backed off.

Rick straightened himself and took a deep breath. "Beth's alive. Let's go get her."

"That's the attitude." Jarred adjusted the rifle slung over his shoulder and pulled the gun from his waistband.

"Wait a second." Rick stared again at the body. "Gus's backpack."

"Yeah, and I saw a second one over there." Jarred pointed a few feet down the tunnel.

"Let's check them out."

Jarred inspected the far pack, while Rick rummaged through the one next to Gus. The main compartment was mostly empty. Rick figured whoever had killed him pulled whatever it was they needed and left only a few minor things: canned fruit and bottles of water. Rick pressed against one of the side compartments, felt something squishy. He unzipped it and pulled out a clear plastic bag stuffed with some kind of a plant. Why in the hell would they bring this? Puzzled, he opened the bag and was nearly knocked back by its minty smell.

*Thyme!*

With a sudden realization, Rick stuffed the bag into his shirt and jumped to his feet. "Forget the pack," he told Jarred. "We have to move, and we have to do it now."

"Quiet," Jarred said.

Rick waved the bag of thyme. "Look what they brought along, they're planning another ceremony."

"Shut up." Jarred held a finger to his lips.

Rick froze.

"Turn off your light."

Rick switched it off, plunging them into near darkness. Ahead of them to the right, a glow, ever so faint, emanated from a tunnel opening. "Another passage," Jarred said. "And someone's in it."

Quickly, Rick pulled his gun and together he and Jarred sided up.

Creeping toward the light, they were soon close enough for Rick to discern a four-way intersection. The glow came from the tunnel on the right.

Rick knelt low and peered around the corner, observing. The passage curved left. Light spilled from somewhere beyond the bend. He nodded to Jarred, and the two leveled their weapons and moved inside.

# 18

MASON SQUIRMED IRRITABLY, mulling over the bullshit reason he was sitting in the truck, getting hot in the head. This was ridiculous, hiding away in the cabin like some kind of forty-two-year-old, thumb-sucking pantywaist.

He peered out the window at the massive cross cut into the mountainside. Carved twenty-five hundred years ago, eh? Alright, so that was pretty cool. But it still didn't make him feel any better. He glanced above the ridge, to where the sun hung suspended in the sky, pouring hues of yellow and gold over the highway. The day was rolling on, and he wasn't accomplishing a goddamn thing.

What good was being the point man now? Mason had watched from the truck as Rick and Jarred whopped the living shit out of those idiot guards, pilfered their equipment, and snuck into the tomb by way of the aluminum scaffold. Now, flashing headlight signals would be pointless. The real action was happening inside.

The more Mason thought about it, the more he realized this was just another trick. In fact, now he was sure of it. Rick probably had plans to throw it all back in his face, on the air most likely. Rick would call him a coward for hiding out in the car, embarrass him again, just like he had when he played the recording of Mason's urologist consultation. Mason crossed his legs. That was just plain wrong. Rick had humiliated him on the air, in front of a national audience, millions of listeners. Mason wasn't about to let him do it again.

With a jerk of the handle, he threw open the cabin door, stepped out into the sunshine. He took a deep breath and stared at the mountainside. The tomb.

He thought of Beth.

Forget the on-air rivalry. He had a bone to pick with Rick, if for no other reason than he was screwing with Beth's chances of rescue. Sure as shit they could accomplish more with three minds than they could with only two. And that was assuming, of course, Jarred was given credit for a full brain, which was a bit of a stretch.

Mason took in his belt a notch. It had been nearly twenty-four hours since he'd even looked at a Ding Dong. He was sure he'd already dropped a few pounds.

The field of strewn boulders was a short jaunt. Mason whistled as he walked. Nearing it, he could see the men Rick and Jarred had beaten and subdued. All four were hogtied and lying on their sides. A couple of them moaned. Mason moseyed up glaring over the sorry-ass group. One of the guards eyed him with a bruised face.

"You losers are lucky I wasn't with them," Mason said. "Had I let loose on you, none of you would be breathing right now."

The tall one mumbled something through his gag tie, but Mason ignored him and continued to the scaffold. An open duffel bag rested in the shade. He upturned it, dug through all the junk, found a flashlight and a water bottle.

A tiring climb up the ladder and Mason was inside the tomb, marveling at the ancient stonework. It was a helluva long time ago, he thought, but these people really knew how to carve a rock. He brushed a hand over the dressed stone. Smooth as silk. Maybe back at the radio station he'd start a history segment, air a piece about ancient architecture. He could bring Beth on as an expert guest. God knew after all this she owed him, big-time.

Beyond the secret wall in the mortuary chamber, Mason descended the gritty staircase, carefully, and real slow. He began to worry. The place was eerie and quiet, and who knew what kind of dangers hid in the shadows. The blackness seemed to swallow his light.

He stopped midway down. Toughen up, he scolded himself, look at this as an adventure. Why not? When he was a kid he used to pretend he was a pirate. He'd wield a mixing spoon as a cutlass, tie a slingshot over his eye, and splash around the pool for hours on end. It passed the time and gave him loads of confidence. I'm a pirate, he told himself as he resumed his descent. And no one screws with a pirate. Amazingly, he felt better already.

By the time Mason entered the main tunnel, his confidence had plummeted again. The corpse he'd found in the cave had given him the creeps and he was beginning to wonder if leaving the truck had been such a good idea. He paused, stared deep into the tunnel's gloom. Strangely, the floor glittered with the color of gold. He sucked in a long breath and reminded himself why he was here. The hell if he'd let Rick embarrass him on the air again. He'd die before that happened.

Urging himself forward, Mason covered what must've been two or three kilometers, taking no more than thirty minutes. He was proud of himself and wondered how long it had taken Rick and Jarred.

Ahead, he saw something. A lump, lying still, obscured in the shadows. He played his light in circles down the tunnel, inspecting the ceiling as much as he did the ground. Slowly, he inched forward.

Closer, he realized what he was staring at.

*Holy shit.* This was no skeleton, like back in the cave. This was the body of a man recently killed. Could Rick and Jarred have—? Mason covered his mouth and edged along the wall, sickened by the sight, giving the corpse a wide berth.

He was so fixated upon the foul scene that when he turned he nearly stumbled back. A rockslide blocked the tunnel. But his light revealed an opening at the top. Eager to get past the dead man, he scrambled up and through, descended the other side.

Once on firm ground, he swung the light in circles to get his bearing. That's when he saw it: the second body, the gnarly-ass beast, the brains all over the wall. Something lurched in his gut, and a burning stream erupted from his mouth. He turned away, spraying vomit over the rocks. After a quick breath, he braced himself against something solid and wiped his lips with the back of his hand. In all his life, he'd never seen anything so horribly grotesque.

Christ, the place was littered with corpses. Rick and Jarred weren't screwing around here. Mason straightened himself with a renewed sense of urgency. Beth was in a world of trouble. He pulled the water bottle from his pocket, opened it, and took a deep swig, swooshing the water around in his mouth before swallowing.

Time to get moving. He had a woman to save. Mason returned the bottle and directed the light down the corridor. A short distance away, he could make out a four-way intersection. As he approached, he considered which way to go. Left? Right? Straight? Why bother changing course? Mason decided. He peered forward and started straight ahead, but upon taking his first step, another thought occurred to him. Could these tunnels and chambers be booby-trapped? The possibility made his nerves prickle. Mason had seen *Raiders of the Lost Ark* and a million other movies just like it, enough movies to know that treasure hunters never got out of these places with their skin still clinging to their bones. The corpse back in the cavern, could it have been the victim of one of these traps? Mason stared at the dusty floor. His next step could very well trigger a pressure-sensitive plate. Poison-tipped darts or spring-loaded knives might suddenly burst from the walls, killing him where he stood. The beam of his flashlight wavered, and Mason looked down at his hands to see them shaking. His unconscious reaction to his own thoughts pissed him off. A trapped tunnel? Get a grip. You're just scaring yourself. Shit like that happened only in the movies, and there sure as hell wasn't a film crew within a hundred miles of this dark and dreary place. He took a deep breath, eased carefully past the intersection, and continued straight ahead, imagining the yellow beam of his flashlight to be a gleaming cutlass. He was a pirate, dammit, and no one in their right mind would ever fuck with a pirate.

For another ten minutes he walked, probing the darkness. The walls of the tunnel were crafted in much the same fashion as the ones nearer the entrance: multi-colored friezes of brick and stone. The scenes here, however, were quite different. Instead of an endless procession of soldiers, the story was of a king and his military campaigns. A larger than life man, who Mason figured must've been Darius, led an army of charioteers against a crush of overwhelming forces.

As Mason walked, he studied the walls, the story. It seemed strangely familiar. At one point, the enemy surrounded Darius and his charioteers, and from the look of things, it appeared all was lost.

Mason skulked further down the tunnel.

The next development in the story was fantastic, and immediately Mason recalled where he'd come to know it—from the etchings around the talisman. The bodies of the enemy soldiers that once surrounded Darius now lay in heaps. And amidst the carnage, the great king stood, the magical stone thrust up high under a blazing sun. Except, Mason now knew, magic and the supernatural had nothing to do with it. The talisman's power was drawn from insects, deadly, microscopic insects.

Mason focused ahead, determined to find Beth.

But before he could take another step, he heard voices, faint and muffled, coming from somewhere down the tunnel. He switched off the flashlight, plunging his surroundings into darkness.

Then, as Mason's eyes adjusted, the tunnel appeared again, pale and in a brassy glow. The light came from far ahead, where the tunnel opened into a chamber. Beyond, a web of shadow and light flickered in a grim and ghastly dance.

Mason crept forward, listening as the voices grew louder and more distinct. A German accent. Son-of-a-bitch, it was the old man, Eckerman. And he was speaking to someone. Probably this Walter character.

Mason inched closer until he reached the chamber's opening. Then, hunching low, he peered inside. And for a moment, he thought his eyes deceived him.

# 19

RICK AND JARRED observed from a distance. An abandoned flashlight lay on the ground twenty feet ahead. "I don't get it," Jarred whispered. "Why would they just leave it there?"

"To keep the tunnel lit, maybe."

"Why?"

"To spot us coming."

"No, it doesn't make sense. They're not expecting us. And even if the flashlight was left as a general precaution, the main tunnel just before the intersection would have been a much better place. I can't figure it."

"Join the club," Rick said, exasperated. "I can't figure the motivation for half the shit these people have done. We're dealing with psychopaths."

"Guess there's no sense dwelling upon it then. Let's keep moving, see what's ahead."

Rick and Jarred crept forward, ignoring the flashlight and continuing along the tunnel's path, which maintained a gentle curve. A few minutes later, they came to an opening. Beyond was a vast, dark space. They approached, guns leveled.

Their pale beams stabbed into the room. From Rick's vantage point, he could see that the chamber was large and circular, a good eighty feet in diameter, crowded with hundreds, if not thousands, of waist-high containers. A narrow path bisected the hoard, running to the far end of the room. A dark, wedge-shaped opening revealed an exit tunnel.

The two moved closer to the threshold, their lights illuminating more of the chamber. Beyond the containers, Rick could see the ancient wall. It was constructed in the same manner as the main tunnel—of colorful bricks arranged to dramatize a series of scenes.

They stopped short of entering.

Rick swept his light over the area to his right. Jarred did the same to his left. The room contained nothing but vases, crowded so closely together each touched one another. They were fashioned of clay, with fat bases, long narrow necks, and two looping handles.

"Look at them all," Jarred said. "This room is seventy or eighty feet in diameter, and it's filled wall to wall. What do you think they are?"

"They're called amphorae," Rick said. "I remember them from a museum trip Beth and I—. The sudden memory caused him to pause. *Beth, he thought. Where the hell are you?* He let out a deep breath and forced away the worry. "Anyway, they were containers common in the ancient world."

"Think they're worth anything?"

"I don't know."

"I'd venture to say the stuffed shirts at the Smithsonian would shit a brick if they saw them all."

"I wouldn't doubt it."

"Why do you suppose there's so many of them?"

Rick picked a vase at random and played his light at the base. Specks of gold shimmered around it. "Remember at the entrance, that explorer and the trail of gold dust?"

"Yeah."

"Look there." Rick nodded to the amphora at the edge of his light. "I think this might be where he found the stash."

Jarred peered closely and grinned. He made a move inside—a little too carelessly for Rick's taste.

"Hold on a second, Jarred. There's no telling what's hidden in here. If Walter positioned a spotter, and he heard us coming…"

Jarred stopped.

"Let's take it slow," Rick cautioned him. "You cover the left side, I'll cover the right. We'll ease toward the exit and inspect the vases, make sure there're no surprises hidden between them."

Jarred nodded agreement and the two began a walk toward the opposite tunnel, slowly, their lights brushing the spaces between the amphorae. Given the size of the chamber and the small area covered by their lights, it took several minutes to scan the entire room.

After reaching the opposite end and deciding it was all clear, Rick peered into the exit tunnel. Shadows, silence, and emptiness.

He turned to Jarred. "Alright, go ahead and satisfy your curiosity. Then we move on."

The big man walked to the nearest amphora with an odd kind of apprehension, as if he were on a battlefield about to disarm a Claymore mine. Taking a deep breath, Jarred angled down his flashlight and carefully lifted the lid. For a long moment, he was silent. His stare was steely and focused.

Rick approached him, directing his own light over the vase. Its opening glared like a miniature sun. He stopped at another random vessel and lifted its lid. Filling it, too, was dust the color of gold and the consistency of fine sand.

Jarred scooped up a handful and let it slip between his fingers. "This can't be real," he said. "I've gotta be dreaming."

"The legend said the chambers were filled with the riches of the empire."

"Legend confirmed, wouldn't you say?" Jarred grinned savagely. "What are we gonna do with it all?"

"We're going to leave it," Rick said. "There's only one treasure I came for, and gold isn't it."

"But we can't just ignore all this."

"We can and we will. It isn't ours."

Jarred frowned. "It ain't anybody's. There must be billions in gold here. What'll it hurt if we take a little along?"

"I remember reading about the Nazis looting diamonds and artwork during World War II. In France, they plundered museums and private art collections, then they shipped what they could back home and distributed everything among the privileged."

Jarred's eyes pleaded. "But—"

"But nothing. What they did was wrong. They stole the culture of a nation and robbed a people of their national treasures. If we take from these chambers, we're no better. I refuse to be part of that legacy."

Shame came over Jarred's face. After a minute of reflection, he lowered his gaze and began rubbing the back of his neck. "I'm sorry, Rick," he said at last. "You're right, I was just thinking of my mother, she…"

"She has a son who's honorable and takes care of her. That's all any mother needs." Rick turned and headed for the opposite tunnel.

"Hey, where you going?"

"To find Beth, where else?"

"Not without me, you're not." Jarred stared down at the gold heaped high in the amphora. Then he straightened himself and hurried to Rick's side. "A guy can dream, can't he?"

Rick looked at the big man and smiled. "A guy can dream."

They turned their flashlights toward the exit tunnel.

"Guess we stay the course," Jarred said, "and go through there."

Rick nodded. But as they started for the exit, Rick's light caught the wall. Something in its relief made him stop. The style of the scenes reminded him of the relief on the talisman. He moved to the center of the chamber and swept his light the breadth of its wall. Images jumped out in the form of a procession. Hundreds of bare-backed men carrying amphorae filed their way toward the gates of Persepolis. And unlike the ruins Rick had seen earlier in the day, the city here was magnificent, built with towering walls and palaces, and embellished with statues of colossal bulls. The entire complex gleamed with the color of turquoise and ivory.

Rick continued his sweep with the flashlight, passing the center of the chamber. Abruptly, the scenes changed. The leader of the procession now knelt before the king, who seemed to accept the gifts with little emotion. Then, the delegate was led away. Rick turned his light to the next scene and observed the poor man's fate. Depicted was a ceremony hauntingly similar to what Rick had witnessed atop the butte. The king, now robed and wearing a Phrygian cap, loomed over the delegate, who lay prostrate upon an altar at the center of a large cave. On both sides, running its length, were simple stone benches. Figures in contorted animal masks stood nearby with outstretched arms.

The next image revealed an identical scene, only now braziers had been lit and plumes of thick smoke roiled in the air. And the king raised a dagger, ready to plunge it into his victim. Again, images of the butte flashed in Rick's mind. He saw pools of blood and rivers of black energy. He felt a sudden rise of nausea.

Unable to tear away his gaze, he turned his light to the final scene.

## 20

MASON RUBBED HIS eyes, then focused again. Now he was sure of it, the gallery that lay before him was real. And it was like something out of a Lovecraft novel. Aglow in bronzed light, the area was rectangular, the size of a large field, with walls that towered at least thirty feet high, disappearing into the shadows.

Opposite Mason, between two massive bull statues, was an enclosed staircase. It ran up five or six steps before ending at a barrier of fitted stones. On the middle steps rested two backpacks.

To Mason's left lay a skeleton, its bones crumbled on the ground, smothered under purple robes. Mason shrunk back and stared. Where the feet once were, a mess of tiny bones lay scattered around a pair of golden sandals. Outstretched at the other end of the skeleton were the remains of an arm that ended in a brittle, claw-like hand. Mason felt his stomach go sour. The sight of the thing gave him the creeps.

He turned his eyes from the skeleton and continued scanning the gallery. At its center, running perpendicular to the tunnel, were two rows of tarnished braziers spaced to form a long pathway. Copper flames leapt from the shallow pans adding to the room's already dark, suffocating atmosphere. Looking to the walls, Mason was shocked to see something strange and unexpected. What he'd initially thought were deep shadows were in fact something else altogether different. The walls were constructed of black stone, polished and glassy smooth. He watched mesmerized as flames from the braziers reflected from the stone, creating the illusion of a moving chamber.

Midway up the far wall ran a horizontal band of relief. Mason looked to his left. There, too, he saw it, just above the skeleton. In fact, the relief encircled the entire gallery. He peered closer, resolving the detail. *Holy Mother of...* It was identical to the relief on the talisman. The encircling band, the depicted scenes, the obsidian walls, Mason suddenly realized, this whole frickin room was a talisman.

He heard a disembodied voice, words faint and indiscernible, yet he immediately recognized the German accent. Eckerman. Mason clenched his tiny fists. The old man's voice had come from the right, beyond the path of glowing braziers, from a large breach in the obsidian wall. Mason was at a poor angle to see, but stretching, he could just make out the opening of a cave, its rough walls disappearing into the gloom.

There came a second voice. This one, Mason didn't recognize. He figured it had to be this Walter character.

But where was Beth?

*Gotta see inside the cave.*

He inched into the gallery, placing each of his steps with quiet precision. More of the rough wall became visible, but still, he couldn't see. He crept further ahead, close enough to feel the heat of the braziers. He stared into the cave. It was dark and oblong, with two stone benches running its length. At the far end, standing with their backs turned were two men. One was Eckerman, unmistakable with his fat rump and mane of unruly white hair. The other man, who stood blocking a large, flattened rock, Mason didn't recognize. He wore a crimson robe and a golden stole, and perched atop his head was a silly little hat. Must be Walter, Mason thought. The guy looked like a total donkey.

But there was no one else. What had they done with Beth? Mason was just about to creep back to the tunnel when the robed man shifted to his side. Lying on the rock-shelf behind him was a body. It was a woman, tan and petite, with short black hair falling across her forehead. She wasn't moving.

*Christ, it was Beth.* For a second, Mason feared she was dead. But then ever so slightly her hand stirred, and he felt a rise of hope, followed by a sense of complete panic. What was he gonna do? He had to help her. He turned and looked down the tunnel behind him. Rick, Jarred, where the hell are you idiots? Carefully, so as not to be heard, Mason began to back up, until he was out of the gallery and again concealed in the shadows.

*Create a diversion and sneak into the cave.* If he could wake up Beth and get her on her feet, the two of them could escape. Hold on, you dimwit. He scolded himself for not thinking it through carefully enough. Even if he revived Beth, how would they ever get out without Walter and Eckerman noticing them?

There was only one solution: Mason had to take them out. He had to unleash an old-fashioned whooping, just like Rick and Jarred had done with those guards. Okay, Eckerman, it's payback time. Mason tried to pump himself up. Used every trick he could think of. The old man was a fat fart, and Walter a complete duffus. Mason could handle them. You're a pirate, he reminded himself, a pirate, goddamn it! And ain't nobody gonna screw with a pirate!

As Mason was preparing, balling his fists in anger, Walter and Eckerman emerged from the cave. Mason shrunk back and observed them. The two men walked to the sealed staircase. Eckerman unzipped a compartment in one of the packs. "I shall attire myself, Father. When your preparations are complete, we can begin."

The robed man rested a hand on the old man's shoulder. "Peter," he said. "We have come far. We have achieved the impossible, and soon, my friend…"

Mason saw this as a chance. With their backs turned, he stepped inside the gallery and scooted along the inside wall. Walter was still speaking when Mason reached the corner of the room. Faster now, he turned in the direction of the cave, continuing along the wall, his shoulder brushing its obsidian surface. Finally at the entrance, Mason stole a glance back, made sure the two men hadn't seen him, then slipped inside.

Beth still lay motionless on the shelf, which Mason could now see was a natural outcropping roughly eight feet long. Its top had been flattened and chiseled smooth. As he neared, he noticed the side of the shelf stained a deep red. It was then he understood the rock's significance. It was a sacrificial altar, probably used by the ancients over two thousand years ago. People were actually murdered on this thing, he realized. He fought back a growing sickness and hurried to Beth's side.

"Beth," he whispered into her ear.

She didn't respond.

He noticed a nasty gash on her forehead. There was dried blood and swelling around it. Her normally tan and exuberant face had become drawn and gaunt.

"Beth, wake up." He pulled out his bottle and opened it. Carefully, he tipped the neck and spilled a little water onto her lips. Her nose wrinkled; her chin twitched. Then she let out a slight moan.

"Shhh," Mason whispered. "Don't try to speak." He tipped the bottle again, pouring more water. This time, Beth opened her mouth and took a small sip. Her head lifted slightly, and she moaned again, bringing her fingertips to her forehead.

"Beth," I'm here to rescue you," Mason said, feeling a growing sense of confidence. "I'm gonna get you out of here and back home."

She opened her eyes. "Rick, Rick…" Her gaze was distant.

"He's here, too, somewhere."

Mason could see Beth's jade eyes fighting to focus. She struggled onto her elbows.

"You're gonna be okay," he reassured her.

With a sudden look of shock, she said, "Mason? What are you—?"

"Don't talk." He put a finger to her lips. "Take this water. Drink. Walter and Eckerman are in the room behind us. But don't you worry, I'm gonna throw down with them and get you out of here. I brought Rick and Jarred along with me. They haven't shown up yet, but I expect them soon."

Confusion was in her eyes. She took the bottle and drank eagerly. Then she touched her forehead again and winced.

Mason looked toward the path of braziers leading to the altar. "If I knock off a dish, I think I can use one these stands as a kind of spear. I mean, how tough can Walter and the old man be?" He glanced back at Beth. "You think I can take them, right?"

But Beth didn't answer. She was staring past him, at the cave wall. Her eyes suddenly widened. Mason wheeled around. In the shadows he could see the outline of a man.

There came a disembodied voice. "You've done well to come this far." The voice was cold and confident, but Mason didn't recognize it.

Then from out of the darkness the figure emerged, lean and insanely tall.

"Who the hell are you?"

The man stepped closer. He held a gun.

Mason's heart lurched into his throat, yet despite his fear, he managed a wisecrack. "You don't have a name? How about I give you one? We can call you Harry Balsack. You okay with that?"

Mason could hear Beth struggling to sit up behind him.

The man raised the gun. "Not a sensible move, coming here and defiling the Sacred Mithraeum."

Mason felt his knees go weak. "You're not going to shoot me, are you?"

There was a pause. Then the man smiled and holstered his weapon. "No. I'll not stain Mithra's womb with the blood of the unconsecrated."

Mason wasn't sure what the hell Harry was talking about, but he was pleased that he'd put away his gun.

"You may call me Sarth," the man said, stepping closer.

"What, you don't like Harry?"

"Run," Beth pleaded from behind him. "He's a killer."

Slowly, the tall man pulled something from his breast pocket. It appeared to be a cord of some kind. He began swinging it back and forth, knocking together its two bulbous ends. *Click, click, click.*

"Run," Beth urged him again.

Still approaching, just feet away, the giant man stretched taut the wiry cord. "I shall rather enjoy this."

Mason peered up into the assassin's eyes. They were dark and lifeless. *Listen to Beth. Run. Don't get yourself killed.* Mason could feel his flight instincts grabbing hold. He looked to the cave entrance.

*Run.*

He had powerful instincts. They were the reason why as a boy he was clever enough to hide at recess from the bullies, clever enough to stow himself away in the library under Mrs. Shelby's beanbags.

*Run.*

Yeah, they were powerful instincts, alright. They were also the reason why as a college student he was always smart enough to lay low and keep his mouth shut whenever a drunk in a bar would ridicule him for being short and fat and freckled.

*Run.*

When it came down to it, Mason suddenly realized with amazing clarity, his instincts were the reason why he had grown up to become such a pussy. The thought of his own cowardice quickly made him sick. He wasn't a man. Who was he fooling? His tough talk on the radio, his belittling of women, it was all just an act, a pathetic front to hide the fact he was a complete coward.

Suddenly, Mason hated himself.

Run? He sure as hell felt the instinct. But he'd be damned if this time he was gonna do it. Beth was hurt and there was no one else here to help her. *If ever you were a man.*

Sarth moved in closer, cord outstretched in his hands.

"Alright, you asked for it!" Feeling a rising heat under his collar, Mason squared himself and charged forward. "Throw down, fucker!"

The assassin made no attempt to dodge the rush. As quickly as Mason was upon him, Sarth had wrapped the garrote two turns around his neck.

Mason felt a pinching squeeze. He sucked in a deep breath of air.

Sarth tightened the cord.

Mason could feel it cutting deep into his neck. His skin burned and his lungs struggled to fill. He threw his arms around the towering man and clenched as hard as he could.

"Let him go," Beth cried out.

Sarth looped the garrote a third time.

Mason's head felt cloudy, but he squeezed his arms harder. *Damn this guy was like iron.*

"You're killing him!" Beth screamed.

Sarth drove Mason back against the rock shelf, pulling the cord tighter.

Mason struggled to breathe, but the air no longer came. He felt light on his feet, strangely ethereal.

Sarth snickered and yanked the garrote again, this time hard enough to spin them around.

Through dim eyes, Mason could see Beth, now behind the assassin, rising on the altar, horror reflected in her pale face.

"No!" she cried.

Voices carried into the cave, Walter's and Eckerman's, getting louder.

Mason's arms loosened, then dropped to his side as he teetered on the edge of awareness. But he didn't plead, nor did he cry. He just smiled. He had fought. He hadn't run.

"I said no!" There came the sound of a wet tear, like a shovel driven into mud. Sarth grunted. The garrote loosened.

Mason, unable to work his legs, slumped to the ground. Darkness was everywhere.

The assassin loomed over him gurgling, something inky running from his lips. He reached out his arms, as would a sightless man.

Consciousness was slipping away from Mason. All was near black. Then a quick, silvery flash registered as Sarth turned his back and collapsed, something protruding from the assassin's neck.

Scissors.

And as Mason's vision gave way to blindness, his only regret was that he hadn't saved Beth.

## 21

RICK STOOD MOTIONLESS in the shadows, surrounded by thousands of gold-filled amphorae. Yet despite the hoards of treasure around him, it was the relief on the chamber wall that captured his attention, its story chronicling the rituals of a Mithraic ceremony. Rick turned his eyes to the final scene. Within the confines of a cave, the delegate who'd delivered the vast quantity of gold now lay helpless on top of a stone altar, while the king towered over him clutching a stone in one hand and a dagger in the other. From overhead, shafts of sunlight penetrated the cavern's ceiling and showered the ceremony in rays of black energy.

Rick was reminded of the Brotherhood and their ceremony at the top of the butte. Technically, Eckerman had been truthful all along. At the radio station, the old man had explained that the Achaemenid kings were not Zoroastrians as history portrayed them, but rather followers of the deity Mithra. So, too, Eckerman had insisted, were the devotees of the Brotherhood. The images on the wall and Rick's experience with the cult seemed to confirm every word.

Rick stared at the culminating act. What he saw was a disturbing scene made all the more gruesome by the sight of the king's victim, the foreign delegate, who now lay dead with the ceremonial dagger sticking from his chest. Blood ran from the gaping wound and pooled in depressions at the top of the altar. Worked into a frenzy by the sacrifice, the surrounding figures exalted. Some lay on the ground, limbs spread and faces euphoric, while others knelt with their heads raised and fists thrown into the air. This was insane, Rick thought. How could the ancients have—

Suddenly, a woman's cry carried into the chamber, so distant it was almost a whisper.

The sound jerked Rick out of his thoughts.

"Did you hear that?" Jarred said.

Without hesitation, Rick turned his flashlight and bolted across the room, toward the tunnel they'd originally entered. "That was Beth!" he shouted back to Jarred. "Let's go!" And all at once, Rick was filled with conflicting emotions—fear and relief. Fear because Beth was in danger, why else cry out? Relief because she was alive! He had to get to her, quickly. Her cry had come from the direction of the main artery, he was sure of it. Rick's legs stretched in great strides as he dashed along the curved tunnel, and in seconds, he found himself back at the intersection.

He stopped, chest heaving with rapid breaths.

Jarred ran up behind him, equally winded. "Which way now?"

"I'm not sure." Rick puzzled at the choice of directions.

There came another cry, louder and more distinct. Definitely Beth, and it came from the right.

As if her scream had signaled the start of a race, Rick and Jarred tore off down the tunnel, the beams of their flashlights bouncing crazily against the ceiling and walls.

For minutes, the only sounds came from their heavy breathing and from the knocking of boots against the ground. Then ahead, Rick could see it. An opening. A room. Light flickered from somewhere inside. *Beth! he mentally screamed, I'm coming for you!*

Years of Ranger training urged him to slow. Assess the environment and enter with extreme caution. Any number of threats could lie ahead. But then Beth cried again, as if fighting for her life, and all sense of vigilance left him.

Pistol in hand, Rick burst through the opening and into a large gallery, Jarred at his side. The area was dark yet strangely vibrant. Burning braziers stood at regular intervals.

Rick's eyes searched for Beth.

A gunshot rang out and Jarred grunted, then stutter-stepped

back, hitting the wall. He slapped a hand over his shoulder. Blood leaked from between his fingers. "Forget me, I'll live," Jarred yelled out, seeing the concern in Rick's eyes.

"You've come uninvited." A familiar voice called out.

*Walter.*

Rick wheeled around and spotted the crazed man, who was dressed in ceremonial robes and standing before the entrance of a cave at the far end of the gallery. Pulled close to him was Beth. The copper light of the braziers revealed her to be gaunt and bruised, her weight shifted to one leg. But as haggard as she looked, when her eyes met Rick's, she smiled, her expression one of tremendous relief.

"I can't believe you're here," she called out to him. "I can't believe I'm seeing your face."

"You can believe it," Rick called back. "And you can believe I'm going to get you out of here."

"Walter will never allow it," she said. "Don't worry about me, just shoot the creep before he has a chance to kill you."

Eckerman stepped from the shadows of the cave, his mane of white hair stark against the black walls. He, too, wore ceremonial robes, and in his hand was a gun, leveled and pointed in Rick's direction. The confidence in the old man's stance indicated he knew how to use it.

Walter grabbed a fistful of Beth's hair and pulled her close. "Is that how it shall be, Mr. Lowell? I kill Dr. Harper, then you kill me?" He pressed the gun barrel harder against her temple.

"Don't give it another thought," Beth said defiantly. "Do what has to be done, and no matter what happens, Rick, know that I love you."

"I'll say this once," Walter said calmly, "and only once. You and your muscle-bound friend there will slide your weapons to the center of the room, or the next sound you'll hear will be the discharge of a bullet. And the sight it will produce, I can assure you, will not be pleasant."

"Don't listen to him," Beth said.

"It'll be okay," Rick told her. Given his experience with Walter, he was convinced the man would pull the trigger, no doubt feeling invincible. He probably thought he had the power of Mithra behind him.

Rick slipped the rifle from his shoulder.

"No!" Beth cried out.

Kneeling down, Rick placed both weapons on the ground, then slid them forward to the center of the gallery. "Jarred, do the same, would you?"

With some hesitation, the big man complied, kneeling and sliding away his rifle and gun.

"How's your shoulder?" Rick asked.

"Caught one in the deltoid, but I'll survive."

Walter breathed in deeply, then took a moment to study Rick. "I'd been informed you escaped the butte, but I must confess, Mr. Lowell, your presence here at Persepolis surprises me."

"It shouldn't. You left town with something precious to me."

Walter paused, then a smirk turned up the edge of his lips. "Was Dr. Harper precious to that man, as well?" He nodded behind him.

Eckerman stood aside revealing the body of Sarth. Bloody scissors jutted out from the assassin's neck. Lying motionless next to him was—*oh God, no.* It was Mason. The sight of the little guy was so completely unexpected, Rick nearly dropped to a knee. He was confused. He and Jarred had left Mason in the truck. How could this have happened?

Eckerman broke the silence, speaking as though amused: "I had figured the diminutive blowhard for a coward. I must say, however, I was quite surprised when he showed up to engage Sarth in a fight for your woman."

Rick's heart tightened. *Mason, why didn't you listen to me? Why didn't you stay in the truck?*

Jarred stepped forward, his hand still pressed against his shoulder. Rick could see the big man's face blistering with fury. "I'm gonna make you pay for this, you prick. If it's the last thing I do."

Eckerman laughed. "Oh, you two were friends were you? Not to worry, you shall meet again very soon, in the netherworld."

Beth struggled against Walter's grip, but she had lost much of her strength, and her tugging seemed to do little more than annoy the crazed man.

"Okay, we've done what you asked," Rick said. "We've thrown down our guns, now release her. We're leaving."

Walter ignored him. He and Eckerman moved toward the center of the gallery where the weapons lay scattered, dragging Beth between them.

Desperate for a way out of this mess, Rick did a quick scan of the gallery. Behind him lay a skeleton, the bones of one of its arm braced against the wall, under a large golden ring. A few feet above the ring, etched into the black stone, was a band of relief much like the series of scenes on the talisman. Wait, it wasn't *like* the series of scenes, it was precisely the same. An exact copy. In fact, the entire gallery appeared to be an enormous replica of the stone. Or perhaps it was the other way around: the talisman was a replica of this gallery. Either way, it didn't make sense to Rick. What was the significance? What could possibly be the purpose? He followed the relief to a pair of towering bull statues that flanked a sealed staircase. Then he glanced up at the ceiling. Though it was shrouded in shadow, Rick noticed the center portion was constructed of a pearly material, limestone probably, but clearly different than the stone abutting the wall.

Walter and Eckerman reached the weapons. The old man bent down and carefully collected them, slinging the rifles over his shoulder and tucking the two guns under his robes into his waistband.

Beth twisted and struggled, and this time Walter released her. Limping severely, she rushed toward Rick, her arms opened wide for an embrace.

When she finally reached him, their arms closed around each other. He squeezed her tightly, and she laid her head against his chest. "We're together again," he whispered. "You'll be alright. I promise."

Walter said, "There's nothing quite as touching as a reunion."

Jarred stepped forward, clenching his bloody fist and peering with hatred at the two men.

Rick eased Beth aside, then turned to Walter. "You have everything you want," he said. "Let us go."

"It's not quite that simple, Mr. Lowell. You see, your very

presence here has defiled the Sacred Mithraeum. And that cannot be tolerated."

"So sue me," Jarred said.

Eckerman took a step forward, his face darkened by the copper glow of the braziers. "Your American court system is woefully inefficient, I'm afraid. I have a much better solution." He leveled his gun at the big man.

With Beth no longer in front of Walter, Rick could now see the talisman dangling from his neck, partially obscured by the folds of his crimson robe. Christ, he was wearing the nest. If guns weren't enough to worry about, there was now the threat of a poisonous insect swarm.

Mind focused on the talisman, Rick suddenly realized something crucial here was missing—the scent of mint. Rick stared at the flames that rose from the braziers. *The smokeless flames.* Of course! Nothing was being burned. He'd found the thyme in Gus's backpack. Walter had neglected to bring it along. Immediately, Rick had an idea. He would have to convince them. "Listen to me. You and Eckerman, your lives are in danger."

There was a pause, then Walter's robes fluttered as he began to laugh. "We're in danger? It seems, my dear boy, you fail to adequately gauge your predicament. It is Peter and I who hold the guns."

"That's not what I mean. If you don't listen to me, you're as good as dead. I have something critical to your ceremony, something you'll need to survive it. Let us walk out of here and it's all yours."

"Don't be ridiculous," Walter said. "We're in no danger. On the contrary, Peter and I have been summoned here by Mithra Himself. You, on the other hand, have defiled His temple. And as a result, your lives are now forfeit."

"Listen to me," Rick said, hearing the desperation in his own voice. "The talisman's a nest. It's filled with deadly insects."

For a moment Walter didn't respond. He appeared bewildered. Rick's extraordinary claim had taken him by surprise.

Beth narrowed her eyes, she, too, baffled.

"That's right. The talisman is a nest. And inside are thousands, if not millions, of microscopic insects. Their stings are lethal. Every bit of evidence proves it—the death of Tanner's Marines, the death of Tanner himself. The surface of the stone is covered with tiny holes, impossible to see with the naked eye. Beth discovered them during her analysis."

"This is nonsense," Eckerman said. He glanced at Walter with a look of irritation. "We must kill them, now."

"Think about it," Rick said. "It all fits. On the butte, that river of darkness we saw. That wasn't a trick of the eye. It wasn't an illusion of weather. It was a swarm, thousands of insects shaken up and really pissed off."

"You're mistaken," Walter said. "What you witnessed was the energy of the stone, the re-awakening of Mithra." Absently, the sick man stroked the talisman. "You know nothing of the signs, and so you invent a wild and ridiculous theory. A nest of insects, you're absurd."

"We're absurd?" Jarred said. "How can you stand there saying that with a straight face? I mean, just look at yourself in your red robes and silly little hat. You're a fucking freak."

Walter scowled at the big man. "The *Telesma* foretells the events, you fool. The Brotherhood has reclaimed the talisman and discovered the Sacred Mithraeum. And now we are on the verge of establishing Mithra's New World Order."

"Yes," Eckerman added. "And upon conclusion of the ceremony we shall complete the prophecy and fulfill the Brotherhood's destiny. Once our bond with Mithra has been realized, He will grant us the ultimate blessing—immortality."

"No," Rick said. "Don't you understand, the *Telesma* is just a book, written when gods and the supernatural were explanation enough for the unexplainable. Don't let your fervor blind you, don't stake your life on an empty prophecy. Listen to me. There's a rational explanation for what happened on the butte, and it has nothing to do with Mithra or what's written in that ancient tome. The talisman's a nest, I'm telling you. The insects are real and they're lethal. And I can give you what you'll need to survive. All you have to do is let us walk out of here."

"If you'll not put an end to this blasphemy," Eckerman said to Walter, his face glistening with sweat, "then I shall." The old man swung the sight of his pistol and trained it on Rick.

"No!" Beth cried.

But her plea was ignored.

Enraged, Eckerman fired.

Instinct taking hold, Rick pushed Beth away and dove for the ground, but even as he turned, he could feel the sting of a bullet tearing into his flesh. He hit the floor hard, sliding into the skeleton.

Beth recovered and scrambled to his side. "Tell me you're okay," she sobbed.

Jarred rushed over, too. "Are you hit?"

Rick touched the wound and knew the bullet had passed without hitting a vital organ. He struggled to regain his breath. "He got me in the side, it's just a graze."

Carefully, Eckerman approached. From the hardened look on his face, Rick knew he was intent on finishing the job.

"He's gonna shoot us, no question," Jarred said. "I'll rush him and hope for the best."

"That's suicide," Rick said. "Tip a brazier and start a fire. With luck they'll panic."

"Nothing here is flammable," Beth said. "The oil will do little more than scorch the stone."

*Scorch the stone.* Beth's words penetrated Rick's memory. *Scorch the stone.*

Eckerman was taking deliberate steps, his blue eyes narrowing as he stared from Jarred to Rick to Beth, deciding who to finish off first.

The gallery's obsidian walls fell into sharp focus, and Rick looked up to the limestone ceiling. The talisman was a nest, an obsidian nest. The walls of the chamber, they, too, were obsidian. No doubt this entire chamber was also a nest. *Scorch the earth!* Rick suddenly realized he had been wrong to assume the insects were roused by agitation. Too often the stone had been jostled without effect. No, what stirred the creatures was something altogether different. And now, what Beth had mentioned days ago about the Scorched Earth Policy made perfect sense: Ancient cities would destroy their own resources rather than succumb to foreign invaders. Ancient Persepolis would be no exception. Everything here in the gallery seemed to fit.

Eckerman stopped about thirty feet away, smart enough to keep some distance between them. "Say your goodbyes. Father and I have a prophecy to fulfill." He lowered the pistol, carefully taking aim.

Slowly, Jarred stood to his feet, his great size looming tall. He squared himself to Eckerman.

*The Scorched Earth Policy.* Frantically, Rick searched for a mechanism, his eyes consuming the walls. *There had to be one, somewhere!*

"Take the shot, old man," Jarred said. "But make it your best, cuz I'm coming to get you."

Rick's eyes darted to the massive bull statues flanking the staircase, but nothing on them grabbed his attention. He looked left. Sidelong, his eye caught something that sparkled, something golden. He craned around and stared behind him. The golden ring! Protruding from the wall, it hung from the nose of a sculpted bull.

*The mechanism. It had to be!*

"You crazy old prick," Jarred said. "This one's for Mason!"

Rick turned in time to see the big man launch himself forward.

A hoarse, yet familiar voice called out from inside the cave. "It's about time you two Bozos showed up."

The voice was Mason's.

Eckerman wheeled around in surprise, his gun firing just as he began to spin. The bullet whizzed past Jarred and ricocheted off the wall, obsidian grit puffing away in a tiny cloud.

"The ring above me," Rick said to Beth. "Pull it with everything you've got."

Beth looked confused, but she knew better than to delay with questions. She stretched forward, grimacing from the pain in her leg. She grasped the golden ring. Then, with a heavy grunt, she flung herself away from the wall. Rick could hear the sound of metal scraping stone as Beth tumbled backward onto her rear side. When she came to rest, he could see the ring in her hand. Attached to it was a thin iron rod roughly three feet long.

Eckerman turned back to finish off Jarred, but the big man had covered a lot of ground. Lowering his shoulder, he slammed headlong into the old man, whose blue eyes rolled senseless as he was launched backward like a crimson missile. With a heavy thud Eckerman slammed to the ground, skidding to a stop near the center of the gallery.

Walter had readied his own weapon and was aiming to fire when a sudden grind, slow and ominous, began to reverberate inside the walls. Within seconds, the ceiling started to shake and the ground began to tremble.

Walter hesitated, looking up into the shadows. At first he stared with wonder, but after a moment a broad smile turned up his lips. "You fools!" he cried out, his voice echoing in the gallery. "You have provoked Mithra!" Walter thrust his arms into the air and laughed hysterically, his dark eyes filling with madness. "Now you shall all suffer His wrath!"

## 22

WALTER STOOD AT the center of the gallery and beheld the mounting fury of God. The dark walls shook and the ceiling trembled. The infidels had angered Mithra and now they would pay dearly.

"Rise to your feet, Peter! Join me in witness to this great event!" But Peter only moaned. The big man had struck a fierce blow and it was clear Peter was having difficulty gaining his senses.

The walls ceased their shaking, but the grind emanating from the ceiling intensified. Carefully, Walter backed away to the Mithraeum. Out of the corner of his eye, he could see the small, red-headed man scrambling across the gallery toward the others, massaging his neck as his little legs carried him rapidly forward. Walter lifted his gun to fire at the infidel, but then stopped. It was of no consequence. Let the fool reach his friends. They would all soon perish together.

From up high there came a horrific scraping sound, and Walter looked to the ceiling, to an area of limestone construction at its center. Huge quarried blocks began to vibrate, while pulverized pieces of rock and mortar showered to the ground.

On the far side of the gallery Harper and the others cowered in fear, as rightly they should, having defiled the temple and enraged Mithra. With great haste, Lowell and the larger man passed around some kind of a plant, and like fools, they rubbed it against their skin and their clothes. What did they think? It would protect them from the wrath of God?

Finally, Peter managed to struggle to his feet and was trying to steady himself when the rock dust began raining more heavily upon him. Walter glanced high above Peter to see a collection of enormous stones working themselves free.

"Peter, hurry here, to the Mithraeum," Walter cried out. "Mithra exacts His revenge."

Face paled by fear, Peter turned for the cave, but even as he took his first step, a massive block dislodged, sliding from between the others. And like a house of cards, they all began to fall, one after another, monstrous pieces of limestone, tumbling and turning as they crashed toward the ground.

Walter focused straight ahead, his stare locked with his Brother's. Panic was in poor Peter's eyes as he reached out a hand, acknowledging the futility. Then suddenly a riot of limestone blocks came crashing over him, and dust and powdered stone mushroomed thick into the air.

*Peter!*

Walter shielded his face as gagging debris spread from the center of the gallery. The room seemed to shake to its very foundation, and blasts of heat surged outward from the collapse. It was all a sign from Mithra, Who was demanding Walter submit to His will. Gathering his robes and dropping to his knees, Walter humbled himself before the great God.

When at last the shaking ended and the dust settled, Walter lifted his head and peered out from his cavern sanctuary. Above, where once stretched a ceiling, a gaping hole revealed a crystal blue sky. Divine light poured like a flood into the gallery. The energy, the heat, it was the arrival of the Sun-God Himself. Mithra! Walter stepped out from the Mithraeum and observed. Copper braziers, toppled and crushed, glistened under the powerful rays. And alas, too, Peter lay dead, his flesh and bones mangled under a heap of stones.

Walter didn't understand. How could this be? Why had his Brother been sacrificed? How could Mithra have allowed it? After a moment of reflection, the answer became clear. This had been a test. Of course. A test by God to measure the depth of Walter's faith and conviction. There was no other explanation.

Regaining his composure, Walter stepped into the ruined gallery and up onto a block of level stone. From there he surveyed the area. Above him, in the foreground of the blue sky, he could see the towering columns of Persepolis. Yellow shafts of sunlight stabbed through the breach, striking the obsidian walls and casting its relief in exquisite detail. It was insanely beautiful.

Harper and the others stood huddled in the far corner, covered in dust and looking like ghosts. Yes, ghosts, what they would soon become. With his left hand, Walter clutched the talisman and yanked it free from his neck. Furious with the infidels, he thrust the relic high into the air. "Here, oh great Mithra, I present to you the sacred stone. For those who have defiled your temple there can be no forgiveness! Strike them down, oh great Mithra!" Under the rays of the sun, Walter shook the talisman and cried in anguish.

Then the call was answered. A sudden high-pitched wail began to resonate from the obsidian walls. Walter could see Harper and the others covering their ears in pain. Yes, suffer the agony! All of you shall burn in the fires of eternal damnation!

Suddenly, in bursts of divine energy, hundreds of black tendrils streamed from the walls and converged at the center of the gallery, where they corkscrewed upward into a thick tower of raven beauty. Then abruptly the tendrils descended again and began a circuit of the perimeter, moving faster and faster with each turn, spreading thin and becoming a single, insubstantial ring.

Walter laughed and he cried. With his hands thrust high into the air, he tightened his grip on the talisman and rejoiced. He had reached his final destiny. Oh, how glorious it was. "Mithra be praised!" Walter lowered his gaze and through the vaporous ring, he could see the others, the infidels who had caused him so much trouble. They were moving from the corner of the gallery and seeking the shelter of the tunnel, Lowell practically carrying the woman. How foolish they were to believe anything could save them now.

The ring of darkness continued to swirl, and then, sensing Walter to be the Chosen One, it broke into a single stream and began to encircle him. The wail of energy had become so incredibly loud he could no longer hear, and barely could he think, the moment of salvation making him dizzy. Indeed, Mithra's grace was intoxicating. Walter peered up through the breach in the ceiling and into the blue heavens and he cried, "Oh, Mithra, Creator and Master of all living things, bless me, for I am your servant!"

A wisp of energy broke from the stream, and Walter felt it cling to his skin. No, not cling, crawl. Then more of the blackness engulfed him, spreading under his robes and between his garments, until every bit of his flesh was covered. How odd, he thought, that Mithra's blessing should feel so unsettling.

The crawling sensation gave way to severe pain as the energy consumed Walter's flesh. His breathing became labored and a sudden tightness gripped his chest.

Something was terribly wrong.

Holding out a blackened hand, Walter brushed the energy aside. He could see his fingers were flayed and bloody, the whites of his knuckle bones peeking through the tendons.

Panic set in, but it was far too late. Walter dropped to his knees unable to breathe, unable to feel anything but agony and betrayal.

Through blurred and teary vision he looked toward the tunnel, to where the others had fled. Lowell was there staring back at him, Harper's face buried tightly into his chest. The other two men stood at his side. Their faces appeared sickened by what they saw. And as Walter slumped to the ground, overcome by pain and suffocation, his final thought was a revelation: Mithra had forsaken him.

# EPILOGUE

LONG SHADOWS FELL over the parking lot at radio station KSND in Phoenix, Arizona. Days ago, the heat wave had broken, and the station's parched landscape had metamorphosed into bright colorful flowers and lawns of thick green Bermuda. Rick pulled the Explorer into his marked space and stared up at the building's glassy façade. Although he'd been back to work for weeks now, Rick felt present only in body, not so much in mind and spirit. Too much had happened in his life, too much with Beth. To each of their delight, they'd rediscovered one another and rekindled their relationship, beginning a new journey together. And so now, Rick's mind was in the clouds, not in his work.

And thoughts of recent events weighed upon him, as well. After Walter's death, Rick and the others had fled the ruins and returned to Shiraz, where they contacted the authorities. With Walter's men beaten and subdued, the police had an easy job picking them up and conducting interrogations. As it turned out, Beth hadn't been Walter's only victim. The cult leader had also kidnapped the wife and daughter of Iran's Ministry of Culture. Both, Rick later learned, had been safely found at a location outside of Shiraz.

While being treated for their injuries and recovering at a local hospital, Rick, Beth, Jarred, and Mason had spent hours explaining to Iranian police and government officials the circumstances surrounding the discovery of the Hidden Chambers. In the end, all four were deemed victims of Walter's criminal activities and ultimately allowed to return home. The crates of "broadcasting equipment" were shipped back to Mason's estate, having never been opened for inspection, and news of Beth's discovery spread like wildfire in the press. By the time she reached U.S. soil, the story had been picked up by all the major networks. Beth had become a sensation—so much so, the university welcomed her back with open arms, eager to share in the immense publicity.

Rick cut the Explorer's engine and leaned back in his seat. "Mason's been working hard to change the format of his show. I noticed he's focusing more on social topics and newsworthy events, less on women and their anatomy. I'd like to encourage him, so I appreciate you giving him first crack at the radio interview."

Beth's jade eyes sparkled in the soft sunlight. "Of course I'm giving him the first interview, he helped save my life." She smiled and leaned close to Rick, gave him a kiss.

The touch of her moist lips made him weak. He kissed her again just to make sure he wasn't dreaming.

Yeah, she was real alright.

The nightmare was over.

Rick opened the car door and jumped out, then hurried around to the hatch and pulled out Beth's crutches. After helping her from the car, he walked her toward the entrance of the building. Beth fussed over the height of the crutch's arm brace. "I need to have these things adjusted," she said. "They're driving me nuts."

Rick smiled. "I'll see what I can do."

When the lobby doors opened, he and Beth were hit by a rush of news reporters and photographers. Barely three steps inside and bulbs began flashing and boom mikes dropped around them. A tall woman in a pinstripe jacket and skirt muscled to the front. "Dr. Harper," she said. "Your discovery is being heralded as the greatest archaeological find since Howard Carter unearthed King Tutankhamen. What are your thoughts on the matter?"

"Howard Carter?" Beth said. "Gee, I don't know. Those are pretty big shoes to fill."

Rick could see Beth beginning to flush, still embarrassed by her newfound notoriety. He worked his way past a few of the reporters, making room enough for her to swing by on the crutches. "I'm sorry," he said. "She's late for an interview."

Beth followed him to the elevator. "Thank you for your interest," she told the reporters. "You can forward your questions to my office at the university."

Seeing Rick and Beth's discomfort with the crowd, good old Security slapped closed his Value Line Survey, adjusted his utility belt, then marched from around his kiosk, waving a hand in the air. "Alright, ladies and gentlemen, you heard Dr. Harper. All questions go through the university."

Rick turned and gave him a thumbs-up.

Security smiled and tipped his head.

The elevator doors whisked open. Rick and Beth stepped inside the car and rode it up to the third floor. "I don't get it," Beth said. "Reporters know where I teach and have already staked out the university, but how did they know to find me here?"

"Mason," Rick said. "He's been on the air touting this interview for days."

The elevator doors opened. Rick could see Elliot standing casually midway down the hall. He was grouped in conversation with Andrea Yacker and the new soundboard operator, flipping aside bangs of silvery hair.

As Rick and Beth walked the hall, the door to the recording lab opened and Jarred stepped out, helping along a small, elderly woman. When the big man saw them, he grinned widely, excitement in his eyes. Rick and Beth stopped to meet them.

"This is my mother," Jarred said.

With a smile, the elderly woman stared at Rick, then at Beth. Her eyes sparkled with an unusual vitality. She was tiny and frail. "I'm Mona, she said with a surprisingly strong voice. "It's a pleasure to finally make your acquaintance. My son has told me all about the two of you."

"Mom just finished recording another commercial spot," Jarred said, sounding mighty pleased. "Mason's gonna run it indefinitely. No charge."

"I provide psychic and palm reading services," Mona explained.

"Yes, I've heard your advertisement," Beth said. "Show me your palm, I'll show you the future."

"That's me," Mona said, pleased that Beth recognized her slogan. "Give me your hand, dear. Let me take a look."

Without hesitation, Beth reached out, smiling.

The tiny woman brushed Beth's palm delicately, but stared at it with the intensity of a surgeon performing an operation. "Yes, yes, wonderful," she said. "Your palm is long and your fingers are slender. You're a sensitive person, yet you possess an adventurous spirit."

Absently, Beth nodded, her jade eyes focused on Mona's reading.

"Smooth and beautiful contours. You see here, sweetheart? This is your lifeline. Its curve is very strong. This tells me you're physically fit, quite a little firecracker."

Beth glanced up. Jarred winked at her, a thank you for indulging his mother.

"And this," Mona said, excited now. "This is your heart line and—oh my."

"What is it?" Beth said, sounding concerned.

"The heart line pertains to relationships. Yours is smooth and uninterrupted. I'm sensing a great celebration in the near future."

Beth blushed. "Rick, you told them, didn't you."

"I didn't, I swear."

"Told us what?" Jarred asked.

"Last night," Beth said, unable to conceal her enthusiasm, "Rick asked me to marry him."

"He did?" Jarred said. "Wow, what did you say?"

The tiny woman nearly had a fit. She turned and slugged Jarred in the side. "Why, she said yes, you big lug."

"Gee, Mom, it was just a question." He rubbed his ribcage.

"It was nice meeting you," Beth told Mona. "You're a gifted woman."

"Good luck on the air today," Jarred said. "Mom and I are heading to breakfast. I'll call you when I get hungry for a steak. You haven't forgotten about the dinner and beer you owe me, have you?"

"Oh, my," Mona said. "As much as Jarred eats, you'd best bring a heavy wallet."

The big man shrugged, then took his mother by the elbow and helped her down the hall. Soon, they disappeared into the elevator.

Rick and Beth turned to the studio door. The on-air light flashed green. "Do me a favor," Rick said. "Mason's been prancing around the studio for days holding up his chin like a red-headed flamingo. He likes people asking about the scars on his neck, and his story gets stretched with every retelling. Say something about his battle wound as soon as you can, get it over with or else he'll spend the entire segment talking to us with his head cocked up at the ceiling."

Beth smiled cheerfully and swiped back a stubborn tangle of hair. "I'll be sure to."

"Thanks." Rick opened the studio door and helped her inside. The light was dim, the way Mason liked it, and the familiar smell of incense burned sweet, drifting lazily in the air.

When Mason saw them, he grinned and spun around to his mike. "Well, look who's here. Joining me in the studio is Dr. Beth Harper from the University of Arizona, the renowned archaeologist and recent discoverer of the treasure hoards beneath the ruins of Persepolis. Stay tuned, we have her story and much, much more, right after a word from our sponsors." He slapped a few buttons and yanked off his headset.

Rick and Beth moved to the sofa and took a seat. Mason rushed over, his head craned slightly upward to reveal his neck. "Hi, Beth, it's good to see that you got color back in your face. I was worried about you." He scratched his Adam's apple. "Ready for the big interview?"

"Sure am," she said. "I've been looking forward to it ever since—" Beth paused. "Wow, is that scar on your neck from your fight with the assassin? It must be a real bother. But you know, I think it makes you look kind of rugged, in an appealing sort of way."

"You think so?" Mason said, excitedly. "I get pains at night. I think my windpipe's still bruised." He turned and took a seat in an armchair, then reached into a box of Ding Dongs on the end table. "Care for one?" Mason didn't wait for an answer. He unwrapped the foil with an expert hand and swallowed the cake in two bites. Then he licked his fingers. "Okay, Beth, just be your sweet little self, and I promise not to keep you out after curfew."

The commercial track ended.

Rick adjusted their mikes over the sofa, while Mason hurried back and perched himself on a chair in front of the soundboard.

The on-air sign flashed green, and Mason spoke, "By now you've all seen on television or heard on the radio the incredible discovery made under the ruins of Persepolis. It's being called one of the most significant archaeological finds of modern history, hell, of all time. Well, today, I have for you in studio the woman responsible for it all, the beautiful and very talented archaeologist, Dr. Beth Harper."

Even in the soft light of the studio, Rick could see Beth blushing at the introduction.

"Dr. Harper... Beth," Mason said. I'm sure you've been busy since news broke of your discovery."

Beth tapped the mike.

"You don't need to do that," Mason said. "Rick has it adjusted. Go ahead and speak normally."

Beth nodded. "Well, let's see, I've given a few print interviews: *Time*, *Newsweek*, and *National Geographic*. And oh yes, I've been asked to deliver the keynote speech at a very important archaeological conference in—"

"Like I said, you're a busy woman," Mason interrupted. "We get the picture. If you wouldn't mind, maybe you could recount some of the highlights of your adventure at Persepolis."

Beth thought for a moment. "Well, to understand this find, I think it's important to first understand its historical context. These chambers were constructed at the height of the ancient Persian Empire, over twenty-five hundred years ago. To give a comparison familiar to most of your listeners, this was at about the time of the great Greek philosophers: Plato and Aristotle, a full five hundred years *before* Christ and two thousand years *after* the building of the great pyramids in Egypt."

"Right, right," Mason said. "But my audience would prefer to hear about your experience in the actual ruins, the chambers beneath the ancient city."

"Oh, sure, the entrance to the tunnels was hidden in the mortuary chamber of King Darius—"

"Right, right, but get to the part where, heroically, I marched into the Mithraeum and found you lying unconscious at the top of a blood-stained altar."

Beth cringed at the reminder.

"Tell my listeners what happened next," Mason said. "Go ahead, Beth, tell them."

"Well, like you said, you came into the Mithraeum."

"That's right, and what did I do? Tell everyone."

"If you wouldn't mind me changing the subject," Beth said. "Since our return to the U.S., Persian archaeologists have already found nineteen other chambers, each filled with valuable artifacts."

"Right, right, but tell everyone what happened when I found you in the cave. Tell everyone what I did."

"Mason," Beth said a little exasperated, "you know what happened when you found me, and I'm sure you've already told your listeners a million times. Can't we talk about—?"

"Oh, come on, the details of the discovery we can read about next month in *Discover* or the *Smithsonian*. What my listeners crave to hear is the heart-pumping drama, the human factor. So what did I do after I found you on top of the altar, minutes away from being carved up by a knife-wielding lunatic? Tell everyone."

Beth sighed, then took a deep breath. "You saved my life. You fought off a dangerous assassin, and you were nearly killed in the process. I love you for it. But did your listeners know the Ministry of Culture has already begun restoration on the gallery's ceiling? They expect to have it completed some time early next year. The tunnels and chambers are soon going to become—"

"That's right, I saved you," Mason said dramatically into his microphone. "But you saved me, as well. You helped me to re-prioritize things in my life and to understand what's truly important. And in the process you made me a better person. And I wanted to say today, on the air, for all my listeners to hear, from the bottom of my heart, thank you."

Beth blinked, unsure how to respond. Mason's gratitude had taken her by surprise. Her lips stretched wide into a smile, and she said, "You're very welcome."

Mason winked at her. "But in the end," he quickly added, "we all surely would have perished had it not been for Rick and his quick thinking. You know, buddy, I still don't understand how it was you knew to pull that ring. I mean, how could you have possibly known the ceiling would collapse?"

"I didn't," Rick said. "At least not for sure. But I was desperate and I had to take a chance. Early on, I realized the gallery was really nothing more than a huge talisman. You saw it yourself: the broad relief on the obsidian walls. Everything was exactly as it appeared on the stone."

"No question," Mason agreed.

"At that point," Rick said, "the pieces just came together. It all fit. The room was a nest; I knew it had to be. But unlike the talisman, I also realized, the gallery couldn't be transported and wielded as a weapon. So what was its point? Then Beth said something that triggered a memory, and I suddenly understood the gallery's true purpose."

"Its true purpose?" Mason said, his eyes opened wide.

"Yes, the real reason the gallery was constructed."

"Tell us."

"To destroy invading armies."

"The Scorched Earth Policy," Beth interjected.

Rick said, "In the beginning, Mason, you and I both assumed that the deaths surrounding the talisman were the result of the insects being shaken into a frenzy. In the gallery, I realized we were wrong. It wasn't shaking the nest that provoked the insects, it was exposing it to sunlight—or some other form of high-energy radiation."

"Of course, sunlight," Mason said. "The relief on the talisman, in the gallery, on the tunnel walls, the sun was always prominently depicted. It all makes perfect sense."

Rick said, "In the cave in Afghanistan, Tanner's men had subjected the stone to the bright light of a halogen lamp. Tanner himself must have made a similar mistake. And at the university, when Beth bombarded the nest with X-ray radiation, the insects went wild. The high-energy resonance they produced shattered fragile parts of the spectrometer. Even on the butte sunlight was present between breaks in the storm clouds. The talisman must have been exposed then, as well."

"Mind-boggling, absolutely mind-boggling," Mason spoke into his microphone, slowly and in a dramatic tone for the benefit of his listeners. "Anyway, tell us how all this fits in with the gallery and the massive nest hidden in its walls."

"The builders of Persepolis," Beth said, "purposefully constructed the gallery and its collapsible ceiling as a means to execute the Scorched Earth Policy."

"I see," Mason said, nodding his head. "Collapsing the roof would have brought in sunlight, which in turn would agitate the nest. The swarms would have wiped out anyone trying to sack the city." Mason paused, allowing the revelation to sink in for his listeners. "Alright, we've yacked enough about this. Let's give my callers a chance to weigh in on the subject, shall we?"

Mason's new soundboard operator patched through a call.

"Frank in Winslow, you're on the air with Mason Manning, and my guest, the renowned archaeologist, Dr. Beth Harper."

"Okay," A gruff voice said. "Let me start off by saying Dr. Harper, I think your discovery is awesome, and oh, by the way, I saw your picture in the paper, and can I just say you're one hot mama."

"Uh, thank you."

"But Mason," Frank continued, "your bit about this Brotherhood organization and a room full of ancient, deadly insects, I mean come on, ain't that a little far-fetched?"

Mason spoke low into his mike. "I'm just giving you the facts, Frank."

"Okay, if the bugs were unleashed after the ceiling fell, then tell me what happened to them?"

"Immediately, we contacted Iranian officials," Rick said, "warned them of the severe danger. We also explained that a chemical in the thymus plant appeared to be an effective repellant against the insects. They sent out extermination crews to take care of the problem."

"Also," Beth added, "entomologists have already begun to study the species. It turns out this rock-boring insect is related to a beetle of the Melyridae family, the same insect eaten as a source of toxin by the deadly poison-dart frog of the Colombian jungles. One milli-gram of batrachotoxin delivered by this newly discovered species of insect is powerful enough to kill twenty human beings. It's extraordi-narily lethal."

"Okay then," Frank said, "for argument's sake, let's say the bugs are real like you claim. And let's say they've spent the last two thousand years hibernating and reproducing in those ruins. If they filled the walls of this gallery like you say, there must've been hundreds of millions of them."

"Yeah, so?" Mason said.

"So, why should Persepolis be the only place for them to lair? I mean, what if there are more of them out there? They could be hiding away in caves and other dark places. Right now. Multiplying. As we speak. All around the world. And we wouldn't have a clue."

Mason didn't say a word.

Rick and Beth turned and stared at each other.

"So what do you have to say about that?" Frank demanded.

Beth shifted uneasily on the couch, then leaned close to the mike. "That, Frank, is a frightening possibility."

www.ingramcontent.com/pod-product-compliance
Lightning Source LLC
Chambersburg PA
CBHW022009110726
47901CB00006B/1452